TWO WORLDS

By the same author

Nine on Nine

TWO WORLDS

Nandita C. Puri

Rupa . Co

Published 2011 by
Rupa Publications India Pvt. Ltd.
7/16, Ansari Road, Daryaganj,
New Delhi 110 002

Sales Centres:
Allahabad Bengaluru Chennai
Hyderabad Jaipur Kathmandu
Kolkata Mumbai

Printed in India by
Rekha Printers Pvt. Ltd.
A-102/1 Okhla Industrial Area, Phase-II
New Delhi-110 020

To Baba, for an enriching childhood
and to my family, thanks

Contents

Acknowledgements *ix*

Book One:
CALCUTTA THEN & NOW 1890–1990

Winds of Change 3
Oona 11
Ela 20
Baba 28
David 37
First Crush 43
Ela's Choice 56
Suitors 66
Sens and Boses 81
Oona's Choice 95
Adieu 107
Turning Point 126

Book Two
BOMBAY 1990–2009

Bombay-Bound 143
Anand 159
All Fools' Day 172
A Bollywood Wife 185
Ears Wide Open 203
Take Two 210
The Breaking of a Legend 219
Strange Bedfellows 230
Riz 236
Coffee Break 250
Mrs Khanna's Lover 265
Charades 280
Crossroads 294
Trouble in Paradise 304
In Transit 320

Book Three
LONDON & WALES 2009–2010

London 343
Flashback 356
Barmouth 373
Keelan 390
The Revelation 407
Two Worlds Collide 418
Destiny Wills 424
One World 430

Bibliography 433

Acknowledgements

First of all I would like to acknowledge the contribution of my editor, Anamika Mukharji, my comrade-in-arms for four out of seven years in my meanderings through *Two Worlds.* Her ruthlessness and passion for this book remains unmatched. *Two Worlds* would not be complete without your gentle prodding and enthusiasm. Thank you Anamika. Sincerely.

I am also grateful to my publishers, Rupa & Co., especially the dynamic father-son duo, R.K. and Kapish Mehra for their continued support.

Also I would like to thank Omendu Prakash for a lovely cover. And his patience.

Sunil Awatramani, Ratin Sharma and others who have helped with information as well as Mita Kapur of Siyahi. Anyone I have missed out inadvertently, thank you nonetheless.

'Out of reality are our tales
of imagination fashioned.'

—HANS CHRISTIAN ANDERSEN

Book One

CALCUTTA THEN & NOW
1890–1990

Winds of Change

'Ela.'

'But what about Indira?'

'Yes. Indira.'

'And what about Charu? Charulata?'

'Yes. Even Charulata. We can give her all three names if it will make you happy, my dear,' Somenath Sen smiled as he gently placed his daughter next to her mother on the bed. 'But we will call her Ela.'

Roma Debi did not argue. She knew that once her husband made up his mind about something, it was final. Even his legal rivals at the high court seldom argued with him. But she also knew she had certain advantages over them. Like her youth and beauty. To which formidable lawyer Somenath Sen had often succumbed in the past.

And now, a few days after the birth of their first child, as she lay on the Burma-teak four-poster bed in her father's house in Manicktola, tired after childbirth, her hair a little tousled, the *sindur* in her parting a little smudged, her sari a little creased, Roma Sen looked even prettier. It was not easy for Somenath to take his eyes off his wife despite the presence of Monu Mashi the midwife, and the maid, Saroj, who protectively stood guard over her.

'Ela is a nice name. But may I ask why Ela?' Roma looked up at her husband. Somenath adored that look in her eyes; innocence laced with a hint of defiance as she held his gaze, studiously avoiding Monu Mashi's shocked expression: women never looked their husbands in the eye. Somenath could not recall his mother ever holding his father's gaze. Or his aunts ever looking into their husbands' eyes. In fact, they always spoke with their heads slightly bowed, covered by their sari *pallu*. This was the *pratha*. The custom. And yet, in her own gentle way, Roma rebelled against these traditions. Perhaps it was these little rebellious streaks in her that made her all the more desirable as a woman to Somenath. As long as he always had the last word, he thought to himself, fondly smiling as he gazed at her.

1893. The year Somenath and Roma's daughter, Ela, was born. But the first time Somenath had met Roma had been over a year ago, at this very house in Manicktola. He had come here along with his parents at their insistence on a bride-hunting mission. Somenath was 26, and his parents felt it was time he settled down with a wife. They had heard of a certain Arun Roy's daughter, Roma, from a common family friend and felt she might just be the right girl for their son.

Roma was the third girl the Sen seniors were seeing for their son within a fortnight. The earlier two girls had been rejected by Somenath as he found them too young, too juvenile and too tradition-bound. Leave alone talk to him, they barely looked at him directly and Somenath found this disconcerting. In spite of hailing from a traditional Hindu family, Somenath was quite liberal in his ways and habits as he socialised a lot with the educated English elite of the Company.* So his criteria for a bride was a girl who would be educated enough to fit into his social circle with ease.

Though Roma had not been to a formal school, the Roys had employed the services of an English lady, Mrs Evelyn John, to tutor her in the elementary subjects, spoken English, as well as to give her some lessons in etiquette. Roma could even recite a few Shakespearean sonnets. But the Roys faced a lot of criticism from some of their conservative

*In the 19th century, 'the Company' referred to the English East India Company.

relatives on this account. For the belief was that if a girl learnt to speak English, then she would be widowed soon after marriage. As a result, not many eligible grooms' parents—fearing for their sons' lives—wanted their sons to marry Roma. And so it was that in a society where girls were usually married off between the ages of eight to thirteen years, Roma was seventeen and unmarried. Most of Roma's friends had children of their own by then, while she was on her way to becoming an old maid.

However, the young and eligible Somenath Sen liked what he saw of Roma Roy that day: elegant in a cream and pink *Dhakai* sari, with Scottish lace trimming the edges of the long-sleeved blouse adorning her delicate wrists. Thick, dark, lustrous braids fell gracefully on her hips. A pair of tear-drop pearls rested on her pale lobes and a delicate pearl brooch pinned the neat pleats of her sari *pallu* as it covered her bosom. So unlike those two other girls he had seen earlier. They reminded him of a couple of Christmas trees, decked in heavy gold ornaments, half their dowry on their persons in an effort to entice the groom-to-be, Somenath thought wryly.

But what helped make up his mind to marry her was the way she answered his customary questions, looking straight into his eyes. She had even gently hinted that some of his questions were puerile.

'You think I would admit it if I did not know how to cook?' she retorted softly to Somenath's questions on her culinary skills. This was part of the routine questions a prospective groom asked the girl: could she cook, if so, what, sometimes even how; did she read and write; could she sing or play an instrument. Mostly mundane, sometimes humiliating. The girl might even be asked to walk so that the prospective groom's family could check whether her hips were large enough for child-bearing purposes. And every bride-to-be had to go through the drill of providing coy, socially correct answers.

'Don't you know,' Roma continued, 'we girls are tutored by our parents in what to say to prospective grooms. We just repeat it like parrots.'

Somenath could not suppress a slight laugh as he looked at her. She smiled at him, half innocent, half flirtatious. That did it. Somenath's mind was made up. It was Roma Roy who would be his bride.

'What are you smiling at? I asked you a question Som?' Roma's voice jolted Somenath back into the present. Every time Roma called her husband by his name, Monu Mashi gave her a disapproving look. Hindu women never uttered their husband's name. They were always addressed with a 'listen', 'here', 'can you hear me', 'Chotu's father', etc. But there was very little Monu Mashi could do to stop Roma.

'Yes. Yes... eh, what was it?' Somenath asked absent-mindedly, still smiling at his recollection.

'Why Ela?'

'Why Ela? Yes. Good question. See. First, it sounds sweet. Second, it is simple and short. And third, it is easy on the tongue. Understood?'

'Yes, I do understand. It is a nice name. But don't you think it is a bit too *feringhi*? Our families might want to choose a more traditional name for our first-born.'

'Roma, that's precisely what I am trying to break free from. Traditions. Conventions. Social prejudices. And I want my progeny to be part of my dreams. Ela will fulfil that dream for me. At least that is what I want her to do and that is why she will be called Ela. Our little Ela.'

Roma Debi smiled back, only half-understanding this explanation.

'And now I want you to get all the rest you can,' Somenath said as he got up and gently touched Roma's hair. 'You have a big responsibility ahead of you,' he said, gesturing towards little Ela. Then turning to Monu Mashi, he said, 'Monu Mashi, I want you to take good care of *didimoni*. And you too, Saroj. You both must see to it that she sleeps well. Understand?'

'*Hanh, dadababu*. You don't worry,' Monu Mashi nodded.

'Then can I take your leave, my love?' Somenath looked at Roma.

'Why the hurry? Why can't we talk some more?'

'We will, my love, but now you need to rest. You know, there is so much I want to share with you. We have a lot to talk about. But all in due course. Right now, just relax,' he gently caressed her hand.

Uppermost in his mind was his decision to become a Brahmo. He desperately wanted to let Roma know about it too. But he held back. He was not sure about her reaction. Would she be happy or upset? After all, Roma was only eighteen and a new mother. Too many things to cope with at the moment. This could wait, Somenath thought to himself as he gathered the folds of his crisply starched dhoti and left the room.

The Brahmo movement began in early nineteenth century Bengal, founded by a group of educated, elite Bengalis who wanted to rethink their Hindu heritage. Its founder, Raja Rammohan Roy, advocated social reform and widow remarriage, denounced the *sati* system and idol worship and other such rituals that plagued the Hindu religion. Drawn to some ethical ideals of Christianity, Roy founded the Brahmo Samaj, a version of Hinduism as defined in the ancient texts of the Vedas and Upanishads. Brahmos believed in the equality of women and worked to improve their condition through education, professional training and by encouraging widow remarriage. They also raised the age at which girls were married off, from childhood to at least puberty.

It was on an afternoon the previous autumn, in 1892, that the young, bright and fiery Somenath Sen first met Shibnath Shastri and Durgamohan Das at his friend Radhakanto's house in Lalbazar. Shastri and Das were two of the stalwarts of the Sadharan Brahmo Samaj. The Brahmo ideals appealed to Somenath and some of his friends from his Hindu College days. He had read with great interest the writings of Rammohan Roy and the young firebrand leader, Keshub Chandra Sen. But the meeting with the quiet, dignified and erudite Shibnath Shastri changed altogether Somenath's perception of life.

'You do not have to convert to Brahmoism to become a Brahmo. It is not a religion. It is a way of thinking. There is Brahma or the Universal Truth within each of us. Just remain a Hindu but follow the principles of the Samaj and the ideals of Raja (Rammohan Roy). After all, Brahmoism is nothing but a refined and reformed version of our Hindu philosophy,' Shastri explained the Brahmo philosophy to Somenath in simple terms.

Somenath felt like a different person since that afternoon meeting with the philosopher. He mulled over what Shastri had said and decided to convert to Brahmoism in order to actively participate in Samaj work. His disillusionment with Hinduism stemmed from the fact that the Hindus exposed to Western education faced terrible social ostracism in their own country on account of their progressive ideas.

Another reason prompted Sen into wanting to become a Brahmo. He longed to be a part of that elite group of Bengalis, the *crème de la crème* of Bengal as the Brahmos called themselves. Apart from embracing Western education and philosophy, the members of this progressive sect also followed European and English ways in their habits and lifestyle. At times it could be called a blind imitation of all things English—food, attire, manner and living, but most importantly, education. So much so that the Brahmos were more comfortable socialising with the Company officials and the local English, rather than with their native Hindu peers.

Some erudite Brahmos felt they could not connect mentally with their countrymen, who they saw as steeped in medieval mindsets, and this snobbery led them to form a very small, elite group, comprising some of the best Indian minds of the time. Sen wanted to be a part of this group. But he had had to put on hold his plans of conversion because of his impending wedding. He did not want to upset two sets of families—his and his future bride's. Once married, he would gradually share his ideals and beliefs with his wife, he thought. He had seen the spark of rebellion in his fiancée's eyes and he knew that Roma Debi would go along with him on this dynamic mission.

'*Eije, jamaibabu*. Where are you off to in such a hurry?' Arun Roy asked his son-in-law mockingly as Somenath walked towards his hackney carriage. Mr Roy had just returned and was alighting from his coach.

'Oh,' Somenath smiled, bending down to touch the older man's feet in obeisance.

'*Thak, thak*. It is okay. Why don't you join me for a cup of tea?'

'Actually, I am in a bit of a hurry... there is something I had to...'

'That can wait,' his father-in-law cut him short. 'Your mother-in-law and I were just discussing the other day that we hardly ever get to see you. You cannot leave without sweetening your mouth. After all you are my only son-in-law. If I don't pamper you well, what will people say?' Arun Roy joked, leading the reluctant Somenath into the drawing room while instructing his servant, Hari to bring in some tea and refreshments.

As they sat down, Arun Roy said, 'So have you decided on a name for your daughter?' Somenath nodded a bit hesitantly.

'I was thinking of Swarnalata?' Arun Roy said. 'What do you think of it?'

'Well, actually we have already decided on a name.'

'Oh, I see,' Mr Roy seemed a little disappointed. 'So what have you decided?'

'Ela.'

'Ela? What sort of a name is that? Doesn't sound like a Bengali name at all. Sounds more *feringhi* to me.'

'No, no. It is not *feringhi* at all. It is just a simple Indian name. Short and sweet.'

'Why give your first-born such a simple name? You must look up the books and think of a nice Bengali name which carries a lot of weight.'

'And sounds complicated,' Somenath could not help adding.

'Now look. All you youngsters don't want to have anything to do with hard work. Always want the easy way out. What is wrong with Swarnalata? A golden flower. That is what my granddaughter is.'

'But it sounds a bit too outdated, doesn't it?'

'Rubbish. Where do you get such ideas? I would not be surprised if it is from those Brahmo friends of yours.'

'Well, there is nothing wrong with my friends. They are all educated and successful. In fact, one gets to learn so much from them.'

'Be careful, my boy,' Arun Roy jokingly told his son-in-law. 'Keep your distance from them. They will soon influence you into becoming a Brahmo.'

'But there is nothing wrong with being a Brahmo. After all it is such a progressive community,' Somenath countered.

'I am sure there is nothing wrong. But the Hindus don't take kindly to Brahmos. You could be ostracised from the community,' Arun Roy said.

Somenath suddenly grew passionate. 'How does it matter? Look at the state of our so-called Hindu community. We marry our daughters off to older men and then burn them on their pyre. We treat our widows with such apathy and let them starve to death. And we treat the so-called lower castes like vermin. Are we supposed to be proud of all this?'

'I agree with you,' Arun Roy nodded. 'But you have a family to look after. Now that you are a father, you have more responsibilities on your head. You should not bother yourself with all this. Concentrate on your family and work. And right now, let us enjoy our tea,' he said, as Hari entered the room, carrying a large, polished brass tray.

'Here. Have one of these *kochuris*. Freshly fried,' Arun Roy extended a plate of savouries towards Somenath as Hari poured the tea into fine bone china cups.

'Thank you,' Somenath said politely as he reached for a *kochuri*. His mind was already made up. It was no use explaining this to his father-in-law. The old man would never understand his reasons. But Roma Debi would. Because she always trusted his instincts. Now, with the birth of his daughter, Somenath Sen felt he was ready to follow the path of the Brahma. The Universal Truth.

Oona

In 1971, apart from the daily news exchange about the Bangladesh War, the most talked-about topic in the Roy household was the fact that Oona would be joining boarding school next January.

There was frantic shopping and several visits to the tailor and New Market as her mother put together her things for boarding school. Her father's younger sister, Oona's Rima Pishi, had remarked that it was almost like putting together her trousseau. Her mother had laughingly replied, 'Well, yes, almost. Except the jewellery!'

Rima Pishi read from a list and ticked off the items as her mother placed them neatly in the steel trunk. Oona's trunk. And hers alone. Oona was excited and happy. For the first time in her small life, she had assets to call her own. A steel trunk containing:

- four dark blue skirts and four blouses with piping and monogrammed pockets to match, for schooldays
- two light blue skirts along with matching blouses for Sundays
- six pairs of white socks
- a pair of black shoes for weekdays and a pair of white shoes for Sundays
- a pair of white canvas shoes for sports
- a pair of Hawaiian sandals for her bath and a pair of leather sandals for after-school hours
- two printed cotton frocks for holidays and special occasions

- eight sets of petticoats
- eight pairs of knickers
- two cardigans, black for weekdays and blue for Sundays

'All done?' Rima Pishi asked.

'Yes. The trunk items are settled and in order,' Sangeeta Roy informed her sister-in-law. 'Now let's check the bedding items, Rima. We will then have to put them neatly in the holdall.'

'Okay. Here we go. Four bedsheets, four pillow cases, two light wraps, one blanket, one oil cloth.... Boudi I hope you have checked all the labels on each item with Oona's name? Otherwise they will get mixed up with the other children's clothes and linen.'

'*Hanh, baba hanh.* I have checked everything. Oona, bring that little steel box over here. Let me check the stationery items.'

Oona was thrilled with the little steel suitcase with a small black handle. She carried it proudly to her mother who checked the contents:

- a dull-orange tube of Forhan's toothpaste
- a red Colgate Junior toothbrush
- a blue comb
- a brown hairbrush
- a brand new bar of Pears glycerine soap in a blue plastic soapbox with the wax paper still wrapped around it
- a big jar of Pond's cold cream
- a bottle of green Palmolive Brilliantine
- a small tin of Cinthol talcum powder

They were all hers. She had wanted a more fragrant body talc like Cuticura or Pond's, but her father had insisted on Cinthol. 'But it does not smell so nice,' Oona had complained to her father.

'But it is medicated, my dear and will help prevent prickly heat and rashes,' he had explained to her. Oona was not very convinced. She still wanted a 'scented powder'. Amit Roy had refused, adding that those were for grown-ups and not small children. He thought she could be quite a precocious little girl at times.

'Oooh. So cute. What is this little *dibba*, Ma?' Oona pointed to a small round tin, the size of an eight-anna coin, which caught her eye.

'Vicks. Vicks Vaporub. Just rub a little on your nose and chest whenever you catch a cold,' Sangeeta explained as she put it in the case.

'Hmm.' Oona nodded in understanding. She decided she would try and empty its contents the first thing on reaching school so that she could play with the small round box. Or put in the two four-anna coins Sumit Kaku had given her. They would fit in perfectly. Oh, this is all so exciting, she thought and was looking forward to going to boarding school. But that was still some weeks away.

As 15 January drew nearer, Oona grew a little apprehensive. She was full of questions.

Baba, what will my school look like? *Oh, it will be lovely and you will have large playgrounds.* Like the Safari Park near the Lakes? *Yes.* And will there be merry-go-rounds and swings and slides and sea-saws? *Yes, yes, all that and more.* Will I have to await my turn for the rides? *Yes, because you must learn to share with your friends.* How will my new friends be? Nice like Soma, or a fighter-cock like Rinku? Chee, *you must not say that. You will have nice friends, but you must not fight with them.*

Ma will you sleep next to me in my new school at night? *No, my baby. You will have your own little bed.* Will I have that pink mosquito net you bought from New Market? *Yes.* But how can I sleep alone? *You will get used to it.* And what if I am scared? Who do I hug? Can I take my bolster with me? *No baby, bolsters are not allowed. You will not be scared. You will get used to it all.* But Ma, I think I will miss you and Baba very much, you know? *I know, but you will have your friends. We will miss you too.*

Do I really have to go to boarding, Ma? *Yes my dear, it will all be for your good.* But why are Rinku and Soma not going to boarding? Why only me? *Because their mothers do not go to office like me. They stay at home and can look after them.* So why do you have to go to office—why don't you, too, stay home and look after me? *I need to work.* But why? *Because we need the money.* And what about Rinku and Soma? Don't they need money? *I will explain it later. When you grow up. Now run along and play with your toys.*

Do you love me Baba? *Yes, I do.* And Ma? *Of course, she does.* Then why are you sending me to boarding school? *For your good my dear.* Why? *So that you grow up to be a smart and clever girl.* Smarter than Rinku? *Yes, much smarter.* Oona clapped her hands in happiness.

It was the day of her departure and the entire household was in a tizzy. Oona enjoyed the attention she was getting. She especially liked the crisp new dress she had just been made to wear. 'Now you be careful and don't mess it up. This is your new school uniform,' her mother warned her as she buttoned her shirt up for her. Oona watched her squeezing the transparent white buttons into their fresh holes.

'Oonifom,' she muttered, trying to figure out this new word as she ran towards the mirror to quickly look at herself. Pleated light blue skirt, with matching light blue piping on white, short-sleeved blouse; white, knee-length socks and a pair of shiny black buckled shoes. Oona noticed the little breast pocket on the left which had the intertwined letters—S, J and C. She had just learnt to recognise the letters of the alphabet and squinted to read them in the mirror.

'Baba, what is SJC?' Oona pointed out the letters in the mirror to her father, who was standing right behind her.

'S stands for Saint, J for Joseph's and C for Convent. The name of your new school.' Amit Roy explained. 'Oh,' Oona said, not quite understanding it, as she put her fingers in the little pocket and imagined to herself what a nice place it would be to keep those small round pebbles, sea shells and Coca-Cola corks. Like most four-year-olds, Oona Roy had a fetish for such odd collectibles.

'*Cholo, cholo*. Hurry up or we'll miss the train,' Oona's father called out to her mother.

'Coming, coming. In a minute,' Oona's mother yelled back from inside the bathroom.

'Meanwhile Sumit, here, take the holdall down to the taxi. It has already arrived.' Sumit hurried down the stairs with the holdall.

'*Ei je*, Ronit. Why don't you take this trunk down also? Meanwhile we will lock up and follow you,' Amit Roy instructed his younger brothers.

'Okay. Everyone, make way,' Ronit Kaku announced as he dragged the shiny steel trunk—four by two by one-and-a-half foot—towards the door. Painted on it in black, bold, uneven letters was her name, OONA ROY. The black ink of the alphabets had trickled down to different points and dried that way, making the paint appear fresh and wet.

When Amit was trying for Oona's admission, they had travelled by train to Chande, pronounced Shandy. Unusual name, Sangeeta had remarked. It is short for Chandipur, Amit had replied. Then why not Chandi instead of this Shandy thing, Sangeeta asked. Because it was a former French colony and therefore it was shortened to 'Chande', pronounced the French way with 'sh' as in chaff and not 'ch' as in champ, her father replied. Oona remembered sitting on her father's lap once they boarded the cycle rickshaw at Chande station. The rickshaw dropped them before a large, imposing, white colonnaded mansion that seemed to run endlessly along the entire street.

Several minutes after Amit Roy rang the bell, the tall, solid rosewood doors of the Convent opened. A dark head popped out and Amit whispered to it. The doors were opened wider and the Roys were led into a prim parlour. The head turned out to belong to a maid with skin as dark as coal in a pink floral frock.

Oona saw her father write something on a small slip-book, tear it and hand it over to the maid, whose name they gathered was Philomena.

'That was a note for the principal, informing her of my arrival,' Amit explained to his family in a self-important manner as they sat in locally replicated Louis XIV armchairs, waiting for Mother Superior.

Oona remembered her father animatedly talking to Mother Superior, a tall, fair and wrinkled *mem* in rimless spectacles with a steel cross hanging from a black thread over her white habit. She later came to know that Mother Superior was Irish, a foreigner. Or a *feringhi,* as all non-Indians were referred to. She seemed firm but somewhat kindly and bent down to say hello to Oona, gently taking her little hands in her own.

'What is your name, my child?'

'My name is Oona Roy. What is yours?'

'Oona! That is a lovely name,' Mother Superior smiled. 'You can call me Sister Michael.'

'We named her after the playwright Eugene O'Neill's daughter. As you probably know, she is married to the great comedian, Sir Charles Chaplin,' Amit Roy interrupted, trying to impress the Irish nun.

'Oh. I see,' Sister Michael smiled, not very impressed. Turning to Oona she continued, 'And how old are you my girl?'

'I am very well, thank you. And how about you?'

'What did you say, my child?' Sister Michael asked, a little bewildered.

'My father's name is Amit Roy and my mother's name is Sangeeta Roy. I stay in Number Sixteen Lake Place, Calcutta Nineteen,' Oona rattled off, desperately trying to recollect the sequence of the few sentences in English her father had made her learn by rote. Somewhere, some link seemed to have gone awry.

'I see,' Sister Michael smiled, quite amused by it all. Most Indian parents were desperate that their children speak English even before they spoke their mother tongue correctly. A silly colonial hangover, she thought to herself.

'Actually, Oona is just learning to speak English…' Amit, tried to explain, a little embarrassed at his daughter's goof-up.

'That is perfectly all right, Mr Roy. She will pick up the language once she joins school. There is no need to pressure her into learning a foreign language so early. We will teach her gradually,' the kind old lady assured the Roys.

ஜ

The following months were full of excitement in the Roy household. 'My daughter has just got admission in St. Joseph's Convent in Chande, in Chandipur. See what a smart little girl I have.' Amit would boast to all who cared to listen. From friends, relatives and neighbours, down to the milkman and newspaper boy, he spared no one.

'It is one of the oldest and finest convent schools in India. Still run by Irish sisters,' he told his colleagues at work.

'But why do you want to put her in a boarding school so far away? There are good convent schools in Calcutta too,' his colleague Ajoy Kundu asked.

'*Arre baba* Ajoy, you don't understand. This one is the best. Since both my Mrs and I are working, Oona will be better taken care of at boarding school. She will be with friends her age rather than left at the mercy of maids. Besides, look at the state of education in the city. The Naxalites seem to have taken over. The schools and colleges are forever closed due to these *faltu* strikes. At least there will be no disruption in her studies there.'

'It must be frightfully expensive, Mr Roy?' Mrs Rozario, the stenographer remarked.

'Well . . . er . . . it is, Mrs Rozario. But then we Roys believe in investing the best in education. For us, education comes first. Above all else. We never make compromises on that front. You know my grand-aunt was amongst the first batch of women graduates from Calcutta University. My mother too is a graduate from Bethune College in English Literature. I know the school fees will be a little over my budget but I would beg, borrow or steal, rather than let this opportunity slip away. My daughter deserves the best in education.'

Jacinta Rozario shrugged. She did not see the logic behind such stubbornness. These Bengalis and their fetish for education. And where does it take them? Most of them end up being clerks in offices. And they call themselves *babus*. Why not pursue a professional course instead of aimlessly following the routine academics? Take her case. She herself did not study beyond her matriculation. Her parents, like many in their Anglo-Indian fraternity, thought it a waste of time and money to go to college. Instead she learnt shorthand and typing and did a three-month course in telephone operation and secretarial work.

That had been a good twenty years ago and for the past two decades she was happy with her job at this prestigious solicitors' firm, Fowler and Co. Once known as Smith and Fowler, it was nearly a hundred-year-old company. She had started as a junior stenographer and now she was the PA, private assistant that is, to Mr P.L. Ganguly, one of the senior partners. She was happy with her three-figure salary and the next increment in a couple of months' time would see her receive a four-figure pay cheque.

It made her feel good that being a woman she drew a higher salary than some of the men, including Ajoy Kundu and the show-off Amit Roy. Not to mention the prestige of being the PA to one of the senior partners.

Come to think of it, these Bengali *babus* spent five years at university trying to understand English poetry and communist fundas which had no application in such firms. What a colossal waste of time! No wonder the Bengalis are stagnating as a race, Mrs Rozario sighed and shook her head as she carried on with her typing.

'Get all the luggage together and be ready to get off. Stand near the door. The next station is Chande. Just check again carefully and don't leave anything behind,' Amit Roy was busy instructing the various family members. Oona saw her uncles gathering together her holdall and trunk and hauling them near the door. Her two uncles and aunt, along with her parents, had come to see her off at her new school.

'I want to carry my suitcase,' Oona suddenly shouted.

'No. No. You just hold my hand now. You can carry your suitcase later,' Sangeeta said, pulling her daughter closer to her with moist eyes, a teardrop gently rolling down her cheeks.

'Why are you crying, Ma?' Oona asked, looking up at her mother.

'No, no. I am not crying at all,' Sangeeta lied, embarrassed, hastily wiping her tears.

'It is all right,' Amit patted his wife gently. 'You must be brave now. Don't make the child feel bad with your crying.'

'I know, I just couldn't restrain myself,' Sangeeta said, wiping her eyes with her *pallu*. 'This is the first time Oona will be staying away from me. It is going to be very difficult for me to stay without her.'

'*Arre baba*, don't worry. Everything will be fine. It is for Oona's good that you are making this sacrifice. For her education. Her future. Besides, we will be visiting her every Sunday. Chande is only two hours from Calcutta. Just think of that,' Amit tried to pacify his wife as the train chugged into the quaint little station with its red-tiled roof. A big rectangular board on the platform proclaimed in bold black letters against a bright yellow backdrop, CHANDIPUR.

'We have arrived,' Amit announced happily while hauling Oona up into his arms and leading his wife and sister to the door.

'Yay! We have reached. I will go to my boarding school now,' Oona smiled, clapping her hands in excitement.

Ela

Somenath and Roma were having dinner. It was a typical Calcutta winter. The year was 1915, and the couple could talk of little other than the recent announcement that Rabindranath Tagore, the Nobel Laureate from Bengal, had been knighted. They were discussing his poetry when Somenath suddenly changed the topic.

'I must tell you something, Roma. I met Biren Roy the other day at the Club.'

'Biren Roy?'

'*Arre baba,* Biren. My old friend, Romen's son.'

'Oh.'

'He has just returned from England. Just completed his Bar-at-Law from Lincoln's Inn. Bright boy. Speaks well. *Khoob bhadra,* really polite. I've quite taken to the fellow,' Somenath added enthusiastically while putting a piece of *luchi* dipped in mutton gravy into his mouth and discreetly licking his fingers. Food always tastes better this way, he thought to himself. Especially when you lick your fingers clean. To hell with table etiquette! Eating with a spoon and fork is like a second-hand experience at gastronomy. The food also tastes second rate. He quickly reached for the spoon when he saw Roma's disapproving look.

'I see. That is nice,' Roma Debi said as her husband quietly nodded. A pregnant silence invaded the room except for the rhythm of the cutlery breaking into it.

Back in 1894, Somenath Sen had finally embraced Brahmoism. His conservative Hindu family refused to accept this, of course, and his father had disinherited him. It had not mattered much to Somenath and his wife, Roma, who stood by him and his decision to become a Brahmo. As Somenath's father refused to accept a non-Hindu in the house, the couple moved out soon after Ela's birth. Relations with Roma's parents also became a little strained. Initially, though Somenath was financially self-sufficient, it was a little hard on the couple, especially Roma who had to raise Ela largely on her own. Her house felt haunted in the absence of grandparents narrating folk tales and young cousins playing around. But that lasted for only a couple of years. Once she herself started going to the Samaj and socialising with the ladies there, she realised that it was a blessing in disguise. There was a world far beyond the narrow confines of the four walls of a Bengali joint family.

Most of the ladies of the Samaj were well educated and accomplished in the fine arts. They read English and Bengali novels and sang songs composed by the dashing young poet, Rabindranath Tagore. They also played the piano, often joined their husbands in ballroom dances with their English friends, and laid out a fine table during dinners and high teas.

Initially Roma felt a little under-accomplished and alien in this milieu. But her lessons with Mrs John stood her in good stead. Besides, she was a quick learner. She was soon serving daintily-cut finger sandwiches and sponge cakes (which she had learnt to bake following Mrs Banerjee's recipe) to her friends from the Samaj. Roma became popular in her circle for serving the best-brewed, finest Darjeeling tea. She took great pleasure in serving it in her finest Doulton cups which Somenath had ordered for her from London along with the sterling silver tea set from Frazer & Haws.

Not just ladies from the Samaj, sometimes she also had 'foreign' ladies visiting her for tea. They were mostly the wives of Somenath's English friends and colleagues. But one of her most memorable high teas was the one attended by a charming social activist, Nellie Sengupta.*

'Where is Ela?' Somenath asked, breaking the silence. 'I have not seen her all evening.'

'In her room.'

'Why is she not eating with us?'

'She is not feeling well. She complained of a little acidity. She ate a bowl of rice and curd a while ago. I told her to go and rest,' Roma Debi explained.

'Oh. Yes. Yes. I see.'

After a while Somenath looked at his wife and said, 'I wanted to share something with you, Roma. I was wondering about Biren and Ela. I think they will make a nice pair. What do you say?'

'What can I say?' Roma Debi replied. 'From what I have gathered about the boy from you, he sounds quite right for our Ela. But let us see what Ela has to say about him after she meets him.'

That angered Somenath. 'What do you mean by what Ela has to say? She says nothing. It is *I* who decides what is best for her. It is *I* who decides whom she marries. In this house, *I* make all the decisions. Why should I take her or for that matter anybody else's opinion on this?'

'I know,' Roma Debi tried to reason with her husband. 'But Ela is an educated girl with modern ideas. We must consider her feelings as well in this matter.'

'Look Roma. You know I am a liberal man. I send my daughter to college despite the fact that there are male students and professors at the University. I have never denied her anything. I have several times

*Born Nellie Gray in England, she met and fell in love with a young Brahmo, Jatindramohan Sengupta, who was at a university in England. She married him and returned to India, where she took up active social work and participated in the freedom movement alongside her husband.

given in to some of her childish demands like going out for college picnics with male students. But in matters like this, I know what is best for her. As long as the boy comes from a similar background, is well-educated, presentable and of sound mental and physical health, how does anything else matter? Obviously, I am not going to marry my daughter off to a moron!'

Roma Debi shrugged, pecking at her food.

Standing outside, Ela overheard this conversation. She had begun to feel a little better, and was coming in to join her parents when she heard her father's raised voice. Deciding it would not be appropriate to enter the room while they argued, she waited outside, and so she overheard her father's plan for her marriage. This came as a big surprise.

Ela Sen enjoyed the company of her otherwise busy father at dinnertime each day. As a rule, the Sens always ate dinner together. This was the only time of the day when the family could catch up with each other's news. Breakfast was a rushed affair: Ela normally ate alone before leaving for her classes while her mother hovered over her, nursing a cup of tea. Somenath came in late and had a leisurely breakfast while he read the newspaper or went through his files. And in between cups of tea with husband and daughter, Roma Debi managed to bite into something that had the semblance of breakfast.

Except Sundays, no one but Roma Debi was home for lunch. So it was over dinner that the family sat together, discussing poetry, politics, philosophy—and almost everything under the sun. Ela did most of the talking while her parents listened indulgently. She would argue with Somenath over various subjects while her father marvelled at his daughter's wit and intelligence. He was proud that his daughter, who read English literature and philosophy at the University of Calcutta, could speak with grace and ease on topics ranging from religion to politics. At such times she reminded him of the young Roma. And at such times, Roma Debi merely made polite interjections. Her efforts went into preparing her husband and daughter's favourite dishes for dinner. Tonight it was Somenath's favourite food—*luchi* and tender lamb curry.

Both Roma and Somenath were surprised when Ela walked in, saying bluntly to no one in particular, 'May I ask what all this is about?'

'Oh. Come in, my child. How are you feeling?' Somenath asked gently as he pulled out a chair for his daughter.

'Better. What were you two discussing?'

'Nothing. Nothing in particular.'

'But Baba, I did overhear something...you did mention my name, didn't you?'

'Yes. Yes.'

'Why don't you tell me what it is all about?'

'Well...it is about you, my girl. About your future,' Somenath said.

'What about my future?'

'Baba has chosen a boy for you,' her mother interjected, while fidgeting with the red ruby ring on the third finger of her right hand. It was Somenath's gift to her on their twentieth wedding anniversary. He had specially ordered it from Asprey's in London after seeing it in their window on his last trip to the city some years ago. He knew Roma was fond of rubies and the stone particularly suited her light complexion.

Roma was a little uncomfortable, anticipating the awkward turn this conversation between father and daughter might take. Ela was an obedient child, but somewhere she did have a streak of rebelliousness. Just like Roma. And at times she could be as vocal and passionate as her father.

'A boy for me? What for?' Ela feigned surprise.

'Why? Tell me, what do little girls do when they grow up?' Somenath mockingly asked his daughter. Ela remained silent.

'Marry, of course,' Somenath answered his own question, looking at his daughter.

'But Baba...what is the hurry?'

Somenath raised his eyebrows and gave his daughter a quizzical look.

'*Ki bolley*? What did you say? What is the *hurry*? What do you mean by that?'

'Baba…I mean…I am still completing my studies…so where is the hurry to get married?' Ela stuttered and looked towards her mother for support. *Get me out of this predicament,* she seemed to plead. But Roma Debi looked equally helpless.

'And may I know who are you to decide about such things?' Turning to Roma Debi Somenath said, 'Heard that Roma? She asks me what is the hurry?' Then turning to his daughter, Somenath asked, 'My dear, do you realise how old you are? Let me guess. You are…Roma, what is her exact age?'

'Errr…she's nearly twenty,' Roma hesitated to give her exact age.

'Twenty! By God! Why was I not informed about this earlier?'

'As if you don't know your own daughter's age!'

'Yes. Yes, of course I do know, Roma. What I am trying to get at is that I have let her remain single for so long. That was because she wanted to go to university and I, too, wanted to encourage this. But there has to be a limit to education also. Especially where women are concerned. In our society, for a woman, her husband and children come before anything else.'

'But Baba…'

'No buts and ifs Ela. Do you know how old your mother was when I married her? Seventeen. And even seventeen was considered too old. Your grandmother was nine when she got married. At your age, she was looking after a husband and running a houseful of children.'

'But Baba,' Ela interjected. 'That was a long time ago. All those customs have become outdated.'

'Outdated my foot. There is a time for everything including marriage. And young girls should be married off early.'

'Please Baba. It does not suit you to talk like this. We are Brahmos. We are supposed to be progressive. What will our Samaj elders say?'

'What will they say?' Somenath retorted. 'They will say that if you find a suitable boy, marry off your daughter at the first opportunity. Never mind her age. Look at what Keshub Sen did? He married off his *nabalika,* underaged girl to the first eligible boy he found,' Somenath laughed. 'Be grateful that I have allowed you to at least study this far.'

'Baba,' Ela said softly after a long silence. 'Just being educated is not enough. I may also have opinions on matters that concern me. Especially my marriage.'

'Opinion. What opinion?' Somenath demanded angrily as he gradually realised that his little girl was no longer little. She had grown into a woman with a mind of her own. But Somenath Sen was not used to women making decisions. And he was in no frame of mind to abide by his daughter's wishes. After all, he had to have the last word. It occurred to him that perhaps Ela needed to be handled more gently in this matter. He decided to reopen the discussion another time.

His thoughts were suddenly broken by Ela's soft voice. 'Baba?'

'Yes. Yes. What is it my dear?'

'Can you not postpone all this marriage business for a while?'

'But why?'

'Because I am too busy with my studies and have not given marriage serious thought till now.'

'Look Ela, I am not rushing you into marriage right now. But we need to prepare for it. You must realise you are of marriageable age. Grooms don't grow on trees, that you pluck one when you want. We have to be on the lookout. What do you say, Roma?' Roma Debi merely looked down.

Seeing that he was not getting any active support from his wife, Somenath tried to explain things to his daughter gently. 'I happened to meet my old friend Romen Roy's son, Biren. He has just returned from England and is a nice and educated boy. Just right for you. I know the family. They are well-off, cultured and extremely sophisticated Brahmos. You should have no problem adjusting…'

'But Baba….'

'Now what? Why don't you let me finish what I am saying?'

'Because it is no use.'

'What do you mean?' Somenath was upset.

'Because I do not want to marry right now.'

'So who is telling you to marry immediately?'

'But Baba, what if I do not want to marry Biren Roy? I may want to marry someone of *my* choice?' Ela blurted out.

'What? *Your* choice? Your *choice*? That is ridiculous. Heard that, Roma? She wants to marry a boy of *her* choice. Listen to me carefully, my girl. *I* decide who you marry. You have no say in this,' Somenath thundered, getting to his feet and storming out of the room, abandoning his much-loved *luchi* and lamb dinner. He stopped short, turned to Roma and said, 'Tell your daughter that I will not allow her to marry a man of her choice. Especially any Hindu boy.'

Ela looked on helplessly after her father, worried and fearful. 'I wonder how he would react if I told him about David,' she thought. And shuddered.

Baba

'Oona Roy.' Miss Lewis announced, reading her name off the white slip Philomena had just brought into the classroom. It was Oona's favourite period. History. With her favourite teacher, Rachel Lewis. 'The principal wants to see you,' Miss Lewis told Oona, referring to Mother Superior.

The Educational Board had recently changed the examination system in the state. In their attempt to become more Indian, the Senior Cambridge examinations were discontinued and even a convent like St. Joseph's had to adhere to the local educational system, following the ICSE (Indian Certificate of School-Leaving Examinations). And likewise, 'Mother Superior' had become simply 'Principal'.

Wonder why she wants to see me, Oona panicked a bit. *After all, I have not played any pranks recently that I can recollect.* At sixteen, Oona Roy was slowly shedding her tomboy image. She was aspiring to be more lady-like, like her friend, Eileen. Eileen Dunstan. The crooner Louise Burns's daughter.

Oona had wondered why Eileen and her mother did not share the same surname. Like she and her mother did. Both were Roys. But Eileen had explained that her parents were divorced and that her mother had remarried and while she, Eileen, had preferred to keep her biological father's name, her mother took on her new husband's name. All this had sounded too complicated to Oona when Eileen had first explained it to her. But that was in kindergarten, a long time ago—in 1972. Now, twelve years later, it made sense.

As a child, Oona had been baffled that Eileen had two fathers. One whom she called Daddy and one whom she referred to as Papa. So who is your real father, Oona would ask her friend. Daddy, would be Eileen's reply. And what about Papa? He is my father too, was Eileen's simple logic. This question-and-answer session was endless till a hopelessly exasperated Oona asked her father one day, 'Baba, why cannot I have two fathers like Eileen? Then I too can get two tuck bags like Eileen gets.' Amit Roy was completely scandalised. It was much later that both Eileen and she realised that the former like everyone else had one father. He was her Daddy. The person referred to as Papa was Eileen's stepfather, her mother's second husband.

Oona gathered Romila Thapar's *Indian History* and her pencil box, lifted the lid of her desk and put them inside. Then she looked towards her friend, who sat across the aisle from her in class and who was as apprehensive as Oona about the latter being called to the principal's office. Eileen discreetly gave her the thumbs up, hope-all-goes-well sign. Oona reciprocated with a quiet nod. She then walked up to Miss Lewis's desk and excused herself from class.

She left the classroom, falling in step with Philomena Didi as she fondly called the parlour-maid. Ever since Oona's first visit to SJC with her parents when Philomena Didi let them in, twelve years ago, the parlour-maid had remained the same. Dark, sprightly, ever-smiling and dressed in those floral frocks cut in the same pattern. Except for a few greys in her otherwise black, tightly beribboned oily hair, Philomena Didi hardly seemed to have changed over the years. A sharp contrast to Oona, who was no longer the little girl entering SJC as a four-year-old. Though she was not too tall, at five feet two inches she was slim and petite, with a shapely body and a glowing complexion. She had long since shed her baby fat. She had small, firm breasts, a twenty-inch waistline which was the envy of her classmates and shapely legs which boys loved to ogle. Oona always saw to it that her socks were rolled down to her ankles and her skirt pulled up high above her knees in order to show them off to the maximum. When you have it, why not flaunt it, was her maxim, much to the chagrin of the nuns in the convent and her equally conservative father.

Her hair, however, remained short. The same cut she had always sported. Except now she did not oil her hair at all. This was a sign of rebellion in her teenage years: a protest against all the years of oily, brilliantined hair she had had to live with. Now her hair with its stylish flicks fell casually on her forehead, in a way modelled after Lady Diana's, which seemed to be quite a rage with young girls these days.

The last few hours had seemed a little hurried. A little unbelievable. Somewhat ominous, Oona thought, as she sat by the window of the Howrah–Bandel local recollecting the sequence of events. She had been happy, surprised and then a little worried to see Sumit Kaku sitting in the principal's office. All well with Ma and Baba? Oona had enquired anxiously, anticipating the worst. Her uncle had assured her that all was well, except that her father was a little unwell and wanted to meet Oona. But nothing to worry about, he had said, though Sister Michael's calm but worried expression belied that. Sister had told her to quickly pack a little bag if she wanted to as it would be only a matter of a few days before her father recovered and she returned to school. Lily Didi, the linen-room maid, had helped her pack a few clothes and books into her bag before she quickly joined Sumit Kaku in the rickshaw heading for the station.

Going home was always a happy event for Oona and her friends. She smiled as she recalled how they all behaved a day before any of their term vacations. The girls used to sing ditties, well out of earshot of the nuns:

After one more day, where shall we be?
Out of the gates of SJC.
No more biscuits, no more buns,

No more scolding from the nuns.
No more pencils, no more books,
No more teachers' dirty looks.
If the teachers interfere,
Give them a shove and send them here.

No one knew who had composed it, but it had been sung by generations of Josephites, as the girls from SJC were known. They would be all over the place in groups, singing this song and throwing confetti.

Days before term ended, each class would collect toffee and chocolate wrappers. Especially the gold and silver ones. The shinier, the better. They would then cut them into fine confetti and store it in a toffee tin. Before the last day of class, these would be sprinkled over the blades of the classroom fans. As the class teacher entered on the last day, the fans would be switched on and everyone would be showered with confetti. Everyone ran around, happily screaming and laughing. Glittering heads with coloured confetti signified the end of each term. No one knew how this custom came about, but it was unique to St. Joseph's. It had been followed by girls in this boarding school for generations before Oona.

But going home suddenly in the middle of the term did not sound good to Oona. And that too just a few days before the Christmas holidays. Something was amiss. She looked towards Sumit Kaku sitting across her, and asked, 'Is all well with Baba? Tell me, what is the matter, really?'

'Nothing to worry about. He will be well.'

'But what has happened to him?'

'He has had a mild stroke.'

'A what?' Oona almost screamed, oblivious to the heads turning towards her.

'A stroke. A cerebral thrombosis.' Sumit Kaku took her hands and gently said, 'Listen Oona. You have to be strong. You are a brave girl, aren't you? You must not panic. It is only a matter of time before Baba gets well. I assure you that all will be well.'

Oona missed her Baba. Especially now on the train ride back home. Amit would always make it a point to take Oona back home for the holidays after each term since Sangeeta could not get time off from work so easily. Her job as a receptionist in the prestigious auditing firm, Price Waterhouse was quite taxing. She worked six days a week from ten in the morning till six in the evening and sometimes even did overtime. Her only off days were Sundays and the second Saturday of each month.

Oona always longed for these days. She enjoyed her mother's company and the house always looked bright and cheerful when her mother was home. She enjoyed eating meals with her mother. The food tasted better somehow. She especially enjoyed the lazy afternoons when she and her mother lay side by side, curled up in the old teakwood double bed in her parents' room. Her mother had said it had come as part of her trousseau along with the rosewood dresser with the Belgian glass mirror, which was now stained with age and neglect. Oona would read her Enid Blytons and Nancy Drews and lately, surreptitiously, Mills & Boons, while her mother would read *Desh* magazines, lying lazily and listening to Hindi film songs on Radio Ceylon. Though Oona was very fond of her father, the mother-daughter relationship was something quite different, quite inexplicable. Something Oona greatly treasured. But these were rare moments. Mostly it was Amit who stayed home.

With her father, life always seemed to be on the run. He was hyperactive and could not remain in one place for too long. The same went for his work place too. Amit's jobs were as flexible as his moods. Every six months or so, Amit Roy would be out of work because of his temper or differences with his colleagues or seniors at work. After a few months of unemployment, which he would spend applying for jobs and going for various interviews, he would eventually land a job. But keeping one for more than six months was not his cup of tea.

It did not bother him much that his wife was the only consistent earning member in the family. That the house ran mostly on her money. That Sangeeta Roy footed Oona's hefty school fees and catered to her husband's silly whims and eccentricities—one of which was buying lottery tickets. Come what may, every week Amit spent a neat amount of money patronising the various state lotteries. Sangeeta could not understand this. Why waste money like this when she ran the house on a near shoestring budget, she fumed. But Amit tried to convince her of the windfall they would have if they won the bumper prize money and how she would not need to work anymore. Sangeeta, ever practical, always scoffed at his fantasies and complained that her hard-earned money was being gambled away.

As a child, Oona believed for years that her father would win the lottery. Amit had promised her a big doll's house and a ladies' bicycle. Much later, in her teens, when she had outgrown her dolls and the doll's house never came, she realised that her father was only a big talker.

But she still did not stop believing in him. Now, with changing needs, he had of late promised to buy her a car. 'By the time you are eighteen, I will win the Bhutan State Lottery which has five lakh rupees as prize money. And then you will have your red Fiat along with your driving licence,' he had promised her. Oona smiled at the recollection. That was Amit Roy. Her Baba. Always positive, brimming with hope in the most adverse situations. Indomitable in spirit. Never say die, Oona thought as the train stopped at Serampore station to the sound of the tea-vendors' cry '*Cha. Cha. Garam, garam cha.*'

'Want to have some tea?' Sumit Kaku asked as the *chaiwallahs* hovered around the compartment.

'No. Not really,' Oona said.

'Have some. You will feel better,' Sumit Kaku insisted.

'All right, if you say so,' Oona shrugged.

'*Eije. Duto cha*—over here.' Sumit gestured to the vendor.

The tea did indeed perk her up. It was nice and hot with a dash of ginger, not too sweet and milky. Just the way she liked it. So unlike the tea Baba prefers. She thought to herself and smiled.

Amit Roy enjoyed making tea at home, several times a day, on any pretext. And Oona hated it. He would boil the milk to a thick creamy texture and add spoonfuls of sugar but very few tea leaves. Oona would hate the thin layer of cream which formed after every sip she took. She hated to have to spoon it out each time. Sangeeta on the other hand cribbed about the extra sweetness.

'No fun if tea is not sweet and milky,' Amit would insist.

'Look at the way he wastes so much sugar. Sugar does not come cheap these days,' she would remind Oona often. Four rupees a kilo was a lot of money, she would say.

But then Amit seldom paid heed to what his wife said. 'Money, money, money, that is all you can talk of,' he would tell her.

'Yes, since I slog hard to earn it, that *is* all I can think of,' Sangeeta would answer back.

When Oona went home for the holidays, she always took something for her parents. Sometimes a purse for her mother or cologne for her father. Inexpensive tokens of love for her parents, bought with savings from her meagre pocket money. This time she had bought a set of handkerchiefs for Ma from the school Christmas fete a week ago.

As for Baba, she had seen a bottle of Tata Eau de Cologne at Luxmi Stores on Main Street. It was a little expensive, but she had told Lal Babu the shopkeeper to keep it for her. 'I will pick it up next week when I get my pocket money. I want to take it for Baba for Christmas.' Lal Babu had nodded, smiling.

'How time flies,' Lal Babu thought, looking at Oona. 'It was just the other day she had come in as a little girl, clutching on to her mother's hand, tight. And look at her now—a young girl, on the threshold of womanhood. Soon she will matriculate and leave Chandipur. And there will be more little Oonas who will come, holding their mothers' hands like her. They will also leave some day. But Luxmi Stores and I will be here, in the same spot, doing the same thing, for years to come,' he thought.

'I hope Baba gets well soon, Kaku,' Oona said. Then I can give him the bottle of Eau de Cologne along with a 'get well' card which I can pick up from The Card Store, she thought.

'Of course, he will. Don't you worry,' Sumit Kaku reassured her.

However all was not well with Amit Roy. The cerebral attack he suffered on 3 December had left him wholly paralysed. He lay virtually brain dead in the ICU of the Presidency General Hospital. Only his heart continued to beat.

It was the same hospital where Oona had been born. The same place where sixteen years ago, Amit stayed up the whole night, holding his wife's hands as she went through labour. Sangeeta Roy broke down as she narrated this to relatives visiting at the hospital. The same hospital, outside which Amit used to take Oona as a child for walks and show her where she'd been born. He would point out the dull brass plaque which stated that Sir Roland Ross first discovered the malaria vaccine during his tenure here. And now in this very same place, Amit Roy lay, with all kinds of tubes piercing his body, virtually a corpse; just a heartbeat away from death.

In spite of her relatives dissuading her, Oona managed to catch a glimpse of her father lying in the iron hospital bed. So different from the Baba she last saw. Or the Baba she knew. Solid, strong, infallible. Yes, he was her God. And somehow she believed that nothing could go wrong with him.

Something did go wrong. More than a month after the attack, Amit Roy passed away on 8 January, having never recovered from the coma he had slipped into. Till now, the date had been significant for Oona as her pop idol, Elvis Presley's birthday. But now it held a totally different meaning. Death was better than living a paralysed life. Amit would not have liked to live like that, his friend and doctor, Asim Sen had said. Yes, yes, most of his friends and relatives chorused. Only that he was too young to die. Just forty-eight years old, his colleagues remarked. Besides, look at Oona, the neighbours added. She is only sixteen. And the poor wife? A widow and so young?

Sangeeta Roy was stoic in her grief. She had to be strong for Oona's sake. What would happen to Oona if she broke down?

As for Oona, she was still too shocked to react. Life had been kind to her all along and she had taken this for granted. Similarly, she took her parents for granted. She had always imagined life with her parents to be like the fairy tales, an eternal happily ever after.

No. This could not be true. She could not imagine this in her wildest dreams. Especially not losing her father. Then why should this happen, and especially to someone as young as herself? God up there must be really mean. And she hated him for this.

Just over two months ago Oona had lost her idol, Indira Gandhi. She had hero-worshipped her for years. More than she did John Travolta or Ryan O'Neil or Neil Diamond. Or even Amitabh Bachchan. Oona admired Mrs Gandhi and had always aspired to be like her. Maybe not the prime minister, but an achiever all right. Mrs Gandhi was shot down by her personal security guards, Satwant Singh and Beant Singh. Oona had not eaten for days after Mrs Gandhi's assassination. And cried non-stop. Now with her father's death, there were hardly any tears left: 1984 was truly an Orwellian year.

She wished her relatives would understand and not insist that she cry. 'The child must cry,' they said. 'Tears are purgative, they will cleanse the system. Or else she will fall ill. You must do something about it, Sangeeta,' they cajoled her mother.

'I wish they would leave us alone. They are not going to pay for our upkeep, Ma, are they? Then who gives them the right to preach?' Oona pointed out.

Sangeeta Roy smiled back at her daughter. 'What could I have done without my wise little lady?' she kissed Oona and hugged her tight. 'You are my reason to live.'

Oona held her mother tight. With her father gone, she was all that she had now. Precious. And not to be taken for granted anymore.

David

Alison would be in any moment, Vincent thought as he heard the horse's hooves and the hackney screeching to a halt on the gravel outside the *gari verandah*. That was how the porticos were known here in Calcutta. Charming word, Vincent thought. He loved the sound of Bengali words. They had such a lilt.

It was a crisp winter day and Vincent loved such lazy afternoons. Especially when he was sitting in his favourite armchair in the drawing room, still in his silk pajamas and kimono, lazing over a cup of tea, doing nothing in particular. Oh, how he loved such days. It had been over twenty-five years since Vincent Anderson Oliver made the city of Charnock his home. In 1891's Christmas Eve Ball at the Great Eastern Hotel, the young Company clerk had first met his bride-to-be, a local Anglo-Indian called Alison.

And now, more than a quarter of a century later, after marriage and two children, Vincent was seriously contemplating returning to England. It was over a year since the War had ended. Not that Vincent did not like India. On the contrary, life was easier here than back home. Alison came into the room and gave him a light peck on the cheek. 'How is your mother?' Vincent asked routinely. Alison was back from her weekly visit to her mother's at Bowbazar. Vincent himself was fond of the old lady. Gutsy old woman, he thought, to raise a child, especially a daughter, as a single parent in such a conservative society.

'Oh, she is fine. She sends you her love as always. Just give me a moment darling. I need to settle a few things. I will join you in a while,' Alison said as she headed towards her room.

Vincent smiled at the way life had turned out for him. Over the years he had risen from the rank of a lower division clerk to the post of a gazetted officer in the Company. He liked the city, with its clubs and colourful social life. He especially liked the laid-back lifestyle. He enjoyed the company of his close circle of friends, his comfortable house and the several servants he employed. They made life so much easier for him and his family. He knew he could ill-afford the luxury of servants back home. Calcutta to him was a mini-England with all its native charms and comforts minus the fierce English winter. Vincent Oliver was one of the many Englishmen to succumb to this.

But then the times were changing. Vincent could see it coming. With Curzon's partitioning of Bengal and O'Dyer's unfortunate massacre of innocent Indians at Jallianwala Bagh in the Punjab two years ago, there was a growing unrest and native resentment building up towards the British. Though these events did not make a marked difference to the Olivers' lifestyle, the atmosphere was nevertheless volatile. Vincent anticipated this and knew life for him and his countrymen would never be the same again.

When Alison joined him, he shared these feelings with her. He knew that it would be difficult to convince his family to relocate but explained to Alison that it would be definitely worth trying.

'But darling,' Alison drawled while puffing up the pink damask cushions, 'I have never really lived there you know. I would be such a terrible misfit, wouldn't I?' Alison said, hoping Vincent would change his mind.

'What balderdash! You will feel totally at home and perhaps adjust even better than me,' Vincent said admiringly to his beautiful, half-English wife, who at times seemed more English than him. Like most Anglo-Indians, Alison never considered herself Indian. Her father was an English doctor and her mother a Bengali *ayah* who had worked for him.

The Anglo-Indians as a community were unique. They largely comprised the illegitimate offspring of British officers and their Indian maids. Most of these men served the East India Company as officers in the railways and as district magistrates in the villages. Their English spouses seldom lived in India with them as they could not acclimatise themselves to the tropical weather. These men then turned to the local women for physical satisfaction.

The children of these liaisons were very often raised as Christians, with English names. They attended missionary schools which had sprung up all over the place, just like the one Alison had attended. Though the men took no responsibility for these children apart from occasionally providing money, these children grew up to be called Anglo-Indians, refusing to identify themselves as Indians. They spoke a pidgin English, dressed in Western attire, ate with a spoon and fork and followed the English festive calendar. It seemed they had been born in India only by accident. The local Indians sneered at them, considered them to be of inferior intelligence and referred to them by the derogatory term 'Dingos'.

It was different for Dr Roland Smith, Alison's father. His wife and daughter Maria stayed with him in their Park Street mansion. But Dr Smith found his wife too frigid—after the birth of their daughter, she refused to have any physical relations with her husband. Dr Smith then turned for sexual gratification to the robust and handsome Bengali *ayah*, Vimla Das. Alison was born out of this liaison, though Vimla kept it a secret from everyone, even her children.

Like other Anglo-Indians, Alison too thought it beneath her station to call herself an Indian. That would be tantamount to calling herself a native. And native she was not, what with her English father and fair colouring. Never mind that she was his illegitimate child. Never mind that her mother was a dark-skinned, Bengali-speaking Christian convert. 'I am English,' she would remind her children often. 'A *memsahib*,' she would add for the benefit of her ignorant menials. And to her social peers, 'We are from Chester. Not too far from London.' She would add,

'My husband spent most of his life in London though.' Of course she never said that she had yet to visit any of these places.

When the English decided to colonise India, their first port of call was Calcutta. It was in 1690 that an Englishman of low birth, Job Charnock, set foot in a small village on the banks of the river Hooghly, called Kalikata—the city of the patron goddess Kali. Charnock liked what he saw. The feudal owners were busy squabbling among themselves and one of them offered to sell the land to Charnock along with a couple of adjoining villages for a pittance. The Englishman could not resist.

It was Charnock who developed Kalikata, Sutanuti and Gobindapur into a town that was to become one of the largest flourishing cities in the world. He christened it Calcutta. Hence the city, born of an Englishman's dream and nurtured by his love, was more English than any other Indian city. It was a place that brought together the best of India and England.

Vincent and Alison's first-born, David, was the product of such a milieu. Calcutta was the city of his birth and youth and he knew of no place he could love more than this. He was most reluctant to go along with his parents' plans of settling in England. Convincing his parents, especially his adamant mother was proving futile. He watched Alison butter her scone while he absent-mindedly stirred his tea. He loved his tea and scones at Firpo's. But right now all his appetite for scones had somehow disappeared. He remembered how as a child he, with his sister Judy, had looked forward to their afternoon outings with their mother. Thursdays used to be known as Firpo's Day in the Oliver household.

Every Thursday after lunch, Judy and David would sit in the coach with their mother as the carriage trudged along. After crossing the fashionable Park Street, the coachman would take the little lane called Tottie Lane, which opened on to the wider Free School Street that connected all the way to Dhurumtolla. David loved the quaint little shops that dotted Free School Street—Braganza's Music Store, Dr Ling's Dental Clinic and Burlington's, among others.

Their destination was the Hall & Anderson's store in Dhurumtolla. Judy and David would bounce up the stairs of the Tudor mansion which housed the store even before the coachman brought the horse to a halt. Once inside, they lost no time filling up their tuck bags even before Alison could retrieve her grocery list from her purse.

Thereafter the ride down the main Chowringhee road alongside the tramcars would be full of anticipation for their next destination. They would pass the Lal Dighi by the Maidan towards Park Street. All the way, their thoughts revolved around the delicious jam tarts and fish rolls of Firpo's. And the cup of fine Darjeeling tea they were allowed once a week.

In the restaurant, old Mr Garney would fondle the piano keys with his gnarled fingers, the green veins brimming over the freckled skin. He would be dressed in an old tailcoat and bow tie. There was magic in those gnarled fingers, David recollected, those tunes always made him feel light. He used to walk up to old Mr Garney once in a while and request him to play a particular favourite. Old Mr Garney would pretend to ignore the lad but as David returned to his table, he would be pleasantly surprised to hear his request being played on the grand old Steinway. Mr Garney had long since passed away, and though a younger pianist still performed at Firpo's, the music no longer held much charm for David.

'Mum. Can I say something?'

'Yes. Go on. I am listening,' Alison said as she put a piece of buttered scone delicately into her mouth.

'I really don't want to go to England,' said David.

'What?'

'Look Mum, I am old enough to be on my own. You all carry on to Chester. I will stay here. I'm due for a promotion, too. Besides, I'm quite capable of looking after myself,' David tried to impress upon his mother. 'Of course, I will be visiting you from time to time,' David smiled.

'I refuse to hear such nonsense. We are all going together and that means you are coming with us. And that's that,' Alison snapped at her son. 'Look David, I myself am not keen on going to that cold, dank country. But as your father says, things are no longer safe here. And since we have to go, it is better we all go as a family.'

'But Mum…how can I make you understand? I do not like it out there. Everything about that country, including the weather, depresses me. I don't think that I will ever be able to live in England.'

'Fiddlesticks. Whoever heard such nonsense! Try it out and see for yourself. You have hardly spent time there.'

'I did, Mum,' David said, referring to a previous trip two years ago, when he had travelled there on work. Smith and Fowler, the legal firm where he was a clerk, had sent him there for training.

'No harm trying again, son,' Alison said firmly.

'But my heart is not there,' David returned.

'That is what happens when you mix around too much with these natives. You must not forget you are English, my boy,' Alison was losing patience.

'But Mum, this is my country and this is where I want to be. My heart belongs here,' David told his mother. What he did not tell her, however, was his other reason for not wanting to leave Calcutta. Ela Sen.

First Crush

'I hope you are coming tomorrow. It is the last day at Lowes. The juniors are giving us a farewell, so dress up in your best outfit,' said Sonia over the phone. 'By the way, what are you wearing?' she asked. Before Oona could reply she went on, 'I am wearing a saree. My mother's chiffon with the kundan set.'

'Let me see. I'll wear that gypsy skirt—remember the one we went to buy together from New Market?' Oona said.

'Yeah. But why a skirt? Why not a saree? Most of us are going to wear sarees. You look lovely in sarees. Remember when you wore one at Vaidya's sister's wedding? All the guys gave you special *bhao*...?'

'Yeah? I know...' Oona muttered as she twiddled with the phone wire. 'By the way, when is the farewell social with the Boys' Hall?' she asked her friend.

'It's Saturday. Not this one. Next one,' Sonia said.

'I'll reserve my saree for then,' Oona said.

'I see. But you can always wear sarees on both days.'

'Yes. I guess I can. But it's too much of a hassle managing it. I think I'll skip wearing a saree tomorrow.'

Oona did not mention that she had just that one green *crepe de chine* saree and could not afford another. Besides, unlike Sonia's mom, her mother wore simple cotton sarees. Mostly inexpensive stuff. Not the kind you wore to your farewell social.

And of course, she did not mention that she wanted to look her best in that one saree for the Lowes' Hall farewell social, which the graduating batches of both the boys' and girls' schools would be attending.

She wanted to look especially good on the occasion for Hector Bose. Fellow student at Lowes. Tall, rugged, good-looking, charming and popular, of part Irish and part Bengali stock. He was in the same class as her, but in the boys' school. Oona had also recently discovered that he was her neighbour, living in the next lane. So every evening, at seven sharp, Oona came out and stood in her verandah. A few minutes later Hector would pass by, casually dressed, on his way to his tuition classes, she assumed. He never noticed her. But she ogled at him. And secretly fell in love. Not so much with him as with the idea of falling in love itself.

At eighteen, Oona was an attractive girl. But she had never had a 'steady boyfriend' like some of her friends. Sonia, Usha and even that dowdily dressed Vaidya. Not that it mattered much. 'I am still young but it is time I fell in love, had a boyfriend and had an affair,' she said to herself sometimes. Hector Bose seemed the ideal candidate.

'How are you going? Alone?' Sangeeta asked, admiring Oona in her saree.

'No, Ma. Sonia will pick me up. We are going together.'

'I see. And how will you return? It will be very late.'

'Sonia's boyfriend, Deepak has promised to drop Usha and me. Stop worrying Ma. I am not a kid. I can look after myself.'

'Of course I know you can, but a mother will always worry,' Sangeeta said. 'You look so pretty in a saree, I wonder why you don't wear it more often instead of those silly tattered pants you wear.'

'Eeks! Imagine wearing sarees daily. How sissy. Besides, how dare you call my jeans tattered? They are so trendy and in fashion.'

'I don't understand what's with you kids these days. Why pay a fortune for torn clothes? At your age, I could not wait to get into sarees...'

'Okay, Ma. *Bas*. Enough. You know my friends will call me a sissy if I wear a saree and they will stop socialising with me,' Oona smiled as she put on her beaded danglers.

'Then you don't need friends like that. They are too posh for you. We don't have money like them. You should spend more time with Babli, the Banerjee's daughter. She is brilliant and—'

'...and a sissy. Such a prude. *Gaiya*. Like a village bumpkin. Please Ma, I am old enough to decide on my friends.'

'*Achcha baba,* okay. Now go and enjoy yourself.'

'Hey,' Sonia nudged Oona. 'Like him?' she winked, gesturing towards Hector as she caught her friend staring at him. Hector was on the dance floor with a pretty date. 'Handsome, isn't he?' Oona blushed innocently as she sipped her fruit punch. Sonia did not fail to notice it. 'Like him?' Sonia nudged again.

'Yes. No. I mean...I don't know him. He is my neighbour', she blurted.

'Looks like you take more than a neighbourly interest in him,' grinned Sonia, puffed confidently at her cigarette.

Oona did not smoke. The one time she tried it, she had choked clumsily, coughing till her face turned red. She admired the way Sonia carried herself in her chiffon saree and halter-necked blouse, smoking away elegantly. Nonchalantly. Oona felt dowdy. Inferior. Gosh, I have a long way to go to catch up on the social ladder, Oona thought to herself as she admired her friend's style.

'Who is the babe with him?' Oona asked Sonia, gesturing towards Hector.

'Oh. Her? That's Sonia. My namesake. Sonia Singh. Ex-Miss Calcutta. She's flying with Cathay Pacific these days. Isn't she stunning?'

'Yes,' Oona muttered. 'But isn't she a lot older than Hector?'

'Yes. So what? She's dating him, has him wrapped around her pretty little finger. Don't you think they make a great pair?' Sonia nudged Oona, who stiffened.

'Hey. C'mon. Relax. Hector's much in demand. He has all the Lowes' girls after him. You are way behind in the queue,' she pulled Oona towards the dance floor and whispered, 'Cheer up. It's not the end of the world.'

The girls were joined by Deepak. Sonia smiled and looked towards her boyfriend and said, 'Deepak, let's find a nice guy for Oona from your group.'

'Please. Sonia, no. I am not such a despo—'

'Who says you are a despo? I just feel you need a nice boyfriend.'

'Yep. Like my friend Sanjeev. You know Oona, he has the hots for you,' Deepak butted in.

'Then what are we waiting for? Let's get them together soon. Are you free tomorrow evening?' Sonia asked Oona.

'Please Sonia. I don't want boyfriends now. Just want to concentrate on college, studies, career… you know the stuff?' Oona quickly added as she thought of the pimply, bucktoothed Sanjeev. She knew he had taken a liking to her, but Oona was not the least bit interested in him.

'C'mon, let's dance,' Sonia shouted over the blaring Bee Gees. 'Stayin' alive, stayin' alive… ' she chorused along. Oona tried to sway with her favourite group, but her enthusiasm was dampened by the discovery of Hector's girlfriend. All her romantic illusions came crashing down as she thought of Sonia Singh. 'Bitch,' she muttered.

'What?' Sonia asked.

'Nothing.'

About a week later, Oona was introduced to Hector by Sonia at the Saturday Club. Sonia was a member and had invited Oona over for lunch at the club. Post lunch, while the two were chatting over a cuppa by the poolside, Sonia saw Hector sauntering in with a friend. 'Hi,' Sonia waved out to Hector.

'Oh, hi there, beautiful. What's up? Where's that bum Deepak?'

'I wouldn't know. Might be helping his dad at the office. What's up with you?'

'Just came with my friend…here…meet Sunil. He is a member. And Sunil, this is Sonia.'

'Hi.' Sunil said. 'Of course, I know Sonia. I've seen you before at the club.'

'By the way, guys. Meet my friend Oona. She was with me at Lowes. Oona, this is Hector, also from Lowes. And his friend Sunil.'

'Hey, I've seen you before,' Hector smiled at her. Oona just melted in a blush.

'Yes…yes…in school.' It dawned on her that Hector was hardly likely to notice her in school, what with the bevy of beauties Lowes was reputed for. 'Also, I think we are neighbours…I mean I live in the lane next to yours…'

'You do?' There was a pause and then, 'But of course,' Hector slapped the table. 'I've seen you in the area. Same *para*. What's your building number?'

'Thirty-three.'

'Oh, that is the Mouchak lane,' he said, referring to the well-known sweet shop next to Oona's house. 'No wonder.'

'Well, if you guys have nothing else planned, why don't you join us for some tea?' Sonia asked.

'Not a bad idea,' Hector said, taking the chair opposite Oona. She was too excited to talk. Sensing this, Sonia added, 'Oh, by the way, Oona, Hector has a super collection of records. Especially Neil Diamond. And Oona here is a major Neil Diamond fan.'

'Is that right?'

'Ah, well, you know…it's just one of those phases…' Oona shrugged.

'I know. But you are welcome to drop in and hear some of my records. I must warn you though that I do not lend any records. I'm over-cautious about them.'

'Same here,' said Oona, relaxing at last.

Oona had discovered Hector's house several months ago. She had grown up seeing the Bose Mansion, as it was called, but now, after realising it was Hector's house, she looked at it more keenly each time she went past. Nice old colonial structure, she had remarked when she passed by it with her friend Rinku. It could do with a coat of paint though. She was especially tickled with the family coat-of-arms gleaming in brass on the ornate teak door. Imagine having a coat-of-arms these days, she had told Rinku. They used to be quite a rich family in earlier times, her friend had replied, hence all the style. Oona realised that the house and garden must have seen better days. Even now, it did not seem too bad.

Rinku had also mentioned the two Bose boys, real studs—Victor and Hector. Victor was in college in England, while Hector was at Lowes, in the final year. Oona merely nodded, pretending not to know anything about the Bose boys, especially Hector. Rinku was surprised at Oona's ignorance of the boys and insisted that no young girl could miss the two handsome hunks. Oona reminded Rinku that she had spent most of her growing-up years away in boarding school.

'Oh, hello,' Oona smiled, surprised to find Hector at her door one day.

'Hi,' Hector said casually.

'Come. Come in.' Oona led the way to her modest drawing room. The room was fairly large by modern standards, as the house had been built in the early 1930s, when space was not a major constraint in the city. The furniture was sparse, comprising the Burma-teak drawing-room set which had earlier belonged to Amit's parents. This included an armed, large double-seater and two individual armchairs along with a round centre-table. On one side of the room was a bookshelf containing the entire set of Encyclopaedia Britannica. The other side had a sideboard which showcased the odd remains of fine chinaware, which must have earlier belonged to a set. Plus the usual souvenirs from across the globe. Though Amit Roy had never taken his family beyond Darjeeling and the local Digha beach, the curios were a legacy from his parents' and grandparents' days, when the family had been better off.

The cushions looked well-used, just like the velvet curtains adorning the windows and the door leading to an inner room. The curtains needed changing, Oona had often complained to Sangeeta. 'Why? What's wrong with them?' her mother had countered. 'They look faded.'

'So?' Sangeeta argued. 'Only faded, *na*, not torn. Besides, I cannot afford velvet curtains these days, they are frightfully expensive. It just so happened that your father got it at wholesale rates from Nitai Babu's factory.'

That was nearly six years ago, before Amit Roy's death.

'But Ma, velvet looks so outdated these days,' Oona would often complain. 'Why can't we have those chic lace curtains like everyone else?' She had seen them at her school friend Rubina's house.

But Oona knew there was no point arguing with her mother. Sangeeta Roy just could not afford new furnishings for her house. At times like these, when friends came home, Oona felt a little embarrassed. Otherwise she was fine with those faded velvets and the strange curlicue motifs on them. She felt more embarrassed than ever right now, knowing this would hardly impress Hector. *I am sure his other girlfriends have fancier houses.*

'Cute place, this,' Hector said as he seated himself on an armchair. He was being polite, but nevertheless Oona replied, 'You think so? It's a little ancient,' she added, 'All this furniture belonged to my grandparents and my parents were just too sentimental about it. So…'

Sangeeta Roy entered. Hector stood up with a polite, 'Hi Aunty.'

'Oh, hello. Haven't I seen you before?'

'Yes, Aunty. You must have. I live in the next lane.'

'Which house?'

'No. 42. Bose Mansion.'

'Oh, so you are Maive Bose's son. I meet your mother quite often. You know in the bazaar, in the library and such places. She speaks such excellent Bengali. Not to mention her English. I had once taken spoken English classes from her at the institute,' Sangeeta rattled on.

Oh did she have to mention that last bit? Oona cringed, nearly dying of embarrassment.

Sensing this, Hector tried to change the subject. 'You know, I really like that dining table there,' he said, pointing to the neat round marble-topped table with elegantly carved legs. The chairs were however mismatched. Later additions, as Sumit Kaku insisted on taking the chairs from their ancestral home after her grandparents' death. Now, cheap bentwood chairs had been added, though Oona thought they did not look too bad.

'Really?' she asked. 'They are also family heirlooms. My house is like a museum, isn't it?' they both laughed.

'Wait till you see mine,' Hector said, 'It will remind you of the ancient history section of a museum.'

Oona laughed, beginning to enjoy Hector's wit.

'Aren't you going to offer your friend something?' Sangeeta asked Oona.

'No Aunty, it is all right. Some other time. I just came to say hello since we stay in the same neighbourhood,' Hector said.

'No. No. How can that be? This is the first time you have come home and you cannot go without having something. What about a cup of tea? Or would you prefer orange squash?'

'Tea will be fine.'

'You two chat. I'll get it,' Sangeeta said as she lifted the curtain and went into the inner room.

'Need help?' Oona offered, reluctantly.

'No. Don't bother,' her mother yelled back.

Oona sat on the other armchair and asked, 'What a nice surprise.'

'Well, I actually got you this,' Hector said, extending a cassette.

'What's this?' Oona took it and scrutinised it with interest.

'I've just recorded some of my favourite Neil Diamond numbers for you since you are a Diamond fan. I'm sure you will like them. These are from my collection.

'Oh that is sweet,' Oona said. 'Song Sung Blue, Sweet Caroline, Solitary Man, Cracklin Rosie, Shilo…' Oona read out Hector's scrawl. 'Wow….hey this is simply great. Thanks.'

'You are welcome.' Oona didn't tell him that she already had those songs on an LP record.

Oona decided to study English literature after failing to convince her mother to let her join Art College. 'A total waste of three years. You'll end up a starving artist with unkempt hair and a *jhola* like the Bakshis' son. What was the point in sending you to expensive schools?' Sangeeta had argued when Oona told her of her plans to take up art. Finally she managed to get admission to the English departments at both Xavier's and Loreto College, but opted for the latter.

'Aren't you stupid!' Sonia had chided. 'Crazy to let go your Xavier's seat. It has a far better faculty and it is co-ed. And also imagine having handsome male professors to teach you.' Apart from Sonia, most of her other friends had joined Loreto. Besides, her cousins had also passed out from Loreto and her mother had insisted she go to Loreto. 'Better prospects on the marriage market,' Rita her cousin had remarked, who, at thiry, was still unmarried. Oona wondered aloud why Rita Didi remained single. 'None of the grooms measure up to my standard, *bujhli*? Understood?'

'Yes of course.'

So Loreto it was. Studying political science and economics with English literature as a major or honours subject. 'English Horrors', they called it jokingly. Honestly, Oona did not think much of her choice of college or the subject she was to pursue for the next three years. She was resigned to her choice and decided to do it more out of duty, than love. But she was certain about one thing—that she would not waste time regularly attending classes and diligently taking notes. Rita Didi had been a first-class literature graduate from Loreto and had promised to give Oona her notes. Another reason to opt for Loreto.

'I will only attend college when I need a break,' Oona told Sonia.

'Break from what?' Sonia had asked.

'From the mundane, career planning etc....'

'Hey, what exactly do you plan to do?'

'Prepare for my future. I need to work hard. Set myself a few goals in life. Do some job-oriented courses like film-making, journalism, advertising, etc. Learn French at the Alliance or German at the Max Mueller. Prospects for interpreters are good, I hear. Maybe even do a course in interiors from Berger's.' Oona had remarked self-assuredly.

'And what about college?' Sonia asked.

'I will attend whenever I have the time. Frankly, Sonia, a degree in English is going to get me nowhere. I don't see myself as a research student or a professor for the rest of my life.'

'Same here,' Sonia giggled. But then she was serious about neither her studies nor a career. She was attending college just to bide her time before she and Deepak settled down. Besides, Deepak's father was one of the biggest distributors of liquor in West Bengal and the family was very wealthy. There was no way any *bahu* from their house would go out and work. 'I am waiting to get married and enjoy life, have kids, and all that,' Sonia laughed, completely carefree.

Meanwhile Hector had left for Delhi to pursue his training in ground studies in order to become a pilot. This was much against his family's wishes. The Boses had been zamindars earlier and like all landed gentry, pursued academics and the arts for generations. Though they were not as rich now as they had previously been, they nevertheless believed that education was above all.

Arun Bose, Hector's father, had read philosophy at Balliol in Oxford, where he met Maive, an Irish fellow student, and fell in love with her. They came to India and got married. Arun Bose, however, was not inclined to work much, so he did not bother to look for a job. He spent most of his time reading, listening to music and managing the family assets and various properties. This in itself was quite a job and more than Arun Bose's laid-back demeanour could handle.

Like his father, Victor, the older boy, was inclined towards academics. After a first-class first in economics from Presidency College, Arun Bose decided to send him to LSE for his master's. And now he wanted Hector to do the same. But Hector had other plans. He wanted to be a pilot. Not because he loved flying so much, but more because of the glamour and money. The starting salary of a pilot was over 30,000 rupees—that was a lot of money. Besides, there was Sonia. His girlfriend. Or so he thought. Hector was madly in love with her and wanted to stay close to her in case some charming pilot swept her off her feet...What if he could land a job with Cathay? Maybe they could fly together...be together.

Oona did not like Hector's decision to become a pilot. She knew the risks involved. That of being in close proximity with the beautiful Sonia Singh. That bitch. But she never mentioned this to Hector. She kept expressing her fears of the hazards of an air accident. Especially after the recent Challenger mishap. But an accident could happen anywhere, Hector had remarked nonchalantly. He could not understand why she was making such a big deal out of it. After all, she was not his girlfriend.

'Hey, how are you liking college?' Hector asked as he seated himself opposite Oona. They were at the local South India Club cafeteria. It had been six months since Hector had gone to Delhi. Now, having completed his ground studies, he had come to meet his family before heading to Ahmedabad.

'College is not too bad. We are preparing for the annual fest. It is going to be fun. Will you be here next month? You could attend too,' Oona said.

'I doubt it,' Hector replied.

'How were your papers?'

'Not too bad,' Hector said. 'The Air Navigation and Air Regulation papers were cool. The Met paper was a bit tough. But I've managed okay.'

'Hmm….,' Oona sipped her coffee.

'It is so bloody expensive, this whole course. I have already dipped into all my personal savings for the ground training course. It cost me fifty grand.'

'Oh! That's a lot of money,' Oona exclaimed.

'That's not all. There is more to go. At least another five lakhs.'

'What!'

'Yes.'

'I am sure your parents will help out,' Oona said, not sounding very convincing.

'Are you crazy! You know they are dead against my becoming a pilot. They are not going to help out at all,' Hector said. Oona smiled wickedly, as she bit into the crisp dosa. Good, she thought to herself. The dosa was beginning to taste divine.

'So how is Delhi?' Oona asked. 'Made any friends?'

'Oh, Delhi is cool. Nice city if you know the right crowd. A couple of good discos too. Fortunately, I have a nice set of course buddies too. Especially this chap called Sajid. He's from Lucknow. Totally crazy. You'll love meeting him,' Hector said.

'Yeah?' Oona tried to sound interested but Hector's flying buddies did not seem to hold her attention. 'Aunty Maive was saying you will be going back again…to do some course…why?'

'Oh, yes. I am going to Ahmedabad now.'

'Right, I heard about that. Why?'

'Now that I have my flying licence, I need to log at least 250 hours before I can fly commercially,' Hector enlightened her. 'For that I need to join a flying club. Therefore I am joining Triple A, that's the Ahmedabad Aviation Academy. One of the best. But frightfully expensive,' Hector added, sipping his coffee. 'A thousand bucks per hour of flying….that's a cool two-and-a-half lakhs!'

'That's a helluva lot of money! How are you going to manage that? Rob a bank?'

'I wish it was that easy,' Hector laughed. He liked Oona's strange sense of humour.

'Ah, well, I have an idea,' Oona suddenly said.

'You do? Let's hear it.' Hector said.

'Why don't you find a job here in Cal and save up enough and then pursue your course,' Oona said, hoping she might persuade Hector to stay on in Calcutta.

'Yeah. And let my licence lapse. I will never be able to save that kind of money in two years' time with the kind of job I get here. And the ground course papers lapse within that period if I don't manage the requisite flying hours.'

'Oh. I see.' Oona said. 'Then? What are your plans?'

'Well, I have decided to borrow the amount from a friend and return it once I start earning,' Hector said.

'Well, I must say you have a very generous friend,' Oona remarked.

'Yes. That she is. In fact, it was her suggestion to lend me the money. She also flies. As an airhostess though. With Cathay,' Hector said.

'Are you talking of Sonia Singh?' Oona asked, in an almost whisper.

'Yes. You know her?' Hector asked.

Oona nodded halfway between a 'yes' and 'no'. The dosa tasted like paper now.

Ela's Choice

It was 1925, six years since the end of the war. With Germany's deep humiliation, England was riding high on its victory. Closer home, the nationalist movement was gaining fresh ground. Frustrated with the moderate stance taken by the leaders of the Indian National Congress, Bal Gangadhar Tilak and other extremist leaders started to pressure the party. After serving his prison sentence in Mandalay in Burma and on his return to India in 1914, Tilak had decided to revive his own political activity while he and his extremist group simultaneously maintained pressure on the Congress to allow them to re-enter the Party. Tilak had realised that in order for any nationalist movement to gain legitimacy, support from the Congress was a prerequisite.

Along with Annie Besant, he started the Home Rule movement in India in 1916, along the lines of the Irish Home Rule League. The main focus of the League was to build up an agitation around the demand for home rule, or self-governance. Besant, who was in her sixties now, had come to India in 1893 to work for the Theosophical Society in Adyar, a suburb of Madras. She had begun her political career in England as a proponent of Free Thought, Fabianism and Theosophy. By 1917, Besant's League had over 7,000 members which included, among others, Jawaharlal Nehru from Allahabad and B. Chakraverti, J. Bannerjee and lawyer Somenath Sen from Calcutta.

Somenath Sen had nothing to complain about. Having made his money as one of the top lawyers in the city, Somenath's mission now was to render his services to his country, to society. It was time to give back. Though he still maintained cordial relations with the English, his reputation for pleading the cases of the 'nationalists' for free was slowly spreading. The British of course termed them 'anti-nationalists' and 'terrorists'.

The Sens had now shifted from their north Calcutta abode to the more posh and centrally located Wood Street. Situated just off the fashionable Park Street, and in a small tree-lined lane next to Bishop House, the bungalow had originally belonged to an English couple, Dr and Mrs Roland Smith. The Smiths had left for their homeland quite some years back and a Paul Smith, distant cousin of Dr Smith's, had been living in the house all these years. Paul had been a lawyer at the High Court for the past two decades and knew Somenath.

When Paul decided to return to England, he happened to mention in passing to Somenath that he would be missing his lovely cottage on Wood Street. 'I will especially miss looking at the flaming gulmohar trees from my window,' Paul said.

'Well, hold on to the cottage. You can always come back every year to beat your harsh English winters and admire the gulmohar,' Somenath had said.

'Well, I wish I could do that. But the house does not belong to me. It belongs to my uncle, Dr Roland Smith. I don't know whether you have heard of him or not. He used to have a flourishing practice here many, many years ago. Dr Smith's Clinic at Dhurumtolla?'

'Yes. Yes, of course. So he's your uncle! Will he be coming back?' Somenath asked.

'Oh, no. He is getting on in age and besides his only daughter is married and settled in England. His wife has no intention of returning either. In fact, they want to sell the place. Do you know of anyone who might be interested in buying it?'

'I'd be interested. Let me think about it. I need to discuss this with my wife,' Somenath smiled.

'Oh, this is news. Why don't you bring your family over for tea? They can see the place. I am sure they will like it and Uncle Roland would be delighted if someone of your standing bought his house.' So when Somenath Sen had bought Dr Roland Smith's bungalow bang in the centre of town, his social standing improved further. There were the Mitters who had a bungalow on Little Russel Street and the Bonnerjees had their mansion near the La Martiniere School on Louden Street; but for a Bengali to own a house near Park Street was a very prestigious affair.

Ela, of course was overjoyed as now she was living close to David, whose home was virtually in the lane next to the Sens'. But that was all there was to it. Neither of the families socialised with the other as they were not acquainted. Besides, neither Ela nor David had told their parents of the relationship.

'Did you know, Mummy, we have new neighbours?' Judy enlightened her mother one day while Alison was busy sorting out things. The Olivers were leaving India for good and there was a lot of packing to do.

'Really? Where?'

'In Dr Smith's cottage. It has been bought over by some Bengali family—Sens or something. David was telling me the other day…'

'Enough,' Alison cut her short. 'I am not interested. The house did not bring any happiness to its previous occupants. It is not a lucky place…'

Mention of the Smith bungalow was painful for Alison. It brought back memories of the father she had and yet did not have. Memories of a deprived childhood, which she could not share with anyone.

'I think David mentioned he knew one of the new occupants,' Judy continued, unmindful of her mother's comments. 'Don't you think it would be a good idea to call on our new neighbours? Invite them for tea or something? Get to know them…?'

'I don't like the idea at all. Besides, what is the point of making new acquaintances when we are leaving? A fortnight from now we will have left.'

Judy was undeterred. 'But since David is staying back, it would be nice for him to know a family close by.'

'He certainly does not need to socialise with the natives. There are still enough good English families in the city for your brother to socialise with.'

Every weekday, at nine in the morning, Ela would take her father's hackney, which would wend its way through the lane next to Wood Street, into Elm Street and stop in front of a small cottage on Louden Street, close to the La Martiniere School for Girls and not too far from the Bonnerjee mansion.

The cottage belonged to Mr Pius, an elderly widower, who lived with his elder sister, a spinster. The Pius siblings had been running a kindergarten school for the past twenty-odd years. Known as Mr Pius's School, it was often mispronounced by locals as Payesh's school (*payesh* in Bengali meant rice pudding). The school catered to European and rich Bengali children—a stepping stone to the nearby La Martiniere and other missionary schools dotting the area.

Ela taught these tiny tots the English alphabet and a few nursery rhymes. Often, she read them stories too. This kept her busy for a good three hours in the mornings, Monday to Friday. She had reduced her commitments to the Samaj some years back, and was enjoying teaching at the school for two reasons—first, she loved the company of children and second, it gave her something to do besides sitting at home, reading Shelley or Keats or doing embroidery. And listening to her parents plan her marriage.

In spite of Somenath's and Roma Debi's persistence, Ela kept postponing her marriage on one pretext or the other. First she insisted on completing her studies. Then she decided to study further, to do her master's. When her father refused, she sulked for a while. Later she started doing charity work for the Samaj.

'All this is fine,' Somenath said, 'but you can still continue to do all this after marriage.'

'What if my husband does not allow me to work?' Ela had argued. But these were mere excuses.

'What rubbish! I will tell Biren. He comes from a very liberal family. I am sure his family will not object,' Somenath had assured her.

Soon after, she had joined Mr Pius's school. It was her friend David who put her on to old Mr Pius. David's sister Judy taught at Mr Pius's and since the Olivers had left, David could think of no better person than Ela to replace her.

'You might find it a little juvenile, teaching kindergarten children, but then you will get used to it. Judy used to love interacting with the children,' he said.

'Oh, I love children too,' Ela said defensively.

'I am sure you do,' David said with a twinkle in his eye.

More than that, Ela wanted to prove to her father that she was capable of some vocation and that was the reason for her not settling down to matrimony. Most days, David would be at the school with some excuse or the other, in order to meet up with Ela. Old Miss Pius would often joke to her brother that the Oliver boy's frequent dropping in on them was not so much to meet them than to chat up with the Sen girl. Her brother would nod without paying much attention.

The Oliver's bungalow had now been occupied by a new family, the Ezras. They came from Armenia and had been living in the city for the past two decades. Like most Armenians, they had come to India with the purpose of trading at least half a century before Charnock set foot in the city. In 1813, there were more than seventy-five merchandising vessels in the Kidderpore Docks in Calcutta, more than in any other city. There were a number of private managing agencies which traded in various goods with the Company. Among them were fourteen Scotsmen, ten English, fourteen Armenians and two Portuguese merchants.

Unlike their more fashionable British counterparts, the Armenian merchants mainly settled near the waterfront in modest houses, causing the area to be known as Armenian Ghat. Mr Ezra owned a small bakery on Park Street next to the more famous Swiss confectioners, Flury's. Though small in size, Ezra Bakery, as it was called, gave the Swiss confectionery a run for its money, becoming famous for rich plum cakes at Christmas time and for making the tastiest rum macaroons on this part of the continent. Over time Mr Ezra had expanded his business and bought a large shop in the newly opened Sir Stuart Hogg Market on Lindsay Street. (The locals preferred to call it New Market.) The shop was next to Nahoum's, the famous Jewish bakery.

The Ezras were kind enough to let out a couple of rooms in the back garden to David. Earlier known as the outhouse and occupied by the *mali* and his family, it had now been renovated and served as cosy living quarters for David. He even had a stove, so that whenever he tired of eating rich food from the Ezra's kitchen, he would boil a simple stew for himself. But what he liked about this arrangement best was that in addition to living in the same area where he grew up, he also continued to live close to Ela.

Since Somenath would be away at work when Ela's classes ended at noon, she insisted on returning on her own, much to the horror of her parents. But as it was a short walk in broad daylight, they yielded. Especially after Ela assured them that she would tell the *ayah* from the school to escort her. In reality, the time she left the school coincided with David's lunchbreak. He would walk the short distance from his office, and stroll home with Ela, the two chatting in earnest, totally oblivious to their surroundings. Once they reached the end of Wood Street, David would wait while Ela crossed the road and disappeared into the corner of the lane towards her house. She would turn back to look at him. David would wave. She never waved back for fear of being spotted by someone from the family standing in the verandah, but discreetly nodded. David understood.

'Oh, by the way,' Somenath Sen suddenly announced to his family one evening while taking a long puff from his *gorgora*—the Bengali gentry's term for the *hookah*. 'The Roys have invited us to tea at the Club tomorrow.'

'Oh, I see,' Roma Debi looked up from her knitting and smiled. 'That will be nice. Are they bringing their son along?'

'Yes. That was the whole point in inviting us. Biren Roy is coming along with his parents. I've been wanting to talk to the Roys about this match, but since Ela was reluctant and Biren has also been working in London for the past few years, I kept quiet. Now he is back in Calcutta and is keen to meet Ela. Apparently he has heard about our Ela's work with the destitute children in the Samaj and is quite impressed.'

'I am sure Ela will be impressed with Biren too. I have been hearing good things about the boy,' Roma Debi added.

She hoped Ela would stop being stubborn and consider the prospect of settling down with Biren Roy. After all, she was getting old. Past 30 and still not married! When would this girl settle down? Luckily the Roys also did not push the Sens regarding Ela and Biren's marriage since their son, like Ela, was also deliberating on the subject.

Roma Debi was certain that the Roys would not find a better match than her daughter in the Samaj. That was why they were still keen on her, she thought to herself and smiled.

Both Somenath and Roma looked at Ela, who pretended not to hear anything and kept reading the *Collected Works of Lord Byron* with affected interest.

'*Eije, shunchho*? I want you to look your best tomorrow. Elegant but subtle…the Roys are very cultured,' Somenath told his daughter, 'So no over-dressing.'

'But Baba…'

'No buts and ifs this time. *Aami kichu shunbo na*….I do not want to hear anything from you. You will do exactly as I say. *Bujhle*?'

Ela nodded reluctantly, 'Well, if you say so.'

She returned to her book. Roma Debi continued with her crochet. She was knitting a set of coasters for the coming Maghotsav Fete at the Samaj. Somenath went back to puffing his *gorgora* and going over a back issue of the *Calcutta Gazette*, which most Bengalis fondly called Hickey Shaheber Gazette. Or Hickey's Gazette.

The Calcutta Club was one of the premier clubs in the city with a select membership of the who's-who of the social circuit. The club came into being in 1907, a few years after the then Governor-General, Sir John Woodburn's eminent Indian guest Rajendranath Mukherjee was subjected to discrimination by the snooty European members at the Bengal Club. Thus emerged this Indo-European club with the Maharajas of Cooch Behar and Burdwan, the Nawab of Murshidabad and the Nizam of Hyderabad as founding members. Leading figures like Motilal Nehru, and Abanindranth and Rabindranath Tagore, were also members.

The Sens joined the Roys in the mahogany-panelled tea room. In keeping with the strict etiquette of the club, the men wore formal jackets. The ladies wore sarees, but with formal leather shoes instead of sandals. Club entry was not allowed in Indian *chappals*. Even sarees were allowed as a concession.

The Roys and Sens exchanged polite words while uniformed bearers served tea and scones and muffins and croquettes. Dressed in an elegant pink crepe saree with embroidered gold *parsee gara* border, Ela seemed quiet throughout and looked a little nervous as she knew all eyes were focused on her. Biren also appeared a little nervous, though he tried covering it up with a laugh every now and then. Ela thought him a funny fellow. So unlike her David, who was charming and sure of himself. Ela's thoughts were so wrapped up in David Oliver that no other man, however eligible, could measure up to him. Not even the pleasant-looking Biren Roy.

Once the tea service was removed, Romen asked Somenath whether he would care to see the famed library of the club, to which Somenath immediately agreed. Mrs Roy announced that she was going to the powder room and Roma Debi promptly decided to join her. This was the elders' way of letting the young couple spend some time together in order to 'get to know each other'.

Once the elders left, Biren suggested to Ela that they take a walk around the club gardens. 'It is quite pretty outside,' he said. Ela agreed, happy to get out of the formal ambience of the tea room.

'So,' Biren said for lack of anything more interesting as they sat in silence on a garden bench after a short walk around the place.

'So?' Ela repeated, surprised.

'So. I mean what do you do, Ela?'

'Oh. I teach, read, embroider, do social work, sing a little Rabindra *sangeet,* apart from eating, drinking, sleeping and waking.' Both laughed heartily.

'And you?' Ela asked Biren, still laughing, 'What do you do?'

'Not much different from what you do except that I go to the *kachari* and in my spare time read law books.' Both laughed again. Then a hush fell.

In the silence that ensued, Ela realised it was quite an effort talking to Biren. I am sure he is an interesting man, but it just so happens that we have nothing in common, she thought to herself. Something definitely is lacking here, she thought as her mind strayed to David. David and I would be talking nineteen to the dozen by now.

'Ela,' Biren cut into her thoughts.

'Yes?' Ela looked up at him.

'It is about time we came to the point,' he said. Suddenly his nervousness was gone. He appeared to be a man in control of the situation.

'I don't understand,' Ela said.

'Let me explain,' Biren continued. 'You know our families have been keen on us marrying for some time now.'

Ela nodded.

'So have I,' Biren said.

Ela was startled. She had not expected this.

'Oh,' Ela said softly, 'I was not aware of it.'

'Though we have met briefly a few times, I have been keeping track of you.'

He smiled at her. Ela blushed. Biren thought Ela looked very pretty when she blushed. 'Your Samaj work, your teaching at Mr Pius's…I like dynamic women.' There was a strange silence that followed. Neither knew what to say. After what seemed like ages, Biren finally said, 'Ela, I think it is about time we got married.'

Men, Ela thought, sounded all alike. Like her father, Biren merely stated they marry. Not once did he ask her opinion on the issue. As if it was of no consequence. So unlike David. Her mind flashed to the picnic in her last year of college, at the Harbour by the Bay, near Chandpal Ghat. Where the boys' and girls' departments had gone together. Amidst the general bonhomie, David Oliver went down on his knees and asked Ela, 'Will you marry me?' Everyone present thought it was done in jest, except for Ela and David. They were dead serious. But what Ela recalled was David had asked her to marry him. 'Will you marry me?' and not just 'Marry me'.

Biren took Ela's silence as a confirmation. 'Then that's settled, right?' he said as if he had just concluded a business deal. 'Please, let us not rush into this…' Ela began.

'Rush?' Biren cut in, 'I have waited long enough, Ela. I cannot wait anymore,' he sounded offended. There are enough girls in the Samaj who are waiting to become Mrs Biren Roy without my having to run after Somenath Sen's spinster daughter, he thought. 'Is there something you want to tell me? Something I should know?' Biren asked.

'No.'

'I take it you do not want to marry me then?' Biren was hurt and upset.

Ela remained silent.

Suitors

'Hey, guess who I met last evening?' Sonia asked Oona as they shopped around for *dupattas* at Satnam's store in New Market. Sonia and Deepak had got engaged a fortnight back in a small engagement ceremony. Sonia was now sporting a ring studded with six large diamonds. Oona thought it a bit too garish, but Sonia kept flaunting it. Oona was now accompanying her friend on her various shopping sprees as she prepared her trousseau. The wedding was just three months away, in December.

'How would I know?' Oona shrugged.

'Take a guess!' Sonia teased. Oona shook her head.

'Hector,' Sonia smiled.

'Oh,' Oona murmured.

'Haven't you met him yet?' Sonia asked.

'No. I am not really in touch with him,' said Oona. 'He last wrote to me ages ago. He was logging in his flying hours, somewhere in Ahmedabad.'

'He is flying these days,' Sonia informed. 'Cathay Pacific. He was at the club yesterday.'

'I see. Alone?' Oona asked.

'No, with my namesake.'

'Oh.' Oona felt a stab of jealousy but quickly recovered her composure. She had realised that day at the South India Club that Hector was not romantically interested in her. He was very much in love with the much older, more beautiful, Sonia Singh. Though he wrote to her on rare occasions like her birthday or New Year's, it was basically to inform and enquire. But Oona treasured even these mundane notes from Hector; they were the closest thing she possessed to 'love letters'.

Oona had almost got over Hector in these last few months, with her demanding college schedule. Now with Sonia suddenly mentioning him, Oona felt a little hurt. More because he had not got in touch with her on returning to town. She was tempted to go home and call him up. Just to hear his voice. No, she would not, she said to herself. Let him call. I do not want to appear to be chasing him.

'He hasn't called you yet, has he?' Sonia suddenly broke into her thoughts.

'No. I told you, we are hardly in touch.'

'But he did ask about you.'

'He did? What did he say?'

'Oh just how you were and what you were doing, etc., etc.' Sonia said, busy examining a red and orange *bandhni dupatta*. 'What do you think of this one?'

'Very pretty,' Oona said without even looking at it.

Hector finally called Oona, the evening before leaving. 'I will be posted in Hong Kong now for the next couple of years. Sorry, I could not call earlier as I was caught up with a hundred and one things,' Hector apologised.

'I can imagine,' Oona was curt. 'All the best for your new posting.'

'Thanks.' Hector sensed the coldness in her voice. 'I wish we could have met. It's just that…'

'Next time,' Oona cut him short. 'I've been extremely busy with college these last weeks. We have the mid-terms coming up.'

'Well, I'll call once I am settled. You take care,' said Hector, giving up.

'You too, and bon voyage,' Oona said, knowing very well that Hector would not call.

With Hector gone, Oona could breathe easy again. She was glad she would not run into him and feel awkward. She met Hector's mother a few times soon after and Mrs Bose wondered aloud why she had stopped visiting them. 'Uncle and I miss your chatter,' Aunty Maive said as they crossed paths near the chemist shop. When Hector had gone to Delhi for his training, Oona had become acquainted with the Boses. She would often visit them for a casual chat while discreetly enquiring about their son, but she stopped visiting them once she realised Hector was still with Sonia Singh. Hector was her first crush. And his memories were too painful for her to endure going to his house anymore.

Craig came into her life a few weeks after Hector had left for Hong Kong. Oona and two of her friends were sitting at Flury's, chatting over fresh lime soda during their lunch break from college, when they noticed Craig watching them curiously from the next table. Dressed in a white kurta, he was a good-looking 'foreigner', which was how all white-skinned people were known, whatever their nationality. Blacks and orientals were not included in this definition of 'foreigners'.

Her friends Shalu and Vaidya were a little wary, but Oona smiled at him. The young man took this opportunity to come to their table and introduce himself. He needed help with an address. Oona and Vaidya explained to him where Free School Street was, pointing him in the correct direction through the window.

'Can I buy you girls a drink?' Craig asked pleasantly. 'It will be a pleasure.'

'Sure,' Oona replied before her two prudish friends could say no. It was always welcome to be treated since most of the time the girls were broke.

Craig Berns was an anthropologist and an Indophile. He had been to India eight years ago as a student and had spent six months in the country, the major part of it in rural Bengal, researching the dying Baul movement and their music.

'Oh,' Oona said. 'Purna Das Baul used to be my neighbour till he moved some years ago.'

'I see,' Craig smiled, eyeing Oona with even more interest. 'You live around The Lakes, do you? Golpark?'

'Bang on.' Oona was very impressed.

'I remember visiting his old pad then. He now has a big apartment in Dhakuria, beyond the bridge.'

'Yeah, Mick Jagger and George Harrison have changed his fortunes.'

'Right you are,' Craig said. Both laughed while Shalu and Vaidya smiled on, clueless.

Craig had never been the spiritual sort. Son of a Catholic mother and Jewish father, he himself was an atheist, or so he boasted. He grew up in the north, upstate New York in Connecticut, then studied anthropology at the University of Vermont. During his first year in college, Craig went to Fort Lauderdale with friends for the Easter holidays. Lying on the beach at sunset on Easter Sunday, he suddenly heard a mystical sound: the clanging of cymbals and a soft chanting of *kirtans* from a distance. Craig looked to where the sound came from and saw a group of white Americans singing and dancing. They appeared to be in a trance of ecstasy. The men were in saffron dhoti-kurtas and clean shaven while the women, dressed clumsily in sarees, danced and sang with equal fervour. They were an interesting contrast to the nude bathers on the beach. Craig and his friends walked over to check it out.

'Have you heard of Chaitanya Mahaprabhu of India?' one devotee asked Craig. He shook his head.

'Have you heard of Krishna?' Craig nodded hesitantly. 'Today we celebrate Krishna's homecoming in Vrindavan with colours. It is known as the festival of colours in India,' the devotee, Bhaktananda informed them. Realising their ignorance, he gave them a glossy magazine called *Back To Krsna*. 'This will tell you about our movement. It is called the Krsna Movement, KM. Spelt Krsna, but pronounced Krishna. And our mantra is *Hari Bol*.'

Craig saw that the magazine cost twenty-five cents. 'Do I owe you anything for this?' he asked.

'Well, if you want,' Bhakta shrugged. 'It costs twenty-five cents, but you can give anything above that as a gesture of your support for our movement.'

Craig pulled out his wallet, and Bhakta saw that it was stuffed with hundred-dollar bills. He said, 'A hundred will be fine.'

'I am sure,' Craig smiled, 'but for the moment I can only spare this,' he said, handing the man a fiver.

'That's fine. Thanks ever so much. Do come by our temple sometime. It is at the Coconut Grove. *Hari Bol*.'

The rhythm of the *kirtans* and Bhakta's confidence had impressed Craig. 'That bald guy sure had a lot of guts asking for a hundred dollars for something worth only twenty-five cents!' Craig told his buddies. Somehow, the gesture had tickled his Jewish veins. Later they went to the temple at the Coconut Grove and had *prasadam* which, Craig thought, tasted divine. Better than anything he had tasted in a long while. At night, he read the magazine. The one sentence which had captivated him were the words of Gurudev, the KM head, 'God himself talks to you through the Bhagavad Gita; it is the song of God.'

Craig bought himself a copy of the Gita and read it on his return to college. When he went home in the summer, he visited the New York KM temple on third and forty-second street, armed with his knowledge of the Gita. That fall, he visited India, the land of Krishna, as part of his college project, where he was studying the dying art of the Baul singers—the travelling folk minstrels from Bengal. Both Mick Jagger and George Harrison were greatly influenced by these singers and were trying to promote their music through their concerts and albums.

In Calcutta, Craig experienced things he had never imagined. The stench and filth of the city coupled with the warmth and love of the people. The religious fervour of the Bengalis during their greatest festival, the Durga Puja, as well as the haunting music of the bauls, especially the much-hyped Purna Das and the lesser known but equally powerful Bhakta Das. His girlfriend Margot had travelled with him, but India had not moved her as strongly as it did Craig, who vowed to come back.

'So here I am,' Craig told Oona as he ended his story and drank up his coffee at the South India Club. They had exchanged numbers at Flury's and today Oona had invited him to her favourite haunt. 'I hope I didn't bore you?'

'No, not at all. Rather interesting, I'd say,' Oona replied, though she found his love for India and Hinduism rather illogical. Gosh, I would give anything to inch my way to the USA. And look at this guy, heading for some mess called India.

'So what do you plan to do now?' Oona asked.

'Join the KM movement.'

'But you could have done that in New York!'

'Yes, I could. But I want to join the movement from here, the land of Krishna,' Craig said. 'I will devote some time to temple services and get my initiation from Vrindavan.'

'But won't that take a long time?'

'Yes. Six months. Maybe even a year. But that is okay. I have all the time to spare.' Craig smiled.

Oona thought his plans rather strange. But she was happy he was staying. There was something in those smiling grey eyes which had held her. A certain kindness maybe. She wanted him to stay.

'Ma...please. I am fed up with this silly soap you watch every day. I hate it. Why do you waste prime time watching such rubbish?' Oona asked exasperatedly.

'Because prime time is meant for prime time serials like this,' Sangeeta informed her daughter as she went back to watching Ridge and his mother arguing over something.

Gosh, imagine watching such inane stuff. 'Why can't we watch the news?' Oona asked.

'When you buy your own TV, you watch what you like. Let me watch what I like now.' Sangeeta went back to watching *The Bold and the Beautiful* and Oona kept quiet.

Suddenly, Sangeeta turned to Oona, switching off the TV. 'Oona, I met Kobir today in the drugstore. He was asking about you. Was complaining that you don't return his calls and that you hardly want to meet him. Why are you ignoring him?'

'Oh c'mon Ma. Stop getting on my case. Why don't you watch *Santa Barbara*?'

'It's *The Bold and the Beautiful.* Don't change the subject. Why do you refuse to meet Kobir? He is such a nice and brilliant boy.' 'Precisely, Ma. The problem is he is too brilliant for my liking. Thinks no end of himself.'

'Oona,' Sangeeta said sharply. 'You cannot talk like this about Kobir. Is this how you talk about your future husband?'

'Oh, Ma please. Not now. Not again. We have been through this a million times. I am not marrying Kobir. He is just not my type.'

'Oona,' Sangeeta was angry. 'How many times must I explain that all these things don't matter? Once you get married, things work out. Even I did not know your father well before I married him.'

'And no wonder you two hardly got along.'

'What do you mean?' Sangeeta was angry.

'Exactly what I said.'

'Stop all this nonsense. Just get married first and things will fall into place.'

'What do you mean?' Oona said. 'How can things work out just like that? Ma please, Kobir and I have nothing in common.'

'I know....but you will get to like him once you marry. The Sarkars are very keen on this match and Mrs Sarkar really likes you. What more can you desire? He's an only son, his sister is married and settled in the US, they have a big house, are an educated family. He's a brilliant boy, will go for higher studies abroad soon. Thank your stars. *Baap mora mei*...fatherless girl...do you think I can get you married lavishly?'

Stopping briefly to gather her breath, Sangeeta started again, 'The Sarkars are such a decent family that they have demanded nothing...no money, no jewellery, no furniture...no dowry. "Just send your daughter in the clothes she is wearing and we will take care of her," is what Mrs Sarkar told me. And look at you...ungrateful girl.' Oona decided it was best not to argue with her mother.

Sangeeta suddenly realised why Oona was protesting. 'Kobir told me that some of his friends have seen you with some man, some foreigner in *kurtas*...some KM guy....Is it true?'

'He must be referring to Craig. Yeah, he is a believer in the KM philosophy though he is not a full-fledged devotee yet. He is an anthropologist and he lives in New York.'

'I don't care where he lives. Kobir did not seem to like the idea of you gallivanting around with some vague foreigner. It spoils your reputation. Don't forget you are a *baap mora* unmarried girl. No decent boy will marry you if the Sarkars call off the wedding. And these Americans will only take advantage of you and then leave you. They have their American girlfriends tucked away back home.'

'Please, Ma...Craig is different from your idea of Americans. He loves India and its culture. You must meet him,' Oona said.

'Enough. I don't want you meeting him anymore.' Sangeeta was firm. 'Kobir does not like it and you will have to respect his wishes.'

'What nonsense, Ma!' Oona was furious. 'Who is he to like or dislike my friends? Besides what about the fact that he keeps going out with that girl...the Seals' daughter. He has been seeing her since his school days.'

'Never mind that. He is a boy, he can do anything. Besides, he is not going to marry her. His mother does not approve of the Seal girl. Anyway, what is it to you? Once he marries you, he will stop seeing her and…'

'Likewise, Ma,' Oona cut in.

'What?' Sangeeta was offended.

'Nothing. I am going to bed now.'

'What about dinner?'

'I am not hungry,' and Oona walked out of the drawing room.

Sangeeta slumped back in her chair, exhausted. These mother-daughter spats were happening too frequently of late, she observed, pulling her sparse hair into a loose knot above her nape.

'Hey this is amazing,' Craig said as he looked at Oona's walls plastered with posters of American pop idols. 'It almost feels like I'm home. You seem to be a big fan of the King's.'

'Yeah, I do like him a lot.'

'You seem to like a whole lot of others too.'

'I had different idols at different ages. They accumulated over the years and I just got too lazy to remove them,' Oona tried to justify her teenage quirks, a little embarrassed.

'That's okay,' Craig laughed. 'We all go through these phases.'

'If I remove them now the walls are gonna look ugly. So I will just have to wait till the rooms get a coat of paint,' said Oona, as Craig began looking through her record collection.

'And look who we have here….Louis Armstrong! You like him?'

'Oh yes,' Oona nodded. 'I am a big fan of Satchmo's.'

Craig was impressed. He gave her a light hug and said, 'Well, that makes the two of us. I used to play the tenor sax for the college band. Nothing major though. We used to call ourselves The Ragtaggers,' he continued. 'I like Satchmo, but I prefer modern jazz. Especially John Coltrane and Miles Davis. What about you?'

'I prefer vintage jazz. Ella Fitzgerald and Satchmo are my all-time favourites.'

'Ella Fitzgerald. Way before your time.' Craig smiled at Oona, pulling her close as he looked through the rest of her record collection. She could feel his body, breathing in tandem with hers. It felt like an eternity.

'You seem to have eclectic taste. Boney M to Bizet's Carmen. Oh and here's the Best of Nirmalendu Chowdhury. I dig him too.' He finally let go of her. Oona was flushed but quickly regained her composure. Craig did not fail to notice it.

'Why don't you sit? I'll get us some tea,' Oona said.

'Oh, good. Tea will be great.' Craig grinned.

One hot, bright afternoon Oona had drawn the curtains and was lying in bed, listening to music. She had bunked college for no particular reason except the heat and was enjoying the treat. Sangeeta was at work and would never know that Oona was lazing at home, missing her classes. She had put on her favourite country album and now it was Dave Dudley singing Rawhide. She looked at the wall clock: 3.30. She should be getting ready to go meet Kobir at the south gate of the Lakes. He had seemed anxious to speak to her. She wondered what he wanted to say.

The Sarkars lived a few lanes away from the Roys and the families had known each other for years. Amit Roy used to be good friends with Saibal Sarkar, Kobir's father. The Sarkars had two children, Maya and Kobir. During her school vacations, Oona had often played with both of them, fondly referring to the siblings as Maya didi and Kobir dada. After Amit's death, the Sarkars had been kind to the Roys, often inviting Sangeeta and Oona home.

The much older Maya was now studying at Purdue in Indiana, in the USA. Oona lost touch with her and Kobir as each of them got busy with their lives. A couple of years back the Sarkars suddenly dropped in at the Roys' to invite them for Maya's wedding. She was marrying her professor at Purdue. 'Thank God he happens to be a Bengali and incidentally from the same *gotra* too,' Oona heard Mrs Sarkar tell her mother.

The wedding was a neat affair and Oona enjoyed herself a lot. For her it was a reunion of sorts, spending time after years with Kobir dada and Maya didi, who she thought looked very chic. Kobir was quite taken by Oona now. She had grown more ladylike in his eyes, especially with her lovely hair which now reached below her shoulders, very different from the short-haired tomboy he had loved to bully. He introduced her to his friends. 'And stop calling me Kobir dada for God's sake,' Kobir whispered. 'It makes me feel ancient.'

'But I've always called you Kobir dada,' Oona said, for she saw him as an elder brother.

'Just Kobir.' He squeezed her hand.

A few days after the wedding, the Sarkars invited Oona and her mother to their house for dinner. They hinted that they would like Kobir to marry Oona once they both completed their studies, if Sangeeta agreed. Sangeeta was overjoyed. On the way home she asked Oona, 'He is quite pleasant looking, don't you agree?' 'Yes, yes,' Oona had replied absent-mindedly. Her mind was preoccupied with Hector at that time.

Taking Oona's indifference to mean 'yes', Sangeeta told the Sarkars that neither she nor Oona had any objection to the match. Everyone was thrilled, except Oona. She had nothing against Kobir, but found it hard to accept her 'Kobir dada' in the avatar of a lover. She got along well with his family though. Maya didi and she were in touch again, through letters. Kobir's mother often took Oona along on her shopping trips, and Oona enjoyed the outings. She even went out with Kobir and his friends a few times, for movies and some dinners, but that was all. She enjoyed Kobir's company but realised there was no chemistry between them.

'Friendship is fine, but if there are no sparks flying, there is no fun,' she had once confided in Sonia. 'I don't go weak in the knees looking at him and if a man cannot have that effect on me what's the point?'

Like Sangeeta, Sonia kept saying all would be well once they settled down. 'Your problem is that you are hopelessly in love with Hector and cannot see anyone beyond him. And Hector is already hitched. So why torture yourself?' Sonia had tried to counsel Oona several times, but always in vain.

Having met Craig, Oona was now even more unsure about Kobir. She had her life ahead of her; was it worth getting saddled with a loveless marriage? She looked out and saw the weather had suddenly softened. Dark clouds had brought in a premature sunset and it was suddenly cool and breezy. The accompanying winds and darkness at sunset always made Oona happy. She loved *kalbaisakhis*—as these windy nor'westers so characteristic of Bengal were called. She found them especially romantic. 'I only hope it doesn't rain,' she muttered to herself. 'I hate carrying an umbrella.'

Kobir walked up to her as Oona reached the southern gate of the Lakes while trying to keep her dupatta from flying off. The *kalbaisakhi* had subsided but there was a light breeze blowing. The area known as the Lakes was quite close to Oona's house. It was a large, wooded expanse, spread over several acres and comprised four large man-made lakes with little man-made islands in them. There were a number of rowing and swimming clubs around the lakes and lots of tree-lined paths for walkers and joggers. On the southernmost tip of the Lakes was a children's safari park with a mini zoo and lots of rides.

Over the years, the Lakes had breathed fresh air into the lives of the nearby residents. The crack of dawn saw the serious joggers followed by the early morning Sorbitrate-popping walkers who discussed current politics and their blood-sugar levels with equal gusto. Mid-morning was the time of the elderly and the aged, when the families preferred them out of their way as they went about their daily grind of preparing for school, college or office. They usually met up just after their daily bazaar visit, as they had time to spare till they were welcome back at home. The prevailing prices of fish and vegetables normally dominated their conversations.

Occasionally it would be a eulogy to a departed friend who would join them no more on their daily meets. Thus they carried on through the seasons and the years, as their numbers diminished and the ones remaining counted the days before they could join their friends again.

Afternoons were peaceful, with dhobis washing clothes and putting them out to dry on the banks of the Lakes. Sometimes cooks and maids from neighbouring homes napped here, gossiped, and even romanced—though the last was hard in the heat and light of afternoon. Early evenings again saw serious joggers, weight-watchers and children with their maids and mothers romping around. Around five, when it would grow dark, it was time again for the elderly to sit and relive their youth as the young passed them by. As it turned darker, most people left and their places were taken by young lovers with nowhere else to go. The Lakes was the best place to enjoy forbidden pleasures. Cops would sometimes make quick money by flashing their torches at random under the various trees and in corners, catching young couples unawares. Embarrassed, the lovers would hand over a few rupees and run, only to return another day.

These goings-on in the dark, and the notoriety of the area as a haunt for drunks and gamblers made it a no-no after sunset. Any young couple out for an innocent walk would call for raised eyebrows. Oona was naturally a little wary. She wondered why Kobir wanted to meet her at the Lakes. Why not at Nirmala Café or even at the Bijoli Grill restaurant?

'Would you like to have something to drink? Shall we go to the café first?' Kobir asked. On the northernmost side, one of the little islands had a café accessed by a hanging bridge. As a child, on vacation from school, Oona remembered jumping all the way along the bridge to make it swing, as she accompanied her parents to the café to have her customary fish fingers and Spencer's ice-cream soda. Now she could see other children doing what she used to do over a decade ago.

She dragged her attention back to Kobir and shook her head to say no. Of average height and complexion, Kobir had a pleasant face with a sharp nose, so unlike Oona's pug little nose. He was trim and appeared neatly casual in his blue jeans and crisp white shirt. He wore his Lennon glasses which made him look rather cute. I am sure a lot of girls find him very attractive....I wonder why I don't? Life would have been a lot less complicated that way. Oona smiled up at Kobir.

'Let's sit here then,' Kobir said, motioning Oona towards one of the many wrought-iron benches dotting the lakes. With the *kalbaisakhi,* it was prematurely dark. There was a gentle breeze blowing. Oona's long tresses kept flying all over her face. She gathered her hair together around the nape of her neck and knotted it into a casual bun.

'Why don't you leave it open?' Kobir said. 'You look lovely. You know Oona, long hair really suits you.'

His remark took her by surprise. It was the first time Kobir had actually said anything near romantic to Oona. She smiled, 'I would love to leave it open, but it will be flying all over my face.'

'That makes you look so sensuous.'

Oona struggled to keep things casual. 'Hey, what's the matter with you? Looks like the weather is having its effect on you.'

'Yes... *kalbaisakhi* always does this to me. And to have a lovely lady so close to me....' Before he could complete his sentence he moved closer to Oona and put his arms around her. Oona's body tensed in his embrace, but Kobir tried to calm her, saying, 'Relax. I won't eat you up.'

'Please... not like...'

'No. I don't want to hear anything. There is nothing wrong. We are going to get married soon,' Kobir seemed to control the situation.

'But I want to say something,' Oona tried desperately to talk as she felt Kobir's face so close to hers.

'Later. We'll talk later. For now, just look at me.' As she turned her head, Oona suddenly felt Kobir's mouth close in on hers. He held her tight. For a moment she went blank and then she could feel his tongue feeling her lips, her tongue while his hand roamed over her bosom, feeling her body and squeezing her breasts. After what seemed like several long, senseless minutes to Oona, Kobir suddenly stopped, flushed with excitement.

'Sorry, I took you by surprise,' Kobir said, smiling a satisfied smile. 'I just could not help myself. I have been wanting you since I saw you at Didi's wedding.' He kissed her on her hair and said, 'Don't worry. I will warn you in advance next time. You will be more prepared.'

It suddenly occurred to Oona that she had just got her first kiss. First serious kiss from a boy! And what did she feel? Nothing. No sensation. Just wet lips and Pepsodent breath. Not her idea of a kiss at all.

Sens and Boses

Returning to India in 1915 after his stint as a lawyer and activist in South Africa, where he vehemently protested against racism, Mohandas Karamchand Gandhi decided to turn his attention to India's freedom struggle. Living a hard life, and travelling by train with the people of India in the interiors of the country, he successfully united the Indians against the British like never before. Ironically, the British inadvertently helped along India's freedom struggle. First by introducing the railways, the postal service and other modes of modern communication which united an otherwise sprawling country. Second, by opening the doors to modern education, they opened the eyes of educated Indians who realised they were being persecuted by the British.

Highly-educated people like Gandhi and the younger lot like Jawaharlal Nehru and Subhash Bose fought the rulers with their own weapons. The first such weapon launched in 1919 by Gandhi, who was popularly called Bapu (father of the nation), was *satyagraha* or passive resistance. This was in protest against the Rowlatt Act which severely curtailed the civil liberties of the Indians.

Somenath Sen and his daughter Ela lost no time joining the Satyagraha Sabha. Somenath gave up Western attire altogether, donning the Bengali, simple cotton *dhuti-panjabi* instead for all occasions. His expensive Savile Row suits and silk shirts were packed away. He even stopped wearing silk kurtas as he felt they looked loud at the Congress party meetings. His family was well provided for, and he now devoted a large part of his savings to fund the work of the party.

Sympathy for the British was at an all-time low and the last straw was the Jallianwala Bagh massacre on Baisakhi day in 1919, when General O'Dyer gunned down more than 400 innocent Indians in a surprise attack. Soon after, the Bengali poet and Nobel laureate, Rabindranath Tagore renounced the knighthood earlier conferred on him by the British Crown.

When the Congress met in September 1920 in Calcutta, their main agenda was non-cooperation and boycotting legislative assemblies and elections. Somenath was part of the brigade led by eminent lawyer C.R. Das.

While the entire country was submerged in nationalist sentiments in the 1920s, Bengal had come to this awareness long before, when in 1861 the Society for the Promotion of National Feelings was founded, as the British termed it, for the 'educated natives of Bengal'. No wonder Gokhale had remarked, 'What Bengal thinks today, India thinks tomorrow.'

The women of Bengal were not found wanting either. Through education, social work and even the militia, the women did their bit. Sarala Debi, an educated young woman from the well-to-do Tagore family of Jorasanko and a distant cousin of the poet Rabindranath, established a gymnasium in her father's house in the city in the early 1920s. She felt it necessary to train the youth in physical fitness and awareness in order to fight the British. Ela, who taught young women knitting and needlework at the Samaj, also helped Sarala Debi in the running of the gymnasium.

Ela had stopped teaching at Mr Pius's school for a while now. She felt she had 'grown out of it'. It was not, as many thought, a protest against the British—after all, the Pius siblings, like David, were hardly racist. There were some among the British who thought it wiser to let the Indians rule the country than face the wrath of the Indians.

'Oh, hello, Ela,' Biren called out rather hesitantly as Ela Sen passed by one day at the end of a musical concert. It was January, the Bengali month of Magh. The Brahmos celebrated the festival of Magh or the Maghotsav at this time, to coincide with the birthday of their founder. Since they did not believe in idol worship, they just celebrated with week-long cultural programmes. It was also a time for young Brahmo men and women to meet, court and eventually marry. The Brahmos, unlike the rest of the Indians, believed in men and women getting to know each other before they married.

'Oh, hello. How are you?' Ela said, a little awkwardness still evident after all those years. After that evening at the Calcutta Club, the Roys had been miffed by Ela's attitude towards their son. So the Roys and Sens did not keep in touch. Ela heard that Biren eventually got married to a Brahmo girl, Somshukla, from another affluent family. Though Somenath had eventually forgiven his daughter, Roma Debi often reminded Ela what a good catch she had missed. Somshukla was supposedly a distant cousin of Ela's, her mother had said, explaining the convoluted connection. Brahmos were such a close-knit community, Ela thought, that she and Biren might just have been related!

'Ela, meet my wife, Somshukla. Som, this is Ela. Remember, I told you about her?' Ela smiled, wondering what he had told her about Ela. She and Somshukla smiled at each other. The awkwardness fell away somewhat after the initial introduction.

'And, by the way, Ela, meet my friend Kshitij. Kshitijmohan Dutta,' Biren said as he pushed a dark gentleman towards Ela.

'Nomoskar Kshitij Babu,' Ela said politely.

'Nomoskar Ela Debi,' Kshitij returned equally politely. Ela noted his polished accent belied his not-so-good-looks.

'Kshitij and I went to college together,' Biren explained as the foursome headed towards the Samaj lawns for lunch.

Singer Atulprasad Sen, who had come all the way from Lucknow, had just rendered some patriotic songs as part of the Maghotsav celebrations. The congregation had now broken for lunch. In the evening some young Samaj members were supposed to sing Rabindra sangeet, or songs composed by Tagore. 'I think Gurudev, too, will be rendering some of his compositions,' Somenath had told his wife and daughter over breakfast in the morning.

Once seated, Kshitij turned to Ela and said, 'I have been hearing about your good work for the Samaj. Also, your work with Sarala Debi.'

'Really! Who has been telling you all this?' Ela said.

'Well, Biren here,' Kshitij gestured to his friend.

'And what else has he been telling you?' Ela asked mischievously.

'Well, nothing much,' Biren butted in. 'Ela let me tell you that Kshitij here is no less accomplished. He has been doing a lot of work for the Samaj at the grassroot level. He has been working relentlessly for rehabilitation of widows in the Nadia district.'

'I see,' Ela said.

'Nothing much,' Kshitij said shyly.

'He is just being modest,' Biren rapped his friend on the back. 'You must try and impress the lady and not be so shy. Shyness will get you nowhere.' Biren then turned to Ela and said, 'You two will have a lot in common I am sure.'

Ela resented the last remark, especially the patronising way it was made. Who was Biren to decide who she socialised with? Was he trying to match-make? He had no business doing so. She noticed marriage had made Biren very ebullient. Anyway, this was getting nowhere. 'I have to go,' she got up politely. 'Nice meeting you Somshukla. Nice meeting you Kshitij Babu. I am sure we will meet again. Bye Biren.'

Meanwhile, at the far end of the lawn, Roma Debi kept an eye on her daughter while she herself chatted with Mrs Banerjee. She sighed, thinking of what a nice pair her daughter and Biren would have made, if only Ela had not been so stubborn.

'I think Biren and Somshukla make a great pair,' Mrs Banerjee remarked cattily, almost as if she had read Roma's thoughts. 'She is quite pretty, and young too.' The last was intended to remind Roma that her daughter was not getting any younger.

'Yes, yes,' Roma agreed, trying to shrug off the veiled barb as she adjusted the folds of her cream-coloured *tant* saree.

'You see the dark boy next to Biren?' Mrs Banerjee asked. 'Well, his name is Kshitijmohan Dutta. Good boy. Does a lot of work for the Samaj. Educated too. He is an orphan though,' Mrs Banerjee said. 'I think you should seriously consider him for Ela.'

'What! He is so dark. And thin. Not at all pleasant looking. How could you think of him for my daughter?' Roma was a little upset.

'Your daughter…well, she *is* a bit over the hill, don't you think? You will be lucky to get her married at her age. You know how men can be demanding. Poor Kshitij, being dark, is still single. He will be happy to marry Ela.'

Mrs Banerjee suddenly realised that Roma had left and walked off. Haughty woman, that Roma. So was her daughter, she thought. No wonder she finds our boys inferior to those filthy Englishmen who hardly bathe. God alone knows what she sees in them, Mrs Banerjee thought, her eyebrows knitted in anger. Mrs Banerjee and quite a few other women from the Samaj had often discussed the rumours of Ela Sen's infatuation with some Englishman.

Winter in Kolkata was by and large good-natured and indulgent. In the evenings, ladies and gentlemen drifted through the Respondentia Walk, the fashionable boulevard on the river front. Though it was an unspoken rule that 'pets and Indians' were forbidden, David would often take Ela down the Walk. Initially, while the other fair ladies swished past her in their fashionable skirts and hats and lace gloves, she used to feel awkward and acutely aware of her 'native' status in her skin colour and saree. But gradually she grew accustomed to this. She often stopped to exchange pleasantries with some of the people she had met through David. Sometimes David and Ela would walk down to the nearby Great Eastern Hotel or hail a hackney to the Grand Hotel which was owned by a distant cousin of the Ezras.

The young couple were in the Tea Room at the Great Eastern Hotel. Some decades before, the SS Tuscany had shipped ice all the way from Boston and introduced it to Calcuttans, changing the face of all parties ever after. Ice-creams and sorbets became popular in the city. Ela loved ice-creams, especially with those wafer biscuits. David studied her as she removed her gloves and placed them by her purse. They were made with delicate white lace from Scotland—his gift to her last Christmas. She would occasionally wear these gloves with her *baluchari* or *dhakai* sarees because the blouses with these expensive sarees were always trimmed with lace after the fashion of the day. They matched the gloves.

David noticed that she had been dressing less and less stylishly of late. Being part of the national struggle, she preferred to wear simple cotton *tants* and at times even coarse *khadis* on Gandhiji's urging. David was not bothered; to him Ela looked elegant in whatever she wore. It was a pity she could not go against her family's wishes to marry him.

'Ela you look lovely when you dress up. I wish you would do so more often.'

'Why, David, don't you like me without my embellishments?' Ela teased.

'Oh, let us not get into an argument now.'

'But it was you who started it,' Ela smiled.

'Okay, end of discussion,' David winked, taking hold of her hand. 'I am going to have my usual cuppa. I hear they have got some excellent Makaibari leaves.'

'You have your Makaibari. I would like the fresh fruit ice-cream with those wafer thins. You know Ma got some nice shortbread fingers and cream wafers from the Hall & Anderson store?'

'Oh? Were they nice?'

'Very. Came from London. Fresh lot. Walker's.'

David nodded, pausing to place his order as the turbaned waiter came up to them. When the man left, David continued, 'Hey, it has been a while since you have called me home to sup. You know, I quite relish the mustard fish these days.'

'Oh really? I thought you said it is very spicy.'

'Was, not "is",' David smiled.

'We'll have to wait for some time. My father will be going to Lucknow next month for the party meet. Maybe you can come then,' Ela said.

'Why should I wait that long? Besides, your father is quite polite to me so long as I don't ask for his daughter's hand in marriage,' David retorted.

'It is not that. My parents are really keen I marry and... you know how people talk...' embarrassed, she left the sentence unfinished.

'I understand perfectly,' he said, squeezing her hand.

David had spoken to Somenath a year ago, but the old man had politely refused to accept him as a *jamai*. After her father's refusal, Ela had become more stubborn and refused all the marriage proposals that came her way. Even Roma's gentle persuasion failed. 'You know your father will never allow you to marry an Englishman. He will never hear the end of it from his fellow patriots.'

'I know,' said Ela bitterly. 'If I cannot marry David I will not marry at all. I will never be able to love another man.'

That brought Roma Debi close to tears. 'Oh please, don't say such inauspicious things. You will die an old maid.'

Stiffening, Ela retorted, 'So be it,' and left the room.

Roma blamed this behaviour on modern education.

Though Delhi became the colonial rulers' favourite city after George V's famed Delhi Durbar in 1911, Calcutta still retained much of its imperial grandeur. It had ceased to be the imperial capital of India on All Fool's Day in 1912, but an Englishman could still make a fortune in real estate here. Of its population of one million, the city was home to 14,000 British and about 16,000 half-caste Anglo-Indians, who were loyal to them.

In spite of the Armenians, Portuguese and Dutch having established their trading interests in the city long before the English, it was the influence of the East India Company and the British Empire that was etched in Calcutta's colonial structure and culture. The city was broadly divided into two parts: the Black Town, where the natives lived and the White Town, where the sahibs dwelled. Churches and lavish homes began dotting the skyline of the White Town in the eighteenth century, prompting Lord Valentia in 1803 to call Calcutta the 'city of palaces'. The White Town grew around Fort William, named after William of Orange to commemorate his Calcutta visit, which stood by the bend of the Hooghly river and housed the English army. It extended to the south and central parts of the city, its heart being the fashionable Park Street.

The sidewalks of Park Street had elite stores and restaurants akin to London's Oxford Street and Knightsbridge. In 1920, the Oxford Bookstore & Stationery Co. was established here and soon overtook giant competitors like Newman's or Thacker & Spinks in popularity. Park Street also offered a pavement where lovers walked unmindful of stares. David and Ela would often visit Oxford if they were not watching the opera at the Globe or a play at New Empire. After tea and scones at Firpo's, they would stroll along the sidewalks and browse through the books at Oxford before David dropped Ela home just off Park Street. The Sens were perhaps among the very few Bengali families living in the White Town.

The Black Town spun its web of narrow, haphazard lanes towards the northern fringes, where, around the temple of goddess Chitteshwari on Chitpore Road, some of the local rajas and zamindars built sumptuous palaces beside a row of untidy houses and crossbred mansions. These were almost always embellished with elaborate columns and plaster of Paris friezes, rising above the general confusion and looming large and ugly on the cluttered horizon.

The merchant aristocracy lived in luxury, patronising the local arts, music, and the famed *nautch* or dance houses. The word 'nautch' originates from the Bengali/Hindi word 'naach', meaning dance. Among these merchants were the Tagores and the Mullicks, the two famous families whose names are deeply entrenched in not only the industrial history, but also the cultural history of the city. The Tagores' elegant house Jorasanko in Paturiaghata was the local seat of art and culture.

Close by, near Chitpore Road, Raja Rajendra Mullick's palatial residence—the Marble Palace—was known as the treasure trove of rich European Renaissance artefacts and paintings, including Dresden figurines, Lalique crystals, Ormolu clocks, Sevres vases, Belgian mirrors and a couple of priceless Reubens. Every room in the palace was rumoured to have been marbled in different designs, all imported from Italy.

It was from these traditional homes of North Calcutta that the *babu* culture came into being. Though Somenath originally lived in Chitpore, he preferred the serene surroundings of Wood Street. Unlike the traditionally rich Bengali families who believed in ostentatious displays of wealth, Somenath's Brahmo affiliations made him frown upon such garish displays.

There were times when Roma Debi did feel odd among her white neighbours, but Somenath and Ela were comfortable in their present abode. Lately, however, Somenath did broach the subject of moving into a more 'Bengali neighbourhood' like Sovabazar or Chitpore up north, but this was more due to patriotic feelings than for creature comforts. Ela on the other hand would hear none of it.

'No, Baba. This is a good area. And why should we leave this nice house? None of us are uncomfortable here, are we?' Ela asked one evening while Somenath was discussing with Roma the prospects of shifting residence.

'I was only thinking in terms of the current situation in the country. It is better we are with our people—not in this white neighbourhood,' Somenath explained.

'But Baba, we have never had any problems while we lived here and —' 'I know,' Somenath cut in. 'But those were different times. Things are changing. Besides, we can find a nice house near Cornwallis Street. It will be easier for you to commute to the Samaj.'

'That is okay…I do not mind the travel. Cornwallis Street is hardly far from here. Those areas are awfully crowded…I would rather be here,' Ela persisted. Roma Debi knew the real reason. As long as her daughter kept seeing that English boy, she would never want to move, or to settle down with a *bhadra* Bengali boy. But as always, Roma Debi said nothing. It was useless arguing with either father or daughter. Both were stubborn as mules.

Her parents let the matter drop for the time being, and Ela sighed with relief as she went back to reading the book David had just presented her. *The Golden Treasury* contained some of the best songs and lyrical poems in the English language, selected by Francis Turner Palgrave. Popularly known as Palgrave's *Golden Treasury,* this was the latest edition, printed in 1919 by the Oxford University Press at Milford. David bought it from the Oxford Bookstore when he caught Ela browsing through it. Ela had remarked absent-mindedly to David how her cousin Kamini had borrowed her copy and lost it. He also gifted her a copy of a 1908 edition of Geoffrey Chaucer's *Canterbury Tales,* published by J.M. Dent & Sons of London. In both the books he simply signed,

'To Ela dearest,
Yours always,
David'

Three years passed and Ela Sen remained unmarried. After a while, the Sens tired of convincing Ela to marry. Roma Debi kept suggesting eligible Brahmo men but gave up in frustration. 'I cannot believe she does not like any of the men from the Samaj,' Roma told her husband one day.

'Then for God's sake, let her marry a Hindu,' Somenath fumed.

But of course, nothing worked. Ela made it very clear she would only marry David or none other. 'Then die a spinster,' Somenath exploded in anger.

One warm summer evening that year, the Sens were invited to dinner at the Bose house on Elgin Road. Like Somenath, Janakinath Bose was a well-known lawyer and the two were friends. Of his sons, Sarat and Subhash, Sarat was about Ela's age. He was well-settled in his career and married with two children. It was the younger son Subhash, who was a source of worry for his father. He had passed the civil service examinations and was ranked first in English but refused to join as a protest against British imperialism. Everyone thought he was being foolish.

News of Subhash's involvement in a number of anti-imperialist activities had also reached Ela, who was naturally curious to meet him. The Sen seniors had set up the dinner gathering for a different reason. Janaki Bose had a distant nephew, a poor cousin, who worked for his uncle and was a bright young man. His name was Nemaikanto and though in his thirties, he was still unmarried. Somenath had discreetly mentioned to Janaki that he was seeking a match with the boy for Ela. Though the Boses were god-fearing Hindus, Somenath was now desperate to arrange Ela's marriage. A decent, Hindu man would do just fine. Unaware of the plan, Ela went along with her parents for the dinner party.

The fare was typical Bengali, served in the traditional manner in huge *kansha thalas* or brass plates surrounded by several small bowls. It was a seven-course meal—starting with *shukto* (bitter gourd cooked in *ghee*), *dal* (lentils), *begun bhaja* (fried aubergines), fish curry, prawn curry and *kasha mangsho* (mutton curry). Of course no Bengali meal could end without an array of deserts. There was *sandesh* and *rosogolla* from K.C. Das and *mishti doi* (sweetened yoghurt) and *boondey* from Bhim Chandra Nag. After dinner Somenath and Janakinath sat down for a smoke, puffing on their *gorgoras*. Sarat Chandra and Nemaikanto were immersed in a serious conversation but Subhash Chandra sat by, looking bored. In the next room, the ladies were busy chatting as Prabhavati Debi, Janaki Bose's wife made *paans* for the other ladies in the room.

Roma Debi was admiring the jewellery adorning Sarat's young wife. 'Young girls look nice when they wear gold jewellery. Look at my Ela. I keep telling her she should not leave her hands bare, but she doesn't listen to me. All she is interested in are those dull *khadis* and shapeless blouses. This nationalism has got too deep into the system of these youngsters.'

'You are telling me,' Mrs Bose replied. 'Look at Subhash. He has no care for the future. He even let go such a prestigious civil service post. All because of this "nationalism". We have tried convincing him to take up a job and settle down, but in vain.'

Ela smiled. She could not endure such conversation. She knew the next topic would harp on her single status. She hurried as discreetly as possible towards the spacious verandah, which ran the entire length of the house. Ela rested her elbows on the teak wooden rails. A shadow loomed behind her and she turned back to see Subhash Chandra. At twenty-six, he was tall and handsome. His round spectacles made him look a little older and more mature.

'Would you mind if I join you?' Subhash smiled.

'Not at all,' Ela smiled back.

'Looks like the ladies could not hold your interest,' he said, gesturing towards the room she had left.

'It's not that. Just that my mother loves harping on her favourite topic and it sort of embarrasses me.'

'And what is that?' Subhash asked.

'My marriage. They are obsessed with it and want to marry me off to any man they can think of.'

'Then it's good you did not join the men there,' Subhash pointed to where the fathers were sitting, chatting over their *gorgoras*. 'They are trying their best to set you up with my cousin Nemai.' Subhash laughed naughtily.

'What!' Ela was a little shocked. 'Well I never suspected *that*!'

'Why, if I may ask, are you so set against marriage?' Subhash asked.

'Well, I am not against marriage. It is just that, well, you will not understand. *Thak*,' Ela said.

'If you don't tell me, I will not understand. But, if you do, maybe I can help,' he said softly.

Ela looked up at him. For a Bengali, Subhash was quite tall, nearly six feet. There was something deep, something soft in those serious eyes. No man since David had had such a mesmerising effect on her. For a fleeting moment Ela wished she had been born five years later. Her expression changed and Subhash threw her a questioning look. Ela suddenly blushed and looked away, fearing he had read her thoughts. Then she told him about David.

'I see,' was all Subhash said. 'I do understand your predicament, Ela.'

Her name on his lips sounded soft and beautiful. She smiled at him and Subhash returned the smile. He held women like Ela in great respect, not because they defied social norms, but because they followed what they believed in. 'I do admire your courage though,' Subhash added.

'Now tell me, why are *you* shying away from marriage? Your mother was complaining about it a while ago. Do you have an English lady-love hidden away somewhere?' Ela asked mischievously.

'I wish it was as simple as that,' Subhash replied. 'But no. Marriage is the last thing I have in mind. Not now. Not for a while. Maybe, not at all.'

After some moments Ela finally broke the silence, 'Why? Have you taken a vow of celibacy?'

Subhash Bose laughed heartily. 'Do I look the celibate sort to you?' he asked with a wicked look. Then in all seriousness, Subhash told Ela his plans for his future. Plans to free his motherland from imperial shackles. First through gentle coaxing. Then if the rulers did not yield, he would use pressure. Build his own army of patriots and fight to free his motherland.

'My chosen path is risky and full of danger. I see no security or stability ahead for myself. How can I lead an innocent girl into such perils? My battle ahead is mine alone,' Subhash concluded.

Mesmerised, Ela asked, 'But what if someone should willingly join you in your struggles?'

'*If* that happens, I will deal with it. Right now I am alone and would like it that way for some time. Women are major distractions, you know.'

'I do not agree with you,' Ela said.

'Look, I think we had better go in. Otherwise our parents will worry we are hatching some anti-government plans out here,' Subhash said.

Ela laughed at the remark. 'I think you are right. We should go in.'

'And one more thing, Ela,' Subhash said as they were entering the room.

'Yes?' Ela said.

'I will see to it that you do not have to marry that cousin of mine,' Subhash grinned.

'Thank you.' Ela smiled back. She had full faith in his words.

Oona's Choice

'So?'

'So.'

'Here we are.' Craig gave Oona his most disarming smile.

'Well...er...I really didn't mean to bother you...'

'You are not bothering me at all, honey. I know you have been going through a bit of emotional turmoil. And as a friend I would like to help, if it means anything...'

'It means a lot,' Oona cut in quickly.

Oona was in Craig's little room, or pad as he liked to call it. He lived in a building right behind the main KM Temple off Louden Street in a quiet, shaded lane. Craig's window looked out onto a huge *champa* tree through which enough daylight filtered in to light up the frugally furnished room. A single cot, a cupboard, a writing table with a table lamp and chair, a telephone, an electric kettle, and a tape recorder were the main things in the room. Cassettes lay on the table, the bed and the floor, and books and magazines were scattered all over the place. Oona stared at the mess.

'Bit of a mess,' Craig said having followed her gaze and reading her mind.

'Quite charming, though.'

'You think so?' Craig asked. Oona nodded.

'Well, I don't.' And they both laughed heartily.

It was almost eight months since Kobir had kissed her. She kept replaying the scene and it rattled her a bit. She had wanted to be kissed, but by Hector. Slowly. Gently. Softly. Sensuously. She had dreamed of it for so long. But being kissed by Kobir was a complete shock. She had no feelings for him. Oona had often tried psyching herself into falling in love with Kobir, tried to find him physically arousing, but it didn't work.

She was upset and confused. She did not call or speak to Kobir for a while after that. He, too, didn't try to talk to her. After a couple of months, he dropped in at her place casually, pretending nothing had happened. Oona was glad Sangeeta was home. After that day at the Lakes Oona always met Kobir in the presence of others. Never alone. And never at the Lakes. Kobir did not insist, and that suited her just fine.

The week before, Kobir had called Oona to say Sonia had invited him to Vaidya's wedding the following week. Vaidya was marrying Sandeep, her penpal of many years. When Sonia had asked Oona to bring Kobir along with her to the wedding, Oona had hesitated. 'Can't we leave him out of this?' she had asked.

'But why? After all, you are engaged to him. It's better he gets to know us well since we'll be seeing more of each other in the future.' Oona hadn't even decided on her present, let alone her future. She did not want to contradict her friend. Sonia took it as an affirmative and decided to call Kobir and invite him on behalf of Vaidya. Soon after, Kobir called her and reminded her that they had to go for Vaidya's wedding together. 'Your friend insists,' he sounded elated. Oona was not. She remained silent.

When Craig called her later, Oona seemed a bit disoriented. He sensed she was upset and when he probed deeper Oona, unable to contain herself, burst into tears and tried to explain what she could over the phone. To Craig, it was a garbled outburst about Kobir, Hector and everything else. 'I wish I could hold your hand, honey,' he said to calm her down. 'You need a hug. Let's meet and talk.' And that's how she had landed up in Craig's pad.

'Sorry, I can't serve you tea or coffee as stimulants of any kind are not allowed here. I can however get you a mango juice. Care for a Frooti?'

'Fine.'

As Craig got her the drink and a straw, Oona sat on the bed and watched him. He had a casual air that made him appear quite handsome. He was wearing a churidar-kurta that sat well on his lean body. Oona wondered how he would look in jeans and a shirt. She imagined him with a few buttons undone, maybe, exposing his dark brown hairy chest. Startled at how sexy she found the vision, Oona blushed, and hurriedly lowered her face. She moved a bit uncomfortably on the cot, fiddling with her *dupatta* and hair, appearing nonchalant.

Craig had noticed the blush, however, and he was not fooled by her attempts to cover it up. He handed her the drink and sat down on the floor. An awkward silence followed. After a while, Craig broke in, 'So what have you decided?'

'Well, I don't know….'

'What do you mean you don't know? From what I gather you think you are in love with Hector. But it's only the notion of love.'

'No, Craig, it's not…' Oona tried to speak but Craig cut her short.

'Let me finish, honey. Don't cut in.' And he proceeded. 'Look, however strong your feelings are, Hector is going to remain a dream. He is hitched and obviously too far gone for you. Look at the present. Now. You have Kobir. You go ahead with him and forget Hector. Unless you have someone else in mind.'

'No. There is no one else. But I do not want to spend the rest of my life with Kobir. He's okay as a friend but not…you know…'

'Yes. I know what you mean. Not exactly lover material.'

Oona blushed again.

'You need someone to make you forget this Hector fellow. And it's high time someone introduced a bit of sex in your life.'

Saying that, Craig got up and pulled Oona up towards him. For the first time Oona did not resist. She let herself go. Craig held her gently but firmly, unpinned her hair and stroked it gently. Before she could speak, his mouth closed over hers. He kissed her gently, gradually building up the pressure, till she felt his tongue explore her mouth with a passion. She responded.

Craig first pulled away her *dupatta* and then he gently touched her breasts. She felt a mild tremor deep within her. He sighed and she could feel him harden close to her stomach. He tried unclasping her bra and Oona put up a token resistance for a few seconds, just so that he wouldn't think she was an easy catch. Craig ignored her efforts, expertly unclasping her bra, freeing her breasts. He went on to gently undress her while caressing and kissing her all over. By the time she was fully unclothed, Oona was moaning in delight and anticipation. Thoughts of what her mother or Kobir would say if they saw her flitted through her mind, but she quickly let it pass. She felt intoxicated. Craig gently pushed her back on the cot and continued kissing her all over. Before she realised it, Craig had parted her legs and was entering her.

'Craig, please,' she moaned. 'I haven't....'

'Sh...sh...honey. Don't worry, I won't hurt you. Just relax. You are going to enjoy this. Just leave it to me...'he breathed, already deep inside her.

Later that evening, Oona couldn't help but look at herself in the mirror again and again. Craig had dropped her home a little earlier, but insisted on not coming in. 'We don't want the neighbours talking,' he grinned. Sangeeta had not yet returned from office. Oona sat by herself and relived the magical afternoon, smiling at her reflection from time to time.

Do I still look like a virgin? She thought of Kobir. Her mind was racing. *What will Kobir have to say if I marry him and he finds out I am not a virgin? Can I live like that with him? Or with any other man? Will these chauvinists accept me as I am?* She stiffened her spine. *I give a damn.*

I am going to live life my way. The only person I will care for is Ma. I will see to it that I don't hurt or embarrass her. But that's not going to stop me from enjoying my life. Her decision pleased her. She looked again at the mirror and noticed her features had softened. *Sex is wonderful. I like it. Gosh! I've beaten Vaidya to the game. She's still got a week more to go. Wow! I've done it before her. I wish I could tell Sonia, but obviously, I can't. She'll be scandalised. Damn society and its silly rules.*

'My, my, look who's here? Someone's looking smashing,' Natasha exclaimed when Oona walked in, in a rust tissue Benarasi saree with Craig in his usual churidar-kurta avatar. The venue was the South India Club and it was Vaidya's wedding reception. Oona's light wheatish complexion glowed in contrast to the elegant saree. She was wearing simple gold *jhumkas* and a dozen thin gold bangles on her right hand. Natasha held up her hands to examine the bangles, 'Gold! Aren't they nice!'

'They are not gold. Just imitation stuff,' Oona informed her.

'Shhh! Don't say it out loud.'

'I don't care. How're you Nats? Long time no see. Oh, meet Craig. Craig, this is my friend Natasha from college.'

'Hi Natasha. Nice meeting you,' Craig shook hands politely.

'Oh, hi.' Natasha smiled.

'See you in a bit, Nats. We'll just go wish Vaidya,' Oona said, taking Craig's hand to lead him to where the bride and groom were seated. Natasha did not fail to notice the intimacy she shared with Craig.

As Oona walked up to her, Vaidya noticed it as well, but she was too busy accepting congratulatory wishes to make a snide remark. After the formalities were over, Oona headed down with Craig. She looked around till she spotted Sonia and Deepak sitting at the far end. Oona waved. Sonia smiled rather tersely. Oona continued to walk towards her, Craig following.

'Hi, Sonia. Hi, Deepak,' Oona said cheerily. 'Have you guys been here a while?'

'About half an hour or so,' Deepak replied.

'Where's Kobir?' Sonia asked brusquely. 'I thought you were coming together.'

'Oh! No, I don't think so…I don't know where he is, do you?' Oona mumbled.

'How should I know?' Sonia said cattily.

'Hey,' said Deepak, pointing towards the entrance. 'Talk of the devil and here he comes.'

Oona turned to see Kobir enter with a bouquet and head straight to the newlyweds. Deepak gestured to him to join them later and he responded with a nod. He hadn't yet noticed Oona. She looked at Craig, obviously uncomfortable. 'Do you want me to leave?' he bent down and whispered.

'No,' she gripped his hand harder and then immediately let go. 'You stay. I am okay.'

'Sure?' Craig asked.

'Sure,' Oona replied.

After what seemed like an eternity, Kobir walked towards them. On seeing Oona with Craig, he almost stopped short in his tracks. As he approached them, his eyes focused on Oona, burning with anger. Craig noticed, and his expression showed his amusement. Kobir ignored Oona completely and went and greeted Sonia and Deepak.

'Kobir,' Oona interrupted him meekly. 'Meet Craig. Craig, this is Kobir.'

'Hello Kobir,' Craig reached out to shake his hand but Kobir ignored him, muttering a steely 'hi'.

'*Arrey*, sit down *na*,' said Deepak, offering Oona a chair as he gestured to Kobir and Craig to sit.

'No, I'll have to leave now. Got another family function to attend. Just came to wish Vaidya. Got to go.' And saying that he strode off, obviously quite angry. The rest of the evening went off very badly. Deepak tried unsuccessfully to make light conversation with Craig. Sonia ignored Oona, who felt hurt and upset and began worrying about facing Kobir, his family and her mother. She spent the entire evening imagining various scenarios, none of which were reassuring.

A few days after Vaidya's wedding, the Sarkars called Sangeeta and asked to meet her. Mrs Sarkar came over the next evening and politely told Sangeeta that they wanted to call off the engagement between Kobir and Oona. She explained that Kobir wanted to pursue higher studies in the US and to concentrate on a career before settling down. Oona needn't wait for him so long. She could be free to settle down with anyone. Sangeeta tried to say that Oona would wait. Mrs Sarkar, polite as ever, said that they would not be comfortable with that, and requested that the matter end there. Oona, of course, knew better. Later, when Mrs Sarkar left, Sangeeta admonished Oona.

'I told you not to see that KM guy. You disobeyed me and now see what you have landed in,' Sangeeta was raving.

'It's okay, Ma. Just relax. I didn't want to marry Kobir da anyway,' she shrugged, reverting to the use of 'da'.

'Now who will want to marry you? Everyone is going to talk about your broken engagement and affair,' Sangeeta ranted.

'Let them. Like I give a damn,' retorted Oona obstinately.

'But I do. And so should you as long as you live with me. After all we live in a *bhadra samaj*. And if you can't abide by my wishes, then you are free to leave. Go and marry anyone you want to. Don't ever come to me. I will not be able to arrange a match for you. You hear me?'

'You don't worry about my marriage. Or me, Ma. I will look after myself. And I'm sorry if I have hurt you. I didn't mean to.'

Later that night, Sangeeta heard Oona talking and crying over the phone. She assumed it was Craig. She was too exhausted to rebuke Oona. She's a big girl now, how far can I control her, she thought to herself, turning in for the night.

Six months on and Oona was deeply involved with Craig. Her friends noticed a certain change in her attitude. She was chirpier and smiled all day for no apparent reason. Her sex life was great. Her face had the soft glow of a woman in love. Of late she seemed to be in a bit of a daze and bouncing high. Sangeeta noticed the change too, but did not comment. In fact, she and Oona were at war. They talked only when necessary and Oona spent most of her time outside the house. This was not just because she was avoiding Sangeeta, but also due to her new job.

Oona had landed herself a job with one of the city's elite PR agencies, called Katy Roy Associates. Katy, an English lady married to one of the wealthiest families of Calcutta, was also one of India's leading public relations experts. Oona had met her some months earlier at an art exhibition and Katy took an immediate liking to the spunky youngster. 'Why don't you intern with me for a few months till your results are out? That way you can decide for yourself whether you would like to work or continue with further studies,' Katy had asked her when she learnt that Oona had just completed her graduation. 'Here, keep my card. And I hope to get a call from you soon.'

When she discussed this with her mother, Sangeeta was impressed that '*the* Katy Roy' had approached her daughter, but she was more keen on Oona doing her MA. Oona of course tried to convince her mother (and herself) that it would be just a temporary arrangement. 'Let's see how I like it.' Craig insisted she join; he felt it would do her a world of good.

Five months into the job, Oona was loving every moment of it. It was completely different from the world in which she had grown up. She loved the high glitz and glamour. Plus there was a thrill and dynamism in working with Katy. She got to meet a lot of influential people. Oona was a hard worker and enjoyed working under Katy Roy, whilst the latter loved having her around. She was like a whiff of fresh air in the office, with her novel ideas. Kobir was completely out of her life. Things had changed a little with Craig, too. Of late, she had found him distracted and a little aloof. Their sex life, too, was not too great. He seemed to have had enough of her and perhaps wanted her out of his life.

All men are bastards, Oona thought to herself. *Once they get you into bed, they want to drop you. To hell with him, she consoled herself.* But it did not help much. She wanted to belong to someone. And Craig's sudden rejection was not easy to handle. *Better I left him, like Kobir, and not the other way round. My ego would never recover.*

On Oona's twenty-first birthday, Katy threw a little party for her at the office. She cut a cake with the staff during lunch. Later Katy took her out to tea and gifted her a lovely silk scarf. Oona spent the evening at home and Sangeeta returned earlier than usual from work. It was customary for friends and relatives to drop by, or at least the few who remembered her birthday. She wished Hector would call. Just hearing his voice would make her day. But she knew it was not to be. Her mind wandered to Kobir, who of course would not call. She had heard that he was seeing the Seal girl and would soon marry her.

She thought now of Craig, who had wished her over the phone while she was at work, and made some excuse for being unable to meet her. It had hurt her. Her ego, not her heart. She just could not handle rejection. She gathered from common friends at the temple that he was seeing a beautiful Polish girl, another devotee. That upset her most. She really wanted to get back at him. She was lost in these thoughts when the doorbell rang and her favourite grand-aunt, Suparna Debi came in to wish her.

Oona loved her and fondly called her Chhordida, meaning 'young granny'. Suparna Debi was the wife of her grandfather's brother, Borun Roy. She was a rich, childless widow. She loved Oona like her own and many of her jealous relatives commented that Oona and Sangeeta sucked up to Suparna Debi so that they would inherit her wealth.

'Oona come on, do *pronam*. Do I have to remind you?'

'I was just about to, Ma,' Oona protested as she bent down to touch Chhordida's feet.

'*Bhalo theko, baba*. Stay well, my child,' said Suparna Debi while patting her head in blessing. 'And a very happy birthday to my most charming and favourite grand-niece,' she said, hugging Oona as she straightened up.

'My, my. You are an adult now. So how does it feel to be twenty-one?' Chhordida asked.

Oona just smiled and shrugged.

'I know you are doing a great job at Katy's. She's very happy with you. She told me the other day at the club. Imagine how proud I felt.' Both Sangeeta and Oona smiled.

'But it's time you looked after yourself a bit. You better start coming out with me and I will introduce you to some fine young men. It's time you got yourself a nice Brahmo boy before one of these non-Brahmo men snatch you away. After all, it's difficult to find a good Brahmo match these days.'

Suparna Debi had been happy when Oona's engagement to Kobir broke off; she had felt he did not match up to her niece's smartness or lineage. 'After all, he is a Hindu. The family may have wealth, but they cannot afford to buy culture,' she had remarked to Sangeeta on hearing the news. Sangeeta did not like the comment but said nothing.

'First things first,' Suparna Debi said and called Oona to her side. 'I have a little something for you.'

'Oh, you shouldn't have bothered,' Sangeeta politely interjected.

'You keep out of this,' Suparna Debi fondly admonished her. 'This is for my Oona. After all, you don't turn twenty-one every year.' She pulled out a square, red velvet box from a *jhola* and opened it. Inside rested a beautiful necklace of pearls the size of peppercorns interspersed with little gold peppercorns. She draped it around Oona's neck and fixed the clasp.

'*Dekhi*. Let me see, oh, you look lovely.'

'Thank you,' Oona exclaimed, admiring her reflection in a nearby mirror.' It's beautiful.'

'Yes, isn't it? It's an heirloom. I got it from my mother-in-law. You know, your grandmother, Nandini Debi inherited the far more valuable *navaratna* set and yet she had her eye on this particular piece. They are genuine South Sea pearls and were set by Harry Winston in London. Take care of it. And always keep it in the velvet box or the pearls will get scratched.'

'But you shouldn't have bothered, Kakima,' Sangeeta said. 'They must be very expensive.'

'I don't care. I am just happy it will stay with Oona. After all, it was her great grandmother's.' She admired the necklace she had placed around Oona's neck, and suddenly remembered, 'And oh, I have something else for you. More family history. Here, take these.' She handed Oona a couple of books. They looked quite old. 'Here, as a student of literature I thought they would interest you. This is Palgrave's *Golden Treasury* and here is Chaucer's *Canterbury Tales*.'

'But Chhordida, I already have them. They were in my graduate course,' Oona said, still distracted by the pearls.

'Of course I know you have them,' Suparna Debi said. 'But look. These are special. Collectors' editions. This Palgrave's *Golden Treasury* was printed in 1919 by the Oxford University Press in Milford. Almost 70 years old. And this is a 1908 edition of the *Canterbury Tales*.'

'Wow!'

'Yes. And it is entangled with a bit of family history too. They belonged to my mother-in-law, Kamini Debi. That's your great-grandmother.'

The surprises still weren't over. 'Wait a minute, there's something more I have in my *jhola*. This.'

She handed over to Oona a twelve-by-six-inch silk box. It was frayed at the edges, the threads sticking out. The small golden hook was slightly tarnished. Oona opened it and saw two beautiful, crystal perfume bottles. They were empty and had an antique look. She looked questioningly at Chhordida.

'These were also from my mother-in-law. These bottles are expensive Lalique crystals. Below is a compartment containing some old letters written to her cousin, Ela Sen. I'm sure you've heard of her ill-fated romance with that Englishman. Poor woman died so young. You may want to see the letters at leisure. It might be interesting to see the style of English written in those days.'

As Suparna Debi explained, Oona had pulled out the bottles and seen the hidden compartment. She saw cursive writing in black ink on yellowed pages. She started to take out one sheet but on touching it realised it was nearly parchment. Later, she decided. She would have to handle this carefully.

'You know, Kamini Debi and her cousin, Ela Sen, were among the first batch of women graduates in India. Way back in 1911. You should be proud to belong to this family,' Chhordida said. Oona, nodded, a little overwhelmed.

Adieu

Ela Sen's association with Sarala Debi went back nearly seven years. Even before she had taught at the kindergarten, Ela had been assisting Sarala Debi with Samaj work for the freedom struggle. A writer, musician and hailed as Bengal's Joan of Arc, Sarala Debi was a dazzling woman. Niece of Gurudev, she drew around her a captivated circle of young men willing to fight and die at her instance. But most important of all and one of history's best-kept secrets, Sarala Debi was the love of Mohandas Karamchand Gandhi.

Sarala Debi first met Gandhi in 1901, when she was twenty-nine. More than two decades later, nearing fifty, married and the mother of a son, she still retained much of her beauty, charm and wit. Gandhi in one of his letters to Anasuyaben in Ahmedabad had mentioned, 'Sarala Devi's company is very endearing. She looks after me very well.'

An unusually talented singer and writer, Sarala Debi also trained Bengali youth in militant patriotism. Even Vivekananda was said to have been somewhat besotted by her and had wanted her to accompany him to the West. She had been widowed the previous year and Gandhiji tried to reinitiate his love for her. She had once rebuked Gandhi as being a bit of a 'Law Giver', but he found it an endearing term. He would write her letters and lovingly sign off as LG, short for Law Giver.

Sarala Debi took a liking to the much younger Ela. She found in her certain traits that reminded her of her youthful self. A few years earlier, Ela had confided in her about her love for David and her reluctance to marry Biren Roy. Sarala Debi had stood by her then and even took up her cause against the formidable Somenath Sen, who really respected Sarala Debi and so gave up forcing Ela to marry Biren.

'Know something, Ela. Do not marry just because you are told to. You should marry when you are ready for it, preferably marry someone you genuinely love and care for,' Sarala Debi sighed. 'I married late. At thirty-three. I refused a number of earlier proposals because I was not ready for matrimony. But then, one day I had to relent to family pressures. Besides, the police were looking for me and my family thought it would be safe for me to be far away from Calcutta. So I was sent away to Lahore. My husband had been married twice before; both women had died. I endured the marriage, but I was never happy.'

Sarala Debi had earlier mentioned her fondness for Bapu (as Gandhi was affectionately called by many). 'If ever there was something close to love for me…it was…' and she broke off. But she did show some of Bapu's letters to Ela.*

In a letter dated December 1920, Bapu wrote to Sarala:

'I have been analysing my love for you. I have reached a definition of spiritual marriage…Have we that exquisite purity, that perfect coincidence, that perfect merging, that identity of ideals, the self forgetfulness, that fixity of purpose, that truthfulness? For me I can answer plainly that it is only an aspiration. I am unworthy of that companionship with you….With dearest love I still subscribe myself. Your LG.'

This was one of the final letters Bapu wrote to Sarala Debi, more so as he was afraid of Ba's (Kasturba's) insecurity due to this affair, which nearly threatened his marriage and took a toll on his emotional state. Societal pressures put an end to what could have been the most talked about and dynamic of historical relationships. Perhaps Sarala

---

*Bapu's letters to Sarala Debi have been shared with the world in his biography, *Mohandas: A True Story of a Man, His People and an Empire*, by his grandson, Rajmohan Gandhi.

Debi gave Bapu the emotional support a man like him—who was always giving—needed. The general of *satyagraha* carried more aches in his bosom than the world realised. The two together would certainly have made an extraordinary political combination. But alas, it was not to be.

Like her mentor, Sarala Debi, Ela too had a brief romance that would be another of history's well-kept romantic secrets. Albeit platonic, it was nevertheless emotionally charged. And heady, brief though it was. This was the bond between Ela Sen and Subhash Chandra Bose.

After that evening at the Bose residence in Elgin Road, Subhash had one day dropped by at the Sen residence. The Sens were elated as Subhash was much in the news, and made him stay for tea. Besides, Somenath, with his *swadeshi* leanings, admired the young man's courage. Ela enjoyed his company and his wit. She harboured no romantic feelings, however remote, for Subhash initially. But Ela did not fail to notice the little flirtatious vibes Subhash sent out while having tea at her place. Obviously he had not just dropped in to socialise with her parents. There was more to it.

Though Ela was emotionally involved with David—and Subhash knew this—she could not deny the attraction she felt for Subhash. Only four years her junior, he had a certain maturity and intensity that attracted her to him. They did interact from time to time. Subhash Bose was completely committed to his mission and yet did not mind some light flirting. It made him all the more charming. Whenever Ela read about one of his several arrests, she would worry and enquire after him. He found her concern comforting.

Every time Subhash went to jail, he wrote to her. And she, infatuated by this young man so dedicated to his cause, was deeply moved by his writing. She loved his letters. He wrote so eloquently. But each time she thought this flirtation through words was going a bit too far, she would chide him gently and bring in a mention of David somewhere in her reply. Gradually, she started to fall in love with Subhash but, so as not to lose touch with reality, she would remind herself of her commitment to David.

In a letter from Alipore Central Jail, Subhash wrote,

> I do not know why you constantly deny my liking for you. I say liking and not love, because you would not prefer the latter word. Is it because you feel committed to your other love? Or the fact that I am younger than you? ('Tch tch', to such social norms.) Or simply because you do not trust me enough? Whatever the reason, I do not blame you. But at the same time I cannot deny the attraction I feel towards you.

Ela blushed when she read these words. She would have loved to share it with the whole world, but she had to stash it away in the deepest recesses of her heart. He used to visit her at Sarala Debi's, and everyone there enjoyed his company. Sarala of course knew the reason for his visits. However, as Bose got busier with his anti-British activities, his commitment to the country took a toll on the budding romance.

One day Biren Roy dropped in at Sarala Debi's, enquiring after Ela. She was not there. Biren discreetly enquired from Mayadi, one of the other social workers, about Ela's timings. A few days later he turned up at the ashram at a time Ela was present.

'Oh. Namaskar, Biren Babu,' Ela asked covering up her surprise with a polite greeting. 'What brings you here?'

'What else but to see your commitment to your cause?' smiled Biren. 'Remember, I had always mentioned that I admired your work,' he said, trying to bring the past into the conversation. Ela ignored the attempt and waited in silence as they sat opposite each other.

After an awkward pause, Biren continued, 'I wish Somshukla would dedicate her life to something more constructive rather than while away her time socialising in the Samaj.'

Taken aback, Ela nevertheless came to the defence of Biren's wife. 'Why? I think she has enough on her hands. Looking after the children, taking care of your parents and the house, and…'

'Oh, no,' Biren interrupted. 'That's not what she does. There are enough servants around.'

'But servants cannot always run the house. It is the lady of the house who runs it. I know for a fact. I have seen my mother at it for years in spite of our staff,' Ela argued.

'Yes. Well, *mashima* is different. You know Som and I keep having our differences.'

'What's new? I believe every married couple has differences.'

'I know, but….I am not happy, Ela.'

'I don't see how I can help you, Biren Babu. Anyway, I have some things to attend to. Please excuse me,' Ela rose to leave.

'Wait. Don't leave yet,' Biren caught her hand.

'*Eki*, Biren Babu. Please. *Haath charun*. Let go.'

'Ela. Please. I will not let you go so easily this time,' Biren sounded desperate.

'Please Biren Babu, people will see us. This is unbecoming of you. Besides, I am already engaged,' and Ela pulled her hand free.

'Yes I know. You are engaged to that Englishman,' snarled Biren in a caustic tone. 'So?'

'So what, Biren Babu?' Ela asked.

'You have not married him, have you? And you will not be able to either if I know your father well. Besides, what harm is there in seeing your old admirer? Or do you prefer younger men in your autumn years?' The last was a jibe about her and Subhash Bose. Ela turned crimson at his audacity and turned away, walking into the staff room as she cursed Biren. 'Just because I am a spinster, he thinks he can make a pass at me.'

That evening David and Ela were out for their usual routine: a walk (mostly by the river) followed by tea and scones (either Firpo's, Flury's or at the Great Eastern), ending with a browsing session at the Oxford Book Store before he dropped her near home. Occasionally, he and Ela took a hackney down to the Hogg Market or would visit the Army & Navy Stores. Today, however, they walked up ahead of Park Street and entered Flury's, the Swiss confectioners reputed for their chocolate pastries and sausage rolls. 'No one can beat the Swiss at their chocolate preparations,' David had once said.

After their tea and pastry treat, Ela and David walked down the avenue as she told him about Biren's visit. David was a bit outraged, but admired Ela for handling it with tact. 'That's the best way to deal with such men,' David said.

'Utter cad,' Ela added.

'Wish I could challenge him to a duel. What do you say?' And they both laughed at such mock chivalry.

'Well, let us see what we can do to cheer you up a bit,' and he swerved left and opened the door to the famous studio photographers, Bourne and Shepherd. He led Ela in as she looked at him questioningly.

'Just a surprise idea,' David smiled.

'What is the purpose?'

'Sh…let me take care of this.' David silenced her.

They posed for a photograph. Old Mr Bourne took the photograph himself using the latest Agfa Box camera he had just acquired and kept boasting about it to David.

'How are your parents?'

'Oh they are doing fine. In London.'

'I know. And how is my dear Judy?' Mr Bourne enquired.

'She's very well, thank you sir,' David replied.

'Ah could you, my lady, just turn a little this way? Ah yes, a little more. That's better.' And he clicked.

For Ela it was a new experience. The Sens had once called in a photographer from this very studio to take a series of family portraits at home, which had been framed since and adorned the various walls and the mantel of the Sen household. But to come to the studio and take a photograph with a male friend, who was not even her fiancé, was a bold step. Ela couldn't help wondering what her family and society would say if they heard of it. But she was thrilled nevertheless.

'Thank you,' she told David when they reached her house.

'You are welcome of course. But for what?' David asked.

'For the photographs. I am looking forward to seeing them. Now, even when you are not with me, I will be able to see you. This way, you will always be near me,' Ela said softly.

'Oh don't you worry about that. I will see to it that I always remain close to your heart.'

A few weeks later, over tea at the Great Eastern, David gave her a square velvet box. 'What is this?' Ela asked, curious. There was a silver S overlapping a gold S on the deep blue velvet. She knew immediately it was the logo of Sen & Sen, the famous jewellers at Sir Hogg Market. Her mother was one of their regular clients. 'Is it jewellery?' she asked.

'Just open it and see for yourself,' David said.

'If it is expensive then I cannot take it. You should not have…'

'Oh, Ela, will you at least open it and take a look?' insisted David, impatiently.

There was a thin gold chain in an 'English design', as jewellers called it, with an exquisitely crafted gold oval pendant attached to it. 'Oh,' was all Ela said.

'Do you like it?' David asked. Ela nodded.

'I am glad,' David said.

'But David, I cannot take it,' Ela said.

'I am hearing none of it,' David said, taking the chain from the box. 'Wait till you see the whole thing.' He operated a small clasp she hadn't noticed, and the locket opened into two halves. He held it forward for Ela to see. David's face in sepia stared back at her.

'Oh!' Ela exclaimed. 'Isn't this the one we took the other day at Bourne & Shepherd?'

David smiled and immediately reached past his collar and pulled out a similar but longer gold chain. There was a slightly bigger oval pendant attached to it. He opened it and turned it towards Ela. She knew she would see her face in sepia.

'Oh!'

'See, when I told you I want to remain near your heart always, this is what I meant. Just like you are near mine. Always.' He pointed to her photograph. 'Ela, there is no one I will ever love more than I have loved you. And I will continue to do so, till the day I die.'

Ela was overwhelmed. And speechless.

After that evening, Ela felt it was time that she faced her father's wrath once and for all, and made a decision regarding her future with David. If need be she would go against Somenath's wishes and marry David. She felt terribly guilty. David refused to marry anyone else (in spite of Ela telling him to do so) and Ela was unable to marry David because of her father.

She decided to talk to Roma before approaching her father. Her mother was sympathetic. 'I know my child, it must be tough on the two of you. It is about time you both settled down. You have my blessings,' she said.

'I know Ma. But I need Baba's blessings too.'

'Well….'

'Well, what Ma?' Ela asked.

'Well, that will have to wait for a bit. You know Baba has not been keeping well lately,' Roma Debi started to explain. The doctor had diagnosed that Somenath was suffering from an ailment of the heart which was further aggravated due to his mild asthma.

'Ma, I know. Doctor Kaku told me about Baba's weak heart and palpitations. And the recent pressure at work has also taken its toll. I think he needs to take it easy for some time.'

'Exactly,' Roma Debi said. 'But it is more serious than mere palpitations. Baba needs a complete change of environment to fully recuperate. Doctor Babu has suggested we go to Darjeeling for a few months. This *swadeshi* movement and all is getting to him. He needs to take his mind off his usual concerns.'

'Darjeeling? For how long?' Ela asked.

'Maybe for three months. Maybe six. Who knows?' Roma sounded a little low. 'I have already spoken to Ganguly Babu,' she explained, referring to Somenath's office manager. 'He has organised a bungalow for us in Darjeeling. It is beautiful. Belonged to some English couple. They stay in London but rent out the bungalow. Ganguly Babu has seen it and says it is quite beautiful, facing the mountains.'

'But Ma,' Ela said and kept quiet.

'*Ki*? What is it?' Roma asked.

'No. Nothing.'

When she later told David about the Darjeeling plan, he seemed a little upset. But he quickly recovered and told her not to worry. 'I think it will do you a world of good. You need a change from all this social work. So does your father. I am sure the old man will be in a better mood and allow our marriage when he recuperates,' David joked.

'But, six months! I am going to miss you.'

'I know. But we will be in touch. Besides, who knows,' he smiled, 'I may just come visiting!'

Situated 7,000 feet above sea level, Darjeeling is known as the queen of hill stations and was gifted to the East India Company in 1836 by the King of Sikkim. It became a popular resort for the British when they wanted to escape the sweltering heat of the plains. Tiger Hill was its highest look-out point for the exotic peaks of the Eastern Himalayas, including Kanchenjunga and—on a clear day—Mount Everest, the highest mountain in the world, named after the 1830s' Surveyor General of India, George Everest.

Soon after Poila Baisakh, the Bengali New Year, the Sens left for Darjeeling. They travelled overnight to Siliguri with their luggage and a staff of three. From Siliguri, a car was arranged for the long uphill drive. Ela was keen to go up in the famous toy train but Ganguly Babu thought that a car would be more comfortable for Somenath. However, Somenath promised Ela that he would take her on the toy train someday. The staff, with part of the luggage, followed in a *tonga*.

Ela loved the bungalow at first sight. It was a lovely old cottage, with four large bedrooms and two big drawing rooms. The dining area was close to the kitchen, which had a nice brickwork chimney. There was a smaller store room and several washrooms. The servants had their quarters outside, near the gate. There was a kitchen garden at the back and a modest lawn in the front of the house. Mrs Kenley, the owner, had cultivated some lovely flowers including some prize chrysanthemums she used to send to the Garden Show in Calcutta. The bungalow was one of many gingerbread trim cottages with English gardens that seemed to dominate the town. Close by was the town centre, the Mall, from where beautiful walkways led off and which was also dotted with popular shops and restaurants.

Ela was happy, though she missed David, especially when she and her parents walked each evening along the Mall. Somenath's health seemed to improve, though not as much as doctors had expected. After a month, Somenath remarked that they may have to stay longer than expected.

'That is fine,' Roma Debi said. 'And good for you, too. You needed this change.'

'It is okay for you, my dear. But poor Ela. She is getting bored. She misses her friends,' Somenath observed.

'I will talk to Mrs Chatterjee. She mentioned a primary school around here. Ela could start teaching again like she did at the Pius's school,' suggested Roma Debi.

'That is a good idea! Trust you, Roma, to come up with it. Why didn't I think of it earlier?' Somenath said.

'Well, that will keep her occupied. But what she misses is friends of her age group, with whom she can interact,' Roma Debi said. She was trying to convince Somenath into inviting David over. But of course, part of Somenath's insistence on Darjeeling was in the hope that Ela might forget David and choose to move on.

'In that case, I am going to tell Debnath to send Kamini and her boys over for the summer vacations. If her husband Soumen wants to join in, he is most welcome. But it's better if she comes alone. Kamini can get a break and Ela will have company. And the house will reverberate to the sound of young voices. *Kemon*?' Somenath asked.

Kamini Roy was Somenath's niece. Her father, Somenath's younger brother, was Debnath Sen Sarkar. Somenath had given up the last family name, 'Sarkar' long before, as he felt it sounded too long for his English clients to remember.

Though Roma Debi had hinted at David, she nevertheless thought Kamini's company would do her daughter good.

'Then you will have to talk to *Bhashurpo* and organise their travel arrangements with Ganguly Babu,' Roma Debi said, referring to her younger brother-in-law.

'Yes, yes,' Somenath nodded absent-mindedly as he picked up the newspaper. 'All that will be organised. Don't worry.'

While Roma Debi sat knitting over tea on the lawns one evening, Ela and Kamini watched Kamini's two little boys run all over the garden, squealing in delight. Suren, the older one, all of six, was daring the younger one, Borun to catch him. Borun at four, tried his best, but just as he drew close, he would fail and sit down in utter frustration. Suren loved it. Kamini and Ela seemed to be enjoying it too.

'Ma, you just finished knitting a cardigan last week for Baba. Now what are you knitting with this colourful yarn?'

'Well, this is for Suren and then I'll knit another cardigan for Borun. Suren loves the blue and red combination. I asked him,' Roma Debi told Kamini.

'That's right, Jethimoni,' Kamini said.

'What about Borun? What is his favourite colour?'

'Let me see? I think he too likes red.'

'Then I'll knit a red and yellow combination for him.'

'*Na, na*. Just stick to the same red and blue. You know how little children are. They will fight over it unnecessarily. Why get into this *jhamela*?'

Roma Debi smiled. 'Fortunately I never had to deal with such sibling rivalry, Ela being the only one. But sometimes, it is fun, isn't it?'

Kamini smiled. She was the only sister of two younger brothers. So she had never had much of a problem either. Her younger brother and close friend, Sibnath, had died two years ago of consumption, leaving her heartbroken. Harinath, the youngest was now studying in college and though six years younger than Kamini, had taken over the mantle of the protective elder brother.

Kamini's husband Soumen looked after his family's business. Though Kamini lived in a joint family, Soumen was liberal with his educated wife. Kamini was the first woman at her in-laws' to have completed her matriculation. She knew about David and had met him several times. David had sent a letter for Ela with Kamini and also two bottles of French perfume. The bottles were in Lalique crystal and came in a beautiful box made of Chinese silk. It occupied pride of place on Ela's dresser and she rubbed on a little perfume every day, thinking of David each time she smelt her wrist.

It was now over a fortnight since Kamini and her boys had come and Ela looked and felt happier. Roma Debi fussed over the boys, and Somenath would sit with them in the mornings and evenings and read to them. Suren and Borun were a little intimidated by Somenath initially, but slowly their fear dissipated as 'Dadu's *golpos*' or stories proved engrossing. Somenath's oratorical skills, acquired during his legal days, had not dulled with his passing years.

Ela and Kamini were like sisters. They bonded over books, Rabindra sangeet, walks down the Mall, chit-chatting over siesta time and of course the men in their lives, David and Soumen. Kamini's had been an arranged marriage and Soumen was the first male influence in her life apart from her father and brothers. Kamini's respect for him had grown over time.

While Ela felt Kamini had missed out on something in life by never falling in love, Kamini was none the wiser and liked the way her life had developed. One afternoon, Kamini asked Ela whether she did not miss being married and having a family.

'Yes. I long to be married and have a family with David. So does he. But....'

'But you know that cannot happen. Jethu will never let it happen,' Kamini completed her sentence.

'I know! Such is my fate!'

'Listen Didi, it is not too late. I know I may sound obnoxious to you, but don't you think instead of wasting your life this way, you could let your parents arrange a match for you. At least you can have children and carry on with your life,' Kamini suggested.

'*Ki rey* Kamini! You too have succumbed to such thoughts? You know all there is to know about David and me. How can you say such a thing?'

'Na, didi. I did not mean it that way. The reason why I even thought of it is I...well...just could not see you wasting your life away like this.'

'*Tui bujhbi na rey*. You will never understand. The commitment David and I have to each other, nothing else matters. No societal pressures, no conventions, nothing. And I do not feel deprived at not being married or having children. I am beyond all that now. I cannot imagine my life with any man other than David. And if perchance we do not marry this life, then sometime in my next birth I will be David's bride for sure.' Ela laughed.

'*Oof*! What rubbish! Next birth and all. Especially coming from a Brahmo like you. What would Jethu say if he heard?' Kamini said.

'Well, he can lay down the rules in my life, but he cannot rule my heart or control my thoughts,' Ela said.

Life went on in Darjeeling. Kamini's holiday drew to a close. It had been almost a month and a half since she had arrived and it had been one of the best times in Ela's life in the small town. Kamini's husband had written that he would be coming in a fortnight's time to take her and the boys back home. Ela was feeling a little low at the thought of the days ahead without Kamini.

Meanwhile David had written her two letters, addressed to Kamini and signed as her husband Soumen on the envelope. In the last letter, David admitted to pining for her and mentioned that he would be coming up to see her. Ela was thrilled but also a little worried about Somenath's reaction.

A few days later David arrived at the Kenley house unannounced. Somenath welcomed him, though he was a bit surprised. Roma Debi and Kamini were very happy. And Ela was ecstatic. David lied to Somenath, saying he was travelling on work and that he would be staying for a few weeks.

'So where are you putting up?' Somenath asked.

'Oh, I am staying with family friends, the Browns. They are down the Ghoom road.'

'Ah yes,' Somenath said. 'But you must come home and have fish curry rice when you have some time.'

'Thank you, Sir, I will.' David smiled, and winked at Ela.

David would meet up with Ela and Kamini during their evening walks down the Mall. A couple of times, Kamini would pretend to be tired and let them both walk up ahead for a while to give them some privacy. Later, after a cup of tea and cakes at the Hillside Café, David would drop the girls home.

One day, while David and Ela walked ahead and Kamini sat in one of the garden benches by the Ridge, reading a book, she suddenly saw

Ela hurrying towards her, looking flushed and upset. She was ignoring David, who was trying to call her back. Kamini quickly collected her book and handbag and asked, '*Ki*? What has happened?'

'Nothing. Let's go home,' Ela said.

Meanwhile David joined them and Kamini gave him a questioning look. David looked a little upset too and politely asked if they would like some tea.

'No. We have to go. *Chalo*. Let's go.' Ela pulled Kamini by the hand and walked towards the Kenleys'.

Later that night, after dinner, Ela went to Kamini's room. The boys had just gone to sleep. 'What has upset you, Didi?' Kamini asked.

'David has to go back to England,' Ela said.

'Oh. Did his parents ask him to?'

'No. He would not if they did. But his office is sending him to London. On a transfer. He cannot say no.' Ela broke down.

'Oh.' Kamini didn't know how to console Ela. 'So what will you do now?' she asked after Ela had regained her composure.

'He wants me to go with him. He wants to marry me.'

'And what did you tell him?'

'I told him that it was impossible. I cannot marry him right now. Baba's not keeping well and he will be very upset. I told him not to go,' and Ela started to sob again.

'What did he say?' Kamini asked.

'He said it was impossible for him not to go to England.'

The days of Kamini's visit were numbered. Soumen had come down to spend the last week with his uncle-in-law's family, before taking his wife and sons back to the city. Ela was a little upset, both at the thought of Kamini's going and David's leaving for England. She was completely lost, not sure what she wanted to do with her life at present. As for her future, she dreaded even thinking of it. She refused to go for the usual evening walks down the Mall, telling Kamini that she was trying to get used to her absence. Kamini of course refused to believe it. She went out for walks with Soumen. One of the days they even met David, who invited them to tea. David looked very distraught and later when Kamini narrated this to Ela, she too got upset.

'I feel so helpless. There is nothing I can do for myself or David and worse, I feel so bad for him. I told him to go to England and marry and not wait for me, but he is so adamant. *Ki korbo bol*? What am I supposed to do?' Ela lamented.

Three days before Kamini was to leave, Ela called her over to her room. 'There is something I want you to keep,' Ela told Kamini as she handed her over the box made of Chinese silk.

'Isn't it the perfume box David gave you?'

Ela nodded. 'Then why are you giving it to me?'

'I am not giving it to you. I am handing it to you for safekeeping.'

'*Maney*? I don't understand,' Kamini asked puzzled.

Ela fondly opened the box and took out the two crystal perfume bottles. She opened the cap of each separately, inhaling their fragrance. Then she put the bottles on the dresser and lifted the inner casing. There were some letters. And the gold chain and pendant David had given her at the Great Eastern with his picture inside the locket. She opened the locket and looked at the photograph for a long time. Gently she placed the chain between the letters. She replaced the perfume casing over it and the bottles in their rightful compartments. She shut the box using the gold clasp and handed it to Kamini. 'Here, keep it with you. Safely,' Ela said.

'But why?' Kamini asked still surprised. 'It's yours. You keep it.'

'My future seems bleak. Who knows what's in store for me? I know you will keep it safely in my memory. *Tui rakh*. Please.'

'Didi what rubbish are you saying! Memory! Bleak! What do you mean?'

'Nothing. *Tui bujhbi na*, you will not understand it now. Just keep this safely. Do this for me and do not ask any more questions. I cannot explain,' Ela pulled out a few books. 'Here, take these too. You will enjoy reading them.'

The books included Byron's collected works and Palgrave's *Golden Treasury*. Kamini knew these were given by David to Ela.

'You are so possessive about them. Why are you giving them away like this?' she asked.

'I want you to have them. And please no more questions, I cannot answer them,' Ela said with finality. '*Jao*. Why don't you go and settle them in the suitcase? You must not forget to carry them with you.' As Kamini was leaving the room, balancing the books and the box, Ela casually remarked, 'Are you and Soumen going for a walk this evening?'

'Yes. Will you join us?'

'No. Will you be meeting David?' Ela asked.

'Yes, I suppose so. Why?'

'Will you tell him that I would like to meet him tomorrow evening? By the Ridge. Four o'clock.'

'Of course, I will tell him, Didi,' Kamini said suppressing a small smile as she left the room.

She was sitting on the usual bench by the Ridge, looking pensive.

'Ela!' David's voice shook her out of her reverie.

'Oh. Hello. It's you,' Ela smiled. David smiled back.

'You wanted to see me? Kamini told me yesterday that you would be here at four.' Ela nodded.

'Is Kamini around?' David asked.

'No David, I am here on my own. I needed to talk to you alone,' Ela said.

'Oh. So let's talk,' David said, looking a little worried. 'Do you want to sit and talk or shall we walk and talk?'

'Let us take a walk,' Ela said as she got up and joined David. They started walking by the Ridge, up towards the Lake by the mountainside. It was a quiet side of town. Ela and David walked in silence.

'I don't know how to begin,' Ela said. This was followed by a long, pregnant pause.

'Well…' Ela stopped.

'Yes?'

'David, I do not know how to put it. We have known each other for such a long time and I am unable to come to a decision. But your decision to go to England has left me heartbroken. I know I should not be stopping you. You have every right to go and move on in life and make a new beginning without me, but I cannot imagine life without you. You are the centre of my being, my existence. I don't know whether I am making sense.'

'Go on. I understand.'

'It is just that I cannot live without you, David.'

'Then marry me Ela. And come with me to England. I have waited so long for you.'

'But I cannot marry you, not right now. You know Baba will never hear of it and besides if I were to marry you against his wishes, anything could happen to him. You know that he is not keeping too well. His health is delicate at the moment. Should anything happen to him, I would never be able to forgive myself.'

'So what are you trying to say, Ela?' David asked.

'Just give me some more time. Don't go to England yet.'

'Give you time? How much longer? Are we going to have to wait for your father to recover or die before you make up your mind?' 'David, please! Don't talk like that.' Ela was visibly perturbed.

They walked further ahead towards the *jheel* and continued towards the mountainside. 'Ela, you know I have always loved you and always will,' David broke the silence. Ela nodded. 'I refused to go to England with my family because I wanted to be near you. That was more than five years ago. And nothing has moved in our lives since then. You are unable to marry me because of family pressures. You are unable to marry another because of me. It is best I go away for awhile. Maybe my absence will help you come to a decision. Should you still desire to marry me, I will come back. And should you decide not to marry me, I will respect your decision. Who knows what the future has in store for us, but let me tell you, my dear, right now I cannot think of loving anyone else but you.' And David reached for Ela's hand. She was crying softly.

'But David, do you really have to go?'

'Yes. I have to. There is nothing I can do about it.' Ela nodded and they both walked in silence.

After what seemed like hours, though it was only a few minutes later, David said, 'Ela, I think we should turn back. I will walk you home.'

'There is no turning back for me now, David. I cannot bear to be without you.'

Saying this she started walking towards the edge of the Ridge. David followed her. Suddenly he realised she was almost running towards the deep gorge. He started to run behind her. 'Ela. Wait. Slow down. There's a deep gorge there. You might slip.' Ela was now running like a mad woman. David shouted to her as he chased her, 'Ela. Stop. Wait. Listen. Ela... please, stop.'

But Ela Sen was beyond anyone's reasoning. She ran straight ahead into the gorge, falling several hundred feet down into wild oblivion. The mountains were waiting readily to devour her as David looked on.

A day later, David Andrew Oliver was found dead in the Browns' guest room. He had bled to death on the bed. His wrists were slit with his Swiss pocket knife. Obviously, death had been slow and painful. The mattress was soaked in fresh blood, prompting Mrs Brown's first reaction, 'Oh dear, I will have to get rid of such a fine downy.'

Turning Point

A lot had happened in her life in the two years since Oona's twenty-first birthday. She was no longer working with Katy, nor had she continued with her studies. Instead she was now a full-fledged upcoming journalist working for one of the city's foremost dailies, *The Herald*. She had left Katy because she could no longer reconcile her principles with her job: advertising and public relations thrived on hard-selling lies. And Oona's ideals would not agree with it. After the initial phase of glamour was over, she realised she could not survive in the world of advertising for too long.

One of her college seniors, Ravina was working on the news desk at *The Herald*. Oona happened to bump into Ravina at a party and took her card. Later she dropped by at her office to seek her advice on something. The dynamism of the newsroom got her adrenalin going. 'At the moment there are no vacancies,' Ravina told her. 'Not even for trainee subs. We've just recruited a whole bunch of nincompoops.' Both laughed. 'I am serious. None of them have any love for news reporting. Not even remotely connected to journalism. Most have done an MA or a BEd and what have you. They are just biding their time before holy matrimony and the stipend comes in handy for make-up and clothes,' Ravina complained bitterly.

'What a waste,' Oona sympathised.

'You're telling me. It's frustrating wasting our efforts training them. The first eligible boy that comes by, they'll happily go and hitch themselves,' Ravina said. 'But what angers me most is this industry. While the hotels and advertising and other fields look for qualified personnel in their respective areas, here no one gives a damn. It's not enough that you can write. It is more important to have a flair for hounding news. Stupid assholes…'

'I know what you mean. Because of some idiot, people like me are deprived,' Oona added.

'I'll tell you one thing. Don't waste your time joining here. Look at me, it's been two years and I am tired of subbing. Just cleaning other people's shit. You don't want to do that, do you?'

'But I do like the idea of writing and reporting. Honestly.'

'Then go across to that cabin,' Ravina pointed to the far end of the room. 'Meet up with Dinks. Dinesh Sharma. He's the feature editor. He's looking out for some freelance writers. He might just put you onto something. And you can drop in your resume any day with me. Whenever there is a vacancy for a trainee sub, I'll buzz you. But seriously, I think you won't enjoy cleaning other people's shit.' And she laughed.

Oona laughed too. 'Thanks. Meanwhile I'll check out Dinesh Sharma.'

When Oona breezed into Dinesh's office, the latter was not exactly pleased. He tried to cut her off, saying he wasn't really looking for writers. But Oona had learnt from her PR experience that gentle persuasion was the key to getting a foothold anywhere. She persisted. She shared some story ideas, including one about a famous cellist performing in the city. Finally, just to get her off his back, he said, 'Okay, bring me a write-up on the cellist. Not just his performance, but also his background. His early years in the orphanage and his rise to becoming one of the world's top concert cellists. Keep it to 1,000 words, maximum 1,200. And I want it by Thursday. You have three days to work on it. Now you may leave.'

'Thank you. Maybe if I have more material, I can increase the word limit? Then you can put it as a cover feature.' Oona was all excited.

Dinesh Sharma stared at her. He couldn't believe the cheek of the girl. She hadn't even cut her teeth and she was dreaming of cover stories. The sheer audacity. But there was something about Oona he liked. Her spunk. So he let her off with, 'Now go. Get cracking, before I change my mind.'

Meanwhile, Oona and Craig's passion for each other had subsided. They were in touch though. They would meet up once in a while, have sex occasionally. But that was it. Initially Oona felt frustrated that Craig did not respond to her with the same fervour she felt for him. But later she realised Craig's whole life was one big chaos. There were certain things about him that annoyed her. He seemed to be floating in and out of the city without an agenda. He would disappear for days and then surface all of a sudden. The last time, a few months back, he had softened up. She had thought it was a change of heart till he asked for a loan. Twenty thousand was a big amount. Oona gave him ten without telling anyone, not even her mother. He had promised to return it in six months' time. Four months had already elapsed and there was no trace of Craig. Oona wondered if she would ever see her money again.

She had meanwhile acquired some new friends. Mainly on the job. Moushumi was one girl with whom she enjoyed spending her spare as well as work time. She still met up with Sonia but not very often as Oona was busy with work and Sonia was busy with her year-old daughter. 'It's an altogether different experience, being a mom. Motherhood is so fulfilling,' Sonia had cooed to Oona when the latter went to visit her after the birth of her daughter, carrying the customary *shagun,* a silver rattle. Oona felt no envy, though her friend's intention was to make her feel it. That had been nearly eight months ago.

Meanwhile her neighbour, Rinku's mother had informed them that Kobir had got married to the Seal girl. That it had been a quiet affair. Oona breathed a sigh of relief on hearing this. Sangeeta of course was upset and spent a couple of sleepless nights before Calmpose helped her settle down.

Oona was too busy to mull over the past. She started out with features for the Sunday magazine of *The Herald*. A rival group, *The Tribune* also started publishing some of her features. Her byline was getting noticed and appreciated. She had a style that was simple, yet dynamic. More than that, she was fiercely honest and wrote straight from the heart. *Dil se*. A quality which comes with innocence and dulls with experience!

Dinesh Sharma did not fail to notice this. He didn't want a rival group to entice Oona with a tempting offer. In a pre-emptive move, he called her to his office. She thought he would tell her to cross-check some fact on her recent copy, which he did from time to time. 'Oh God! I'll have to go back to the Kalighat *basti* to recheck with Das Babu. And the *Tribune* deadline is tomorrow,' she groaned to herself as she entered Dinesh's office. She still hesitated to call him Dinks.

'Hi.'

'Oh, hi,' said Dinesh, looking up from his monitor. 'Sit. Want coffee?'

Coffee, she thought, he's actually offering me coffee? So unlike Dinesh. What is he up to?

'Well, I don't mind.'

Dinesh buzzed the peon to fetch two sugary coffees from the machine. What he told her next, took her by complete surprise. He had been noticing her hard work and was quite pleased by the way she was progressing. He thought it would be only fair to absorb her in the paper.

'But I don't want to work full-time,' she countered; Ravina's words of cleaning other people's shit rang in her ears. 'I earn more as a freelancer and I am not tied down.'

'Wait a minute, young lady. Let me finish.' He told her he did not expect her to work full time in the office. He would give her assignments and she would have to complete them from wherever she wanted, either from home or she could use the office. She would be given a monthly retainership of Rs 2,000, plus extra for every assignment, at the rate of one rupee per word! Oona could not believe her luck at what she was hearing. She knew there had to be a catch somewhere.

'Just one more thing. You cannot take up assignments for any other publications or newspapers. And that includes magazines as well.'

Ah, so there it was! But at the moment it did not seem to matter. *The Herald* was by far the most widely circulated and respected paper in the city. She was happy to be a part of the team for the moment. And it was too good an offer to let go. Oona smiled and nodded.

'Good,' Dinesh smiled for the first time. 'So from next month you are on. Meanwhile tie up your other assignments. C'mon, get cracking.'

'Thanks, I appreciate this. Thank you.' Oona smiled and left, bursting to share it with Moushumi or Ravina. Unfortunately, neither girl was at her desk. So she sat with Dasu, one of the senior photographers, and shared another cup of the sugary machine coffee.

Craig called her from Connecticut one day, out of the blue, and said that he would be coming to Calcutta in a few days. He wanted to catch up with her. Though Oona did not jump with excitement, she was keen to meet up with Craig for two reasons—first to try and persuade him to return her loan, or at least part of it; and second, she wanted to have sex. It had been quite some time since they had made love and there was nothing much happening in her love life anyway. So it was the body's yearning rather than the mind's.

When Oona caught up with Craig, her desperation for sex was obvious. She did not hesitate to make the first move. Craig was quite taken aback by her. She was so different from the shy, hesitant girl he had deflowered some years back. 'My, my! Someone is really becoming a veteran,' Craig remarked, amused.

'Shut up! I've missed you so much,' Oona replied, not sounding very convincing.

'Me too,' lied Craig.

'Really! I thought you were busy with your Polish lady love? Or have you found someone else?'

'Are we gonna discuss my love life or get on with it?' Craig sounded irritable.

Oona grabbed him and began kissing him hard. Craig responded with equal fervour and soon they were making wild, passionate love.

'Hmmm... that was rather good!' Craig sighed after they had finished. 'You came thrice.' He kissed her. She just cooed in contentment. 'Just give me a second, honey, will you? I need to use the loo,' Craig told her, heading to the bathroom. Oona waited. Craig seemed to be taking more time than usual. Maybe he was smoking a joint. She got up and got dressed. She walked across to the table to pick up her hair clip and purse when she saw a leather-bound black planner lying on the table. *Let's check out some of the girls he is dating. I am sure he will have their names in here.* As she was about to go to the telephone index section, something caught her eye. Written on it was:

> *The international Krsna Movement (KM) was founded in 1960 by the great spiritual leader from India, Gurudev. Though this movement officially continues around the world, today it is no longer the movement founded by Gurudev, but rather a massive hoax. This hoax has been well-documented but evidence of the hoax is largely unknown to many of its supporters and members who, blissfully ignorant, continue to follow and fund the movement*
> *Fifteen years after Gurudev died...*

Oona heard the click of the bathroom door. She quickly put the planner in her bag and clasped it shut. Her curious mind had scented that she was on to something really big and she did not want to lose out on a story. As Craig came up to her, she decided she had to leave before he noticed his missing planner.

'I think I'll have to leave now. Some people are coming over for dinner. Besides I have an early press conference to attend to tomorrow,' Oona said.

'Are you sure? I thought we could have dinner or something....'

'Yes, I know. But I completely forgot about the dinner at home. Maybe tomorrow or the day after? I'll call you. I'll have to rush now.'

'Okay,' Craig shrugged. 'I'll see you off.'

On the way home in the bus, Oona quickly started to read through the diary. It was a goldmine of information on the KM movement which of late seemed always to be mired in one controversy or the other. *This could be a huge exposé, her journalist's mind reasoned. I have to play my cards right. This could be the story of the decade. Not just national, but of international interest.*

The first thing she did on getting off the bus was to go to the friendly neighbourhood photocopy shop and get the entire planner copied, telephone index *et al.* Then she went home and called up Craig.

'Hi,' she said almost breathless.

'Hi. What's up? Are you okay? You sound breathless,' Craig replied.

'Yeah, I'm okay. Just reached home. Climbed the two flights up.'

'Oh.'

'Craig, when I opened my purse to buy my bus ticket I realised I'd put your planner in my bag. I must have picked it up by mistake along with my purse off the table.'

'That's okay. But I need it,' Craig sounded urgent. 'It is my lifeline and I cannot survive without it. I'll come right by and pick it up.'

'Oh, no, you cannot do that. We have guests coming and besides my mother will be furious if she knows I am still seeing you,' Oona sounded worried.

'But honey, I need...'

'Please. I'll drop it off first thing tomorrow morning. Seven. Eight. Whatever time you say. And I promise not to peek at your girlfriends' numbers,' Oona tried to sound casual. Craig laughed.

'Promise?'

'That's a promise.'

'Then see you at eight tomorrow morning and…'

'Bye,' Oona said and hung up.

Oona had often visited the KM Temple with Craig, and had always felt that the organisation was a little shady. She had overheard Sangeeta discussing with relatives how such organisations lured young men and women into the world of free sex and drug abuse and so on. She had initially thought Sangeeta, upset at her being with Craig, was inventing such things.

She once lied to Sangeeta, saying she was going out of town on an assignment whereas she had actually gone with Craig to Mayanagar, a little town by the Ganges where KM had its world headquarters. She had heard Craig boasting about the temple and was finally persuaded by him to go there. It was simply mind-blowing: very ornate, with the idols of Krishna and his consort Radha moulded in gold and lavishly studded with precious and semi-precious stones. The spacious temple compound fed hundreds of hungry pilgrims and villagers each day with free *prasadam* or meals. The food was vegetarian, cooked in the purest ghee and served with the finest-grained basmati.

Adjoining the temple was the guest house for international pilgrims. Only select, rich Indian donors were allowed to stay here. The rooms were basic but expensive, designed with the best of Carrara marble. The bathrooms had gold-plated fittings. Oona was impressed. 'When I introduce you as my fiancé, just nod; illicit sex is forbidden here,' Craig warned Oona. 'And no wearing any Western outfits. You can wear sarees and salwars, but keep your head covered always. I know you don't smoke, but just to spell it out, no smoking, no drinking…not even coffee or tea. Got it?'

'But what do I do without tea?' Oona cried. 'I will not be able to surface without my morning cuppa.'

'Relax,' Craig smiled. 'I'll walk you down to the tea stall outside the temple premises and we can both have our tea there. It's just that it is not allowed *here*.'

Oona spent four glorious days with Craig. That was the time when she was still in love with him. Besides great sex, they enjoyed walking down the river front. In the mornings and evenings they attended the *aarti* at the temple. And the *prasadam* was simply delicious. Craig did introduce her to a few people, including the head priest, Surananda Prabhu and his assistant, Dhananjoy. Both were Americans and Surananda, in spite of his clean-shaven head—like the rest of the initiated devotees—and saffron attire, was a handsome man. Oona found him charming and at times got the feeling that he was trying to flirt with her. But if so, it was very subtly done.

On some of those afternoons Craig would be away for hours on some 'temple work', which he was rather vague about when she asked for details. Oona used the time to read or take a nap. Some of the time she noticed Craig returned heavily doped. She thought it better to ignore this behaviour. While returning to Calcutta, Surananda insisted they travel in his personal van. Dhananjoy saw them off. Craig had a shiny steel briefcase with him, which remained cuffed to his left wrist throughout the three-hour journey. Oona thought it strange but Craig brushed it off as containing 'some important documents'.

Now, reading through the diary, Oona's suspicions were confirmed. It opened up a whole new world of drugs, sex abuse, paedophilia and money-laundering. Craig went on to state that Gurudev had appointed twelve disciples who would, after his death, look after the KM temples and the more than 50,000 devotees worldwide. But within a year of Gurudev's death, these devotees became self-appointed 'gurus' or 'prabhus', manning different centres. One of these was Surananda Prabhu, the Guru of the Eastern India headquarters—Mayanagar, which oversaw the whole of India and Southeast Asia.

After carving out twelve zones for themselves, these 'gurus' started funnelling huge amounts of temple funds into their personal Swiss bank accounts. Slowly, the number of self-appointed gurus doubled and then trebled whilst the number of devotees reduced to one-third of the original strength.

Power struggles and confusion are common in the history of religious cults following the passing of a charismatic founder. In this case, the document left behind by Gurudev on how he visualised the continuation of the movement was misinterpreted to suit the personal whims of the new 'gurus'. Craig described in minute detail instances of sexual abuse of young, nubile devotees by the gurus, flouting their vow of abstinence. He recorded cases of paedophilia in the *gurukuls* (schools for the temples' children) on the pretext of education. He also talked about drug abuse on temple premises everywhere, links with the South American drug cartel, laundering of drug money and the siphoning of temple money into personal coffers. Most of the claims were substantiated with names, dates and places and even bank security numbers.

Reading through the detailed notes in Craig's diary, Oona gathered that he was planning to publish an exposé of the rot within the Krsna Movement. Little did he know that she would beat him to it.

When Oona showed Dinesh the photocopied diary, he was initially sceptical and then very impressed. She admitted how she had got the diary and the first thing he said was, 'We have to get you round-the-clock security cover. This Craig fellow may be crazy, but the other guys will be dangerous. And once the story breaks, they will be out to get you.' He paused and looked at Oona and asked, 'Do you want to break the story under your byline or shall we just put it as "Our Special Correspondent"?'

'My name, of course. It's my story!'

'Relax,' Dinesh said. 'I did not mean that. I just thought it might be safer…'

'No, Sir. I don't care. I would rather it goes under my name,' Oona said.

'Okay, as you wish lady. But you will learn from experience that it is not always wise to be brave.'

A week later *The Herald* carried the story 'Krsna Movement: The Inside Story, Part I' by *Oona Roy*. The complete story came out in three parts, over a period of three days.

Two days before the story went to print, Oona was given a 24x7 security cover. Two armed guards from the local Top Dog Securities stood guard in front of her house, alternating on a 12-hour shift. Anyone who wanted to visit the Roys had to go through them first. Initially Sangeeta was a bit wary, but she soon got used to their presence, supplying them with cups of tea and biscuits from time to time. Dinesh Sharma saw to it that Oona was provided an office car for her assignments and otherwise. Oona insisted Sangeeta go to office in her car rather than take public transport. 'You never know with these crackpots. Where they get you,' she reasoned with her mother.

The week after her story was published, the papers were full of reports of investigations into the workings of the Krsna Movement and interrogation of key members.

Oona was enjoying being the centre of attention. The neighbours were a little awed by her new-found power. Her relatives boasted that they had known all along she would be famous some day. Jealous colleagues looked at her through the corners of their eyes. Envious ones lauded her courage. 'Wish we had been in your place,' they said. Friends who had been out of touch for many years suddenly reappeared in her life. 'We got your number through so and so,' they chorused. 'Congrats.' She even got some fan mails and calls. And some threat calls too. She lodged an FIR, and her phone was tapped for her security. At parties, which she attended very infrequently nowadays, she was the cynosure of all eyes as the gutsy young journalist from *The Herald*. One party-goer flippantly remarked over a Scotch, 'Had this been the US, Oona Roy would have definitely got the Pulitzer. Unfortunately, not only do we *not* honour our journalists, we do not even pay them well. Imagine the risks they take for such pittance!'

A week later, Craig headed off to the US. He called Oona from the airport, hurt and abusive. 'You have betrayed my trust. Wait till I get back at you. You will have to pay for this dearly some day, honey.' Oona felt bad, not at Craig's departure but because she had to bid farewell to her money as well.

Oona was wearing a simple white salwar-kameez with a bright yellow and green *bandhni dupatta* when Moushumi entered her house.

'Sorry, can I use your loo, honey? Need to touch up my face.' Moushumi was dressed to the hilt. She looked at Oona and asked, 'Are you going like this?'

'Why? Do I look under-dressed?' Oona asked.

'No....you are okay. It's just, all this white ethnic stuff...a bit too simple don't you think. After all, it's a filmy party with the Bombay stars. Sultana Ahmed and Badshah Khan. And that dude Anand Khanna.'

'How can you call that Anand charlie a dude? He is ancient history. I saw his film as a kid...maybe I was in the first or second grade then...' 'What are you talking about? Who is ancient history?' Moushumi gave her a weird look.

'Rajesh Khanna. Right?' Oona faltered, realising she had made a mistake.

'Oh God! No, no. Wrong. Absolutely wrong. Which world are you living in Oona? I am talking about Anand Khanna,' Moushumi said.

'Who's he?' Oona asked, indifferently.

'*Yaar*. Anand Khanna is the producer of the superhit *Aaj, Kal aur Aaj*. He is kind of dishy. I bet tonight all the women are going to fall over him. He's been an eligible divorcee for years. He is hot property these days...and loaded!'

'Well, I'm not in queue for his attention. In fact, I haven't even seen his films. Just heard the names. Big deal. I'm comfortable as I am.' Oona said.

'Suit yourself,' Moushumi shrugged, applying another round of *kajal*.

Anand Khanna was one of the top producers of the Hindi film industry—the largest film industry in the country, churning out nearly 500 films a year. Most of these films were inane, feel-good type films or in-your-face slapstick. The intelligentsia and the elite had a condescending attitude towards them whilst the great Indian masses thrived on their feel-good escapism. On a lighter note, of late people had begun referring to the Hindi film industry as 'Bollywood', after the term was jokingly coined by a screenwriter as an obvious spin-off on its more successful Western counterpart, Hollywood.

Anand Khanna's last three films, *Heera aur Patthar, Mister Gambo* and *AKAA (Aaj, Kal Aur Aaj)* had been mega hits, breaking all previous box-office records. Anand had unconventional good looks and was quite a charmer, with a long list of female admirers. A complete ladies' man, Anand never spurned any attention from the opposite sex.

He was in the city with his stars Sultana and Badshah, for a film called *Jaaneman,* made by Bollywood hit director, Kapil Desai. Anand was rumoured to have had a scene sometime earlier with Sultana. She had been the cause of his earlier divorce, according to the rumour mills. Anand's presence on the sets and in the city for so long meant a possible rekindling of their earlier romance, though Sultana was married to ace director Suleiman Ahmed. Moushumi had done a big interview with Anand some days ago in the *Herald*. But contrary to rumours, Anand had also admitted to Moushumi during the interview that there were no sparks flying between him and Sultana this time and had even obliquely referred to her as being '*thanda,* rather cold. And besides I am single, ready to mingle,' he joked.

'Look, there's Anand. Isn't he gorgeous! What a bod, man! Come, let's go and say hi to him. I hope he remembers me,' Moushumi said, pulling Oona and trying to wend her way through the crowd towards Anand. Before she could get to him, Anand spotted her and came towards her with a big grin and hugged her. Moushumi was left speechless.

'Hi Moushoomi,' Anand said with a hint of a charming Bengali lilt.

'Oh, hi Anand,' Moushumi recovered from her reverie, and tried to sound nonchalant. 'Good to see you again. How have you been?'

'Great. And you?'

'Not too bad. Busy with work as usual,' Moushumi said.

'Oh that was a nice piece you wrote on me,' Anand said.

'You liked it? I'm glad,' Moushumi smiled.

'Hmmm, what can I get you to drink?' Anand asked.

Meanwhile Oona was feeling rather stupid hanging around them but was also amused at the way Moushumi was trying her best to impress Khanna. She realised that Anand was merely humouring her. He seemed leaner than what she vaguely remembered of him in his photos. Besides, he was tall, well-built, and craggily handsome in a Harrison Ford sort of way.

Anand was wearing beige, pleated, slightly loose-fitting trousers and a white shirt with light brown pin-stripes. His sleeves were folded back and she noticed his lean, muscular arms. But what impressed her most were his hands: big, strong and sexy. They spelt power. Especially the way he moved them whilst talking. For Oona, it was love at first sight with those strong hands.

'Hi.' It was Anand's voice.

'Oh, sorry, I was a little distracted. Hi,' Oona said almost blushing at her thoughts. 'I am Oona. Oona Roy.'

'That is a beautiful name. An unusual one though. I have never heard it before. Bengali names are beautiful, just like the language,' Anand said.

Oona blushed again. 'It's not actually a Bengali name. My father named me after Oona O'Neil…'

'I know, Eugene O'Neill's daughter. She was married to my favourite film-maker, Charlie Chaplin.'

Oona was very impressed. After all, Bollywood folk were supposed to be real duds. *Seems like this Anand Khanna has brain to his brawn.*

'Let me get you charming ladies a drink,' Anand said, leading the girls towards the bar. Suddenly, Oona's left eye began to twitch. Sangeeta would have said that it was a good omen.

I wonder what good fortune is coming my way now.

Book Two

BOMBAY
1990–2009

Bombay-Bound

It was 22 December. Calcutta was cold. Oona was flying to Bombay that afternoon. She had told Sangeeta that she was travelling on an assignment and would be gone at least a fortnight. Sangeeta was a little worried as it was the first time Oona would be on her own for so long. 'Do you really have to take on outstation assignments?' Sangeeta had asked.

'Of course, Ma. And don't worry. I'm old enough to look after myself.'

'Better take some extra warm clothes. Don't catch a cold in this chilly weather,' Sangeeta warned.

'Relax, Ma. Bombay is not as cold as Calcutta,' Oona replied, still lazing around in bed.

'You never know,' Sangeeta persisted.

Sangeeta would have been shocked had Oona told her the real reason for her trip. She was going to meet Anand Khanna. It had been six months since the party where Moushumi had introduced Oona and Anand. Soon after, Anand invited Moushumi and Oona for dinner. In fact, he personally called Oona, taking her telephone number from Moushumi. Oona was flattered. They had a quiet dinner at the hotel and Anand flirted with the young women throughout. In the taxi on the way home, Oona remarked, 'You are right. Anand Khanna is quite a flirt.'

'Yeah,' Moushumi sounded a little bored. 'He seems quite taken by you.'

'Oh, c'mon!' Oona protested, and the rest of the journey went by in silence.

A few days later, Anand asked Oona out again, this time for a fashion show. Though she was quite busy that particular evening, she did not say so and turned around a few plans to accommodate him. She did not want to lose a chance to go out with Anand. Later that weekend, she called Anand. 'The Calcutta Symphony Orchestra is playing under this American conductor, Russell Jeston. Would you be interested?'

'I would love to come,' Anand drawled. 'I enjoy listening to Western classical music.'

By the end of the evening Oona realised that Anand knew as much about Western classical music as she knew about Zulu music. But she was flattered nevertheless that he had tried to pretend, for her sake. She also enjoyed the envious glances she received on being seen out with the macho producer. Soon Anand and Oona started going out. There was some mild gossip about them. One or two colleagues at the paper would hint at the relationship, but Oona brushed them off. Some evenings Anand dropped her home and soon her neighbours were talking about her late night rendezvous with the 'Hindi film producer'.

She didn't tell too many friends about her relationship. Moushumi seemed to suspect something, but was also a little aloof nowadays. Oona had hinted about Anand to Sonia, who seemed happy for her friend, but also issued the usual warnings. 'I hope it works out. You never know with these filmy people. They are all out to have fun. So don't give in too much to him. Get what I mean?'

Oona nodded. Damned if I am going to listen to her, she thought.

'Oh by the way, do bring Anand over for dinner when he comes next. I'd love to meet him. Never met a Bollywood type before,' Sonia told Oona.

'Sure,' Oona smiled at how everyone fell for glamour.

The shoot was drawing to a close. Anand and his unit would leave town in a few weeks. Oona and he were at his hotel room one evening, drinking tea. She was feeling quite low about his imminent departure, and he admitted that he would miss her too. Slowly they started talking about their respective lives. He about his past marriage. She about Craig. Anand gave her a sympathetic hug and then kissed her on the forehead. Oona relaxed in his arms, secure and comfortable. Soon he was caressing her back and she kissed him.

When Anand undressed her expertly, she did not resist. It had been a while. Craig was history. They shifted from the couch to the bed. 'Are you okay?' Anand asked. Oona nodded. 'Should we....?' he asked again. Oona nodded and breathed, 'Don't worry. I won't pretend I am a virgin.'

'Thank God!' he muttered, kissing her passionately. Realising that Anand seemed to reciprocate her feelings, she let herself go, enjoying every moment of their love making. Later, they had dinner and Anand dropped her home. This became a routine. He would return to the hotel after shooting, she would drop by and they would make love. Then they would have dinner and Anand would drop Oona home.

On the last evening, Oona broke down. 'I am going to miss you,' she sobbed.

'So will I,' he said sincerely, stroking her forehead.

'No you won't. You will forget me once you reach Bombay.'

Anand smiled. 'Don't worry,' he soothed her. 'We will stay in touch.'

He kept his word, calling almost every other day. Once, he even came to Calcutta for a few days just to meet her. She lied to her mother about another assignment and stayed with Anand at his close friend's house. But when he left, Oona found herself distracted by thoughts of him. 'Why don't you come down again? We can take a short holiday to Darjeeling or somewhere,' Oona had asked him.

'*Jaan*, I am busy with my shoots,' he would say.

'I miss you so much,' Oona sighed.

'Me too.'

One day Anand asked Oona to come to Bombay. 'But how will I explain to Ma?'

'Tell her that you have to go out on an assignment. I will send you the ticket. And we'll go to Goa for New Year's Eve!'

And so, Oona was off to Bombay.

Bombay's domestic airport, Santa Cruz, had of late had been renamed the tongue-twisting Chhatrapati Shivaji Terminal at the behest of the local political fanatics of the Narangi Dal. Narangi Dal was the political epicentre of Bombay just as Bombay was the financial epicentre of the country. The public snidely referred to it as the Kachrapati Terminal, '*kachra*' in Hindi meaning garbage. The airport had served as a base for the Royal Indian Air Force during the Second World War and after India's independence became known as Santa Cruz Airport, named for the suburb of its location.

Anand was waiting for Oona at the arrivals terminal. Suddenly he heard a voice behind him, 'Hi.'

Turning to respond, he saw it was Mimi Saluja.

'Oh, hi! Nice surprise.' Anand was at his charming best. Mimi was one of the most feared Bollywood gossip columnists. 'You, here?' he asked.

'I've come to pick up my daughters. They live with my ex-husband in Calcutta and are coming to spend their holidays with me. We are headed to Goa for New Year's,' Mimi said, stylishly drawing her locks together with her Dior shades. Her long, crimson nails stood out like the tip of her pointed pen. Sharp. Menacing.

Mimi Saluja was a stunner. She had started out as a model alongside the 1970s' Bollywood sex-bomb Zeenat Aman. While Zeenie baby became a star, the closest Mimi came to stardom was to date the intellectual Bollywood star of the 1980s, Shishir Kumar. But he dumped her to marry according to his parents' wishes. Driven by ambition, she had married political commentator and editor of *Calcutta Tribune*, Khokon

Day, not just because she wanted to have children but also to gain respectability as a writer. The first she accomplished immediately by producing a set of twin girls with Khokon. For the second, she used her husband's newspaper to foist herself on people as a columnist. *Day to Day with Mimi Day* dealt with everything under the sun from motherhood to masala chicken.

She was married to Khokon when she met the dapper Bubbles Saluja, who in those days claimed to be a shipping magnate. Tabloids said Mimi had seduced him on a Bombay-Goa flight. Mimi dumped Khokon and married Bubbles, resettling in her native Bombay. Soon after marriage the bubble about Bubbles burst. She realised he was not the shipping magnate he had seemed to be. In fact, she later realised that even the baubles he had wooed her with, including a twelve-carat solitaire, were excellent fakes. His business was in bad shape. Never one to give up, Mimi packaged herself and Bubbles in such a way that they became the most happening couple in Bombay. They were a regular fixture at every Page 3 event, long before the term 'Page 3' was even coined. She capitalised on her good looks and started the trend of glamour writing, or what laymen called 'gossip'. She began the tradition of gossip rags, launching *Star Tips,* where she routinely took apart film stars and films. Her first victim was of course her old flame, Shishir Kumar, who quickly left Bollywood and settled in Nashik, where he ran a small motel.

Mimi was the country's highest-paid gossip columnist. Most newspapers syndicated her columns and some tabloids sold by virtue of her name. She also had some Jackie Collins-style novels portraying the sleazier side of Bollywood which sold like hot cakes. Everyone in Bollywood was in awe of her and made sure not to annoy her.

Naturally, standing at the airport, Anand smiled and went in for flattery. 'Tell me, how do you always manage to look so lovely?' Used to these tactics, Mimi ignored it and asked a question in response, 'What are you doing here?'

'Come to receive a friend,' Anand mumbled, almost stumbling on his words.

'From Calcutta?' Mimi asked. Anand nodded.

A little later, Oona walked towards the luggage carousel, scanning the crowd for Anand. She spotted him talking to Mimi Saluja. She's gorgeous, Oona thought, walking up to them. When all she got from Anand was a limp 'hi', she immediately realised he was being cautious in front of Mimi. Determined not to allow him to hide her away, she walked up to Mimi, hand outstretched, saying, 'Hi. My name's Oona. And I simply love your columns. They are so immensely readable.' What she actually wanted to say was, 'They are such crap.' Mimi smiled in acknowledgement.

'Were you on the 8.45 flight from Calcutta?' Mimi asked. Oona nodded.

'So are my daughters. Then Reema and Raima will be here soon,' Mimi said.

'I'll just get my luggage,' Oona told Anand as she left for the luggage carousel.

Mimi asked Anand casually, 'So she is the friend you have come to receive. What does she do?'

'She's a journalist.'

'Hmm. I see. Bright kid.' And she gave Anand an all-knowing smile.

By now Anand Khanna was feeling very awkward. He knew Mimi would mention it in her next column and he had been trying desperately to hold on to the 'single and unattached' tag like most of Bollywood tended to do. Besides, though Oona was nearly half his age, all of twenty-five, he hated being reminded that he was a cradle-snatcher. Bloody bitch, he thought to himself as he politely smiled back at Mimi.

Bombay, the capital of the state of Maharashtra, lies on India's west coast, by the Arabian Sea. It is India's most populous city, and the world's fourth-most populous. Besides being famous as the home to the Hindi film industry and most of its stars, the city is also the financial capital of

India, housing important financial institutions like the Reserve Bank of India and the Stock Exchange. The corporate headquarters of many of India's leading companies and industrial houses are also situated here. Bombay is one of the rare cities to accommodate a national park, Borivali, within its city limits. A dream destination for business opportunities, Bombay attracts migrant labour from all over India and its high standard of living makes the city a potpourri of various cultures and communities. Bombay usually seems to be bursting at the seams.

The cluster of islands that make up Bombay have existed since the Stone Age. They were part of the Buddhist empire, and some of the oldest existing edifices of the archipelago are the Elephanta Caves and the Walkeshwar Temple complex. The name Bombay derives its origins from the local goddess Mumbadevi. She was the patron goddess of Koli fisherfolk, the original inhabitants of the islands that make up Bombay. In 1534, the Portuguese appropriated the islands from Bahadur Shah II of Gujarat and named the place 'Bom baiya', meaning 'good bay'.

The islands of Bombay were brought together into the single peninsula we see today through the active reclamation of land. When the Portuguese ceded the group of islands in 1661 to Charles II of England as dowry for Catharine de Braganza, the English anglicised the name to 'Bombay'. In 1668, the islands were leased to the British East India Company for a sum of sixteen pound sterling per annum. The deep harbour was ideal for the British to set up their first port in the subcontinent and Bombay's population has risen at an alarming rate ever since. It soon replaced Surat as the East India Company headquarters and later on came to be known as the Bombay Presidency. In 1853, India's first passenger railway line was established between Bombay and Thane.

In the mid-nineteenth century, during the American Civil War, Bombay became the world's chief cotton trading market. The resulting economic boom enhanced the city's stature. The opening of the Suez Canal in 1869 transformed Bombay into one of the largest seaports in the Arabian Sea. Over the years, as capital of the Bombay Presidency, it was an important base for India's independence movement, with Mahatma Gandhi launching his Quit India Movement from here in 1942. Post independence, on 1 May 1960, Bombay became the capital of the state of Maharashtra.

A construction boom in the 1970s and the influx of migrants made Bombay India's most populous city, overtaking Calcutta. To safeguard the rights of the 'sons of the soil' a local political outfit, the Narangi Dal, was formed in 1970. This was the first seed of unrest to penetrate the city's secular fabric.

Nearly a quarter of a century later, when Oona landed on a nippy December evening, Bombay was growing rapidly—industry, real estate and films. Real-estate prices were so high that at one point Bombay had beaten New York and was next only to Tokyo. Everyone wanted to be in Bombay and share a piece of its glory. Though Oona was not really enchanted by the city, she was nevertheless curious. And of course, her idea of Bombay began and ended with Anand Khanna.

It had been a few days since she came, and Oona was getting dressed for the evening. It was going to be her first Bollywood party. The music release of *Shankara*. The film starred two upcoming youngsters who had absolutely no experience in acting but were the lead pair purely by virtue of being the children of yesteryear actors. One of their fathers had also financed the film. That was Bollywood. Completely feudal. Actors and directors with talent and experience languished whilst rank newcomers made it big due to their 'filmy connections'.

The music launch was at the suburban five-star hotel, Juhu Centaur. Anand Khanna loved attending these filmy dos, however inconsequential. 'One has to be seen circulating at the right places to stay afloat in this industry,' he told Oona.

Earlier in the day, Oona and Anand had had their first little spat. He had mentioned the party to Oona but was hesitant about taking her along. 'You have to understand *jaan*, in Bollywood, your value increases if you are unattached.' What he meant was it was easy to woo heroines if you were rich and single.

But Oona was upset and took him to task, 'Is that why you called me here? To keep me under wraps? Screw me and then tire of me and pack me home while you are seen in public with your heroines and your model arm candies?'

'Oh, damn! You don't understand.'

'Of course I don't and I don't want to either. Book my ticket. I'll leave tomorrow.'

'Now listen, *jaan*...'

But Oona stormed out and closed the door behind her. Anand heard her sobbing in the bedroom. Oona was not the average Bollywood babe—the kinds he had dated earlier—no strings attached, wham-bam-thank-you-ma'am. She was intelligent and smart and genuinely cared for Anand.

'All right,' he knocked on her door. 'Open up. We're going for the party tonight.' Oona slowly opened the door, feigning hurt. But she was happy inside. She knew she had triumphed.

Anand kissed her on the head and wiped away her tears. 'C'mon, cheer up. Make me a cup of tea.' Oona smiled and headed to the kitchen.

Anand had sacked Parvati, his maid of many years, a week before Oona's arrival. Parvati had, since his divorce, begun interfering too much in his life. She would smother him with her concern and conveniently forget to pass on messages from his lady friends. She had many times lied to Oona over the phone about Anand not being at home. When Anand discovered this, he decided to do away with her services because he knew she might cause more trouble with Oona's arrival. He gave her 5,000 rupees and told her to go to her village and rest. Parvati wailed loud and long, but finally left with the money. Later, Anand heard that she had found a job in a neighbouring building.

As a replacement, Anand had hired a young Nepali boy. Santosh was a bad cook but he managed the odd jobs around the house. Still, most of the time he hung around in the building lobby, chatting with the building watchmen and smoking *beedis* on the sly. This was not too bad as it gave Anand some privacy with Oona. They enjoyed sitting over drinks and cosy dinners by themselves. Oona loved Anand's company and he enjoyed her intelligent chatter. There seemed to be no age gap between them.

'Here,' Oona handed him a cup of tea. 'Just taste it. I hope the sugar is right.'

'Should be,' he said, taking a sip without looking at it. The next instant he'd screwed up his face in disgust and ran to spit it out.

'What happened?' Oona followed him, concerned.

'Nothing,' Anand said. 'It's bitter as hell. Tastes strange. What did you put in it?'

'Well, tea leaves, milk, sugar…why?'

Anand led her to the kitchen and asked her to show him the tea leaves. Oona brought out the jar to show him. Anand studied it and shrieked, 'This? What is wrong with you? This is not tea. This is *kasuri methi*. Used to flavour mutton. No wonder it tasted bitter.'

'Oh,' Oona sounded sheepish. 'I thought it was Darjeeling leaf tea.'

In silence, Anand began making a fresh pot of tea. Oona stood and watched.

'Looks like you have never entered the kitchen, girl. Your mother should have taught you a thing or two about cooking.' Oona smiled.

'Never mind,' Anand went on. 'You will have to learn.'

'Why?' Oona asked. 'Santosh is there *na*.'

'Yeah. But I like my women to serve me tea. And food, madam.'

'Honey, are you looking for a maid or a girlfriend?' Oona asked feigning annoyance.

'Bit of both,' Anand kissed her. 'A servant and a slut.'

Oona did not know how to react to that.

Anand looked at Oona in the car on their way to the party. She was dressed in a heavy silk kanjeevaram saree with a lot of make-up. 'It is a nice saree,' he remarked casually. 'But you need not have dressed up so much.'

'Why? Am I looking overdressed?'

'Well... it's only a music launch. Not a film premiere or an awards' night. Don't forget we are the largest film producing country in the world. Nearly 750 films a year, out of which Bombay alone churns out 500. That is an average of a film and a half a day. At this rate there is a film or music launch every other day. So you can save your best sarees for the big events.' He squeezed her hand and said, 'But you look smashing. I hope you don't steal all the attention away from me.' She thought he was joking but Anand actually was somewhat apprehensive that Oona would attract the press photographers with her overdressing.

Anand was right. Everyone was in casual but designer jeans with a snazzy black top at the most. Some starlets were oozing out of their little black dresses. 'Looks like Bombayites know no other colour than black. And coming to a party in jeans... no one would be seen dead in them back home,' Oona thought to herself. But she actually liked the idea of dressing down. Lesson No.1 learnt at Party No.1 in Bombay. Dressing down.

Oona walked alongside Anand, feeling a little awkward in her saree, as he went about hi-helloing people. He did introduce Oona to a few of them. Anand was suddenly assaulted by a voluptuous girl in black tees and jeans. 'Hi ji. How are you ji?' she said, in distinctly Punjabi-accented English, which sounded totally fake. 'Oh. Hi Kulvinderji. How are you?'

'Good ji. Santoshji is also here ji.'

'I see. Oh, meet my friend, Oona. Oona, this is Kulvinder, my friend Santosh Mangat's wife. You have heard of Santosh Mangat, haven't you? Who played the deaf *pitashree* in the telesoap *Balaji*?'

'Oh yes, of course. How do you do?' Oona replied not quite placing Santosh Mangat as she rarely watched TV and least of all soaps.

'I am fine, Oonaji. Good to meet you. We must meet more often and you must come to our humble home ji. Anandji, you must bring Oonaji over someday,' and with that Kulvinder tightly hugged her. Oona was completely taken aback; she was not used to being over-friendly with strangers. 'Okay, bye ji. See you soon ji.' Kulvinder quickly left as she spotted one of Bollywood's top directors, Prakash Ghai making his way into the party.

Anand was amused to see the shock on Oona's face. 'You will meet many more such characters. All ji-jiing all the time. Sycophancy at its best. This is only the beginning. Bollywood is full of such surprises.'

'Hello there. My all-time favourite producer.'

'Oh, hi Aradhana. Good to see you. What a nice surprise!'

'Yes. Good to see you too,' Aradhana Gupta said as she looked to Oona. Anand took the hint.

'Oona, this is Aradhana. You must have seen her brilliant performance in *Tatkal*. Well, we have worked together once. And Aradhana, this is…'

'Oona,' Aradhana cut in.

'How do you know?' Anand and Oona were both surprised.

'Just got the info from Mimi Saluja's *Date with Mimi* in the *Daily*. Apparently she bumped into you at the airport where you had gone to receive a young journalist from Calcutta? Am I right?'

'Yes,' Anand looked a little embarrassed. 'Trust Mimi…'

Aradhana smiled pleasantly at Oona. The latter reciprocated. She was also quite pleased at hearing about Mimi's column, though she knew Anand must be cringing inside. *Serves him right! Soon we will be the talk of town and I'll see how he keeps me under wraps then!* Oona grinned to herself.

They were at the business class lounge at the Santa Cruz Domestic Airport. While Oona nursed her coffee and looked excitedly around,

Anand went to the foyer to pick up a newspaper. It was a bright morning on the second last day of the year and they were headed to Goa. Oona was really excited. She had heard so much about Goa. The hippest place to be at this time of the year, with half the jetsetters of Bombay and the film stars all headed there. As Anand returned with his paper, he suddenly stiffened. He made Oona exchange seats with him and sat glued to his paper. Later, he leaned forward and whispered to Oona that the well-known film critic and columnist Wahid Ahmed was seated opposite her and that it would be in their best interest to avoid him. 'See the reed thin guy with the rimless specs? Just avoid making eye contact with him. And warn me if he heads this way,' said Anand, hiding behind his paper.

After security check, the Goa-bound passengers were politely asked to wait some more. It was the usual excuse of the flight being inadvertently delayed by a few minutes. Suddenly Anand realised that Wahid Ahmed was seated in the row next to his and that it would be impossible to avoid his gaze. So he quickly closed his eyes and started snoring loudly. Oona was embarrassed when people began staring at Anand. Wahid also looked hard at him and Oona. Each time he did so, Oona tried her best to look away.

'*Bechara*,' a passenger next to Anand told his neighbour, 'Must be so busy chasing actors and making them do double shifts and minting money that he gets no time to sleep.' His neighbour laughed.

It was enough having to dodge Wahid Ahmed without having to endure the passengers' sarcasm. But this was a small price to pay for stardom. Oona wanted to defend Anand, but thought she might end up in a verbal duel which would attract undue attention from Wahid and the others. That would surely upset Anand even more. So she kept quiet.

The Goa trip was splendid, except for the fact that Anand practically refused to leave his room once he found out (on making discreet enquiries at the reception) that four of his actor friends with their family or official girlfriends were also staying there. Sunil Kapoor with his wife Anita and the kids, Rahul and his girlfriend Rita—also an actress, Samir Shah and wife Seema, and Ram Gulati and a very close male buddy.

Oona did not mind. They stayed in the room, watched the glorious sea and the sunsets, made love, ate, made love again and took turns going to the poolside. In the evenings, Anand would hire a car and take her around Goa, explaining the differences between the old Goa and the new, the North and the South and showing her the various churches and beaches. Oona was excited to see the Church of St. Francis of Assisi, the patron saint of the land. She was especially tickled to see the nudist beach Anjuna, though it was only from afar. The old Portuguese houses and villas had a romance of their own. It was unlike any other place in India.

The Goans were a laid-back but friendly lot. Anand, a frequent visitor to Goa with his ex-wife and sundry girlfriends, was quite familiar with the hotspots. One evening they had seafood at one of the best 'shacks' or small seaside eateries on the beach. So popular was this place that even liquor magnate Ajay Sajnani, whose palatial mansion spread over several acres, frequented these shacks. However, after Anand spotted a few of his industry friends there, he and Oona spent the following evenings in the privacy of their hotel room over wine and lobster thermidor.

Back from Goa, the year started on a busy note for Anand. While he was away, Oona enjoyed gazing out at the sea. She never tired of it. She loved waking up to the sea in the mornings with the cup of overcooked sugary and milky tea that Santosh served, although to be honest she would have much preferred her English breakfast or Assam tea. It upset Oona that Bombayites could never brew a proper cup of tea. In fact, they never brewed their tea at all, cooking it instead, over-boiling it to the point of a thick creamy layer, which reminded her of the way her father used to make tea.

Her afternoons were spent watching the sun glistening on the waters from the air-conditioned comfort of Anand's bedroom. The guest room did not have much of a sea view. In the evenings she made her own cup of ginger tea and sipped it languorously, watching the sun go down. And at night, she enjoyed the fierce darkness of the sea with a few fishing dinghies popping up now and then. How lucky Bombayites were to have the sea.

She liked Bombay. It was a huge, huge city and Oona was looking forward to exploring it. Its people, its life, its alleys. The city excited her. Calcutta was beginning to get a bit tedious, with the same faces, the same lifestyle and the same streets. Besides, people here kept out of each other's daily lives as they were too busy living their own lives. The neighbours were less curious and less interfering. Bhabhiji from the flat across would smile a knowing smile every time their eyes met, but seldom probed into Oona's affairs. Had it been Calcutta, by now the whole city would have been abuzz with their affair. Here no one could be bothered. Live-in relationships were not uncommon.

Unlike the Calcuttans, Bombayites were hardworking and enterprising. At times a bit too enterprising. And of course less helpful than Calcuttans. Since the Bengalis were a lazy lot and did less work and discussed more football and politics, they had all the time in the world to over-help others, to the point of interference. Oona remembered once looking for an address in Calcutta. She had asked a passer-by, an elderly gentleman. Since he did not know the exact location, he asked another passer-by and took the trouble of locating it for Oona, even though it required him to deviate nearly half a kilometre away from his destination.

Oona contrasted this with another incident which happened soon after her coming to Bombay. She was supposed to catch up with an old college friend from Calcutta, who was now in Bombay. She lived on Johnny Wodehouse Road in Colaba, the southernmost tip of the city. It took the better part of an hour and a half for Oona to get there in a taxi and then the cabbie stopped at a building to ask the gateman where the particular address would be. The gateman shrugged. Meanwhile a courier delivery man standing next to the gateman insisted he knew the address.

'Explain,' asked the cabbie.

'It is complicated,' the courier boy replied. 'I can take you there though.'

'Then come on,' said the cabbie, motioning to him to enter the car. After taking the cab through narrow twists and turns, the fellow suddenly yelled, 'stop!' He got out and walked away.

'Hey,' the cabbie shouted behind him. 'Wait a minute. You were supposed to show me the street. Where is it?'

'I don't know,' the courier fellow shrugged and ran into an office building.

'*Saala*!' the cabbie swore. 'He brought me all the way for a free ride.'

Oona could not help laughing. She admired his cheek. To survive Bombay, you had to be enterprising. *Zara hatke, zara bachhke, yeh hai Bombay meri jaan,* she hummed the old Hindi number from the film *CID*. The lyrics could not have been more apt.

Anand

Oona went to a couple of film sets with Anand to watch the shooting or filming of various films. She found the whole procedure rather boring, with endless takes and retakes. She quite enjoyed talking to a few of the known faces instead. She attended two shoots, one for *Prem Kahani* with the reigning Bollywood heroine Madhuri Dixit. The other was a small budget film called *The Train*, starring Sultana Ahmed. Anand had put some money in both films and introduced Oona as a journalist from Calcutta who had come to interview him. When he took her for the shooting of *The Train*, he saw to it that Sultana was not filming that day. Sultana had already met Oona in Calcutta and Anand didn't want her to recognise the young girl and start putting two and two together. Sultana had a loose tongue and Anand was taking no chances.

In his spare time, Anand drove Oona around the city. He showed her some of the old landmarks, including the Gateway of India. They entered the Taj and had tea at the Sea Lounge, watching the sunset. Anand told Oona how, many years ago, with just ten rupees in his pocket, he had come in and had a cup of tea for a princely five rupees!

'I just wanted to tell people that I had tea at the Sea Lounge,' he explained to Oona. Now, even at forty-five rupees, it was very affordable for him. 'Those days I could not even afford a snack with the tea,' Anand explained. Oona smiled and listened as Anand narrated stories of his 'struggle' before he made it big in Bollywood. She seemed to be falling more and more in love with him.

Anand's was not a conventional rags-to-riches Bollywood success story. But it was a lot of hard work and clever thinking. Anand grew up in the industrial town of Ludhiana, Punjab as Anand Raj Khanna. His father, Harkishan Khanna was a *halwai* and owned one of the most popular sweet shops in the city, Anand Sweets, named after his only son. It had been previously called Khanna sweets. They specialised in *kaju-kesar katris* and *gajak*, especially in the winter.

Anand grew up in a patriarchal Punjabi home, the much pampered only son. He had two sisters, the elder Rukman and the younger Sheila. When Anand was around six, his mother died and Rukman, then 12 years old, virtually brought up her little brother and sister with the help of the old family wet-nurse, Harmeet. When Anand was 12, Rukman got married and settled in Chandigarh. By the time he was 20, Sheila was also married, to an NRI Punjabi doctor and settled in Sacramento, California.

Harkishan Khanna's sole attention was now focused on Anand. Father and son never got along, and Harkishan thought Anand was quite spoilt. Anand was reasonably bright and topped mathematics in his board exams. He went on to major in mathematics and tried to go abroad for further studies, but failed to get admission anywhere. Harkishan of course only wanted Anand to handle the family business. The young man couldn't visualise himself sitting behind the counter at Anand Sweets, selling sweets, looking increasingly prosperous over the years and greasing himself with wealth, married to a fair and plump Punjaban from an equally prosperous business family and going out on family picnics with two fair and cherubic kids in their Ambassador. He wanted more out of life than Anand Sweets could give him. And he wanted out of Ludhiana. His friend Sunil Kapoor was trying to catch a break as an actor in Bombay and was studying film acting at Sheroo Khan's Academy, a private acting school in the city. He asked Anand to join him.

Harkishan threw a fit when he heard of his son's acting aspirations, thundering 'NO' and stamping his feet on the floor. Father and son did not talk for days. Eventually, one fine day, twenty-five years ago, Anand sought his father's blessings, touched his feet and left for Bombay, telling the old man he was leaving. Harkishan was too stunned for words. Anand's first stop was Chandigarh, where Rukman didi gave him a little money. With that and a bit from his savings, he took the Punjab Mail and landed at Bombay Central. He shacked up with Sunil who was staying as a paying guest with an old Christian lady in Khar. This was done on the sly, else Mrs D'Costa would start charging rent for two instead of one.

Anand could not afford the acting course at Sheroo Khan's, but he would hang around the school daily, waiting for Sunil and chatting with the other students. One day Sheroo noticed him and called him into his office, asking him what he wanted to do with his life. 'I want to be an actor,' Anand said simply.

'I like your confidence, young man. But I would have much rather heard you say that you "want to act" rather than "be an actor". Do you really love acting?'

Anand was confused, but intelligent enough to realise that if he said yes, Sheroo would figure he was lying. So he said instead, 'Well. I love the fame, glamour and money associated with the profession. Hence I would like to be an actor.' This time Sheroo was really impressed by his spunk.

'Okay you can work as an office assistant. You can keep the accounts and I will pay you 250 rupees a month. You can save up and join the acting course. Or do the evening crash course at a discounted fee.'

Anand chose the latter. He kept accounts by day and did the crash course by night. And he changed his name from Anand Raj Khanna to Anand Khanna at Sunil's insistence. 'How can you debut as Anand Raj Khanna? Too long. Raj Khanna is too wannabe considering Rajesh Khanna is such a superstar. Just Anand Khanna is good. People can wonder if you are related to Rajesh Khanna. All the better. Just like people assume I am related to Raj Kapoor. Ha ha...!'

'But it's my family name!' Anand had protested. 'Bauji will disown me.'

'He already has, so big deal.'

Though the course finished in six months, Anand held on to his job as an accountant. He befriended Shamira Khan, the choreographer who taught dance at Sheroo Khan's. She taught him the typical Bollywood dance, with all the pelvic thrusts. Shamira took a fancy to the young man and soon they were seen together, with Anand known as her toy boy. Eventually, he quit his job and began accompanying Shamira when her troupe performed hit Bollywood song and dance numbers in other Indian cities and abroad, especially the Middle Eastern countries where the money was good. Though Anand was a lousy dancer, his intimacy with Shamira got him selected for the shows.

Director Mansoor Khan, who made Hindi musicals of the sleazier variety, happened one day to meet Anand with Shamira. The young man fitted the part of the villain for his forthcoming project, *Chaalis Percent*. 'Good choice, Mansoor,' Shamira cooed. 'He has done an acting course with Sherooji.'

'Who gives a fig about that! He just has one rape scene and one dance sequence with the heroine. Not much to say. But he has to look evil throughout. He has got the body. Rest we will see,' Mansoor said.

Chaalis Percent bombed, and along with it Anand's dreams of being the next big baddie of Bollywood, let alone a hero. A couple of smaller roles in low-budget films followed, but were not enough to sustain Anand. He soon parted ways with Shamira, who had to choose between her husband and her toy boy. She realised that Anand could not afford to indulge her expensive tastes, so she went back to her husband. Heartbroken though he was, Anand was also footloose and fancy-free now.

Sunil Kapoor had meanwhile become some sort of a star with his clean-cut good looks, and so he had lots of women running after him. Anand still struggled along, looking for work, dating various women, mainly starlets and wannabes. The top actresses eluded him. He envied

Sunil's luck. Anand swore he had to make it big, even if it meant changing tracks.

In the meantime, back home in Ludhiana, Harkishan Khanna went into deep depression after Anand left for Bombay. His main concern was not Anand's aspiration, but Anand Sweets. His health was failing and Rukman spent more and more time looking after her father in Ludhiana. She'd never really got along with her in-laws, especially her mother-in-law. Her husband and father-in-law were both government employees and so they were not as well off as her father either. When Harkishan had arranged this match, his primary demand had been an educated boy. Taman was different from the boys of the business community and his future looked promising. However, things did not work out as expected and several years after marriage and a young son Bobby, Taman Mehra lived mainly off his wife's savings. Rukman never let him hear the end of it and as a result fell out with her in-laws.

At Rukman's suggestion, Taman resigned from his low-paying government job, collected his provident fund savings and shifted base to Ludhiana to assist his father-in-law with Anand Sweets. 'If we play our cards well with Bauji and keep him in good humour,' Rukman advised him, 'we will inherit this business. And it is worth a goldmine.'

'How can you be so sure? What about your brother Anand and sister Sheila? I don't want to work like a donkey when someone else will enjoy the fruits.'

'Don't worry,' Rukman consoled him. 'Bauji is upset with Anand, especially after he dropped the middle name Bauji so lovingly gave him. He says he wants nothing to do with him and has in a way disinherited him. Sheila will not bother much as she is rather well-off.'

'I don't care. I want it all on paper. I need to be assured of it,' Taman insisted.

So Rukman got Bauji to prepare a will leaving fifty percent of the stake in Anand Sweets to her and Taman. Anand and Sheila stood to gain twenty-five percent each. The huge family mansion was of course bequeathed to Rukman and her husband for looking after the family patriarch in his twilight years.

Bauji passed away soon after the release of *Chaalis Percent*. Though he never spoke to his son after Anand left Ludhiana, he was quite proud of him, especially when friends and customers mentioned his bit roles in films. For a Ludhianvi it was a big achievement to be seen on a Bollywood screen, however briefly. Anand did not bother to go to his father's funeral. 'Taman bhai, I am in Dubai, performing for a private party for Mastan Mian's relative. There's no way the organisers will let me leave. You were more than a son to Bauji, please perform the last rites. I am sure he would have liked that.'

And thus ended Anand's connection with Ludhiana. Though he visited his sister once every few years, especially if he was filming anywhere close by, he never bothered to contact other friends or relatives there. The city meant little to him now. But he called Rukman didi almost every other day. Their bond was as strong as ever.

One good thing came out of Harkishan's death. Anand sold his twenty-five percent stake in Anand sweets to Taman and used it to make a film. He managed to convince his friend Sunil, who was quite a star by then, to act in it, almost for free. Made on a small budget in a short time, but with a big star, *Deccan Queen* became an instant box-office hit. Ecstatic, Anand quickly invested a part of the earnings in a similar film, this time called *Golden Guns*. This too was a super hit. And with his third film, *Heera aur Pathar*, Anand Khanna became a name to stay in Bollywood. And later, to reckon with.

Anand spent the next two decades establishing himself as Bollywood's most successful small-budget film producer. He aptly named his production house 'No Budget Films'. He was slowly wending his way upwards and giving big-time producers a run for their money. Soon, he shifted out of his PG digs with the Gonsalveses in Bandra West to his own apartment on Yari Road. It was the first house he bought with his own savings and his first own shelter in Bombay.

Bandra was the most hip and happening suburb in Bombay. It was the right blend of the quaint and the modern, where old Christian families survived the onslaught of the neo-rich, the tall sea-facing apartments contrasting sharply with the old Portuguese style bungalows in stone and tiles. Bandra was where Anand had stayed when he first came to the city and he loved it. It was familiar. But unaffordable. The apartments there were well beyond his budget. Besides, living on rent was not good for his image. It was all about appearances. His secretary, Mannuji would advise, 'When you become a big producer, the first priority should be a car. The fancier, the better. Because everyone should see you get out of a fancy car. Once the paparazzi notices and you are talked about, it will be easier to sign on the stars. And even easier to get your future projects financed.'

'How?' Anand asked.

'Simple. Stars will see you get off a fancy car and think you will be able to pay them well. They start befriending you. Star-struck businessmen with lots of unaccounted cash will come forward to finance your projects knowing you know the stars. You take from Pappu and pay Pannu *and* stash away some in your pocket.'

'But that's like being a broker!'

'Precisely. And the second thing, Sirji, you should buy your own house. If not a bungalow, at least buy an apartment so you can call a few close stars and businessmen over for drinks and dinner from time to time.'

Anand's first car was a second-hand Fiat, but soon after the success of *Heera aur Pathhar,* with a loan from a prosperous industrialist, he bought a second-hand Toyota. 'I forget the model though,' he narrated to Oona. He got a good paint-job done and this, coupled with his flamboyant dress style, impressed the producers.

In the late eighties, when Anand moved there, Yari Road was a back-of-beyond suburb. There were few buildings, as the place was a mangrove area protected by the wildlife department. But nothing in Bombay is protected by law. A little greasing of the right official palms in the right places, and little loopholes in the laws are dug out to accommodate law-breakers. In spite of environment activists crying foul, the top echelons of government officials and ministers gave permission to leading builders like Bawejas and Dhokhawalas to develop multi-storeyed buildings in protected marshland and mangroves. These builders even flouted rules in conjunction with corrupt officials and raised structures on land reclaimed from the sea. This despite the fact that Bombay lies on the tsunami belt and human dwellings should start at least 500 metres away from the high-tide mark. Yet, slums and fancy buildings dotted the entire beach-line of the city.

Anand's apartment was on the tenth floor in a sea-facing Dhokhawala building. Though he had eyed the penthouse on the fifteenth floor, that had already been taken by a top television actor. With real-estate prices soaring in Bombay, Juhu and Bandra, which were the earlier hubs of the film fraternity, were extending further north to Yari Road and Lokhandwala. These neighbourhoods became the dwelling for the emerging television stars and producers and became known as the most nouveau riche areas of the city.

Initially it was his girlfriends and wife who added amateur touches to the house's decor. Later, Anand hired one of Bollywood's top set designers to do up the interiors. Ketan Desai insisted on a steel and glass look to match Anand's bachelor boy image. The centrepiece was the huge glass and steel bar which housed expensive liquor. Anand loved his Red Label and got an endless supply from his bootlegger. It was said that all of Scotland did not produce as much Red and Black Label as was served by the Bollywood fraternity! In the spirit of demand and supply, most of this 'Scotch' was distilled by USA, otherwise known as the Ulhasnagar Sindhi Association.

The walls were another eye-catching feature. By the time Oona arrived in Bombay, the walls of the entrance foyer were plastered with neatly framed awards and citations Anand had received over the years:

Best Producer of the Decade from Ludhiana by the California Punjabi Association or the Yari Road Welfare Mandal Diwali Chief Guest citation and others. The living room wall was dominated by Anand's photographs with all the major Bollywood stars and directors, including some Hollywood greats. The latter were taken mainly at Madame Tussaud's! The dining room had a large sideboard running along the entire wall with gleaming trophies of popular film awards. The not-so-important awards and citations were housed in the guest bedroom. There was no mistaking who the owner of the house was.

Oona would sometimes wonder whether it was Ketan's design or Anand's suggestion.

In Bombay, Shamira Khan was Anand's first serious lover, and she also groomed him in Bollywood etiquette. After his break-up with Shamira, Anand did not have a steady girlfriend, but rather a string of one-night stands. He tried to consciously remain unattached on the advice of Mannuji. 'Good for your image Sirji. Projects will keep pouring in and you will have a chance to play a hero someday.' When Anand moved to production, Mannuji also changed tracks to be with him, but he continued to warn, 'Women are extravagant. No need to waste your money on a wife but rather invest it in films.' Of course, Mannuji stood to make ten percent on each venture.

A few years later, Anand met upcoming singer Surily Shah. She was a Gujarati girl who had grown up in Benaras. A trained classical singer of the Agra *gharana*, she was discovered by a Bollywood music director and rendered a couple of semi-classical songs for a film based on Mirabai. The songs were a success and Surily shifted base to Bombay hoping to make it as a playback singer. But her success was modest as her classical voice definitely did not suit the yodelling style of commercial playback singers. With only odd songs coming her way, Surily was undeterred. She continued her *riyaaz*, gave music tuitions and when called for a recording did so with equal ease.

A few months after meeting Anand, Surily decided to move in with him. In her, Anand found a stability he had missed in his life. He tried to deny the affair to the press but tongues would wag. Still, when she had spent eight years with him, and he continued to deny their presence to the public, she gave up on ever marrying him and walked out. Not only did this hurt his ego, he realised that he did actually love her. He barged into Surily's apartment one morning six months later and, on the spur of the moment, they went to Bandra court and quietly got married. It was a dream come true for Surily.

'Marry in haste, repent at leisure,' they say. Here was the opposite. Anand and Surily took eight years to decide to get married. And in less than three months they decided it was a big mistake. Surily took Anand for granted after marriage and all the care she had showered on him just flew out of the window. She stopped giving tuitions, nagged Anand no end and was always keeping tabs on him. Anand felt suffocated and this time round he could not walk out. Small arguments led to nasty fights and accusations flew back and forth. Finally, they decided to file for divorce, mutually agreeing on mental cruelty and torture. Also, after having walked out on Anand earlier, Surily realised that Anand was not the beginning and the end of her world. The six months without him overshadowed the eight years spent with him. And no one, not even Anand Khanna, was indispensible.

Once the divorce came through, Anand started dating other women, albeit cautiously. He had met a starlet, Loveena, at a party. Tall and fair with thick pouting lips, Loveena was pretty in a sensual way. She was the oldest starlet in the city. A beauty-pageant winner in her native Rajasthan, she had come to try her luck in the movies but her stammer was her enemy. She couldn't speak a line without stammering. Though stars like Sridevi could hire dubbing artistes to cover up their poor Hindi, Loveena was not so lucky. With no acting skills and no godfather, she ended up doing small, unnoticeable roles in C-grade films. What she became known for were her blue films, where she was not required to speak much but to perform. Though she was not exactly the reigning porn queen like Silk Smitha and Thunder Thigh Rita, she nevertheless managed to stay afloat in the city thanks to her various liaisons with Bollywood producers and small-time actors.

Anand was smitten by Loveena. It was lust at first sight for him. Loveena did not mind. She latched onto Anand thinking he would do wonders for her career, and happily moved in with him. Meanwhile, Anand produced a film with one of Bollywood's hotshot directors: a hard-hitting film on the underworld, based on real-life characters, and called *B for Bhai.* One night during the filming, Mannuji got a call at midnight from Dubai. It was the don's right-hand man, Kasim.

'*Kya* Mannuji! Tell your boss to portray me positively. Any mess-ups and I will castrate the two of you!'

'Yes, Kasimbhai....yes...sir....' Mannuji had peed in his pants. How had Kasim got his home number?

'*Chal chutiye.* Go to sleep. Goodnight!'

B for Bhai was the year's blockbuster. Anand got the Filmdust award for Best Film. He had always coveted the lolly during his days as a struggling actor. And today he had won it, though as a producer. Anand Khanna was definitely making it in Bollywood. Stars and financiers were queuing up at his doorstep.

Kasimbhai had called to say he liked the film. '*Saala*, your boss did a good job. Hey Mannuji, what about my cut? After all, your boss is making money at my boss's expense. What do you say?'

'But Kasimbhai...he is still recovering from debts...'

'Then tell him to host my niece's birthday party at Dubai. Will send you two tickets. No fees,' Kasim said.

'But Kasimbhai, no dates available....'

'Stop *chutiye*....Unless you two want to be castrated.' And Kasim hung up.

Anand did go to Dubai. Later, he asked for twenty-four-hour police protection due to extortion calls. This further increased his market value. One day Kasim called again. 'Mannuji, tell your boss there is Bhai's family wedding in Dubai. He must get stars to perform some dance numbers. Some hot item number types. Also he must get that *randi* of his. Bhai will pay well.' The word 'Bhai' was enough to get Mannuji to say yes; he felt a moisture in his pants.

'Who ... *randi*?' Mannuji asked Kasim.

'Arrey, that tart your boss keeps in his house. Lovely or whatever that starlet's name is. We want her too.'

Over the next few years, Anand, most reluctantly, and Loveena most willingly, made regular, discreet trips to Dubai and other Middle Eastern cities at the behest of Kasimbhai and Bhai to entertain their guests. Anand knew it was not good for his image, but he was not complaining as the money was good. He also noticed that Kasim had taken a fancy to Loveena. Anand had outgrown that initial passion and thought it best to let her go.

However, Loveena would not go easily. She was happy hanging around Anand while earning big pocket-money as the Bhai's moll. Kasim was also happy this way, as he preferred his long-standing Serbian girlfriend, Mania, to what he thought were cunning Bollywood tarts. Every time Anand tried to shake off Loveena she would complain to Kasim and he, fearing Mania's wrath, would threaten Anand to hold on to Loveena.

The solution came in the form of Sultana's husband. Suleiman was one of Bollywood's commercially successful directors. Anand was filming with Sultana in Manali and Suleiman joined her. A day later, Loveena joined Anand. Suleiman had a roving eye and Sultana and Suleiman had what Bollywood called a very 'open marriage'. While Anand and Sultana spent the whole day working, the spouses bonded in the comfort of the five-star hotel.

One afternoon, Anand finished work early and walked into his room. He caught Suleiman and Loveena in bed. Anand quickly checked into another room. The first thing he did was to call Mannuji and instruct him to gather all Loveena's belongings from his apartment and send them to her aunt's place in Malad. And the second call he made was to *Filmdust.* He spoke to the editor, Reena Bachchani and told her about the incident. Then he settled down with a glass of Scotch at three in the afternoon.

Anand was relieved and in a way thankful to Suleiman for bailing him out of his predicament. In the evening he sent Suleiman and Sultana a box of *motichoor laddoos* with a card marked 'For the good times ahead'. Anand knew it would become messy to work with Sultana, 'but what the heck, her days are gone, she is a hag now,' he thought to himself.

He swore he would never marry again or even have a live-in relationship with any woman remotely related to the film industry. They were like sharks. Casual flings were fine. Affairs were okay. If women were hard to come by, ex-heroine Sweety Sharma's escort service provided decent girls. And if all else failed, there was something called masturbation.

Anand Khanna had had enough of marriage and women.

All Fools' Day

Their wedding was a small and quiet affair. On the morning of All Fools' Day, Anand and Oona signed as man and wife at the Bandra court. Mannuji and a friend were the two witnesses. Oona wore a light pink salwar kameez and Anand wore a half-sleeved khaki shirt and jeans. There was no ceremony, no exchange of wedding vows, no walking around the sacred fire, tying a *mangalsutra* or filling the middle parting of the bride's hair with vermillion. Neither remembered such details. It was Oona's first marriage and Anand's second. Oona would always hold it against Anand for forgetting to tie a *mangalsutra* around her neck or filling her *maang* with *sindur*.

The wedding feast comprised simple vegetarian fare at a nearby Udupi. Later that evening Sangeeta called to congratulate them. Oona had called to invite Sangeeta who, hurt, had refused, though she sent her blessings. Anand called Rukman after the ceremony; she slammed the phone down without even congratulating them. She was feigning hurt at not being informed earlier. She would have definitely stalled it had she known. Oona suspected that she wanted Anand to remain unmarried so that all his wealth would pass on to her good-for-nothing son, Bobby.

Sheila, on the other hand, was thrilled. She spoke warmly to Oona and later told Anand to get her sister-in-law decent jewellery. She was aghast to learn that Anand had not even tied her a *mangalsutra*. Later, Anand took her to Mannuji's family jeweller and bought her a light and sleek *mangalsutra*. 'You can wear it all the time,' he told her.

'What about a diamond ring?' Oona asked coquettishly.

'What about it?' Anand asked, feigning ignorance. Champakbhai had already brought out his best diamond rings. Oona immediately opted for a traditional cluster with nine diamonds. Anand chose a plain band with a single stone.

'But I like this cluster. It is such a classic design. I have always wanted one.'

'Never mind,' Anand was firm. 'I am supposed to be giving you the ring, so it has to be my choice. I like this simple band. Immensely wearable.' He feared the cluster would be way too expensive.

'Okay,' Oona shrugged. Champakbhai made the calculations.

'Forty-five thousand.' Anand nearly choked. He was curious to know how much the cluster would have cost. 'What about this one?' he pointed to the cluster. Champakbhai calculated and said, 'Eighteen thousand.'

'What! Why so cheap? It has so many more diamonds.' Anand exclaimed.

'Yes, but they are smaller stones. This is a solitaire, a half carat princess-cut diamond,' Champakbhai explained.

Anand swallowed. Oona smirked.

'Why don't you keep the cluster since you like it so much?' Anand asked Oona.

'No way, I prefer the solitaire. After all, it is your choice and I am happy with it.' She slipped the ring onto her third finger and it fitted perfectly. 'You are right Anand, it is immensely wearable.' Oona smiled at Champakbhai. 'And it looks sleek, not garish.'

Champakbhai laughed as Anand looked on helplessly.

'Women, they are all the same,' he said to no one in particular.

Anand had not had any intentions of marrying Oona. After hanging around in Bombay for several weeks, Oona gave Anand an ultimatum. Either he could marry her or she would leave. She lied that she was facing family pressure to agree to an arranged match. Anand did not believe her. So one fine afternoon, while Anand was away on location, Oona took the flight out to Calcutta.

When Anand returned and called her, she was curt. Anand sensed her hurt. A couple of weeks later, Anand decided to go to Calcutta and bring her back.

'On one condition. And that is marriage,' Oona insisted. Over the next few weeks he tried convincing Oona of the futility of marriage. She remained adamant.

Finally he relented. 'What the heck, I will give it one last shot,' he declared to Suraj, his friend

'Who knows, you may be second time lucky.' Suraj and his wife Heena were Anand's friends and Heena and Oona, too, got along well.

'Hopefully.'

Anand was tired of high-maintenance arm-candies. After Surily, Oona was the first to bring him a sense of stability. He also thought that Oona, hailing from a non-glamorous and non-filmy background, would be more grounded and less extravagant. And just in case it did not work out, there was always the last resort of 'divorce'.

For Oona it was a dream come true. In spite of being ambitious and having wanted a career, Oona had always envisioned herself having a husband and a house full of children. Maybe, having grown up as a single child in a nuclear family, she yearned for the cacophony of a normal, noisy household. For her, marriage was for keeps. And there lay the ideological difference between Oona Roy and Anand Khanna.

The only condition Anand had was that Oona should lie low and not talk to anyone about this marriage. 'We will reveal it in good time. Right now I have signed a film with Madhuri as the leading heroine. And I don't want her to back out,' Anand explained.

'But why should she back out if the money is good and she has agreed to work on your next project?' Oona asked, astounded.

'You know these heroines....very moody. All *nautankis,*' Anand said unconvincingly. What he did not explain was that he was secretly dating Madhuri so that she would cut down her rates for his film.

Mid-way during the shooting of *Biwi To Hona Hi Tha,* an overenthusiastic cub reporter from *Filmdust* broke the news of Anand and Oona's marriage, even publishing a copy of the marriage certificate. Anand was upset. Oona was delighted. The financier was furious. Madhuri, disgusted and hurt, left the film halfway citing date problems. Her secretary told Mannuji that her next available date was two years away. Anand Khanna shelved the project, blaming Oona's hurry to settle down.

That was the end of Anand's short stint as a big budget film-maker. He reverted to what he was best at making, low-budget films. Surily called Anand after reading the news of his marriage to congratulate him. She also expressed her dismay and sympathised with Anand about *Biwi To.* The first seeds of discontent in his marriage with Oona had been sown by his ex-wife without Anand or Oona realising it.

Oona loved the city. People did their job and work was more easily accomplished here than in any other city in the country. People worked hard and partied harder. No wonder Bombayites were called *bindaas,* or 'chilled out'. There were no power failures, no water shortage and no rationing of food items here. In fact every kind of vegetable and fruit was available all-year-round, unlike seasonally as was the case elsewhere. This was mainly because Bombay preserved most of its fresh products in huge cold storages. But the produce did lack the fresh taste of seasonal vegetables in smaller towns. It looked luscious but was largely tasteless, full of preservatives and colouring.

Another thing Oona loved about the city was that people dressed as they pleased. There was no moral police to determine how people, especially women, dressed. Calcuttans were conservative in their dress style; in Delhi, women had to dress down to ward off the city's notorious eve-teasers. In Bombay, you dressed the way you wanted, just *bindaas.*

Bombay never sleeps. Life begins after ten. It is a city of night clubs, discos, pubs and the famous dance bars. Most shops remain open late and restaurants and coffee shops function till the wee hours of the morning. Only between 2.30 a.m. and about 4.30 a.m., does the city doze off for a bit. But soon the humdrum existence begins, with the sound of the milkman's cans clanking away as he cycles the streets.

Still, Oona did miss her friends and home from time to time. She sometimes wished Sangeeta was close by. Her mother, too, missed Oona but was happy she was settled, though she did not much approve of Anand Khanna. They spoke on the phone from time to time but their lives were very different now.

In Heena, Anand's friend Suraj's wife, Oona found a friend. Friendly and caring, Heena was a Bombay girl with most of her relatives in Bandra, except her parents, who lived in Hong Kong. Having just quit her job after delivering a baby, Heena would often drop by or call Oona over when Anand was away. On their way to Vile Parle Market one day, Heena, who was driving, took a wrong turn into a 'no entry' and before they could reverse, a cop had knocked on her window.

'Sorry,' Heena begged, 'Please let me off this once.'

'No way,' the cop said. 'Give me your licence.'

'Please, don't confiscate my licence. Or my husband will never let me drive the car,' Heena pleaded.

'Well you don't deserve to. Now licence, Ma'am?'

Very gingerly, Heena pulled out a fifty-rupee note from her wallet and handed it to the cop. He took it awkwardly and put it in his pocket and straightened up. As Heena was about to drive off, he said, 'Wait. One minute.' He pulled out a twenty-rupee note from his pocket and handed it to her. 'It's okay. You can keep it too,' Heena said.

'No. I don't take more than I deserve. Here, take the change.' As they drove off, Oona could not help laughing. 'Imagine an honest cop who takes bribes! What do you make of it? This can happen only in Bombay.'

With Heena, Oona enjoyed exploring various markets, shopping at Elco Arcade and Lokhandwala, buying knick-knacks from the home stores. Anand appreciated Oona's little touches to the house. She put up sheers, nice paintings on the walls, kept the brass polished and chose bright-coloured upholstery. When he was in town, meals were served in style on chic and muted ceramic crockery Oona brought from Pondicherry.

'At last this house feels like a home. A woman's touch makes all the difference in the world,' Anand told Oona over dinner one day. For Oona it was the biggest compliment she had received from him. It was worth leaving Calcutta. It was worth missing her mother and her friends. It was also worth sacrificing her career.

Soon after her marriage, Anand told Oona not to bother with a job. 'All the newspaper offices are located downtown and it will take you two hours to reach there. Besides, you are not used to the Bombay traffic. So forget it. I'll give you enough pocket money to compensate for your salary.'

A few months later, Anand forgot about the pocket money. Oona hesitated to remind him, feeling awkward to ask for money. She started saving a little from the household expenses. This was Heena's advice. 'That is how we women manage to save. Husbands' generosity is like the honeymoon....over after the first flush.'

One day Kulvinder, Santosh Mangat's wife called Oona, overwhelming her with her over-friendliness. 'Helloji, Oonaji. How are you ji? Congratulations ji. I read about your wedding and I told Santoshji that I had known something was up between you and Anandji. I am very happy for you ji and you must come home for dinner ji. I am very good cook myself Oonaji. Also you must call me home for mustard fish curry ji. I am big fan of fish ji. Very healthy food you know.' Oona could not help smiling to herself as she accepted the invitation. The thing that irritated Oona most about Kulvinder's English was the American accent she put on with her heavily Punjabi-accented diction. The whole combination was annoying as well as funny. Kulvinder Mangat came on heavy, just like her broad Jat frame.

Kulvinder grew up in a small village near Hoshiarpur in Punjab. Her parents were farmers and land-owners in the village. Her mother, Balbir Kaur, was involved with the Khalistani movement and worked closely with Bhindranwale, demanding a separate homeland for the Akalis. During Operation Blue Star in 1984, where the then Prime Minister, Indira Gandhi sent the army into the Golden Temple to rid it of Sikh terrorists, Balbir Kaur was one of the lucky few who escaped.

The Sikhs could not forgive Mrs Gandhi for letting the army into their holiest place of worship, even though the army had adhered to all their religious sentiments by entering barefoot with their heads covered. And so, later that year she was gunned down by her very own security guards at her home. To the Sikhs, Mrs Gandhi was an enemy of the faith whereas to the rest of the country, she was a ruthless politician but a martyr. After her assassination, Balbir fled to her brother in Canada to escape the police round-up of Khalistani militants, taking along Kulvinder and her sister Simranjit. Like a large number of Khalistani militants, they took refuge in Surrey, near Vancouver. Know as Mini Punjab, Surrey is a place where for miles together billboards are seen not in English, but in Gurmukhi.

In 1985, Khalistani militants in Canada blew up Air India jumbo Kanishka over the coast of Ireland, killing all 326 people aboard. At the behest of the Indian government, the Canadian police rounded up a number of Khalistani sympathisers in Canada. This time Balbir Kaur escaped with her daughters to her sister's place in Orange County, California. Here, Kulvinder met Santosh Mangat at a Bollywood stage show, and she followed him back to India after a one-night stand. She mistook it for love, and in any case, she dreamt of being a movie star.

But the broad-built, voluptuous Kulvinder didn't fit the image of the heroine. Her only audition call was for *Dacoit Queen*. She looked the part, but her acting abilities were weak. Kulvinder then decided to turn producer of television serials, banking on Mangat's fame. She never stopped telling people who cared to listen that she almost became the Dacoit Queen and that the director, in spite of promising her the role after sleeping with her, did not honour his promise. 'All work went to waste,' she would giggle when Mangat was not around.

Anand was most upset that Oona had accepted her invitation. 'Why the hell did you have to commit? I am going to get bored with the Mangats. We have nothing in common.'

'But I thought you and Santosh were friends. Same city, same *mohalla*?' Oona said, getting ready for the evening. 'That is why I said yes.'

'Yeah. I know. Santosh is nice. But that wife of his with all her ji-jiing is very irritating. Besides, socialising with them is tricky. She will expect a bit role in return. I have had enough of such people. Next time check with me before you commit. We should be careful with whom we socialise. After all, I belong to the film fraternity and Santosh is only a television artist.' Oona made a note of that. Classism existed even in Bollywood, she smiled to herself.

Kulvinder was a decent cook. But the joy of eating the delicious meal was marred by Kulvinder's constant reminder of 'how tasty the chicken is, have more ji' and 'very delicious *saag* please eat more ji' and 'Santoshji loves my *makki di roti* so you must have another ji'. Later, Kulvinder gifted Oona a pair of small gold loops. 'A wedding present. It will suit you ji. You must wear and show me ji,' she smiled.

'Thank you Kulvinderji,' Oona smiled politely.

'Call me Kul. No ji. And I will call you Oona.' Oona had no say in the matter.

The evening ended with Kulvinder landing a resounding slap on her husband's face over a disagreement. Both Anand and Oona were visibly embarrassed. Driving back home, Anand warned Oona not to mix around too much with Kul. 'She has a reputation of beating her husband even on the sets in front of the whole unit.'

'Are you scared I may imbibe some lessons from her?' Oona laughed.

'Just try that on me and you will never know what hit you!' Anand warned his wife.

After the initial anger had subsided, Rukman didi made it a point to drop in on Oona and Anand quite often, whenever she was bored of Anand Sweets and her husband. Anand, though he loved his sister, found her a bit overbearing. He preferred Rukman didi from a distance. The other irritant was her good-for-nothing son, Bobby, who acted like he owned the place, calling his friends over and messing up the house. Oona resented his behaviour, but when she complained to Anand, he shrugged. 'You've got to bear with him. I cannot do anything.'

Bluntly, Oona said, 'Well, I did not know you had a baggage called Bobby when I married you.'

'Shut up!' Anand suddenly yelled.

Oona tried to reason with him but he wouldn't listen. And so began the small arguments, which would grow into nasty fights later. Oona slowly realised that Anand was like most Indian men, a complete male chauvinist pig. He expected Oona to behave like a typical Indian housewife, cooking, cleaning and pampering him, never complaining. The honeymoon days of chivalry had vanished.

Soon after Oona's marriage, Anand's servant Santosh went off to his native village. He had never been much help in the kitchen anyway. Oona hired a woman to come in daily for the cleaning and cooking. When she rang the bell at seven the first morning, Oona was fast asleep. Anand was already up and lazing in bed. He shook Oona awake and told her to go and open the door. In her sleepy state, Oona did so, but when she came back and saw Anand awake, she asked, 'You were up. Why did you have to wake me up to open the door?'

'That is because as a wife, it is your duty to open the door and bring me a cup of tea in bed,' he proclaimed. Oona thought he was joking. She was wrong.

'Hello?' Oona answered the phone.

'Can I speak to Anand?' cooed a female voice sexily.

'Well, he is not home. Can I take a message?' Oona asked.

'And who am I speaking to?' the voice asked.

'I am his wife. Oona,' Oona said.

'Well, Oona, this is Rehana Khan. I am a friend of Anand's.'

'Oh!' Oona exclaimed. 'I am quite a fan of yours.'

'Thank you. I wanted to invite Anand for a party at my place tomorrow evening. I wasn't aware he was married. I would love for you to come too. I live in the next building. Arcadia. The penthouse,' Rehana said.

'I know, I know. Anand told me. But he is out of town,' Oona said.

'That's all right. I want you to come. Be there eightish. And by the way, what are you good at cooking?'

Oona was a little puzzled. 'I think, mustard fish, Bengali style,' she said hesitantly.

'Hmm…sounds good. I love fish,' Rehana purred, diva style. 'We are having potluck. Bring enough for about fifteen of us. We will have fun. And I am looking forward to meeting you.'

Rehana Khan was an icon and Oona was flattered at being invited to her do. She went over sharp at 8 o'clock with a casserole of steaming mustard fish, which she had instructed the *bai* to cook. No one had arrived and Rehana herself was luxuriating in her bath. When they met, Rehana was warm and friendly and both sat down over a glass of wine. 'Tell me about yourself, Oona,' Rehana asked. The young Oona rattled on and on. Rehana found her innocence charming. They enjoyed each other's company till the guests finally began arriving.

First it was Sweety Khanna from the floor below. Sweety was a fresh divorcee, bitter about her ex-husband. She went on and on about him and the women he was seeing. 'It's okay, honey. You don't own him now. So forget him. Move on in life,' Rehana told her.

'You don't understand. By the way, Oona you better be careful,' said Sweety, suddenly looking at Oona. 'Your husband, like mine, is a typical Punjabi and they make very dominating husbands.' Oona nodded in understanding.

'Oh, don't believe her,' Rehana laughed. 'Anand's such a sweet guy.' Oona bit back a sarcastic response to that.

The next to arrive was Dolly D'Souza, Rehana's next-door neighbour. Oona thought she looked familiar. 'Have I seen you somewhere?' Oona asked.

'I don't remember seeing you though, maybe in the park?'

'Oh Dolly flies Indian Air,' Rehana interposed, 'Perhaps you two met on a flight?'

'No, I don't think so,' Dolly replied cautiously, turning away. Oona was puzzled.

Dolly had brought a case of Grover's white as her contribution for the evening. Sweety had brought grilled chicken in mushroom sauce. Later a couple of other girlfriends dropped by, one with a cottage cheese preparation whilst the other got *jeera parathas*. Rehana of course served the salads and peanuts with the drinks in her black and white Pottery Barn crockery. It matched the décor of her apartment, where everything was in black and white, including the books on her shelves and the DVD cases. Even Rehana was dressed in black trousers and a white tee!

It was nearly ten when the first male guests arrived. Director Vindoo Chopra came in with his girlfriend; actor Randhir Kapoor with his ex-wife and finally, one of the hottest stars of Bollywood, Mona Ghatge. Mona was beautiful and friendly, but was soon completely sloshed. She took out her anger on Vindoo, whom she had dated a couple of months earlier. Vindoo looked embarrassed. Mona abused him of being a user, growing more and more shrill, till she tugged his girlfriend's little black dress off her shoulder, embarrassing the gathering. Randhir had to physically carry Mona away and Vindoo got busy placating his near-hysterical girlfriend.

'Sad,' said Sweety to Oona. 'She is such a talented actress and yet she lets men and alcohol ruin her life. She changes men quicker than she changes her tampons. Every time she breaks up, she drowns her sorrows in alcohol; and every time she falls in love, she celebrates her happiness with alcohol. Another Meena Kumari in the making.' Oona felt genuinely sorry for Mona.

A few minutes later, Dolly passed by, and Oona decided to ask Sweety about her.

'You know, Dolly looks so familiar and yet I am not able to place her. I am sure I have seen her before.'

'I'll refresh your memory for you. But on one condition,' Sweety piped up.

'What's that?'

'I want passes for the Filmdust Awards next month. Anandji will get them and you must give me one at least. Promise?'

'Okay, promise,' Oona laughed.

'If you read the papers some months ago, Dolly was in the news for all the wrong reasons. Her boyfriend is Vinodbhai, you know Big Bhai's right-hand man. Dolly flies Indian Air and a few months back she was caught smuggling—cocaine stitched into her panties. She was in lock-up for a week before Vinod bailed her out,' Sweety relished every word as she recounted it to Oona.

'Of course, now I remember,' Oona said.

'She leads a lavish lifestyle. Apparently her fabulous penthouse was Vinod's gift for losing her job. Lucky girl,' Sweety continued. 'She throws the most amazing parties. She is a generous host but a great bore. Great food and wine flowing freely at her dos. Not like Rehana—she is such a miser. Every time she hosts a dinner, the guests have to bring their own food and drinks. She only provides the crockery and cutlery!'

'Then why do you bother to come?' Oona asked Sweety.

'*Arrey*, to socialise. To catch up with the Bollywood crowd. It's nice to be seen at Rehana's dos.' Spotting Palsekar bhau, the yesteryears Marathi screen heartthrob, Sweety abandoned Oona, walking away as she practised her best smile.

It was nearly three a.m. and the party was going strong. Oona was feeling a little high though she had managed to space out her drinks. She was no longer hungry. She went up to Rehana and said, 'It was lovely. I enjoyed myself. I must go now.'

'I am glad. We must have you here more often. Are you sure you can go alone?' Rehana asked.

'Of course, I am only next door. Besides, the gateman will be there. Don't worry. I'll be fine,' Oona said.

'Come, let me walk you to the door.' Rehana looked as lovely off screen as she looked on screen. 'You and I must catch up over coffee or dinner when Anand is not around. Just the two of us,' Rehana said huskily, obviously high and happy. But Oona was nevertheless flattered. As she reached the door, Rehana went out and pressed the elevator button.

'Don't worry,' Oona said, 'I will manage. You look after your guests.'

'Okay, bye,' Rehana hugged her tight. As the lift arrived, she felt her breasts being squeezed. Rehana smiled. Oona smiled back weakly and entered the lift. Alone, she rubbed her eyes to bring her back to reality. Was she dreaming or was it for real? Did *the Rehana Khan*, who was supposed to have been having it off with India's super star, the Badshah, did she really go for her boobs? 'Anything is possible in Bollywood,' Anand had once told her. Walking home, Oona repeated it to herself and giggled.

A Bollywood Wife

'How long has it been since you and Anand got married?' Sangeeta suddenly asked, looking up from the newspaper she was reading. Sangeeta was visiting Bombay for a few weeks. Oona was busy downing a cup of tea as she made her grocery list. She turned towards Sangeeta in surprise.

'Why do you ask? As if you don't know!'

'No. Just like that. I am wondering what you are doing with your life.'

'C'mon Ma, I am married. I have a house to run and look after. What more do I have to do?'

'I know Oona. Even I have been married. I rose at the crack of dawn, cooked, washed, cleaned the house and then went and worked at a full-time job. And in the middle of it all I also raised you,' Sangeeta said.

'So what are you implying?' Oona asked, though she knew where this was going.

'Just don't waste your life. You have been blessed. You do not have to face financial hardships like me. Anand is earning well. There are servants to take care of the house. You have a cook, you have a maid, you have a driver. You don't physically have to do anything. So why did you give up your writing? You could have still worked. That is the only thing which will stand you in good stead. See it was my job which saw you guys through....'

'But Ma,' Oona cut in. 'Your life and mine are completely different. You had just me and Baba and your days revolved around us and maybe the occasional friend or relative. Here it is different. Anand has to keep up his image of a film producer. He has to pamper the stars. He also has to call financiers, directors and colleagues over frequently and have lavish dinners. It just cannot be a simple meal. Planning an elaborate menu, drinks, snacks…I cannot leave it entirely to the staff. I have to supervise it or they will mess things up. We also have to socialise so much. Besides I also travel with Anand to locations during his longer schedules.'

'You don't have to,' Sangeeta interrupted. 'You do so because you have nothing better to do.'

'Not true Ma,' Oona tried explaining. 'One has to be around. Otherwise you know all these women in Bollywood. They are always there to latch on to men. Married or single, they don't care as long as there is money!'

'Well if you have decided to be a housewife, you can at least have a baby. You have help around. After all, you aren't getting any younger. You're nearly thiry and Anand is nearing sixty.'

'Then all the more reason for us not to have children. Why burden a child with parents who have one foot in the grave?' Oona joked.

'*Chi chi*, don't say that. You aren't that old!'

'Ma. Please. Can we postpone this discussion for another time? I am busy right now. Sultana and Suleiman are coming for dinner.'

'Don't change the topic. Okay, if you have decided not to have a baby then at least you should work. Start writing again.'

'Ma, Anand has made it clear that I should not work.'

'Who is Anand to decide on your career? Men don't like financially independent women. Even your father tried to dissuade me from working when we first got married. Thank God, I stuck on. Men feel threatened when women are empowered. Think about it seriously.'

'I will,' Oona said.

'But I still think it will do you a world of good to have a child. At least you will be secure. I don't trust Rukman and that loafer Bobby.'

'Ma. Please. I really have to leave for the market now.'

'What are we doing on our anniversary?' Oona asked Anand pleasantly one morning as they lazed in bed. 'It's a Saturday. Why don't we have a nice dinner at the Sun & Sand?'

'Saturday? What is the date?'

'Anand! April 1st!'

'Oh yes, of course,' he laughed. 'April Fool's Day. I really did get fooled on that day.'

'Anand! You are disgusting. I hate you,' Oona's eyes blurred and she threw her pillow at him. He pulled her closer and kissed her on her forehead. 'Hey, I was just joking. We'll do whatever pleases you. What do you want to do?'

'Let's call some friends and colleagues and have a party at Sun & Sand. We never really had a wedding reception. This will be a good way of calling friends over.'

'That is going to cost a bit…'

'Come off it, Anand,' Oona cut in. 'How can you be so cheap?'

'And, anyway, I have an important meeting that day,' Anand sounded relieved.

'Then cancel it,' Oona said.

'I am meeting Badshah Khan. I cannot cancel it.'

'Well you are not meeting him throughout the day. Only in the morning…'

'Please, Oona. Stop bullying around. We will go for a quiet dinner. Okay?'

'And save all your money in the bank. Not okay.'

'My money is your money,' Anand said gallantly.

'But I never get to see it.'

'Okay, *jaan*. Tell me what you want for your anniversary.'

'It is our anniversary,' Oona corrected.

'All right, *jaan*. What can I give you on *our* anniversary?' Anand asked.

'Let's go to Champakbhai's…'

'I knew it!' he groaned.

Later, at Champakbhai's, Oona chose very expensive diamond chandelier earrings, exquisitely set with red rubies surrounded by small brilliant cut diamonds.

'Pretty isn't it?' she asked Anand, trying to get him excited.

He was not amused. 'How much?' he asked instead.

'I'll give you the best price Sir. Besides, Oonabhabhi is my favourite bhabhiji,' Champakbhai rattled off his standard lines while calculating the cost. 'Coming to 2.75, but, Sirji you pay 2.5. Okay?'

'Thousand? Twenty-five thousand?' Anand asked.

'What's wrong with you *jaan*? As if you'll get diamonds set in white gold so cheap!'

'Then what?'

'Tell him *na*, Champakbhai.'

'Of course he knows, Oona bhabhi. He is just joking around,' Champakbhai added cleverly.

'You mean lakhs! 2.5 lakhs! What? Listen baby, do you know how expensive it is? Have you gone crazy? Besides, you never wear such heavy earrings. It will not suit your small face.'

'But Anand, how can you be so cheap as to put a price to our anniversary? If you had a dinner party it would have cost you more than a couple of lakhs. Besides, you wear expensive watches. I am your wife. This is the least you can give me considering you barely give me any pocket money. What happened to all the promises you made? "Don't work, I'll give you more money than your work will pay you!" Just because your previous women have fleeced you, does not mean you make me suffer. This is getting unbearable.'

Oona was hysterical. It was nothing new. These spats over money and other sundry topics happened every now and then. Anand was embarrassed at being made to look like a miser in front of Champakbhai and his staff. He did not want to tarnish his public image of an extravagant Bollywood producer.

He tried to dissuade her, pointing to a similar design that was cheaper. But Oona refused, saying those diamonds weren't the same quality. '*Saali* has developed expensive taste,' he muttered as he fished out his wallet. Oona turned away to admire her anniversary gift.

Later they stopped for dinner at an old Tandoori joint in Dadar called Gypsy. It used to be Anand's favourite during his struggling days. 'This place still retains its old charm and they have maintained the quality of their food,' Anand said as he sipped his whisky with water.

Oona was still admiring the earrings, and she said, 'I am feeling a little bad, Anand.'

'Why?'

'I should not have insisted on it. It is quite expensive actually.'

'Oh, c'mon. Nothing is too expensive for my pretty wife,' Anand Khanna said in an expansive mood. The whisky was already making him feel generous.

'Hi Oona, what's... oh hi Kulvinderji!' Anand stopped in surprise when he walked in one evening to find Kulvinder and Oona chatting over a cup of tea.

'Helloji, Anandji. Returning from a shoot?' Anand nodded.

'Which film ji?'

'Some edit work for an old film,' Anand proferred half-heartedly. Oona knew Kul was not welcome and quickly got up to bring him a cup of tea. Suddenly she heard him scream, 'Ouch!!! What the hell is this?' He came up to her with a tiny dachshund scampering behind him. 'What's, err, who's this?'

'*Beta, aa, aa, aaja*. Come baby, come to mamma,' Kulvinder gestured to the pup.

'Your dog?' Anand asked Kulvinder.

She nodded. 'But now she is yours ji. She's part of the litter my dog just delivered. I have just gifted her to Oonaji. For your anniversaryji. Happy belated anniversary.'

'What the fuck,' Anand began, but Oona interrupted, 'Please *jaan*, please. Don't say no. You know how I like dogs. I've always wanted one. Can I please keep her?'

'But you know I am not very fond of dogs....there will be fur all over the place.'

'Anand, please. It's a dachshund. Hardly any fur. Besides, I will potty train her myself. Just trust me. Please, Anand.'

'Well, okay,' he grinned suddenly. 'But on one condition. I will decide its name.'

'But Kul has already named her Kitty,' Oona began, then stopped. 'We can always change the name. She is anyway too little to recognise her name. What do you have in mind?'

'Sridevi.'

Kulvinder laughed, 'Very goodji. You have a great sense of humour ji.'

'Send my tea in,' Anand told Oona as he went off to his room.

Oona was a little shocked. Sridevi was the reigning Bollywood heroine and had refused Anand's recent projects. 'I don't want to spoil my reputation working with low-budget producers,' she was heard telling people. It was a small revenge for Anand. Oona suddenly burst out laughing, wondering how Sridevi would react if she ever found out.

Later that night, after wrapping up the puppy comfortably in a small rug, Oona cuddled up to Anand. 'Thanks, honey. I really appreciate you letting me keep her.' She could not bring herself to call it Sridevi. It sounded rather odd. 'It would have hurt Kul's sentiments if I refused her gift.'

'Nonsense! That woman has no sentiments. She beats up her husband and maids. Besides, she has to get rid of her dog's litter and found you an easy scapegoat. I've told you earlier, stop socialising with her. She is a foul-mouthed social climber and I have my reputation to maintain. I do not want my wife socialising with the television fraternity.'

'C'mon *jaan*. It is not that I go out with her to parties. We just share a cup of coffee or tea now and then. Besides, she is the one who keeps calling me over and over again.'

'Just ignore her calls. Someday, these coffees are going to prove expensive. Kulvinder Mangat is quite a *matlabi* woman.'

Oona held her peace, deciding not to antagonise Anand unnecessarily. She would continue to meet Kul, but in his absence. Kul was weird, and, as the Bombay lingo went, total TP, or time pass. But she provided Oona with all the industry gossip, especially who was bonking whom.

Apart from running the house and going out to parties and on locations with Anand, Oona did not have much of a life or too many friends of her own. She was close to Heena and was very upset that she and Suraj were planning to relocate to Hong Kong. Kulvinder, of course, was there, but Oona couldn't meet her too often. Lately, Rehana had been inviting her over. Anand was pleased. 'Yes, you must bond with her. The right people to be seen around with,' he added.

Recalling how Rehana had squeezed her breasts, Oona was a little wary of meeting Rehana alone at her apartment. One day Rehana called and asked her to accompany her to the *Bombay Times* annual bash. Anand would be out of town that day, and Oona hesitated.

'Don't worry. I can't rape you amidst hundreds of people,' Rehana said over the phone. Oona laughed. That ended the awkwardness.

'Of course I will come,' Oona said on impulse. *What the heck, I am old enough to take care of myself.*

'Great, but we shouldn't make our appearance before midnight. Will pick you up after eleven,' Rehana said before hanging up.

For Bombayites, even at midnight, the night was still young. It was typical of the stars in Bombay. Each tried to outdo the other in entering fashionably late. The later the entry, the higher the star value. Oona was slowly getting used to this life. Whenever Anand and she had to go for a party, they would sit around idly watching TV till the clock showed nearly midnight. By the time they set out, Oona would be trying her best to stifle her yawns and Anand would have downed several pegs of whisky. On reaching, a hungry Oona would tuck into all the food that came her way, making social conversation with her mouth full, much to Anand's embarrassment.

One night while returning home from a party, Anand turned to Oona, 'Why the hell do you go and attack the food instead of interacting with people? It's like I don't feed you enough.'

'But it's way past my dinner time and I am famished. My brains don't function on conversation mode then,' Oona replied cheekily.

'In that case eat dinner at home before you go out.'

Oona did not argue further but decided to heed his advice. It helped. Anand had the same problem that afflicted most Punjabi men: he could not drink once he ate and once he ate, he needed to turn in. Oona had no such problem.

Rehana's Mercedes, an old E-class model, came round to the main entrance of Oona's building on Saturday night, well past eleven. Oona had eaten dinner and was dressed in well-cut black trousers and a slinky black jersey. As she entered the car, she saw Rehana resplendent in a gorgeous black and white ikkat silk saree. She had tied her hair in a high knot and tucked some flowers in it.

'Hey you look great,' Oona could not help admiring. 'I wish I had worn a saree too.'

'Forget about me. Look at this sexy lady! You look so different! I am seeing you after such a long time. My goodness! You have had a complete makeover. What have you done to your hair?'

'Well I just decided to cut it off. Easy to manage,' Oona said.

'You've lost some weight too. You've got a new persona altogether,' Rehana went on. 'Well, the city's touch has got you, honey. I quite like it. In fact, short hair does suit you well. Anand must be charmed.'

From the reigning Bollywood stars to the wannabes, everyone wants to be seen at the *BT* annual bash. When Rehana and Oona entered, the place was packed. Flashbulbs popped as both the ladies wended their way into the party.

'Can I get you a drink, honey?' asked the dashing Kabir Bedi as he gave Rehana a hug. He turned to Oona with a friendly 'hi' and asked what she'd like to drink. Oona almost went weak in the knees. Bedi did not fail to notice it.

'So when did you get here, Kabir?' Rehana asked.

'Just a couple of days back. Especially for this do. Besides, I'm trying to relocate to Bombay. There seems a lot of scope for work here. Let's see.'

'And how's Nikki?' Rehana asked.

'Oh, she's fine.'

'Hi there. The gorgeous Rehana Khan. And Kabir Bedi. What a pleasant surprise to see you two.' David Dhawan walked over with his wife.

'*Arrey,* look who's here! Bollywood's Director No.1,' Kabir ribbed. David was famous for making films with the No.1 tag: *Biwi No.1, Hero No.1* and others.

'Hi David. Meet Oona. She's Anand's wife, Anand Khanna,' Rehana introduced Oona.

'Of course I know Oona. We have met before. Where's Anand?'

'In Hyderabad. On location.'

'Yes, yes. I know. Is he funding that new director?' Oona nodded. '*Yaar,* that bum did not finance my film for that kiddo's. Just because he offered to do it for less *moolah*. Doesn't matter, its all part of the game,' David chuckled.

Just then Oona spotted Raunaq, an old friend of Anand's. She excused herself from Rehana and company and waved a pleasant 'hi' to Raunaq.

'Hi Bhabhiji, good to see you. Where's Anandbhai?' Raunaq asked.

'He's out of town. How're you?'

'Good, good. You've lost so much weight bhabhiji! Exercising?'

'Well, a bit yes. Actually I had lost more but have put on a few kilos in the past few weeks,' she said as she noticed a suave gentleman standing next to him with a drink in hand. He looked familiar.

'But bhabhi you are looking so slim and sexy! I can flirt with you *na,* since I am your *devar*. Besides, Anandbhai is not in town,' Raunaq added. Oona wished he would not refer to her as bhabhi, it did not make her feel sexy at all. She noticed his companion's amused smile. Their eyes met, and she proffered her ever-friendly 'Hi'.

'Hi, my name is Riz. Riz Ali.'

'Oh, but of course, I know who you are. I've seen you in so many ads and hoardings,' Riz Ali had been one of India's best-known models. He must be in his forties, but he still looks gorgeous, Oona thought to herself. Riz smiled as if he had read her mind and she blushed.

'I'm Oona.'

'Oona. That's a pretty name. Bengali?' he asked.

'Yes. But how did you guess? My name's not Indian.'

'Just a guess. You look Bengali,' Riz shrugged.

'Riz, Oona bhabhi is Anand Khanna's wife,' Raunaq explained.

'Ah! Good to meet you. I've met Anandbhai occasionally. Always socially though, as I have never worked with him. I think it is every Bollywood actor's dream to work with him once. So what do you do Oona bha-'

'Please call me Oona,' Oona cut in before Riz could complete the word. 'No bhabhi-shabhi business. I keep telling Raunaq here that I do have a persona of my own besides being Anand's wife.'

'Sure,' Riz agreed. She noticed a slight American twang. 'So what do you do, Oona?'

'Well, I am a journalist. I'm taking a break these days but I plan to start writing again soon,' Oona said on an impulse, suddenly realising she meant it.

'Great! So which paper are you planning to write for?' She was stumped. Riz seemed to be taking a little more interest in her career plans than she had anticipated.

Raunaq butted in, 'Well, bhabhiji here used to be a very famous journalist in Calcutta. Now she is too busy being Mrs Anand Khanna.'

'Why don't you let the lady talk?' Riz told off Raunaq pleasantly. The latter laughed and went off for a refill. Oona enjoyed Riz's company for the better part of the evening. They found much in common, including a love for Nana Mouskouri's music.

Much later, Rehana walked up and Riz went and hugged her. She was surprised to see Oona with him. 'So you two know each other?' she asked Oona.

'Just met her, honey,' Riz responded. 'We were having a very interesting conversation till you interrupted us.'

'Quite the flirt, aren't you Riz? Beware of him, Oona. He is a complete ladies' man and quite a charmer. Riz, you should know Oona is married to Anand Khanna. So watch out,' Rehana smiled.

'Yes, I gathered as much,' Riz said. 'My bad luck.' Both women laughed

'I'm hungry,' said Rehana. 'Care to join us for a bite?'

'You ladies carry on, I'm okay. I'll catch up with you later, Oona. Have a great evening.'

'Bye,' Oona said with her best smile. She wasn't really hungry and would have much preferred to hang around with Riz, but she didn't want to offend Rehana.

As she and Rehana walked away, Kulvinder appeared in front of her and hugged her. '*Arrey dekhoji,* Santoshji. Oona is here ji. What a surprise!' she shouted.

'Hi,' Oona muttered, a little embarrassed by Kulvinder's volume.

'Hello ji. You are the great Rehana Khanji. I know. I am such a big fan of yours ji. I did not know you were Oona's friend. Myself, Kulvinder Mangat, Santoshji's better half.'

'Hi,' Rehana replied rather curtly. 'Oona, I'm headed to the food counter. Join me once you are through, honey.' With that Rehana walked away. Like Anand, Rehana too did not approve of Kulvinder. Oona tried to excuse herself from the Mangats. 'I'll have to go. See you later, Kul.'

'No problem. I have just sent a brilliant script for our next tele-serial to Mannuji and I want Anandji to produce it. I'll get in touch with him but you must convince him to do it. Once in a lifetime opportunity, ji. All awards guaranteed, ji!'

'Yes. Yes. I will tell him. I'll have to go now. See you.'

'Bye ji. See you soon,' Kul's voice trailed off behind her as she hurried to catch up with Rehana.

'Sorry,' Oona smiled at Rehana who was seated at a table with a glass of wine and a plateful of salad. 'Just one of those unavoidable people.'

'You have to learn to sort the chaff from the grain. There will be many such people who will hang around you because of your relationship with Anand, and you just have to learn to ignore them.'

'You know, Anand always tells me the same thing. I guess I am just a sucker when it comes to people.'

'You will learn soon, my dear. Now, don't you want something to eat?'

Oona went and brought back some dessert. 'Ooh, the chocolate trifle looks sinful!' Rehana said, taking a spoonful off Oona's plate. 'I wonder why all good things in life have to come with baggage.'

'Hello, Rehana ji,' a plump, heavily painted chiffon-clad lady, with oversized chandeliers dangling from her ears, came up to them and did a *namaste* to Rehana.

'Hello Madhuri.' Rehana was a little curt.

'I was wondering when I could meet you. Remember I told you about a script I had in mind when we met last,' Madhuri began.

'Yes, yes. But this is hardly a place to talk of such things. Call Rameshji tomorrow and he will fix up an appointment.' Ramesh Ahuja was one of the top Bollywood secretaries, including Rehana Khan's.

'Okay ji,' Madhuri then turned to Oona and said, 'Hello ji. You don't know me but you are Oona, no? Anandji's wife? I have seen your picture with Anandji in some magazine. I know Anandji well. I met him the other day at Loveena Yadav's place. You know Loveena Yadav, no?' Madhuri seemed a little too keen to bring up the name.

Oona managed to cover up her shock, but not before Madhuri had noticed it. 'He told me he was going to Hyderabad for his new film. Said we would all have a meal together at my place on his return. You must join us, too.' Oona could just about nod and smile.

When Madhuri left, Oona asked Rehana who she was. 'I guess some television actress past her prime. She now wants to direct a film she has written. The latest trend for failed and retired actors is to turn director or screenwriter,' Rehana smirked. 'They think it's child's play. No wonder we have such crap dished out in the name of cinema.' Oona was not concerned about Madhuri but she was upset on hearing that Anand had been seeing Loveena again. More so because he had told her she was completely out of his life.

Two days later, Oona heard her driver Pandey answer the home phone, 'Helloji. Ji. I am Pandeyji. One minute, madam....' He brought the cordless to Oona.

'*Arrey* Pandeyji, how many times have I told you, you don't call yourself Pandeyji, just Pandey. Others will call you Pandeyji.'

'A *memsaab* for you,' Pandey said, handing the phone to Oona. 'Who is it?' Oona asked.

'Not saying name. Wants to talk to you.'

'Hello. Oona Khanna here.'

'Helloji. Just wanted to let you know that while you are looking after Anand's house in Bombay, Anandji is having the time of his life with Loveena Yadav in Hyderabad. *Bahut mauj kar raha hai woh udhar.*' Oona was shocked.

'Who are you? Why are you telling me this?'

'*Main apki shubhchintak hoon,*' said the voice, implying she was a well-wisher.

'Yes, but what's your name?' Oona tried to engage her in further conversation but she hung up. She was obviously uncomfortable conversing in English but spoke in chaste Hindi. It tallied with Anand's description of his ex-wife Surily. Besides, the voice sounded familiar. Early in their marriage, a lady would call up and mutter 'bitch' and hang up each time Oona answered. Once, Anand had picked up the extension and recognised Surily's voice. 'Ignore her,' he had told Oona then. She now realised that this was the same voice.

Upset and shaken, Oona fought the impulse to call up Anand immediately and scream at him. That's exactly what Surily would have wanted. She had had a string of short-lived affairs after Anand. Now pushing 50, with no alimony, husband or career, she was eyeing Anand Khanna again.

On his return, Oona confronted Anand about Loveena. Though surprised, he explained that Loveena was also in Hyderabad and that they had bumped into each other accidently.

'What was she doing there?'

'I did not ask. And please, I am not interested in explaining anything to you. Just mind your own business.'

'Your business is mine too.'

Anand was not interested in hearing her out. He got up to go, then stopped and said, 'And by the way, I will not be funding your Kulvinder's silly tele-soap. So don't try and convince me on her behalf. I have told Mannuji to tell her a firm "no".'

'I don't care about her serial. She's not *my* Kulvinder. You and Santosh are from the same village,' Oona began. But Anand had already left the room.

'I quite like this place,' Oona said, looking around the compact coffee shop at the Sun & Sand Hotel. One wall of glass windows overlooked the poolside and the other looked onto the sea.

'Me too,' Heena said as they settled down after a hectic round of shopping. 'I'm gonna miss it.'

'And I'm gonna miss you,' Oona added. 'You can still rethink your plans. Suraj will do anything you say.'

'Oh please, now, don't start it again. Don't make me feel bad. As it is I am already miserable,' Heena said, opening the menu.

Since Suraj's career had not quite taken off in the city, Heena's brother insisted they come to Hong Kong and work for the family business. Heena was not keen but Suraj took the offer, despite Heena's opposition. Bombay was where her heart was and where her friends were. As for Oona, Heena was one of the few genuine friends she could confide in.

As Heena's departure date came closer, Oona wanted to spend every waking moment with her friend. They shopped together for all the utensils, spices, clothes and gifts Heena wanted to carry with her. They spent their time running from the tailors to the jewellers and snacking at their favourite joints in-between.

Over her cold coffee Oona confided in Heena about Anand meeting up with Loveena.

'These exes are all *matlabi*. Just want money out of him. If I warn him, then he says I am being mean. Damn. It is frustrating....'

'Don't worry, all will be well. Anand really loves you otherwise he would not have married you after so many failed relationships. I think it is time you guys had a baby. It will settle him down and you will be too busy to pay attention to his silly philandering. A man will be a man, there is no point trying to change him. A child is the best option in these circumstances,' Heena explained sympathetically.

'But you don't understand, we cannot have a child,' Oona trailed off.

'Why?' Heena asked, before noticing that Oona had tears in her eyes. 'Sorry, I don't want to probe but what is it? Do you want to tell me, Oona? Can I help?'

'Well, Anand is... how do I explain? We've been having some problems and the doctors suspect erectile dysfunction.' Oona looked away.

'Oh poor you! Can't you do anything? Maybe adopt a child?'

'I would love to, but Rukman didi has brainwashed him into not adopting. She wants that loafer Bobby to inherit his wealth,' Oona said bitterly, sniffling as she stopped her tears and wiped her eyes.

'But that is not fair,' Heena was upset.

'I know. And I guess he goes around with women just to show off...' before Oona could complete her sentence, a voice interrupted.

'Sorry to bother you, but I had to come and say hello. You are Oona, aren't you? Oona Roy?' Oona looked up at an elderly lady, clad in a mauve *tangail* saree, with salt and pepper hair cut in stylish flicks, smiling at her. Elegant from head to toe.

'Yes,' Oona smiled back.

'I am Bina Ghosh. Your grand-aunt Suparna Roy is my aunt-in-law. Her first cousin was my mother-in-law. She is now no more. So we are very, very distantly related. I met your mother at Suparna Mashi's place in Calcutta some years back. She told me you are married to Anand Khanna. I have seen your photos in magazines,' the lady explained.

Oona got up and politely hugged her. 'Good to meet you,' Oona said, feeling drawn to this lady.

'You can call me Bina Mashi. You are just like my daughter. She's about your age. Married and settled in Chicago. So nice to meet you, especially after hearing so much about you from Suparna Mashi. She is so fond of you and so proud of your achievements.' Oona smiled.

'Would you like to join us, Bina Mashi? This is my dear friend, Heena,' Oona introduced the two.

'Hi Heena. No thanks, I am with a friend,' Bina pointed to another elderly lady sitting a few tables away. 'But we will exchange numbers and must be in touch. Where do you stay?'

'Yari Road.'

'Oh. That's pretty close to me. I stay in Model Town. Here, give me your number.'

As Oona rattled off her number Bina neatly entered it in a handmade diary she pulled out from her purse. She then gave her number to Oona, who saved it in her Casio electronic telephone book.

'Wow! You kids are so tech-savvy! My son also uses one of those. I haven't a clue how to handle it but he says it's so simple,' Bina said.

'It is, Bina Mashi. You should try it,' Oona said.

'Not in this lifetime. By the way, did anyone ever tell you that you bear an uncanny resemblance to Ela Sen? Have you heard of her?' Bina asked.

Oona nodded, 'Yes. Vaguely. Chhordida did talk about her. Some great-aunt who was among the first batch of Indian women to graduate, something like that.'

'Exactly. She was Suparna Mashi's grand-aunt. That makes her your…let's see…great, great…yes, great, great aunt. She was said to have been in love with an Englishman. Even Netaji Subhash Chandra Bose was besotted by her. I have seen her photograph in Suparna Mashi's house and you look so much like her.'

Oona smiled. 'So I have been told.'

'We must meet and dig up our family history. Besides you remind me so much of Koel, my daughter. I miss her.'

'I get homesick too. It will be wonderful to have tea and good old Bengali *adda*.'

Three months later Heena and Suraj, with baby Jahnvi, left for Hong Kong. Oona saw them off at the airport, trying to fight her tears. 'Say bye to Anand from us. I know he is busy and therefore could not come here. We will miss you Oona,' Suraj told her.

Zindagi Ka Ek Pal, a fifty-two-episode tele-serial produced by Anand Khanna was launched starring Loveena Yadav opposite a young newcomer with much fanfare. It was Anand's television debut as a producer. The

TRP ratings for the first few episodes were good as the audience was keen to see Anand Khanna's foray into television. Within a few episodes they realised a C-grade starlet doing the Miss Goody-Two-Shoes act with a hero young enough to be her nephew was intolerable. Thirteen episodes later, the serial was pulled off the air due to poor TRP ratings. Anand lost a lot of money and decided never to venture into television again.

Kulvinder called up soon after *Zindagi Ka Ek Pal* was launched and expressed surprise that Anand, in spite of refusing to put money towards a tele-serial, had done so. 'Why this sudden change of attitude ji?' she asked Oona.

'Search me.'

'After all, she is his ex-girlfriend ji. Whatever the status, you cannot erase the feelings from the heart,' was Kul's explanation to Oona, who realised it was meant to provoke an outburst. She kept silent. After that, Kul did not call. Though initially perturbed, Oona was relieved to have got rid of Kulvinder Mangat at last. And Anand seemed happy.

Ears Wide Open

Mannuji came to their house one day with a shady-looking character called Pony. Initially, both Oona and Anand were irritated at this invasion of their home by a stranger. But over a few pegs Anand seemed to loosen up with Pony, who turned out to be a real-estate broker of sorts. Despite losing money, Anand was not too badly off after all. Having lost money on Loveena, he had nothing more to do with her. Surily was now seeing Dada Palsekar, the veteran Marathi playwright, and as it was a serious relationship she, too, rarely called Anand anymore. This also meant fewer fireworks at home.

Pony took Oona and Anand along with Mannuji to see a dilapidated bungalow in Versova, close to Yari Road. After years of wanting to own a bungalow and considering innumerable properties around Versova and Juhu, Anand finally zeroed in on this seafront one. It was in a state of disrepair but Anand was as excited as a little boy and soon began talking to architects about renovation work. Although Mannuji had always wanted Anand to make a good impression, he was concerned that Anand was taking a huge bank loan. 'How will you pay it back, Sirji?'

'I'll manage. Raise as much money as possible, promising to get whichever star they want. We'll decide later which of them we will complete. As for now, try and get as many films off the floor as you can under No Budget Films. Try and raise funds from every corner. Avoid financiers with underworld connections. In case we cannot deliver, we will get jacked. Understand?'

'Exactly Sirji. I was thinking along the same lines,' Mannuji smiled. '*Chutiya saala*,' Anand said as Manhuji left. 'If he thought like me then would he not be in my place today?' Oona giggled.

Oona was not keen on the bungalow as she knew it would invite trouble. Relatives from Punjab as well as Rukman didi and family would take up permanent residence here. Besides, wannabe actresses would latch on to him with one hare-brained scheme or the other in order to extract money. But Anand was not interested in listening to her opinion.

One evening, Anand had called his friend, a producer called Shetty, for dinner. Mannuji was also present. Shetty owned a big bungalow in Lokhandwala. When Anand told him about his plans to buy the bungalow, he asked about the location. Once Shetty had figured out the exact bungalow they were talking about, he said 'I remember, I too had an interest in that one. Don't buy that property. There are problems.'

'Don't be vague, Shetty saab. Please explain that. You are my friend,' Anand coaxed.

'Well, it belongs to Bhai. He wanted to build a small motel for his business associates to use when they come from Dubai and the Gulf. After the bomb blast however, he had to cover his tracks, so he quickly sold it to the Kakkadawalas and after they went to TADA, they sold it *benami* to builder Shah. Was it he who approached you?'

'Yes.'

'He approached me too. But don't go near it. My *khabri* in the B-Gang tells me Bhai still has his eyes on it. He will eventually try and get it back, by hook or by crook. You know Bhai's methods... all your hard-earned money will go down the drain.'

There was a shocked silence as everyone digested this news.

'No wonder it was cheaper than the going rates. I was wondering,' Mannuji broke the silence.

'But haven't all the Siddiqui properties been sealed by the government?' Oona suddenly asked Shetty.

'Yes, bhabhi, but there are some properties which the government does not know about. They are *benami*. In false names.'

'I see,' Oona nodded.

Anand spoke, 'Why don't you start getting dinner ready? Shetty saab, you must stay and have dinner. There's nice Bengali fish curry.'

Oona knew this was Anand's way of telling her to shut up and leave.

The following day, once Anand left the house, Oona called up Dinesh Sharma, her ex-boss at *The Herald* in Calcutta. She told him about Bhai's *benami* property. 'Still got your eyes and ears open, Mrs Khanna?' Dinesh joked.

'Oh c'mon, Dinesh. It's been a while and I am bored of being plain Mrs Khanna. I think I'm going to start working again. Meanwhile, I thought I'd let you know about this.'

'Yes, thanks. I'll call my Bombay office and tell them to send the concerned guy on the beat. They'll get in touch with you.'

Anil Dharam, the Bombay crime reporter for *The Herald*, called her the next day for the details. Oona had meanwhile discreetly gathered a few details by calling Shetty. She shared these with Dharam. 'Keep me posted,' she said before hanging up.

A fortnight later, Dharam called her, saying there was nothing much to the story. Oona couldn't believe it. 'What do you mean? I know it for sure. I can get you more details.' 'Listen, my dear, you don't know what you are up against. This could be dangerous. Just keep off this, will you?' Anil advised.

'But precisely. Everyone's keeping off it. At least you guys should expose the truth.'

'But we aren't just dealing with political heavyweights or petty criminals. We are dealing with the underworld. With Bhai. The B-Gang. So just keep out of it.'

Oona called Dinesh and updated him. He seemed to know it already, 'I cannot do much if he refuses to budge,' he sighed.

'Then let me do the story.'

'You? Are you sure? Won't Anand object?' Dinesh asked.

'Don't worry about him. Trust me. I'll deliver. Besides, I'm itching to get back to work.'

'Okay. But it's dangerous ground. The KM organisation was a *bachcha* compared to the B-Gang. You have to be careful, my dear. Cool off if you sense trouble. And another thing, we will carry the article under another name.'

'That's not fair,' Oona cried.

'What's not fair?' Dinesh asked.

'Why shouldn't I get the credit when I do all the hard work?'

She didn't want to spell out how much she loved seeing her byline, just like Anand got a high seeing his name as the credits rolled. It had been years since she had seen her name in print. Dinesh understood.

'All right. I was just trying to protect you. After all, Bollywood and the underworld seem somehow connected. Since you move around in Bollywood circles, well, I thought you might not want undue publicity.'

'No that's okay,' Oona said.

But Dinesh knew her well. One thing Oona Khanna did not shy away from was publicity.

'Do you have change for five hundred?' The woman asked at the building porch as Oona got out of her car. She was standing next to an auto, and looked the same age as Oona. Clinging to her was a six- or seven-year-old girl, dark, with black ringlets framing her face.

'No, sorry,' Oona said.

'Oh, you are Anand Khanna's wife, right?' the woman smiled in recognition. 'I'm Shalini. I live on the third floor. I'm stuck with the auto driver, as I owe him twenty bucks and he does not have change for 500 rupees.'

'Oh,' said Oona, pulling a twenty-rupee note from her wallet and handing it to Shalini.

'Thanks! I'll come by later to return it.'

'Sure,' said Oona, heading into the building.

Later that evening, her doorbell rang and Oona opened the door to see Shalini standing there with her daughter. 'Hi. Came to return the money.'

'Oh. You could have done that later. Anyways, thanks.'

There was a brief silence. Shalini stood there smiling.

'Err…Do you want to come in?' Oona asked hesitantly.

'Well, I'd love to!' Shalini breezed into the apartment. 'Guess what, I've lived all my life in this building but never been here. I have visited all thirty-one apartments in this building except this one. Been hearing about Mr Khanna's swanky apartment.' She talked nineteen to the dozen, Oona realised. But though she was overfriendly, she was not overbearing, Oona observed.

Shalini told Oona about herself. She was the Deshpandes' daughter from the third floor. Hers was a 'love marriage', when she slept with the first man she dated, Dasharath Menon, a Malayali. Angry that she had chosen a man outside their Maharashtrian community, her parents cut her off from even the small family inheritance to which she was entitled. Dasha's mother was equally upset and threw him out. As the only child, he would inherit the house one day, so Shalini was just waiting for 'the old witch to hit the bucket'. Dasha did the odd production job on film sets and they rented a single room down the road from Oona's building. Shalini used to work for a television channel but was now housebound because her daughter, Sana, was too young to be left alone. It was obvious the Menons were hard-pressed for money, Oona gathered, though Shalini did have a few airs about her. She noticed with amusement as the entire plateful of over a dozen biscuits disappeared in minutes between mother and daughter. Oona also concluded that her parents, especially her sister-in-law, did not treat Shalini well.

She soon realised why. The woman thrived on gossip. Within half an hour, she filled Oona in on Anand's personal life before he'd married her and also mentioned a few women even Anand had not mentioned. She made Anand sound like a sultan with his harem. By the time Shalini left, Oona was thoroughly amused and entertained. She could fill the vacuum created by Heena and Kul's departure from her life.

'I'll come again,' Shalini promised as she left. 'I'll take you around. You won't get bored of my company.'

'That I have no doubt about,' Oona said, waving goodbye.

The Herald broke Oona's story about the *benami* bungalow under her own byline. The headline said, 'Shah plays caretaker to Bhai', with a photograph of the bungalow splashed across the front page captioned: *Whose bungalow is it anyway? For details, see Page 8.* Oona fearlessly spelt out in bold the nexus between the underworld, the builders' lobby and Bollywood. Essentially a Calcutta-based daily, *The Herald* had poor circulation in Bombay, but by the third day Bombay's leading tabloid *The Afternoon Post* carried a gist of Oona's story. Soon, other papers picked it up. One even carried a file photograph of Oona and Anand along with the article.

Anand was upset. Mannuji got calls from two financiers—obviously acting on the underworld's instructions—demanding he return their advance for two forthcoming films. Surily, who had broken up with Palsekar, reminded Anand how Oona had jeopardised his position in the industry and with the underworld. Shetty called him about the story, saying it was not the wisest thing to rub Bhai the wrong way. 'You had better apologise and request Kasimbhai to intervene on your behalf. He is, after all, Bhai's right-hand man.'

But Oona got a kick out of it. She got calls from well-wishers including Bina Mashi and Rehana. Shalini called in to say she was surprised to learn she was a former journalist. 'Practising,' Oona corrected her.

'Ah, in that case you must write about my husband Dasha. He wants to be a director someday.'

'Like hell, I will,' Oona muttered under her breath.

One afternoon, Oona answered the phone to a surprise caller.

'Hi. This is Riz. Riz Ali. Remember me?'

'Yes, of course. How are you?'

'Reasonably good. I am on my way to the US. Just got your number from Rehana. Wanted to congratulate you on your story. That was rather daring.'

'Thanks. We must catch up soon,' Oona smiled over the phone.

'Yes, we sure will Madame, once I return. That will be in a couple of months' time. I will call as soon as I get back. All the best.'

'Bye, and have a great trip,' Oona said.

'Thanks. And happy writing to you.'

Take Two

Oona's feature in *The Herald* elicited a lot of praise. One day the editor of *The Post*, Shahnaz Ejaz called her.

'Hi, Mrs Khanna. This is Shahnaz. Shahnaz Ejaz from *The Post*.'

'Oh, hello!' Oona said. 'I really enjoy your editorials.'

'Is it okay if I call you Oona?' Shahnaz asked.

'Absolutely.'

'How is Anandji? I doubt he remembers, but I had interviewed him years ago.'

'Oh, did you? He is fine, but unfortunately not in town. You'll have to wait for a week to interview him. I'll tell him to call you when he returns, if it isn't urgent,' Oona offered.

'But who said anything about an interview? I don't want to talk to Anand. I want to talk to you,' Shahnaz laughed.

'Oh.'

'I have a letter from Pinky Shah for you. You know the investigative journalist and author?'

'Yes, of course,' Oona replied.

'Well, she has written in, appreciating your bungalow story. We're carrying it in our Letters to the Editor in tomorrow's edition. I thought you should keep the original, so if you give me your address, I'll post it to you.'

'Oh, thank you,' Oona was touched, and gave Shahnaz her address.

'I also thought it would be a good idea to catch up with you one of these days,' Shahnaz said. 'A work-related chat, of course,' she added, to gauge Oona's interest. Oona jumped at the opportunity. She had anyway been making a list of editors to visit and Shahnaz was on top of that list.

'Sure. You tell me when.'

'Well, let me see…maybe you could swing by the office on the coming Friday? Say three-ish?'

'Sure. I'll be there.'

'Good. I'll see you then.'

On Friday over coffee, Shahnaz offered her a job as Assistant Crime Reporter at *The Post*. Oona was excited at the prospect of being on the beat again. The first thing she did was to call up Dinesh and inform him. She looked up to him as her mentor. 'That's great news. I wish you could work for me. But you'll have greater exposure there than you could ever have had here. The crime world there is rocking,' he congratulated Oona.

'Listen, *Herald* is my baby. I can never abandon it. I'm always there for you if you need me. I can use another byline,' Oona assured him.

When Oona shared the news with Anand he didn't react until the next day, when he said, 'Listen. I did give it a thought. But you need to be around the house. Besides, you travel out with me so often. You will never be regular with your job.'

'Please *jaan*,' Oona pleaded. 'I don't travel much these days. You're the one who keeps going without me, saying that the airfare is expensive. I get bored here when you are not around.'

'Listen. Don't argue. I don't like my wife parading around as a reporter. If you really want to do something why don't you join an NGO part-time? Do social work. "Mrs Anand Khanna the social worker" sounds better than "Mrs Anand Khanna the reporter". It's better for my image.'

Oona left the room in a huff. 'Always your bloody image,' she muttered.

She lied to Shahnaz, saying that she travelled too often to take up a full-time job.

'Well, in that case, write a weekly column for us. You don't have to come to office. Just fax in your copy every week, from wherever you are. You can write on Bollywood as seen from close quarters. Scoops, gossip, everything... since you have a ringside view of the industry...'

'But I have never written on films,' Oona protested.

'Then start writing. I'll give you three rupees a word to begin with. Not more than 500 words. That is 1,500 rupees a week, 6,000 a month. You can start from next month.'

Oona took a deep breath. She could not argue with that. And that was how 'Take Two' began.

It started off slow. The words just would not come. She envied Mimi Saluja, who captivated readers down to the last word, even though half the time neither Mimi nor her readers knew what she was talking about. And she did it daily. Oona found it hard to sustain even her weekly column, rewriting her copy several times. Luckily, she had access to a computer. Anand, who was technologically savvy and always made sure he had the latest gizmos, had a computer and a fax machine in his office, making life much simpler for Oona.

But the office was very noisy. Mannuji was constantly on the phone, making loud deals using his freshly coined English words. Oona was amazed at the confidence with which he spoke grammatically incorrect English, non-stop. If he ever had trouble thinking of the right word, he would make one up on the spur of the moment.

'Don't worry, Vickyji,' Oona overheard him say to actor Vicky Lal, as she laboured her way through her article. 'I will signatory it on the documentary with Anandji and will by speed-post the copy. Details of the shedulology will be there. You be *bindaas*. I am at your service.'

Oona often wondered whether people even understood Mannuji. But they obviously did, or he would not have lasted with Anand for over two decades.

Mannuji's loud chatter and Chotu the peon's equally loud banging of files on the table, clattering of tea cups and dragging his sandals as he walked spoilt her train of thought as she sought the right word or the right opening sentence. But she gradually got used to this cacophony and found that she worked better amidst the noise.

Mannuji's endless telephonic conversations also proved to be a blessing in disguise. Oona was now privy to a lot of trade secrets that helped in her columns. She often broke industry news much before any other film journalist. Gradually, her columns caught public attention and were taken seriously. They were much read and talked about, sometimes even more so than Mimi Saluja's.

Oona's success hit Anand hard. Some of his Bollywood buddies now joked that they would not tell him juicy details as his 'journalist *biwi*' would spill the beans. Some producers bluntly told him that it was not wise to allow a journalist—even if she was his wife—to sit around Mannuji and overhear sensitive industry information. Luckily, Surily had settled down with Palsekar (this time it seemed to be for keeps) and stopped bothering Anand.

Anand told Oona to stop writing for newspapers and do some NGO work. 'And if it is a question of money, start a small business like chocolates and flowers. I'll fund you,' he said expansively. When Oona ignored this suggestion, Anand decided to buy a computer for the house. 'Now, you can work at home, in peace,' he smiled. Oona had been writing her column for a year, and had grown very comfortable at the office. She tried to dissuade him, but Anand said he did not like people talking about Mrs Khanna sitting at the 'shop'. Anand's office, like most production offices, operated out of a renovated *gala* or godown in Andheri.

Now able to type up her column at home, Oona—always a people's person—missed the constant activity of the office. She had loved observing people and their characteristics. So whenever she went in to the office to fax her copy to Shahnaz she would spend some time chatting with Mannuji over a cutting *chai*. Of course, this was only possible when Anand was not around. But soon, the Internet ended that, too. Though Oona marvelled at the way the world could be connected at the touch of a button and at how easy it had made her job, as an armchair writer, literally, she missed the buzz of the newsdesk. Or, in this case, Mannuji's desk.

In a couple of years, Take Two, which had started out as a chatty column on cinema, had evolved into a more constructive column encompassing industry news, views and overviews. The tone was reader-friendly, much like Mimi Saluja's. But Oona's column, unlike Mimi's, was taken a bit more seriously, as it went beyond pointlessly slamming films and film stars. Mimi Saluja belonged to serious tabloid reporting. Oona Khanna belonged to light mainstream journalism. Therein lay the difference.

As time went by, Take Two was popularly referred to as Oona's Take. Besides the fees of actors and the price of real estate, Bollywood party topics revolved around Oona's Take and Mimiii's Date.

With the change of 'Bombay' to 'Mumbai', Mimi Saluja had also changed the spelling of her name, to end with a triple 'i'. While Bombay became Mumbai because of the Narangi Dal, Mimi became Mimiii because of Chumani Baba. Ideologically, too, the reason for the change differed. The Narangi Dal's demand was an attempt to invoke provincial pride, while Chumani Baba's suggestion was a solution to enhance the finances. Of course, jealous South Bombay socialites and ignorant Mumbaikars wondered how Mimiii could possibly need more money or luck!

Mimiii did need more money. Bubbles' business, always dodgy, had sunk. But Mimiii continued to project an image of being wealthy and was seen at all the right places, with Bubbles as her arm candy. The media loves the rich and the beautiful and went out of its way to woo her. She raked in the moolah. Mimiii Saluja knew exactly how to market her failures. To the intelligentsia she could be an air-head for all she cared. But to the average Indian women, she was an icon: the great middle-class success story.

Unwittingly, Oona was inspired by Mimiii's enterprise. Not by her deceptive packaging, but by the way she had turned adversity to success. Oona, on the other hand, had everything going for her, including money and talent, so why should she cry over a bad marriage?

Oona sat down to her early morning cuppa with her customary choco-chip cookie. She rarely took sugar in her tea or coffee but made it a point to have a cookie on the side. This was her morning ritual as she speed-read the paper, slowing down only if a particular headline captured her attention.

As she flipped through *The Daily* this morning, she noticed Mimiii's Date was titled 'Kudos to the Mallu babe'. She wondered who the concerned Mallu or Malayalam babe was. To her surprise, she discovered that Mimiii was talking about Mira Nair the film-maker and her film *Monsoon Wedding*, which had won the Golden Lion at Venice.

Oona immediately called up her friend Sunita Sharma at *The Daily* and told her how their most senior and highest-paid columnist had blundered. 'We all know that Mira Nair is as Punj as they come, and *Monsoon Wedding* is all about a big fat Punjabi wedding. This is common knowledge.'

'You're telling me! Forget her facts, her grammar and spellings are pathetic. We have a tough time redoing her copy. But then our editor and she are great pals. Hey, why don't you call and tell her the lapse? I'll give you her number,' Sunita suggested.

'Forget it. None of my headache. You guys be careful next time.'

In her column the following week, Oona gleefully mentioned the serious lapse in a perfectly innocent tone.

That evening Oona got a call. 'Hi Oona. This is Mimiii Saluja.'

'Oh, hi,' said Oona, not quite sure what to expect.

Instead of giving her a dressing down for berating her in her column, Mimiii very charmingly said, 'Oona, you do write well and I really enjoy reading your column. In fact, I look forward to it every week.'

'Thanks,' Oona still did not know what to make of her words.

'I read today's column and let me tell you that I am perfectly aware of the fact that *Monsoon Wedding* is all about a big fat Punjabi wedding,' almost mimicking Oona's words. 'I have also seen the film.'

'Ji,' Oona said.

'But that still does not make Mira Nair a Punjabi. You can be from Kerala and make a film on Punjabis,' Mimiii coolly stated.

'I agree with you on the last bit. But to put the facts right, Mira Nair is Punjabi,' Oona insisted.

'Honey,' Mimiii sounded exasperated, as if explaining something to a slow learner, 'the Punjabi surname is "Nayyar". "Nair" is a Keralite surname. That is the difference.'

'I know, but in Mira's case her Punjabi surname Nayyar was misspelt as Nair in school and it just stuck,' Oona explained.

'Oh, I see,' Mimiii seemed to accept her mistake. 'How was I to know such nitty-gritties?'

Oona explained, 'Since it is our job to inform others, it therefore becomes our responsibility to know the facts first, before we part with any information. Sorry, I did not mean any offence.'

'No, no. None taken. That was nice of you. In fact, with a daily deadline over your head, you tend to slip up at times. But do keep up your good work. And thanks, Oona,' Mimiii said warmly.

Given Mimiii's reputation, Oona couldn't help wondering if she genuinely meant it or was being deadly polite.

Mannuji did eventually manage to find a bungalow for Anand. It was in a complex of row houses in the lane close to their current home. It had been a hard task for Mannuji. Whenever the builders realised he was scouting for homes for Anand Khanna, they either upped the price or gave some reason for not wanting 'film stars' in the complex. One builder even said he was afraid 'Anandsaab's journalist *biwi* might dig out a story on him.' Finally, Anand saw and finalised the house while Oona was in Calcutta. 'Anyway, how does it matter what she thinks?' he told Mannuji when the latter mentioned that Oona had not seen it. 'I am paying for it, so I should approve of it.' Mannuji agreed wholeheartedly.

'Oh, by the way, you never told me Anand meets up with this Prerna Singh woman!' Bina Mashi exclaimed one day over tea.

'Prerna who?' Oona asked.

'Prerna Singh. The former model,' Bina Mashi succinctly added.

'Why should I mention it? Is it important? Anand meets so many famous models and actresses that I have lost count.' That shut the old lady up.

In the few years since Heena's departure, Oona had grown closer to Bina Mashi, meeting the old lady quite often. They formed a close bond and Oona sometimes even poured her heart out. While she could usually count on her sympathy, Oona had realised that at times her aunt could get on her nerves. She dropped Anand's name to anyone who would listen, embarrassing Oona, but luckily she was harmless. She was somewhat estranged from her daughter, who lived in the US, and her son was too busy climbing the corporate ladder. Oona enjoyed her company as she was a great raconteur, like Shalini. But unlike Shalini, she was not malicious.

Besides, Bina Mashi was always available if Oona needed company. Whenever Anand was out of town, Oona loved to call Bina Mashi and Shalini over for dinner. Bina Mashi to alleviate her loneliness and Shalini to alleviate her boredom. With Bina Mashi she enjoyed going shopping and eating *chaat* and *panipuri* at Elco. Shalini was reserved for parties and plays. And both took turns sharing Oona's lonely evenings. But while Bina Mashi often returned the hospitality, Shalini lived off Oona's largesse, taking free rides, free meals and hanging around with Oona as her willing sidekick at parties. She even took Oona's old clothes, bags and other hand-me-downs. But none of that stopped her making digs at Oona. She once casually joked about how Oona came all the way from Calcutta to 'nab' Anand Khanna while she, living in the same building, missed a good catch. Oona could not trust Shalini.

She could trust Bina Mashi, but still decided to avoid discussing Anand's liaisons. Over the years, Oona was gradually beginning to develop a thick skin if not a hide. During her initial days of discomfiture with Anand's women-friends, her mother gave her a sound piece of advice: 'It is better to be exposed to a lone wolf than a whole herd.' Oona kept that in mind and tried to focus more on her work.

'I have to go, Bina Mashi.' Oona got up to go.

'Okay. But listen, don't do anything rash. Don't fight with Anand. You have to learn to handle these things maturely. After all, you need him, not the other way round. So be careful what you say to Anand.' Oona nodded and left.

She was truly developing a hide now.

The Breaking of a Legend

Friday, 24 January 2003

Chandragupta is a must-see film.

*The Daily*****

The film of the year, if not the decade is undoubtedly *Chandragupta.*

*The Post*****

Chandragupta is a film well-made and well worth the watch.

*Indian News****

After *Chura Liya, Chandragupta* is this year's biggest blockbuster.

*Cinema Weekly*****½

Chandragupta is a great and entertaining lesson in history. A must watch for every school-going child.

Oona scanned all the papers for reviews of Sameer Shah's latest venture, *Chandragupta,* a feature film on the legendary Indian emperor, Chandragupta Maurya.

The film opened to a complete 'housefull'. In fact, tickets for the entire week were booked in advance, mainly by schools.

Shah, the current Bollywood superstar, had not only essayed the title role but also directed and produced the film. It was supposed to be a film on a grand scale, on par with *Mughal-e-Azam*. It was one of the most extravagant and lavish productions of recent times. Close to twenty crores, industry insiders whispered, had been spent on the film. The costliest by Indian film standards so far. Shah had not only put in most of his money but also a great effort into faithfully portraying the angst and passion of Chandragupta the Great.

Everyone had been talking about the film for the past few months. Expectations were high. And a person's importance in Bollywood was measured by whether or not they were invited to the premiere of *Chandragupta*. Anand got a call from Shah's office asking if he would attend the premiere. He was travelling abroad and asked Oona whether she would like to go with a friend. Oona refused—on principle, she preferred to buy her ticket and watch any film she was going to write about. She would sit along with the common cine-going audience over popcorn and *samosas*, the intention being to gauge public response while forming her own, independent views on the film. This was why, unlike most reviewers and cinewriters, Oona seldom attended private screenings or 'trials' as they were called. As she once explained in her column, 'it takes away the honesty from a reviewer; especially, having eaten the producer's salt, in this case having drunk his alcohol, it makes you feel obligated to him.'

She knew every writer worth his salt would be writing on *Chandragupta*. So she could happily give it a miss in her column. She decided to go and watch one of the private screenings to which her party-circuit friend, Rohit was invited. However, on the morning of the screening, Rohit called her up and told her the screening had been cancelled. 'Keep me posted about the next one,' Oona told him.

'Yeah, okay,' Rohit said, though she thought he sounded cagey.

A week before the release Oona bumped into Rohit at a party and he let it slip that '*Chandragupta* was a fuck-all film' and that it would be very difficult for Shah to recover his money.

'Hey, when did you see it?' Oona asked.

'Oh, err, a few days back.'

'Why didn't you tell me? We were supposed to go together!' Oona exclaimed.

'Actually, Oona, it happened quite suddenly….'

'Stop lying,' Oona caught him.

'Sorry babes,' Rohit broke into a wide grin at being caught. 'Shah's production chap Ratin called me for the screening. When I asked him if I could bring you along, he told me strictly no journos. Sorry.' 'That's all right,' Oona understood. She knew film-makers rarely called rivals and journalists to private screenings. The idea was to get honest opinions from well-wishers rather than have journalists spread the word on the film before release.

Rohit was also an out of work film-maker, and Oona valued his opinions on films. They were always sharp and incisive. Oona had once suggested that he write about films for a living, rather than try unsuccessfully to raise funds for his films.

'Tell me seriously, is it really bad?' Oona asked again to be sure.

'Very. You take my word for it,' he firmly said.

Saturday, 25 January 2003

> *Chandragupta* releases to packed houses. Already a superhit.
>
> *The Daily*

> No tickets for *Chandragupta* available. All sold out for the coming week. No tickets even in black. Advance booking opens for the following week.
>
> *The Post*

Amazing! Oona thought to herself as she read the papers.

Sunday, 26 January 2003

> Shah has truly outdone himself and given the performance of a lifetime. If *Chandragupta* makes it to the Oscars, Sameer Shah certainly deserves to win. That is how good the film and the protagonist are.
>
> Mimiii Saluja

> Outstanding film, outstanding performance. Sameer Shah is undoubtedly India's No. 1 superstar. The Shah amongst stars.
>
> Ashwin Sinha

> Amazing performance.
>
> Wahid Mohammed

Oona again found only praise for the film in her Sunday read. Ashwin Sinha's 'Shah amongst stars' was a direct hit at the other reigning Bollywood superstar, Badshah Khan, Sameer's arch rival. Having read all this and more, Oona was now all the more determined to see the film. Rohit's remark echoed in her mind.

She called Shalini. 'Hi, let's go watch *Chandragupta* tomorrow. You organise the tickets and I'll arrange the car and popcorn!' she suggested.

'But it's going to be tough to get tickets! The theatres are booked a week in advance,' Shalini sounded doubtful.

'I know. But try through your friend Vincent at Andheri Talkies. I'm sure you'll manage,' Oona convinced her.

Twenty minutes later Shalini called to say that the tickets had been organised for the next day's matinee show.

'I knew you could do it,' Oona laughed.

Monday, 27 January 2003

Venue: Andheri Talkies
Film: *Chandragupta*
Time: 2.30 pm
The theatre: Near empty
Audience reaction: Deadpan
Sound: No laughter. No gasps. No tears. Only the munching of popcorn.

Friday, 31 January 2003

The Breaking of a Legend

TAKE TWO

Oona Khanna

The Post

I went to see *Chandragupta* after reading all the rave reviews, a week after it released. Tickets were apparently unavailable, even in black. I had a tough time procuring tickets. They were indeed sold out. But not to the public, because the theatre was nearly empty. And this on the fourth day of the release of a 'superhit'!

There was no audience response or reaction. The only sound was the munching of popcorn, the crunching of wafers and the slurping of *chai*. As for my view on the film:

I draw a blank. I cannot comment. Either I'm ignorant and the film is beyond my comprehension. Or I'm arrogant and it is way beneath my intelligence. Therefore I shall refrain from commenting.

It is not the fault of the film-maker. He starts out with noble intentions and if he fails to accomplish his goals, you cannot blame him. The effort has been made.

What is despicable is that the media, which is supposedly the conscience-keeper of the nation, can be so easily bought. This has been demonstrated in the case of *Chandragupta*.

I hang my head in shame at being a part of this fraternity.

Chandragupta the film was not about the making of a legend, but rather the breaking of it.

The following day, *The Chronicle*, a well-respected daily, carried a two-page feature on *Chandragupta* vis-à-vis Oona's column in the previous day's *Post*. Senior journalist Sudhakar Shinde slammed *Chandragupta*. He concluded with:

> It was like the Emperor's new clothes. None of us could really see the beauty of it but we all agreed unanimously that it was exquisite for fear of ridicule. We were all blind. Till Oona Khanna, like that innocent little boy, opened our eyes by saying, 'Look at the King, the King, the King, the King, the King. He is as naked as the day he was born.'
>
> Unfortunate but true. The few so-called sensible critics are so easily bought over, as Ms Khanna writes.
>
> And now that she has opened my eyes, I must admit that *Chandragupta* is indeed a terrible film.

Thereafter every writer/critic/journalist who had been too afraid to slam Shah's epic, went to town crying about the terrible waste of effort.

People wanted their tickets refunded. Some theatres offered free popcorn with the film ticket. A fortnight later, most theatres withdrew the superhit film.

People were talking about Oona's honesty. Some openly admired her style and guts.

People were talking about Mimiii and Sinha being on Shah's payroll.

People from the fraternity warned Anand that his wife could prove to be a liability in future.

Overnight, Oona became a mini-celebrity in Bombay—a talking point in the Page 3 circuit.

Wednesday 5 February 2003

A DATE WITH MIMIII
The Post
Mimiii Saluja

Some chit of a youngster who claims to be a journalist says we, the media who praised *Chandragupta,* have been paid off by Shah.

Serious accusation.

Maybe I am too partial to Shah. Maybe I saw the film with blinkers on, being an unabashed fan of his.

Nevertheless, I decided to watch the film again.

I still say, Sameer Shah rocks.

Anand handed the paper to Oona after reading the piece. They were on a flight to Delhi. 'I think this column is dedicated to you,' he said dryly to his wife.

To: *oonakhanna@vsnl.com*

Hi Oona,
My name is Ashwin Sinha.
I thought you were a bit too harsh about Chandragupta.
I still think it was a beautifully shot film….whether or not I have been paid to say so.
Best,
Ash

To: *asinha@hotmail.com*
Hi
I still disagree.
Anyway, to each his own opinion.
Ciao,
Oona

'Five hundred rupees, Madam? Please give me change,' said the waiter, returning the note to Shalini. She and Oona were sitting at the Prithvi Theatre Café with Sana. While Oona was just finishing her tea with a *samosa,* Shalini had downed a chocolate brownie, two cups of tea and two *samosas.* Sana was still struggling to finish her brownie, and Shalini eyed it eagerly, waiting for her daughter to give up on it.

'I don't have any. You bring me change, *na*,' Shalini insisted, looking expectantly at Oona, who studiously looked the other way. This was nothing new. Every time they went out and it was Shalini's turn to pay the bill (which was very rarely), she would always produce a five hundred-rupee note and demand change, and Oona would end up footing the bill.

'No change, Madam,' the waiter was firm.

'Do you have change?' Shalini asked Oona directly. Oona took the note from Shalini, looked at the bill and put a hundred-rupee note in the folder. She put the five hundred-rupee note into her wallet and sat back. After a few seconds, Shalini asked, 'Where is my change?'

'What change? Ah, you mean that?' Oona quickly pulled out a notepad and pen from her bag. She began rattling off figures and scribbled them down. 'Last week you took forty bucks from me at Alpha to buy dates for Sana because you did not have change for five hundred. I bought your tickets for *Pukaar* because you did not have change for five hundred rupees. That's hundred. Then the last three times you did your eyebrows at the parlour, I paid for them because they could not give change for five hundred. That's a total of thirty rupees. At Foodland the other day, you bought the strawberry milk for forty rupees. Again no change, I paid. Day before yesterday you did not pay for your coffee at Barista as you did not have change again for five hundred bucks, so another thirty rupees. On the way here you picked up the ten-rupee packet of baby potatoes. And now, you insisted on bringing me here for *chai* and *samosas*. Said it was your treat. The total bill is sixty-four bucks, which again I paid because you have no change.' Shalini gaped as Oona added up the numbers.

'That's 304 rupees,' Oona announced pleasantly. 'Here,' Oona handed her two hundred-rupee notes. 'You can pay me four rupees later.'

Shalini swallowed and shamelessly said, 'Why don't you return my five hundred rupees now? I will pay you later. I have to buy vegetables.'

'Oh you have enough to buy vegetables for the week,' Oona said, indicating the change as she got up to leave.

'Where are you going?' Shalini asked.

'I also have to go pick up vegetables. Don't rush poor Sana. You can always take an auto back home. There will be enough money left after buying the vegetables,' and Oona walked off to her car, parked outside the theatre. She had had enough of Shalini's penny-pinching habits. *The girl's a leech. It is time she learnt to spend rather than investing every rupee in long-term deposits at the post office. Gosh she is the epitome of miserliness.*

Oona was lost in her thoughts when she heard a male voice, 'Have I caught you at a wrong time, Madame?' Oona had not even noticed Riz Ali standing before her.

'Oh, hi! No, no. It's all right. Actually I was just heading home. You?'

'Just going in to watch a play. Have you seen *Anokhi*?' he asked.

Oona nodded, and said, 'It's been quite a while since we met.' 'Yes, I remember. But I've been away. Mostly in the US. But I thought of you whenever I read your column. I enjoy your take on films. It's such fun and yet so damn correct.' Riz smiled.

'Thanks,' Oona smiled shyly.

'Why don't you give me your number? I don't have your cell number.'

'Sure,' Oona rattled it off. 'Text me yours, too. Do call and we must catch up one of these days soon. Oh wait, I'm headed to Calcutta the day after for a month. We'll catch up after I return. Enjoy your play.'

'Thanks. And see you soon, Oona,' Riz said, as suddenly Shalini came huffing up to them with Sana in tow. Riz looked at her in surprise.

'Yes?' he asked. 'Can I help you?'

'No, no' Shalini was still panting. 'Hi, I am Shalini. Oona's friend. You are Riz Ali, right? I am a TV producer,' Shalini extended her hand to Riz, who hesitated before shaking hands with her. He turned to Oona and said, 'Okay, bye Oona.'

'Bye.'

'Bye,' Shalini chimed in, but Riz was already walking away. She turned to Oona and said, 'Quite the looker still, isn't he? I did not know you knew him.'

'Vaguely.' Oona was curt. 'What do you want now?'

'A lift back home. Sana just finished her brownie, so I thought I would come with you.'

'Oona Aunty, Mamma did not let me finish my brownie. She ate it up, saying I had to hurry otherwise we would have to go home in an auto and she would have to pay the autowallah. But with you we can take a free ride home in the AC car.'

'Your mama is always saving. God knows for what?' Oona could not help smiling at Sana.

'For my daughter's dowry,' Shalini added cheekily.

'And when did you turn into a television producer?' Oona asked sarcastically.

'Well, I did work with Zee and Sony,' Shalini replied.

'For a month each, and years ago!' said Oona.

'Listen, here you have to push yourself all the time. If you work as a production assistant, say you're an executive producer. If you're an EP, say you're the producer. Who's going to find out, but your *izzat* goes up. If I were you, I would tout myself as the Editor of *The Post*.'

'You are incorrigible, Shalini,' Oona sighed.

Shalini just laughed.

Strange Bedfellows

'That was a very stupid thing for your husband to do, Oona,' Suparna Debi, Oona's grand-aunt told her. She was reading *The Herald* in her easy chair while Oona sat on the magnificent four-poster Burma-teak bed, going through an array of precious ornaments in the bedroom. Oona had been in her hometown for a few weeks now, commuting between her mother's place in Golpark and her grand aunt's in Rainey Park. Suparna Debi had been rather unwell lately and it was on her insistence that Oona had flown down to Calcutta. Now Kolkata.

Oona had taken her grand aunt for a variety of tests, and the final verdict was incurable and fatal. Stomach cancer. The brave old lady refused chemotherapy and decided to live out her last days at home, free of doctors and painkillers. Practical to the core, she made Oona go through her will with the lawyer. Her sprawling bungalow in Rainey Park was to go to the Bengal Home Industries to train destitute women in various crafts and make them self-sufficient. A major chunk of her money went to Oona and Sangeeta and the rest was divided among faithful domestic help. Jealous relatives didn't see why Oona needed any more money, married as she was to the 'rich producer'. But Suparna Debi had sensed that Oona was not happy in her marriage. This was her way of securing Oona's future.

Oona also received some priceless family heirlooms and jewellery. Even more valuable was Suparna Debi's commentary on each item. The *navaratna* set was 'a gift from Gayatri Devi's paternal uncle in Cooch

Behar'; the rose-cut diamond necklace and matching chandelier earrings were 'set in Amsterdam in the early part of this century', and the golden South Sea pearls 'came from Tagore's side of the family you see. It was meant for Victoria Ocampo* but poor chap never got around to giving it to her!'

But now Suparna Debi's commentary was directed at Anand. Oona looked blankly at her grand-aunt as she continued railing against him. 'Why must he campaign for Surendra Modi? Is he out of his mind? I'm die-hard Congress, but even if it was the BJP he chose to support, did it have to be Surendra Modi?' Oona had also been horrified by the news, until she discovered that Modi's friend, Bachchubhai, was interested in funding Anand's next venture.

'Chhordida, Anand does exactly what he wants. How can I stop him?' Changing the topic, she pulled out a delicate gold filigree brooch, studded with small rubies and elephants and shaped like a peacock. 'This is nice.'

Suparna Debi got the hint. 'It doubles up as a pendant,' she informed Oona.

'Oh, wow!'

'Do you like it?' Suparna Debi asked.

Oona realised that Chhordida would give this to her as well if she said yes. She quickly toned down her enthusiasm. 'Okay, okay types. There is so much you have given me. Give this to somebody else.'

'I have distributed all that I had to. These are all yours. You can give the brooch to Bina. She's a nice girl. Let her have it if you don't want it,' Suparna Debi said.

'Oh, Bina Mashi will be thrilled. Wait till she sees this,' Oona said. 'But Dida, are you sure you want me to have all this?' Oona stared at the jewellery spread on the bed. It looked straight out of the Nizam's catalogue!

---

*Famous Argentine writer and intellectual, Victoria Ocampo was known to be Tagore's muse.

'Listen child, I don't mean to intrude but if things do not work out between Anand and you, the money I have left for you and your mother will see you two through for a while.' Pointing at the ornaments, she continued, 'These are family heirlooms, not just priceless but irreplaceable. Just for a rainy day. Part with them only if you absolutely have to. But I am sure it'll never come to that. You're smart and your career will take you places. Then you can pass them on to the children I hope you'll have some day.' Her eyes twinkled as she added, 'Preferably with some nice Bengali, maybe even a Brahmo boy.'

Oona couldn't help smiling.

On her flight back to Mumbai, Oona met Shreya Dutt, the young, dynamic politician. Daughter of yesteryear-star Dev Dutt, Shreya belonged to the educated breed of second-generation Indian politicians. She had worked her way up from the grassroot level, contributing to youth welfare projects, and was now contesting the general elections from Oona's constituency, Bombay North West.

They formed a mutual admiration society. Shreya admitted she enjoyed reading Oona's columns and Oona lauded her social work and guts. They exchanged telephone numbers.

'I'm really busy campaigning,' Shreya said, 'but call me.'

'Sure,' Oona hesitated before adding, 'and I'd also like to help if you need anything, maybe by way of the press...?'

'You've snatched the words from my mouth. But my only issue is that your husband's campaigning for the BJP. For Modi. So I'm unsure,' Shreya confessed.

'Actually my side of the family have always been die-hard Congressmen,' Oona clarified. 'My great-great-uncle worked alongside W.C. Bonnerjee and S.N. Banerjea and Subhash Bose. I don't agree with the BJP ideology at all. Nor does my husband. But between you and me, he got roped in. Know what I mean?' Shreya smiled and nodded. Everyone knew these campaign fees were hard to resist.

'Well such things happen. Anyway, I want you on my team. We'll ensnare Anandji later. So that's a deal then,' Shreya concluded with a firm handshake, as they went their separate ways.

Two weeks later, Oona was back in Kolkata. Suparna Debi had passed away, peacefully, in her sleep. After the funeral, Oona stayed on for a few days with her mother. While looking through some of her old shelves, she discovered the pearl necklace Suparna Debi had gifted her on her twenty-first birthday. Oona had never taken it to Mumbai. Along with it came Ela Debi's letters, in the silk perfume box with the false bottom. Oona had meant to read them later, but later never happened. Now, as she carefully removed the letters, she found nestled below them an oval pendant on a thin gold chain. *Perhaps even Chhordida was unaware of it, or she'd have told me. Maybe she never read the letters, just tucked them in and forgot all about them.* Noticing a clasp on the pendant, Oona carefully prised it open. The faded, sepia-tinted face of an Englishman stared back at her. He was quite young and handsome. She looked closely, then closed the pendant and examined its back. The inscription read: Sen & Sen Jewellers, Hogg Market, Calcutta. Below, in tiny print was etched, '*For Ela from David, 1929*'.

'Sen & Sen, Hogg Market,' Oona muttered to herself. Then realisation dawned. *Oh of course! It's our Sen & Sen Jewellers from New Market, which used to be called Sir Stewart Hogg Market. I must go and check with Sen Babu who this David is. They might just have preserved their old order books. But it's over eighty years ago.*

Oona knew about Ela Sen, the grand-aunt she bore an uncanny resemblance to.

So Ela Debi had had an English lover. David. How exciting!

Oona decided she must find out more. Sangeeta called her for lunch at just that moment, so Oona carefully replaced the long-ago letters in their box and left the room.

'So after marrying the famous film-maker you have forgotten poor Sen Babu,' the friendly proprietor welcomed Oona into his shop with a smile. 'We have become an air-conditioned shop now, though no comparison to your Bhimji Zaveri.' Oona laughed.

'So tell me, Oona Debi, what will you have? *Cha*, coffee, cold drink?'

'Nothing, Sen Babu, just wanted some information about something I got from Suparna Debi.'

'I am sorry to hear about her death,' the old man said. 'She was our very old and valued customer. More than that, she was a nice person. No airs. We hope we will continue to serve you like we served her,' Sen Babu shifted his weight in the chair.

Oona handed him the chain and pendant. 'Can you tell me more about who ordered this? It says Sen & Sen at the back. Very old. In case you have your old records?'

'1929,' he muttered, looking closely at the pendant. 'Yes. Made by us. During my grandfather's time. In the British days.'

'I need to find out who ordered it, if there is a forwarding address . . . any information will do.'

'Oona Debi, this will take time. I have to pull out the old record books. Give me some time and leave me your Mumbai address. I will send you whatever information I find.'

The Times of India's Mumbai edition carried a small news piece a week later:

> Well-known film producer and former actor, Anand Khanna campaigns for BJP candidate Surendra Modi. His journalist wife, Oona Khanna joins Congress candidate Shreya Dutt as Media Manager. What will the verdict be?

Anand was furious. 'You cannot work with this Dutt woman. You are my wife,' he blasted her.

'But I have a mind of my own,' Oona retorted.

'Then keep your bloody mind out of my life,' Anand screamed.

It was all-out war now.

Riz

The year 2004, 6 February. Another day on the calendar. Another day in Oona's life as she turned a year older. For a change, Anand remembered her birthday and gave his wife a kiss on her lips first thing in the morning. Though his breath smelt of stale cigarettes, Oona was touched. *God knows when he will kiss me again. It feels good to be kissed by a man after a long time.* Anand gave her a bunch of carnations and a packet, clumsily gift-wrapped. Oona opened it and found no card, no message but just a bundle of crisp 1,000-rupee notes. She looked up questioningly at Anand. 'Thirty-six thousand rupees. For your birthday. A thousand for each year of your life. Count and check. And buy yourself something nice,' Anand said with a self-satisfied smile. *Does he have to be so fucking crude? No little words scribbled on a card, no finesse, just handing out hard cash...does it make up for all his bad behaviour? These Punjabi men can be really crass.*

Usually, this was the one day Anand tried in his own way to make up to Oona for the whole year. He wined and dined her in five-star luxury. If he didn't, Oona would never let him hear the end of it. This was a lesson he had learnt in their marriage. But this time things were different. Their cold war had begun with a political showdown. Both their candidates won. Surendra Modi, the 'Hindu fundamentalist', routed his adversaries in Gujarat while Parliament saw the influx of GenNext politicians like Omar Abdullah, Rahul Gandhi, Sachin Pilot and Shreya Dutt, among others. People pinned a lot of hope on these rising political figures for their open mindsets and understated dignity. Anand had tried to coax Oona against campaigning for the Congress. Gentle persuasion turned to threats of divorce. When Oona remained unshakeable, the cold war began. Anand moved out into the guest bedroom.

While Oona fumed over the 'gift', Anand walked away. 'Have a great day. I have meetings all day but if I am home early maybe we'll go out for dinner.'

Oona nodded without looking up.

A little later, she went to the bathroom. She splashed water on her face and looked closely at herself. She still looked pretty. Some men would find her very attractive in spite of a couple of very fine lines around her eyes. There was also a hint of a double chin. She had begun working out at the gym and hoped to shed the unwanted kilos she had piled on lately. She glanced sideways at her reflected profile and was happy to note that her high cheekbones, though less angular, still showed.

Thirty-six. So now I'm in my late thirties. This year I promise to pamper myself and look good. But why? And for whom? After all, Anand pays no attention to my emotional and physical needs any longer.

Roger Riter, the Pulitzer prize-winning author was conducting a two-day workshop at the Sheraton for professional writers. Oona was among the select invitees to attend the workshop. 'Lucky you,' Shalini had remarked when she heard. 'Isn't there a way you can get me in?'

Oona could not fathom why on earth Shalini would want to attend a writer's workshop, other than that she wanted to have a finger in every pie to boast to all who would care to listen that she kept herself busy attending workshops and parties.

The workshop was interesting but the best feature were the ample coffee breaks where Oona met up with a number of well-known authors. On the first day, as they were re-entering the workshop after lunch, Oona's phone rang. She saw Riz Ali's name flashing on her screen.

'Hi Riz,' she answered.

'Hi Madame, I am so flattered you saved my number. How are you?'

'All well. I am just in the middle of a workshop. Can I call you back?'

'Oh, okay. Don't worry, we'll talk later. Just wanted to meet up briefly to discuss something.'

'Sure. But it will have to wait till the day after. I am attending this two-day Roger Riter workshop.'

'Wow! Go ahead, I'll call you the day after. Bye.'

'Bye.'

Later that evening, Oona was at home when she got an SMS from Riz: *Luking 4 2bhk flat 2 share wid friend around Lokdwla-Versova. Evn 1bhk for self wil do. Riz.*

She immediately called him from her landline. He answered with a hesitant 'hello'.

'Hi. This is Oona. Oona Khanna. Just saw your message.'

'Oh, hi! Is this your home number? And how was the workshop?' Riz asked.

'Yes it is. The workshop went off pretty well. What is your budget for the rental?'

'Ummm, about 10,000-15,000 for a two-bedroom place. And about 7,000-10,000 for a one-bedroom. Actually, my actor friend, Siddharth was keen to share with me. But he has backed out. So a one-bedroom is fine.'

'Well, I have a good agent. Will check with him and let you know, say by tomorrow?' Oona asked.

'Sure. In fact, why don't we meet for ten–fifteen minutes tomorrow?' he suggested.

'Okay, let's make it post lunch, say around 2.30ish. I'll give you good coffee and will call the agent over too.'

'Sounds great. You can assure your agent that I am a good tenant. I don't throw noisy parties, don't entertain girlfriends or even boyfriends, and only rarely have visitors. My mother may come over occasionally. My wife and I are separated, so no question of her dropping by either.'

'Okay,' Oona said, wondering why he had seemed to emphasise the last bit. Was it for her benefit? 'See you tomorrow, Riz. I'll just text you my address.'

'Looking forward to it,' he said as he hung up.

❧

It was nearly 2.30 by the time Oona mailed off her column. She was in the studio apartment she used as her office and had texted the address to Riz. She preferred meeting her friends here rather than at the house. She quickly brushed her hair and sprayed on a bit of her favourite Issey Miyake. Smiling at her enthusiasm, she justified it to herself. After all, Riz Ali was a top yesteryear model. And quite a looker. She remembered back in school, her friend Rubina used to be a major Riz Ali fan. She would paste cuttings of his magazine ads in her scrap book—cigarettes, suiting, woollens and other products. 'Who's this guy?' Oona had once asked Rubina.

'He's the top model these days,' Rubina informed her. 'Isn't he good looking?'

'I can see that. What's his name though?' Oona asked.

'Riz Ali. I just love him. Big fan of his. Love to marry someone like him some day,' Rubina gushed.

'Why don't you just marry *him*?' Oona joked.

'As if he is waiting to marry me! He must have all those gorgeous girls falling over him. You think I stand a chance with those glamour babes?'

'No harm trying,' Oona remembered having told the pretty Rubina. Oona smiled at the memory. Who would have thought then that he would come by to visit her someday? She wished she could tell Rubina, but they were no longer in touch. Last she'd heard, Rubina was somewhere near Los Angeles, married to an NRI doctor and a mother of two. The doorbell interrupted Oona's thoughts. Must be Rubina's hearthtrob, she guessed, going towards the door.

'Hi,' Riz said, looking handsome in blue jeans and a white shirt with the sleeves rolled up. Oona realised he was lean and did not look too different from his pictures of twenty years ago. The few lines that had appeared on his face since then no doubt added to his mature good looks, Oona decided. Besides, the glasses he now wore suited his profile just fine and softened his otherwise too-finely chiselled nose.

They chatted over coffee, getting to know each other better. The agent arrived soon after. Oona was about to introduce them when Riz said, 'Oh, we've met before. Sharmaji, right?'

'Ji, Riz Saab,' the agent said, doing a *namaste*.

'You know each other?' Oona asked.

'Yes,' Riz replied. 'I met him some days back after my landlord gave me marching orders. He has not been able to help me much, though,' Riz smiled at Sharma.

'Well, he told me he has four places for you to check out,' Oona said. 'Right, Sharmaji?'

'Madam, only one. The one on Yari Road. Saab has seen that one.' 'What about the other two in Lokhandwala?' Oona asked. Sharma seemed to hesitate. '*Kyon? Kya hua?*' Oona asked.

'*Kya hai na* madam, it will be better for Sir to take the Yari Road one. Good Muslim landlord. Lokhandwala is a little strict…you know what I mean?'

'I get it. They don't want a Muslim tenant. That is what he means. I think I'll have a look at the Yari Road once again,' Riz said in a matter-of-fact manner.

'I'm so sorry,' Oona was embarrassed.

'I don't see why you should be sorry. I am quite used to this. After the '93 riots the secular face of Mumbai has taken a complete battering. But such is life.'

She called Riz soon after he left. 'I just remembered you came to meet me over something which we didn't get to talk about. We got busy with Sharmaji and your house-hunting issue,' Oona said.

'*Ji*. I too realised it later. But I'll come by again soon for that. I'm leaving for Singapore tomorrow morning for an ad film shoot. Only two days. Will buzz you the moment I get back. Anything I can get you from there?'

'Nothing, thanks. What are you shooting for?'

'Lime Fizz. I play the girl's father. After all, that's about all I can do in this country in my forties!' he joked.

'Well, I can confidently say you look much younger than 40,' Oona said, giggling.

'Thanks for the compliment, I'm flattered. But I'm not joking,' Riz said. '*To thik hai ji. Inshallah, jaldi mulakat hogi*. We shall catch up soon.'

'*Inshallah*. Looking forward to that. And have a safe flight. Bon voyage,' Oona responded.

'Merci, Madame.'

Oona was in high spirits as she hung up, hoping to meet him soon. Something about him felt good. Maybe his genuine politeness. Or simply his charm. Both of which she missed in Anand.

Am just down d rd 4rm u. Cud I drop by 4 a min 2 drop a packet?

Reading Riz's message, Oona wondered about the packet. She was at her office, sorting some paperwork. She dialled his number.

'Hi. How are you doing?' Riz asked, in the slightly nasal voice which Oona found sexier than Anand's baritone.

'Good. And you? When did you get back?' Oona replied.

'This morning. I'm in your neighbourhood and I have a packet for you.'

'What packet?'

'Why don't you see for yourself?' Riz said.

'Can it wait? Am down with a terrible headache,' Oona lied. She was in really casual clothes and didn't want Riz to see her that way. Besides her periods were giving her terrible stomach cramps.

'Don't worry,' Riz persisted. 'I'll only be there for a minute. Am on my way to Pune by the 5 o'clock flight, so I shan't take much of your time.'

'Okay,' Oona said, hurrying to the mirror to tidy up.

'Be there in five,' Riz said. 'See you.'

Riz arrived in less than five minutes. He refused to come in. 'I can see you are not feeling too bright,' he commented.

'Bad headache,' Oona feigned as he handed her a packet. 'What is this?' she asked as she opened the packet. 'Oh. Lindt Dark. I love them,' She looked up at him and smiled.

'I know. You had mentioned. So I picked them up for you when I saw them at the airport. Got myself a packet too. Hope you enjoy them and see you in a few days' time when I return from Pune.'

'Okay. See you. And have a good flight. But why aren't you just taking the bus?'

'I know I can,' Riz shrugged. 'But what the heck, I like to fly.'

'Have a great flight and thanks a ton,' Oona said, but Riz was already on his way out.

She was touched that he had remembered to get her dark chocolates. That too her favourite Lindt. She felt bad that she hadn't even offered him coffee, and decided to thank him with a text message:

Sorry for being a bit abrupt. Feeling down with the headache. Touched by your thoughtfulness and the Lindt Darks. Have a safe flight and enjoy your trip. Ciao.

A little later Riz messaged back:

Ur welcom madme n may ur headache dissolve. Wil call when i return. Tk cr.

It had been nearly a week since he dropped by and Riz had neither called nor turned up at her door. He'd said he would return in a couple of days.

Maybe he'd been held up? Or was he busy with other things? *Should I call him to say hello? He might think I'm pursuing him. Anyway, who cares!* Oona's fingers were already tapping the buttons of her cellphone:

Goodmorning! Long time no news? Hope all's well. Have a great day

An hour later Riz texted back:

Ah. Bonjour Madame Oona. Still in Pune. See you soon. Ciao.

Oona smiled. She loved his old fashioned use of Urdu and French words. Both her favourite languages. She remembered mentioning to Riz about her schooling in Chande and how they were taught French as a second language in school. Of course, her French had dulled over the years that she'd had no practice, but she still managed reasonably well. Riz was impressed and admitted he had spent a few years in France. 'Doing what?' she had asked then.

'Oh, with my wife's family. She is half French and half American.'

'That's a deadly combo.'

'You bet,' Riz agreed. 'She almost killed me!' He sounded rather mean. Oona let the remark slip and changed the topic. It was enough to know that his relationship with his wife was not great, but she did not want to probe deeper and appear inquisitive.

Let me kno if u r free day after i.e. 20th. There is a jazz prog follwd by dinner at Taj. Wil reserv 2 passes. Oona messaged back. She waited for his reply, but when he was silent even by late evening she realised he was probably not interested.

She called up Shalini next morning and asked if she would be willing to come along with her for the performance on Saturday. 'Okay. Am more interested in the dinner though,' Shalini was her usual self. 'Can't give a shit about jazz.'

'Be ready by six then and stand at the usual place. Will pick you up.'

'Okay. Bye.'

On Saturday morning, Riz called her.

'Oh, good to hear from you. When did you get back?' Oona asked.

'Last night. And how have things been with you, madame?' Riz asked.

'Good. And you?' Oona wanted to remind him of the jazz performance but let it go.

'Not too bad.'

'What were you doing in Pune?' Oona asked.

'Just hanging around with friends in the ashram,' Riz said.

'Which ashram?'

'Osho.'

'I see. So you're a follower?'

'Yes. Have been ever since I was 20,' Riz said.

'Wow. I've been there once. Years ago. Had taken my mom there. Nice place.'

'Yeah, sure,' Riz said. 'You did mention something about a jazz programme today?'

Oona was relieved. 'Yes I did. But since you didn't text me back, I thought you weren't interested.'

'Oh, I thought I had texted you on that. Why? Have you made some other plans?'

'Not really, except that I was trying to take along a reluctant friend who doesn't like jazz. Let me check with her if she still is keen on coming,' Oona said.

'I don't want to upset your plans. Why don't you go ahead with her?' Riz said.

'Oh, believe me, you won't be upsetting her, but doing her a favour. Give me a minute,' Oona said. 'I'll call you back.'

Oona quickly called Shalini and cancelled the evening's date, making up a vague excuse about having to go with Anand for a music launch. Shalini sounded a little unconvinced—Oona had done this before and Shalini had found out when she saw Oona in a photo on page three of the *Post*. She hated being treated like a second-class citizen but swallowed her pride each time. Oona was her only ticket to Bombay's party circuit.

It was her first evening out with Riz. For some strange reason Oona felt the excitement she had felt on her first date as a teenager. She dressed in stylish black trousers and a slinky top with an ochre pashmina stole draped casually around her. She went to the parlour to blow-dry her hair and Jenny, the owner, wanted to know where she was headed.

'To town. For a jazz performance.'

'Hubby's going with you?'

'No, am going with a friend. Will be picking him up shortly.'

'No wonder,' Jenny grinned.

'No wonder what?'

'No wonder you're glowing.'

She told Riz she'd meet him at the petrol pump near her house. That was her first stop anyway as she needed to tank up. The attendant mentioned that Anand had just driven off with a full tank some time back. 'That was close,' thought Oona. People had already gathered that she and Anand had drifted apart. He would be seen with a different arm-candy at each film-do. Riz, being a looker, would attract Anand's attention if the two met, and Oona didn't want to give Anand ammunition for their next argument. Besides, given Riz's deadly reputation with women, she'd best keep him under wraps. It was her reputation at stake, too.

She knew her marriage with Anand had only survived because he did not want to divorce her and have to shell out a huge figure as alimony. Having been taken to the cleaners several times before, he no longer had the energy to build his fortune from scratch. If he caught Oona with another man she knew he'd nail her for mental cruelty and infidelity.

Riz stepped out of an auto and slid in next to her.

'Good to see you, Madame,' he gave her a light hug, looking dapper as ever. 'I did not realise earlier but you have gorgeous dark hair. It is rare to see natural black hair these days with women colouring them in all hues. And I hate Indian women with coloured hair.'

'Thanks,' Oona blushed. So going to Jenny's had not been in vain.

It took nearly two hours to reach NCPA from Juhu. Oona had joked that Riz would tire of her company on the long ride, and in return he promised to tell her his life's story. 'Then you can write about it someday,' he smiled.

His father, Habib Ali, was a moody man, a gentleman of leisure who did not do much for a living. They had a family mansion in Delhi's Nizamuddin East. Habib Ali took up the odd writing job now and then. He sounded like a very stylish man, and Oona could see where Riz inherited his style from. Habib Ali had passed away some years back. Riz's mother, Khushnum, was the typical Indian wife, barely educated and patiently tolerant of her temperamental husband. Her elder son lived in the US and her daughter worked for Cathay Pacific as a flight attendant. Riz was her younger son and it sounded like he was spoilt as a child.

'I've always been a waster. Was a *charsi* since the age of 20, smoking hash, not the hard stuff though. I was happy to live off my parents, go out with friends and girlfriends. One day my brother Feroz called from the US to speak to my mother and I answered. He abused the daylights out of me. Said at my age I had no right to be sitting around doing nothing. That it was time I went out to fend for myself.

'It set me thinking. I was twenty-seven then. My sister, Attiya, who flies Cathay, was stationed in Bombay at that time. I came to live with her, got my portfolio done from my photographer-friend Victor Bose, and the rest, as they say, is history.'

'Did you say Victor Bose?' the name rang a bell, though Oona couldn't quite place it.

'Yes,' Riz said. 'He used to model part-time as well. He was my contemporary, though a bit younger. You may have seen his ads.'

'Maybe,' Oona said. 'Anyway, continue.'

'Without really meaning to become one, I was soon a supermodel,' Riz continued. 'I have never gone out of my way to achieve anything. Opportunities just fell into my lap, clichéd though it sounds. And I am thankful to God for it.'

'I remember seeing you on hoardings during my schooldays in that cigarette ad. Camel Lites? Was it?'

'Now don't make me sound like an old fogey when you say school days!'

'Sorry. I did not mean it that way, but I really was in school then,' Oona grinned.

'Just joking, I know,' Riz said.

'My classmate was a major fan of yours. She even had a scrapbook with all your ad clippings. That's how I first heard of you,' Oona said.

'Wow!' Riz was flattered. 'And where is she now?'

'Rubina? She's in the States. Somewhere near LA. Married to some doctor with two boys. I am not in touch with her but our mothers meet once in a while.'

'Is she pretty?' Riz asked naughtily.

'Very. Used to be a stunner in school.'

'Well then you must give me her number and when I visit LA next, I shall go and look her up. See for myself what I missed!' They both laughed and the remaining drive passed in easy banter.

It was nearly ten when the jazz show ended and Oona and Riz headed to the Taj for dinner. On the way, Riz picked up some *gajras* from the flower-girl at the traffic signal. She took them eagerly and breathed in their fragrance. 'I love them,' she exclaimed.

The dinner was a lavish spread and they bumped into some common friends. Anand called Oona a few times during the evening, asking where the Tylenol was and when she would be home. She told him where she was without mentioning her companion, who drew a lot of attention. Dilnaz, the marketing head of Louis Vuitton in India, and a casual friend of Oona's, cattily remarked on seeing Riz that Anand was looking different these days. Anand's friend, actor Hari Singh asked where he was. When Oona said he was back home, Singh's wife Deepti asked Oona to call him over. Singh told his wife, 'Honey, why don't you realise she is better off without him?' looking pointedly at Riz.

On the way back, Oona offered to drop Riz home. 'Please don't bother. Just drop me off at the gas station and I will take an auto.' 'Why would you take an auto when I can drop you?' Oona asked, genuinely concerned at that late hour.

'Honestly, I am quite used to it. I am so used to autos and trains. I have no hang-ups. In fact when people see me using public transport, they feel sorry for me. "Poor Riz Ali," they must think. But it does not rattle me in the least bit. I am a very frugal person. I don't like to spend on unnecessary luxuries. And I am quite comfortable. This is my second innings after a long gap, so I don't mind starting from scratch notwithstanding my age.' He gave her a hug and a light peck on the cheek. 'Thanks for a great evening, Madame. Have a good night and talk to you later.' 'Good night,' Oona said.

Reaching home, Oona gently held up the *gajras* and smiled. She kept them by her bedside table, the fragrance reminding her of the evening. She heard Anand stir beside her. Lately, Anand took turns sleeping in the guest bedroom and the master bedroom, according to his mood, though they hardly ever had sex. This was more to assert his ownership of the house than any emotional motive. Oona wondered which of his girlfriends had given him this idea.

'What time is it?' he mumbled in his sleep.

'Must be around half past twelve,' Oona lied, knowing very well it was past 2 a.m. A few minutes later, Anand got up and went to the bathroom. Oona knew he was just checking the time. When he joined her, he remarked, 'It is nearly three in the morning.'

'Is it?' Oona asked.

'You should know better,' was all Anand said and turned away to resume his snoring.

Coffee Break

The new bungalow at Yari Road had been renovated over a year and at considerable expense. Anand had got Rozanne Khan and Rimple Kumar to do up the interiors. Rozanne and Rimple, apart from being high-profile designers, were also star wives. Rozanne was married to Hyder Khan and Rimple to Ajay Kumar, two of Bollywood's reigning idols. This was Anand's trick to ensure these stars' presence in his future projects.

He was really proud of the bungalow. 'Can you imagine what my folks back home in Ludhiana would say? *Anand ka Bambai mein bangla hai.* Our *munda* has made it.'

'But you don't need to have a bungalow to impress your folks. There are other ways. Your hit films. Besides, a bungalow is high maintenance,' Oona wanted to reason. But it would be wasted on Anand. He wanted to keep up with the Joneses, in this case the Johars, the Khans, the Shahs and the Chopras.

Two things Oona loved about the bungalow were its location—close to their old home and all that she had grown familiar with in her years in Mumbai—and the sense of space it afforded her. The master bedroom was two bedrooms converted into one. Anand's study housed the home theatre and a film screen. He fondly called it his 'den'. So typically filmy, Oona rued. Nowadays it was the fashion to buy huge apartments in the far suburbs like Oshiwara and Goregaon and have a 'den'. This always comprised a home theatre with Bose speakers and foreign film DVDs. One room was designated for Rukman didi, who visited often, and one for Bobby or other relatives. The last room was meant for Sangeeta, on the rare occasions she visited Oona, and for other guests the rest of the time.

What Oona loved the best was her walk-in closet. She could display her sarees and dresses and choose her wardrobe with ease. She had an Imelda Marcos fetish for shoes and bags, and finally had ample space to house them without thinking twice about buying new ones. Oona realised that over a decade she had accumulated so many material goods, that she could use them over several lifetimes. 'If you have not worn a dress or used something in over six months, chances are you will never use them,' she remembered reading in some feng shui magazine. 'So it's better to do away with the clutter in your life. It will bring you peace,' the article had concluded. Oona thought this was an ideal time to clean out the clutter from her life. She ruthlessly gave away clothes and other items to her two bais. Shanta bai and Renuka bai were ecstatic, fighting like children over the loot. A large number of her shoes went to her neighbour's college-going daughters who were fans of 'Oona Aunty's style'. Shalini was upset that none of the shoes fitted her.

Oona started sorting out her jewellery and realised she hardly ever wore most of it. She set aside a few as gifts for close friends on their special occasions. She earmarked some items for Sangeeta, keeping just a few rings and earrings for herself. The rest had to go. 'I'll tell Champakbhai to give me a fair price for all this gold,' she decided.

Now the house looked sparse but well furnished. It gave her a zen-like feel. Oona sat down to sort through old letters and other memorabilia. Sridevi had the run of the house, bounding up and down in all the open space. Anand walked in.

'We need to buy some more furniture. The place looks empty,' he remarked.

'Just let it be. Don't cram it up. It gives a sense of peace,' Oona said.

'To hell with your sense of peace. We need to display. Look at the other producers' houses. This looks like a sadhu's den. *Kuch to dikhana hai.*' Oona detested the typical garish display of wealth in the star homes, but decided not to argue. 'I will look into it later. Do you want some *chai*?'

'Yeah. Tell Shanta bai to get it. What are you doing?'

'Sorting out old photographs and letters,' Oona replied, immersed in her chore as Sridevi tried to nuzzle in between.

'*Arrey*, why keep such stuff? Just throw it away. Who reads old letters?'

'Some of these old family photographs are priceless,' she began. 'I think we Bengalis value our paper assets more than metal assets. We value our books and letters and even old magazines…'

'Yes, I can see that,' Anand cut in. 'But start valuing the right paper assets.'

'*Matlab*?' Oona asked, perplexed.

'I mean stocks and RBI and mutual fund bonds!' Anand laughed at his own clever statement. 'Including this,' he raised the magazine he was reading. A cheap looking trade guide on Bollywood called *Box Office*.

Oona had just taken a break from sorting out the photographs. The previous day she had bought several albums and begun arranging family photographs in chronological order. They'd been kept bundled up in packets for too long and many had got spoilt. Oona wanted to preserve them. It was a mammoth task and took nearly three days to complete.

Now everything was done and Oona decided to sit back and enjoy a cup of coffee. Suddenly she remembered the silk box Chhordida had given her. She realised she hadn't followed up on that research. She rose to fetch the box when her cell beeped: *Can I c u for 5 in 15. Riz*

Oona did not know what to make of it. It had been quite a while since Riz had called. After the marathon date they had not even met. She had got busy with shifting houses and had forgotten to call him. She dialled his number. 98200 98098. It had a certain ring to it.

'*Hanji. Sab khairiyat?*'

'*Ji*,' Oona replied. 'All well. Did you just message me? Sorry but I could not quite figure it out.'

'Was just wondering if I could drop in for five minutes for a cup of coffee? Am just around the corner from your pad,' Riz asked.

'Sure. Make it as soon as possible because I'm craving some coffee myself.'

'That makes two of us. Be there in less than 15 minutes.'

He arrived as promised, and Oona poured out the coffee. 'What were you doing in this area?'

'Just shifting my things,' he said, taking a sip. 'I decided on the Yari Road dig. Will be moving in next month. So over the next few days I will gradually move my stuff here.'

Oona was secretly delighted that Riz would be her neighbour soon, but she managed to hide it. She didn't know that Riz's main reason for moving to Yari Road was to be closer to her.

'It'll be nice to have you as a neighbour,' Oona remarked casually.

'Yeah, guess I'm just a holler away from you,' Riz tried to sound equally casual.

'Why don't you just hire a truck and shift all your stuff together at once?' Oona asked.

'No. I prefer it this way. It also gives me time to sort out and throw away a lot of junk. Besides, I'm not working these days, so I have enough time on my hands.' Riz said.

When Riz left after half an hour, Oona was feeling pleasantly recharged. She compared this little chat session with the coffee outings she and Anand had sometimes. *There's nothing to talk about. Anand is just keen to drink up and get it over with. Like a chore. As if it was a duty, not pure pleasure.*

Oona turned her attention back to the silk box. She took out the two crystal bottles and kept them on the display shelf above her desk with the handmade Ganesh in ceramic and the frames with family portraits. It had been nearly two years since Suparna Debi had died. Oona felt bad that she still hadn't got around to reading through the old letters or to sort family photos she'd brought away from Chhordida's place.

She carefully unfolded the letters and read them. They were mainly love letters from David to Ela. Once, some years earlier, Suparna Debi had told Oona about the love affair between a family member Ela Sen and an Englishman, David Oliver. Ela Sen was the aunt of Surendranath Roy, Suparna Debi's father-in-law. Surendranath's mother, Kamini, had been Ela's first cousin, as their fathers were the brothers Somenath and Debnath.

'Ela Sen was a woman much ahead of her times,' Oona remembered Chhordida saying. 'She was amongst the first batch of women to graduate from Calcutta University. She was a social worker who worked with Sarala Debi and was also Subhash Bose's friend. She died a spinster because her father would not let her marry the Englishman she loved. Back then, it was even harder to follow your heart and not give in to social pressures.'

As Oona read the few letters David had written Ela and remembered Chhordida's words, she grew more curious about Ela. The story and its tragic end moved her deeply, and it also prompted the writer in her to want to know more. *Maybe I could write a historical romance someday. But I have only David's letters and his state of mind. I wonder what Ela Sen's perspective was. Did David also preserve her letters this lovingly? He seems so sincere in these letters, I am sure he must have. Wonder who has them now? Maybe some distant great-niece like me? Or have they been destroyed? I would love to look at them. I would love to see how my great aunt expressed herself in English all those years ago.*

Oona began putting the letters back, already thinking of sharing them with Riz. He'd been a history student, he'd said. Perhaps he'd find them interesting too. Suddenly, Oona remembered about the letter from Sen & Sen Jewellers. She'd put it aside when it came because she was busy finishing her column. That was a year and a half ago. And she'd never gone back to it.

It was time to head to the gym, so she made a note to look for that letter. She hoped it hadn't been lost in the shifting. As she walked to the gym, she decided she must work extra hard. Her thoughts were with Riz again. *Look how toned he is. Says he never gyms. Must have great metabolism. And I have to work to lose every single calorie!*

The next evening, Oona's phone flashed with an SMS: *In the vicinity. Cud I drop by 4 cofe.*

Sure. She texted back.

C u in exactly 5. By now Oona was able to decode his texts.

This went on for the next few days. Every afternoon, Riz brought some of his belongings to the new house, and would come by and have coffee with Oona a little after five. He enjoyed the serenity of her office, the aromatic brew she served with ginger and hazelnut cookies and her company. And she, too, loved his company and his charming ways.

One evening it was past five and there was no news of Riz. Oona decided to call him. 'Where are you?' she asked, when he answered.

'At home. Resting. Why? All well?' Riz asked.

'Oh, yes. Just wondered whether you wanted to have coffee or not?' she asked.

'Sure. Don't mind. You will have to give me half an hour at least to get ready and come over,' Riz said.

'Please. Don't bother. Just wanted to…'

'It is no bother, Madame. I will be there soon. Just keep the kettle on the boil ten minutes from now. See you.'

Over coffee Riz told her he would be out of town the next few days. He was headed to visit his mother in Delhi. She had just had bypass surgery and Riz felt she needed him around. 'Anything I can get you from Delhi, madame?'

'Nothing. Just enjoy, and bring yourself back soon,' Oona smiled.

Oona worked furiously at her computer the next day. By five in the evening she looked at her cell expectantly when she remembered Riz was in Delhi. But her hand was drawn to the phone anyway and she was dialling without thinking. 98200 980 98. How easily the number came to her mind these days.

'*Adaab arz.* Calling from the office?'

'*Ji. Adaab.* I'm sorry, I know you are in Delhi but I suddenly realised it was coffee time and I am missing my coffee mate. Your company has kind of become addictive,' Oona said.

'Ouch!' Riz said.

'So all well at home?' Oona continued.

'*Ji.* And you? All well? How is Anandsaab?' Riz asked.

'All well. He's well too,' Oona replied, noticing it had become 'saab' from 'bhai'.

'You take care and enjoy your coffee and *inshallah* I will see you soon,' Riz said.

'Thanks. Bye.'

The next day at five Oona's phone beeped: *Bonsoir, madame Oona. Enjoy your coffee and have an extra ginger cookie on my behalf. Enjoy your evening. Riz*

Oona messaged back: *Thx. Wil do. And you have a great evening too.*

Riz texted back: *Merci madame Oona! C u soon! Warm regds. Riz.*

Her coffee tasted good, but the cookie even better.

One afternoon a few days later, Oona's phone flashed a message: *Good Afternoon ms Oona. Hope u're jumping about like a grasshopper. Jus hedng home frm Airport. C u soon. Riz.*

So he was back. Oona smiled. By half past five in the evening he called. 'I know it is too late now. You must have already had your coffee?'

'Well, I did actually. You must be tired. Let's meet for lunch tomorrow if you are not too busy?' Oona asked.

'Lunch is fine by me. Shall we make it around 1.30?' Riz asked.

'Sounds perfect,' Oona said, trying to figure where Anand would be at that time. She dialled Anand's secretary, Mannuji and asked about Anand's schedule for the next day. 'He has meetings lined up back to back in Film City from noon till about five or six in the evening.'

Mannuji was quite used to Oona's question. He knew husband and wife barely communicated, and also knew Anand often hid information from his wife for no reason at all. 'Better keep her guessing about my whereabouts,' he would say. But to keep tabs on Oona, Anand often returned from outdoor locations ahead of schedule. Oona always asked him to inform her so she could send the driver to the airport, but he would say Mannuji had dropped him home.

Oona knew he was trying to catch her on the wrong foot so that he could throw her out without a penny. But she was too smart for him. She would never give him that pleasure. She wished she could just walk out of the marriage, but this was Mumbai, and accommodation did not come easy. Having lived like a queen in a seafront bungalow, coping in a PG dig in some eastern suburb of the city was unthinkable for Oona.

Lunch with Riz was a relaxed affair. Oona ordered food from the local Chinese joint down the road and laid a table for two on the kitchen counter of her studio. She brought out her white Italian crockery and the Sheffield cutlery which caught Riz's eye. 'Sheffield! I remember those from my childhood days. They don't make these anymore,' Riz said. Oona was happy he noticed such details. Anand would have never done so.

After lunch, Riz went out on the little verandah that opened into the garden for a smoke, as usual. He knew Oona abhorred smoking and therefore respected her feelings by going out for a smoke. Oona chatted with him through the wire-mesh door as she went about odd jobs. 'Sorry. But I don't allow smokers in my space,' Oona had sounded apologetic when she'd first told him her rule.

'That's perfectly all right by me. In fact, I don't like smoking myself. But *kya karoon? Adat ka majboor hoon.* This damn addiction. Wish someone would lay down such rules for me at home,' Riz said.

'Well, rules at home are always broken. Anand just saunters in anytime and smokes without asking, dropping ash all over,' Oona said.

Riz laughed. 'After all, he has the right. *Aapka mian hai bhai.* He is your husband.' Oona shrugged disinterestedly. Riz did not fail to notice it. 'Hey, I just noticed, this marble slab on the rail seems to be a bit loose?' Riz said, lifting its loose end.

'Yeah I know. Will have to get the mason to fix it before it comes off,' Oona said.

'It better be fast, Madame, otherwise an accident could cost a passer-by his toes,' Riz joked.

Next morning Oona was busy meeting a couple of deadlines when a message flashed: *Can I drop in for 15? Am round the corner. Riz.*

She checked her watch. It was 11.30 a.m. and rather an odd time for Riz to meet her. Besides, she had oil in her hair and did not want Riz to see her this way. She called back. 'Hi. Am in the middle of some work. Can we catch up later in the evening?'

'I'm in the neighbourhood. At the hardware shop. Will need exactly 15 minutes with you. Won't take more of your time,' he insisted.

'Well, okay,' Oona said reluctantly. She did not mind Riz spending more time with her. What bothered her was her greasy plastered look. There was nothing much she could do, she sighed. *He might as well get used to me in all my avatars.*

As Riz hugged her, she said, 'Sorry, am all oily. Just had an oil massage. Can I make you coffee?'

'Well, if it is not a bother, please.'

As Oona went about preparing the coffee, Riz pottered around the verandah. When she went to call him in, she saw that he was putting M-seal dough under the loose marble slab, his hands black with the sealing plaster.

He smiled at her and continued with his job. 'Just trying to save some poor bloke's toes,' he said.

It touched her. His thoughfulness. His ingenuity. And as Riz Ali worked on that slab, his hands blackened with M-Seal, Oona fell in love with him. Many years ago, something similar had happened when a young Oona had noticed Anand Khanna's powerful hands at the party in Calcutta. Today, another pair of hands were making her heart skip several beats.

He left the dough to dry while they drank their coffee. Half an hour later, Riz checked the marble slab. 'It worked. It's fixed. Come and try lifting it!' Oona did. It would not budge.

'It really is fixed. I am impressed. I hope it will not come out later?' she asked.

'I don't think so ma'am. Now that will be five hundred rupees ma'am,' Riz joked.

'You are way too expensive. I'll give you a hundred,' Oona joked back.

'Labour does not come so cheap these days,' Riz replied. 'Okay. Gotta head out. See you soon and thanks for the coffee.'

'Hi,' Oona called Riz some days later. She sounded chirpy. Anand had just left town for Dubai to promote his forthcoming film, *Lock, Stock and Barrel.*

'What's up? All well? And how's the marble doing?' Riz asked.

'Super. Stuck for good I guess. Thanks a ton. I meant to call you earlier. I am touched,' Oona said.

'The pleasure is all mine,' Riz said.

'Are you busy this evening?'Oona asked.

'For coffee? Yes. Am in town. Won't be back before six or so,' Riz said.

'What about dinner? Say 7.30-8ish? That is the least I owe you for fixing the marble.'

'Ah! I see. Dinner sounds fine.'

'Okay. Then let us meet at my office and then we can go out somewhere nearby? How does that sound to you?' Oona asked.

'Sounds good. See you at 8 sharp then,' Riz said. Oona wanted to invite him over to see the new bungalow. But she decided against it as the servants would be hanging around. Besides, Anand's driver, Pandeyji was a big gossip.

When Riz arrived on the dot at eight, Oona had put on dim lights and soft music. The Emperor Waltz played in the background. 'Wow! The place looks quite different in the evenings,' Riz remarked.

'Yes the mood lights have their own effect,' Oona said as she brought out the bottle of single malt. She had raided Anand's bar and reserved this for special people, those who would understand its worth.

'Water or soda?' she asked.

'Soda.' He looked at the bottle, 'I like Glenfiddich. What about you?' he asked her, pouring his drink.

'Well I don't drink much. But I will join you today.'

'Soda or water?' Riz asked.

'I like my malts neat,' Oona said.

'On the rocks?'

'No. Just plain neat.'

'Sure,' Riz shrugged, impressed.

They chatted over their malts about life, about Riz's rocky marriage, about Chinese horoscopes and tarot cards. 'According to the Chinese calendar, I was born in the year of the monkey. And I have characteristics similar to the species,' Riz said. Oona could not help giggling.

'Which animal species do you belong to?' he asked her.

'No idea,' Oona laughed, telling him the year of her birth.

Riz calculated and told her, 'That places you in the year of the pig. It also makes you a decade younger than me. Shall we drink to that?' and they raised their glasses.

It was almost ten when they decided to have dinner. 'And where would you like to eat?' Riz asked. 'Papa Pancho da Dhaba?'

'It's your choice today. Why not move further towards Juhu? I am tired of the Yari Road eateries.'

'Okay. Let's see….something Italian? Say Al Fresco?' Riz asked.

'Sounds perfect. Great food, great ambience. Belongs to friends of mine, Sushant and Rohini,' Oona said.

'I know them too,' Riz said. The glamour fraternity was really a close-knit world in this city.

Oona and Riz were the last to leave the restaurant. It was past one in the morning and every guest had left. The waiters stood conspicuously around the couple, who seemed unaware of their surroundings. When Oona and Riz ignored the broad hints, the lights were dimmed, and finally Riz noticed. 'I think we need to go. Or soon they will be serving us breakfast,' he said with a smile.

Riz called for the bill but the waiter glanced at Oona and said that it was already paid. Riz looked accusingly at her. 'Did you have to do that?' 'It was my treat. Remember? For fixing the marble.' Oona said and they both laughed. It gave her an odd feeling of power to pick up the tab.

Walking out, Riz lit a joint he had rolled in the powder room just before leaving Al Fresco. 'Care for a drag?' he offered, holding out the cigarette to Oona. She tried clumsily but returned it to Riz saying, 'Don't waste it on me. I don't know how to handle such stuff. I can neither exhale nor inhale properly.'

'Then you are blessed, honey,' Riz said, taking the cigarette from her and taking a deep puff. 'And *inshallah* I hope you stay that way. Shall we call for an auto?' he asked.

'Can't we walk for a bit? Actually I don't mind walking back home, I love walking,' Oona said. She was enjoying Riz's company. She did not want the night to end. Ever. Besides, she did not have to worry about returning home as Anand was away.

'Walk? From Juhu to Yari Road? You must be joking!' He looked down at her feet. 'And in those stilettos?'

'Oh, I can run in them. I was born in heels,' Oona said, increasing her pace. Riz tried gallantly to catch up with her.

'You should have met my dad. He passed away two years ago. He could walk for miles together,' Riz said as he puffed away.

'La lalala, lala lalalala, lal lal la lalalalala....,' Oona hummed an old Nat King Cole tune.

'...walking my baby back home,' Riz sang the rest of the words for her.

Oona smiled at him. 'It's one of my favourites,' she hummed again. Riz nodded. Wish he would at least hold my hand, Oona thought, but Riz continued puffing at the joint.

Oona considered reaching for Riz's hand, but she did not want to scare him away with a bold gesture. As they were about to cross the main road that separated Juhu from Versova, she pretended to look on haplessly as cars whizzed past at maddening speeds. It worked—Riz grabbed her hand and helped her cross the road. As soon as they reached the safety of the pavement, Riz let go. Oona was disappointed. They walked together in silence for a bit. 'You walk really fast honey. I need a lot more energy to keep up with you. Don't forget I am much older,' Riz smiled.

'Shall we take an auto then?' she asked. Now that it was clear holding hands was not on the agenda for Riz, there was no point walking all the way home in the dead of night.

Riz whistled and stopped a speeding autorickshaw. They got in, riding in silence for a minute. As they neared Oona's place Riz suddenly asked, 'Can I hold your hand? At least for the next forty-five seconds or so?' Oona held out her hand willingly and Riz took it. He entwined her fingers in his. She moved closer to him and squeezed his hands. He pressed her hand. Her bungalow arrived.

'Can you tell him to stop here?' Oona asked, barely audible. Riz nodded and motioned to the driver to stop. He disentangled her fingers from his. Oona got off and waved bye to him.

'Good night. Take care. Talk to you later,' Riz said. Oona nodded, still not believing what had happened a few seconds back.

As she switched off the lights in her bedroom, the phone beeped.

It was 1.50 in the morning. Oona got up to check the message: *Thanks once again. Nite, nite. Riz*

Oona messaged back: *And don't let the bed bugs bite.*

Oona was not quite sure whether to call Riz the next evening. But he called her at five. 'Can we meet at Barista for a cuppa say in fifteen minutes?' Riz asked. Oona was relieved to be meeting on neutral ground. She walked in to find Riz waiting for her at the far end of the café. He got up and gave her a hug. She smiled. 'All well?' he asked. 'It's too dark indoors to be wearing your sunglasses, why don't you take them off?'

'No,' Oona was curt.

'Okay,' he said, sounding puzzled. 'What would you like? A cappuccino?' She nodded, taking off her glasses because she had to wipe her eyes. Riz noticed they were red and swollen. She had obviously been crying. 'All well at home?' he asked again.

'Yes.'

'How is Anandsaab? In Hyderabad did you say? Or was it Dubai, I forget?' Oona just nodded.

Riz decided not to probe further. Gradually, as she relaxed with her coffee, Oona admitted to being upset with Anand. He had called up just as she was leaving the house and the conversation had turned into an argument over Bobby coming over yet again. Oona had protested and

Anand insisted that she tolerate him. Sensing Rukman didi's interference, Oona remained adamant and Anand grew more and more abusive.

Riz listened sympathetically. 'My sister's interference caused my marriage to break up. I realise it now,' he admitted.

Changing the topic as they waited for the bill, Riz asked if she was free the next evening. 'There's a party at the Four Seasons, 9 pm onwards. Sponsored by Hum TV. I'm invited. Would you like to join me?'

'Sure,' Oona agreed.

'Let's leave at say…9.30?'

'Sounds fine by me. I'll pick you up then, across your building at 9.30?'

'Great,' Riz said. And, giving her a light hug, he left.

As Oona entered her car she received an SMS: *Atta girl! Cheer up! Riz.*

She smiled. Actually her spat over the phone with Anand was one of those routine ones. But she had captured Riz's attention by making a big deal out of it. She enjoyed playing the harrassed wife, she thought, grinning to herself.

Mrs Khanna's Lover

As Oona turned the car to pick him up, she noticed Riz leaning casually by the street-lamp, smoking. He was in a light pink shirt unbuttoned mid-way, revealing a white tee below. He looked like he had stepped straight out of a magazine ad. Oona loved his sense of style. Conservative and yet not wild. He dressed in what he knew suited his looks best.

Riz looked at her appreciatively without saying anything. Since the dress code was casual, Oona was in close-fitting brown stonewashed denims, topped with a Ritu Kumar chikankari shirt. She had accessorised it with an amber resin neckpiece and bracelet picked up on her last trip to London. Oona wished he would be more vocal in his compliments. After all, she had spent more time in front of the mirror this evening than she had done in a long while, trying out several outfits in order to look chic but not overdressed. And all for Riz.

Suddenly Riz said, 'Please stop if you spot a chemist.'

'What do you need from the chemist?' Oona asked.

'Just some boric powder. Cut my wrist. Don't want any infection to set in.'

Oona examined his wrist at the next red light. 'I think you'll be fine. It's only a minor nick.'

'No. I don't want to risk an infection.'

Oona found it strange but kept quiet, stopping at a nearby chemist so that he could get the boric powder before reaching the hotel.

As they entered the party lawns, television cameras flashed. Oona was careful to stand a little away from Riz as she did not want the media to catch on to her and Riz. Suddenly she noticed Honey Khanna, one of television's top producers. Anand had done some work for Honey and the latter was quite fond of Oona. Both hugged each other like long-lost friends. 'Good to see you. You are glowing!' Honey said, looking deliberately from Oona to Riz. 'And who do we have here? Mr Riz Ali. How are you, Riz?'

'Am good,' he hugged her. 'And Honey, you look gorgeous as always. How do you manage it?' Oona wished he would pay her the compliment instead. But she knew Riz hesitated because she was married to Anand Khanna.

Over drinks Honey and Oona talked more. 'You are such a talented writer. I really enjoy your columns. Why don't you write a short telefilm for me?' Honey asked.

'I would love to,' Oona began, fishing for excuses. She knew Honey was a poor paymaster. Suddenly she spotted Riz calling her from the opposite end of the lawn. 'Oh, Riz is calling me, excuse me,' she said, hurrying away.

'What's up?' Oona asked Riz.

'Shh…this.' He held up a cigarette.

'A cigarette? You could have smoked it at the table,' Oona exclaimed.

'Oh. Bad boys don't smoke cigarettes,' said Honey, coming up to them. She'd followed Oona. 'I'm sure Alex must have rolled it for you?' Alex was a beefy six-foot-tall American, Honey's latest toy boy.

Riz took a long, slow drag and inhaled slowly. 'Gosh! This stuff's strong. I will be dead in six months' time if I have this regularly,' Riz said. He offered it to Oona but Honey pushed his hand down, 'Don't spoil her. I'm protecting her, since Anand isn't here!'

Oona realised that Riz stiffened at mention of Anand. She herself wished his name hadn't come up.

'*Chalein*? It's past midnight. Ready to leave or would you like some dinner?' Riz asked when Honey left to say hello to a friend.

'No, I don't like hotel buffets. Besides, I ate at home.' 'Me too,' Riz smiled. 'What about heading out to the coffee shop? A cookie and coffee perhaps?'

Oona was delighted at the prospect of prolonging the evening. 'Great,' she said.

But the coffee shop was closed and the twenty-four-hour restaurant was packed with people. As they wondered where to go, Oona suddenly offered, 'We can go have coffee at my office. If you don't mind that is?' 'I don't mind, honey. But is it okay to go to your office this late?'

'I don't see why not.' Oona was sure she could trust Riz. And even if she couldn't, what the heck, he was sexy and she liked him!

The watchman gave Oona a knowing smile as she walked in with Riz. *I'd better remember to tip him on some pretext so he doesn't squeal.* Entering her office, she dimmed the lights before starting up the coffee. She didn't want curious neighbours wondering why Mrs Anand Khanna was working so late. She suddenly felt very tired of the charade of being Anand's wife. Pouring out the coffee, she sat down next to Riz with the box of cookies. 'Just help yourself. Am feeling too lazy to serve them on a plate.'

'That's all right, honey,' Riz said, setting aside the coffee and cookies. 'Can I give you a hug?'

Oona looked up at him, surprised. *Is that his pick-up line?* Polite as ever, he added, 'I feel like hugging you. Can I?'

'Sure.'

As Riz held her close, Oona's arms immediately encircled him. It felt divine to be held by a man who smelt that good, especially after Anand's alcohol-breath and sweaty armpits. She sighed, and Riz drew her even closer, rubbing her back in a soothing gesture. 'Thanks. It feels good,' Oona said softly.

'Honey, you deserve it. Let me give you a good massage,' and he began to gently massage her back. She moaned in pleasure and arched her back unconsciously. And suddenly, it was no longer just a massage. As she relaxed in his arms, Riz reached under her shirt, touching her soft flesh. When Oona didn't protest, he expertly unclasped her bra, fondling her breasts.

'Enjoying it, honey?' Riz asked, his voice hoarse. Oona moaned again. She could feel him hardening near her thighs. *I hope it's not a dream. It feels so good.*

'I want to kiss your breasts,' Riz said, as he started to undo her buttons. He lifted her on to the counter as he took off her top and bra. 'You're so beautiful,' he groaned, kissing and caressing her breasts, neck and then her whole body. His tongue went below her navel. Oona was moaning in delight. Riz reached for her zipper and unzipped her jeans, gently pulling them off. When he touched her black lace panties, Oona stiffened. Riz noticed and asked, 'Is it okay?'

Oona smiled. 'Actually, it is just that you are the first man I have known other than my husband in so many years of marriage.' Riz kissed her forehead.

'You sure, honey?' he asked again. Oona nodded.

'I don't know, but how do we go ahead with this?' Riz almost whispered. 'No strings attached?' he asked as he bit her earlobe. Oona was already in love with him, but she nodded, looking down at herself naked on the kitchen counter.

'So do you still want to go ahead?'

Oona hugged Riz and kissed him on the lips.

'Let's not stop... what the hell! You only live once,' Oona whispered. Riz's fingers were curled between her legs. She wanted him to strip. *Not fair. He's still fully dressed while I'm sitting here stark naked!*

Riz gently pushed her till she was lying back. 'You are so bloody sexy, Oona.' He touched her intimately, 'Gosh! You are wet!' he exclaimed, parting her legs further. She felt his tongue probing deep inside her.

Her heartbeat raced madly. She had never experienced such pleasure before. His tongue went into a frenzy as her excitement built. His hands clasped hers. Oona was in ecstasy and came with a loud cry. 'Riiiz,' she moaned as her body quivered. Riz lifted his head and Oona saw his chin glistening in the dark. He wiped his face and grinned, 'Boy! What a volcanic eruption!'

Oona lay back and smiled. 'I feel bad.'

'Why?' Riz asked.

'You need to feel good too,' she said, trying to rub his penis through his trousers.

'But I feel twice as good when you feel good, honey,' Riz said, gently removing her hands before he could harden in response to her touch.

Oona found this hard to believe. Men were such a selfish lot. She had thought Riz just wanted easy sex with her. Anand always looked for his own gratification during sex, seldom Oona's. And here was Riz trying to pleasure her as much as he could.

Is he a masochist? Or a saint? Why is he doing this for me?

It was in the wee hours of the morning that Oona and Riz finally left her office. Riz left first, on foot, and waited for her at the head of the road. Oona drove up to him a little later. She turned towards his building but Riz insisted she drive on till her house.

'I will not be comfortable leaving you alone at the wheel at this hour,' he said, brushing aside her protests. Finally, just a building away from Oona's bungalow, Riz got off, giving her a light peck on the cheek. Oona watched him in her rear-view mirror as she drove to her gate. By the time she woke the night watchman and had the gate opened, Riz had whizzed by in an auto. She went to bed, but lay awake, replaying the events of that magical evening. Oona wished it had not ended. She wished it would continue.

'Hi,' Riz called her later in the afternoon. 'Did you sleep well?'

'Not really. You? Did you get some sleep?' Oona asked.

'Nope. Not a bit. I actually had to leave for Delhi—there's a fundraiser for an HIV NGO I helped organise.'

'Oh,' Oona didn't remember him mentioning it. 'I see. Okay, try and get some sleep now so that you are all fresh by evening.'

As Oona drifted to sleep early that night, her cellphone beeped: *At US embsy. Sleep like an Angel! Gud nite! Riz*

Four days later, Riz called her. 'Am back this evening. How are you? And Anandsaab?'

'Am well. Anand's still in Dubai. What time is your flight? I'll pick you up at the airport—I'm relatively free,' Oona lied. She had a press conference to attend but decided she'd depute one of the trainee subs.

'Oh, please don't bother. I would much prefer taking a cab. What if the flight is delayed?'

'Okay, Riz, then let's have dinner together. At my office.' Oona had not met him since they'd made love. 'I missed you.'

'Me too. See you for dinner then. I'll call the moment I land. Bye for now.'

At five minutes past eight, Riz messaged: *Just landed! C u in abt 45 mins or less dependng on trafic. Riz*

Am waiting. C u soon. Oona texted back.

He arrived nearly an hour later, looking dapper in a light beige suit, with a Calvin Klein overnighter and a box of *chhena murgis*. 'For you. Delhi's specialty,' he said, handing her the box. 'Gosh! Bombay's warm,' he said, taking off the coat. 'But I had to wear the suit as I had an embassy lunch. One of those suit-and-tie affairs,' he shrugged. Oona wished Riz had hugged her.

'All well back home?' Oona asked. 'You kind of overstayed your visit.'

'Yes. I had to meet my psychiatrist. I've been a bit stressed out with family problems. I mentioned you to her,' Riz said.

'Oh.'

'Here,' Riz pulled Oona close and kissed her lips. 'Honey, I missed you.' He started to caress her. Oona loved it and responded with equal fervour. Before long, Riz started to undress her. Not to be outdone, Oona began unbuttoning his shirt. As she started to unclasp his belt, Riz lifted her, naked, onto the kitchen platform and started kissing her inner thighs. Soon his tongue was inside, probing at a furious pace. She came quickly, moaning loudly in sheer ecstasy. Riz had to quickly stifle her moans so no passer-by would hear. After all, it was barely ten o'clock and Bombay at this hour was wide awake and kicking.

ꕥ

Oona lay awake half the night thinking of Riz. He sure gave great blow jobs! Better than any sex she had had with Anand or Craig. But she was puzzled by his refusal to undress, in spite of having an attractive body. And he did not force himself on her though he knew she would not mind. Maybe he was biding his time. She was not complaining.

ꕥ

R u free this eve? Riz messaged a few days later.

Ji. Oona texted back.

Want 2 c a film @ 8? he asked.

Sure.

Mr & Mrs Smith or Parineeta, madame?

Mr & Mrs.

C u @ 7.30 in front of gas stn

OK.

After the film, Riz asked where Oona would like to go for dinner. 'Want to try the new restobar Echoes near Juhu beach?' he asked.

'What about my place instead?' Oona countered. 'We can order whatever you feel like.' It had been a while since Riz had given her a blow job and Echoes did not sound like the ideal place for that.
'Sure. Let's head there then,' Riz said with a smile as they exchanged knowing looks.

As Oona was clearing the counter post dinner, Riz came up and pulled her close. 'Can't that wait, honey?' He kissed her.

'It can but I like to clear things up before I leave the kitchen area,' Oona returned with a smile.

'Go ahead. Actually I kind of like my women tidy considering I am such a messy sort,' Riz went off to light a joint.

While doing the dishes, Oona noticed that Riz had gone to the bathroom but left the door ajar. Finishing up, she went to the door to see Riz busy working on the tubelight above the sink mirror.

'Don't bother,' Oona said. 'It's not been working for some time. I'll get the electrician to fix it tomorrow.'

'It's almost done. Just get me a screwdriver,' Riz asked, fitting the holder back in place. Oona had a tool box in a cupboard and brought it to him. She watched him work. Ever since Riz entered her life, he had been using his skills to fix things in her studio. First it was the marble, then he had lubricated a door handle with something as simple as Vaseline. 'You know my wife used this to lubricate herself before sex,' he had said, holding up the jar of petroleum jelly. 'You, of course, don't need it.' Oona had blushed. He had fixed up a couple of her wobbly tables. He also got her a set of four small whisky glasses when he realised she only had wine glasses. He fixed the speakers of her music system up on the wall for better acoustics. And the previous week he had also repaired the sink tap, which was leaking. *Gosh! The whole place is a reminder of Riz.*

'Done,' Riz said, showing her his handiwork.

'Can't say I am impressed. I am bowled over by your ingenuity. You are a genius!' Oona cooed.

'Hey, someone else said that to me before. My ex-father-in-law.'

'I wholeheartedly agree with him.'

Riz could see the look of admiration in her eyes.'Now, want a hug, honey?' Riz asked with a mischievous glint. Oona nodded naughtily, knowing very well what would follow. After a bit of foreplay, Oona told Riz hoarsely, 'Let's go there,' she pointed to the inner room, where her study was located. The kitchen counter was a little uncomfortable for the two of them. They went in and Riz looked around, pulling out her yoga mat and spreading it on the floor.

Slowly, he undressed her, only to realise that she was undressing him simultaneously. 'Ouch! You've managed to undress me completely,' Riz said, trying to suck in his already flat tummy. Oona pulled in her abs too. Both stood completely naked, admiring each other's bodies. '*Chaliye*. You have seen me completely naked now,' Riz sat down and pulled Oona down towards him on the mat.

'Big deal,' Oona returned. 'As if I have been in a *burqa* all along!' They started kissing passionately. She could feel him harden. She held him gently and tried to guide him inside her. Riz almost entered her but suddenly pulled away. 'Riz,' Oona was hoarse. 'I want you inside me. Now. Please.'

Riz caressed her hair and kissed her. 'Not now honey, some other time. Please.' Before Oona could react his tongue was already probing her.

She enjoyed it but her mind was distracted. She wondered what made Riz hesitate. *Is he worried I might get pregnant? He'd mentioned a rich socialite who tried to tie him down with a pregnancy.* 'Thank God she miscarried,' Riz had remarked earlier.

But he should know me better by now. We made it clear no strings attached. Besides, I'm married. She came eventually, after a long time, 'erupting like a volcano' as Riz liked to say. Oona lay back in bliss and Riz lay beside her, watching her.

'Something worrying you, honey?'

'Why don't you make love to me, Riz?'

'Then what am I doing here? Masturbating?'

'No. Not that. I mean…'

'Well, I told you I haven't been keeping well,' Riz tried to explain. 'The doctor says erectile dysfunction or some such thing. So it will take a while before I am able to…'

'Please,' Oona cut in. 'I am not a kid. I've felt you harden several times. And Mr Ali, I know what erectile dysfuntion is. Mr Khanna suffers from it. Are you scared of getting me pregnant? In that case get a rubber next time.' Oona turned away.

Riz leaned over and kissed her ears. 'Honey, try and understand. I am not a masochist. It's just that I am a bit of a coward knowing Anandsaab's hold in the industry. I cannot afford to jeopardise my position at this stage. Next time we will use a rubber,' he smiled. Oona pulled him towards her and bit his lobe.

'Ouch!' he screamed, feigning pain. 'Don't! I have a shoot for that silly shaving cream tomorrow. And I bruise easily.' He tried to get up.

Oona held him down. 'Let's lie down for a bit,' she hugged him. He patted her bum.

'C'mon now. It's late. I have an early morning shoot. And I don't have a car or driver. I am a one-man army. C'mon honey. Upsadaisy!'

Mid-morning next day Oona's phone beeped: *On d set. Stil somtime 2 shoot u bet! Take a nap when u can my angel, I hope 2 do d same in d vanity van!*

Oona was touched. She kept reading and re-reading his old messages throughout the day.

At 11 a.m. she got a call from the *Post* reminding her to send in her copy. Oona realised she had almost slipped up on her deadline. 'Ouch' she said aloud.

While coffee with Riz had become a minor addiction, dinner with Riz became an even stronger one. Almost an affliction. For the fortnight Anand was away, she and Riz met almost every other day. At her office pad. Almost like criminals. Like Constance in *Lady Chatterley's Lover*. When Oona had first read Lawrence's classic in college, she'd wondered why it was such a big deal. Now, in twenty-first century Bombay, stealing moments with Riz, she was in the same boat, and realised the social consequences. She empathised with Connie's predicament despite a near-century separating their haplessness. There was not much difference in the circumstances of Mrs Khanna's lover and Lady Chatterley's.

She wished Anand would never return. That she would never have to go through a messy divorce. Hurt her mother. That Riz would continue to make love to her, showering her with charm and attention. That his wife would stay away from him. And that this moment in her life would continue forever.

'Hi Madhu,' Oona said into the phone when she saw Madhusudan Mishra's name on an incoming call.

'Hi, babes. Believe you enjoyed *Sadak*. Considering all the other critics have panned it, why don't you write something nice about it in your column?' Mishra was an upcoming Bollywood director and *Sadak* was his second film—a damp squib after his debut hit *Madhushala*. A complete washout, Oona had thought. Riz had taken Oona to see it some days back as he had a bit role in it. 'I always do bit roles. Before you can rub your eyes, I am gone in a flash,' he had said. Oona loved his self-deprecatory comment. So refreshingly different from Anand's vanity.

'How did you know I had gone to see *Sadak*?' Oona asked, about to add that she hated the film.

'*Arrey*, Rizbhai told me. You guys had gone together to see it.'

'Yup, I'll see what I can do,' Oona politely hung up. She got the drift. Riz must have taken her name praising the film to the director, knowing a film critic's comments carried more weight than an actor's.

That way, he was ensuring his bit roles in future Mishra projects. A bit unlike Riz, Oona thought.

ꕥ

Anand was back in town and Oona told Riz they would have to be careful for the next few days. He sounded upset, responding with a sarcastic, 'Lovely!'

'It's just a few days, honey. He's scheduled to leave for London next week. We'll have all the time in the world to ourselves then,' Oona assured him.

'Anandsaab will obviously want his wife there with him!'

'Well, I do usually accompany him. But I would rather be with you. I'm planning to use work as an excuse,' Oona shrugged.

'Honey, don't have to change your plans for me,' Riz said, hanging up. Oona was hurt.

ꕥ

Sory 4 being nasty yesterday. Apologies. Can v meet for a drink at ur pad this eve? Lov. Riz.

'Riz,' Oona called him. 'Anand's in town. I'm not sure we should meet. But I've been meaning to tell you a few things for some time.'

'Yeah, I know I was a bit abrupt. A little upset. But I need to see you for a bit. Been missing you,' Riz insisted.

Oona felt wanted. 'Okay. Let's catch up. I'll cook up some excuse for Anand. See you at 8.30. Bye.'

'Thanks honey. Bye.'

ꕥ

'Who else is going out with you and Deepa?' Anand asked as he watched his wife taking extra care over her appearance.

'It's just the two of us. Why?'

'No,' Anand remarked idly. 'Just wondering why you are dressing up so much to go for a movie with Deepa.'

Oona ignored the comment. 'Pandeyji will drop me to the theatre and Deepa will drop me back,' she said. Anand nodded. Oona used Deepa's name as a ready excuse. She was one friend Anand wouldn't bump into. He knew her only vaguely and she lived mostly in Nashik with her brother. Shalini and Bina Mashi were complete hazards, as Anand could easily check with them.

After Pandeyji dropped her, she pretended to wait for her friend. As soon as the car was out of sight, Oona hopped into an auto and headed to her office. She was just putting on some music when Riz rang the bell.

It was past eleven when they finished dinner. Riz had drunk a lot and topped it with a joint. As he held her, Oona felt him harden. He began to undress her when she stiffened. Riz stopped halfway. 'What is the matter? You seem preoccupied.'

'Just a little worried,' Oona said. 'Anand is virtually next door. He knows I have gone for a night show with a girlfriend. What if he just walked in and saw us....'

Riz pulled himself away. 'Okay, let's go honey.' He was upset.

'Please. Riz. I did not mean it this way. I love you... you know,' she held him and kissed him. 'I don't care about Anand. I'll take the risk.'

It took a few minutes for them to get back into the mood. This time Riz first undressed himself and then her, carrying her to the inner room. He laid her down on the yoga mat and gently put a cushion under her head. He kissed her passionately and she could feel his erection against her legs. She held him and tried to guide him inside her. He paused, and Oona raised her head to see him putting on a rubber. 'Just a second, honey,' his voice was hoarse with desire.

'I'd love you without that rubber. I don't want anything coming in between us,' Oona whispered, only to gasp as Riz entered her. She was in heaven. This was the moment she had been waiting for. She moaned in pleasure.

'Liking it?' Riz asked gently. As Oona nodded he started pushing harder. Oona wound her legs tight around him and came like a maniac.

Not once, but twice. Finally, Riz asked, 'I am ready. Would you like me to hold on while you come again?'

'No…yes….' She pushed again. Moments later she moaned, 'Ah… aah…Ri…riiiz….I love you,' as Riz and she came together this time.

'Love you baby,' Riz whispered between pants.

She didn't care if Anand walked in. Riz was worth the risk. Oona was in love and she let her heart rule her head.

'So how was the film?' Anand asked. He was awake, reading a book in her room. 'Which film was it?' Oona was surprised to see him in the bedroom. He had of late taken to sleeping in the guest bedroom again.

'*Black Friday*. It was okay,' Oona said as she changed into her pyjamas. She hesitated to slip into bed, and hovered around the edge of the bed instead, waiting for Anand to leave the room.

'Long film! It's nearly half past twelve.'

'Yeah, kind of,' Oona said, getting up. 'Goodnight, Anand. I think I'll go sleep in the guest room.'

'*Abey*,' Anand pulled her down on the bed, facing him. 'Who said anything about goodnight. I have missed my wife. What is the point of keeping a wife if I am not allowed to fuck her?' Anand was drunk and began to rub himself against her.

Oona tried to turn her face away when he kissed her, his breath smelling of a stale mixture of cigarettes and alcohol. Riz's breath never smelt though he too smoked and drank, Oona thought. She did not want Anand to overwhelm the beautiful memories of Riz's love making, barely an hour ago. She could still feel Riz all over her mind and body.

'Anand,' Oona pleaded. 'Please, I don't want to….please don't force me.'

'*Chal saali*,' he cursed. 'It takes just a few minutes. Who told you to tire yourself watching silly films? You should be looking after your husband. I've been away so long slogging for you!'

'But Anand, please. I cannot go on living this charade with you…'

'In my house you have to do as I say. If you leave, you can go do whatever…' Anand said cruelly.

He started to rip off her pyjamas, not bothering with her shirt or his own. He just pulled off his own pyjamas and lifted her shirt to chew on her nipples. Oona decided it would be best not to resist Anand. She spread her legs and let him enter her though she was sore from the marathon lovemaking with Riz.

'Bitch!' Anand groaned as he entered her. Oona wondered whether he was on Viagra. She had discovered some once when he came back from a shoot out of town. 'I love you, you bitch.' Anand grunted as he humped her. '*Saali*, you've have been using my perfume again,' Anand said groaning with pleasure. *Oops! That was close.* Oona knew it was Riz's aftershave he could smell. 'I love my little Bangalan,' Anand said, panting and then screamed her name as he came.

Oona felt like a slut. Two men in the space of an hour! Tears streamed down her face. She did not know why.

Thankfully, Anand did not see them in the dark. He had slumped over on the other side of the bed in complete carnal satisfaction.

Charades

The next two months were pure bliss for Oona. She refused to go to London with Anand, though he insisted. She had begun ignoring Shalini, too. She had no time for gossip anymore. Shalini missed her passport to high-society events and criticised Oona to anyone who would listen. Oona missed Heena of course, and even Sonia, but after a long time, she had a good companion in Riz. They had similar taste in music, literature and art. They argued over Louis Armstrong (Oona's favourite) and Bob Dylan (Riz's favourite) but had fun teasing each other the whole time. When he was in town, Riz spent almost every other day with Oona, meeting in the studio in the evenings over drinks, staying till the wee hours. They also went for movies, plays and parties, making sure the shutterbugs didn't catch them.

One evening as they dined out, an elderly lady walked up to their table and greeted Riz. 'Remember me? Mrs Rosario. You stayed as a PG in my Hill Road bungalow twenty years ago? I am Brendon's mother.'

'Oh yes, Ma'am. I remember,' Riz got up to hug her. 'And how have you been? How is Brendon?'

'He is fine. Sailing. Somewhere near Florida at present. And you? How have you been? Don't see you much these days.' Mrs Rosario turned to Oona and smiled, 'Your wife?' she asked Riz.

'No. Not yet,' Riz smiled at Oona.

'Oh! How sweet! I must tell Brendon I met you. All the best to you two. Enjoy your meal. Bye.'

Oona could not help blushing as the lady walked away.

'Hey!' Riz nudged her. 'All well?'

'What do you mean "not yet"? Was that an indirect proposal?' Oona asked.

'Who knows?' Riz shrugged. 'Next time I'll take you around in a *burqa*.'

Oona did not quite know what to make of that. She wished she could marry Riz right now. No messy divorce, no mudslinging. Just run away with Riz without the moral police chasing her.

After years of boredom and stagnation, these were the best months in her life. She and Riz spent more nights discreetly in her studio. The watchman was the major beneficiary of Oona and Riz's clandestine love. Oona tipped him regularly so that he would not sing. Riz would also flatter him with a *namaste* and Ramu would give him an extra attentive salute. It was a windfall for the young man. And no one found out.

Though they managed to keep the secret, the affair reflected in their lives. The late nights with Oona and increased alcohol and hash intake were taking their toll on Riz's health. He had bouts of dizziness and insomnia. He was up all night and slept through the major part of the day.

As for Oona, while her columns were as spunky as always, she began slipping up on major assignments. Shahnaz called to ask if all was well. 'All well, why?' Oona seemed in a rush.

'You're missing major assignments these days. And there have been complaints of some howlers in your copy. So I thought I'd check on you,' Shahnaz said. 'You are my favourite columnist and I would hate to see you mess up like Mimiii Saluja. Get it?'

Oona thanked her and apologised. 'Sorry, just busy settling in at the new place,' she lied.

One day Riz brought some old photos to show Oona. 'That's my dad, and this is mom. Here is my brother Feroz, Attiya, my sister. And here is the wife,' he pointed indifferently.

'Why do you hate her so much?' Oona asked.

'Because she fucked up my life big time,' Riz said.

'Hey, chill. It takes two to tango,' Oona said. Riz glared. 'Okay *baba*, sorry. Then why don't you divorce her?'

'She is happy this way. Besides, till I find somebody, it's fine by me.'

He of course did not mention that she sustained him financially, which Oona had found out from some other source. He pulled out another album. 'These are some photos from my modelling days.' He pointed, 'Here, this is the Camel Lites ad. And this is the Brent Suitings ad which I did with my friend Victor,' he pointed to the handsome model next to him.

The face looked familiar. So was the name. 'Victor who?' Oona asked.

'Bose. You asked me before,' Riz said.

So this was Hector Bose's elder brother, Oona realised. She had never met him. He had gone to London to pursue his higher studies but returned mid-way to pursue a modelling career in Mumbai. He had done well as a model though not as well as Riz.

'I know him,' Oona said. 'Rather I know *of* him. He is from Cal. My neighbour. Lived in the next lane. In fact I knew his brother well. Hector. Is this the same Victor?'

'Oh you know Hector as well,' Riz said. 'Small world.'

'How do you know Hector?' Oona asked.

'Well, I met him a couple of times through my sister Attiya. They used to fly together for Cathay. He is junior to her in service years though.' Riz said.

'I haven't met him in years. Is he still flying Cathay?' Oona asked.

'I don't think so. Last I heard, he was working in London with British Airways. I caught up with Victor four years ago in London when

I was there—he isn't doing much. Works as a freelance photographer. He promised to make my current portfolio but we never got around to doing it,' Riz said. 'I can check with Attiya about Hector or maybe through Victor.'

'Yeah, please. I would love to connect with Hector. Used to be a good buddy. I was quite close to his parents. You know, his mom is Irish. I wonder where Aunty Maive and Uncle Bose are now. When I last went to Cal, I heard they sold their house, Bose Mansion, to some builder. It was the prettiest bungalow in our lane.'

'I think their father passed away some years back. That is what Victor told me when I last met him. And I think his mother lives in England. I can find out if you want.'

'Please. Aunty Maive was such a darling,' Oona recalled fondly.

Busy whole day 2day on projct. Will tel u later. Spoke 2 attiya. Hector B stays in London. Left Cathay. With BA when attiya last met him 2 yrs bak. Not in touch now. Wil find out frm Vic n let u kno. Ciao.Riz

Thx. Catch u latr. Miss u. Oona.

Later in the day, Riz messaged her: *Victor B, 18/21, Lexham Gardens, Kensington, Lond SW1 Cell: 00447882188203 email vicbos@aol.com. Ciao and take care.*

My Name is Khanna

Anand returned to the city in the best mood Oona had seen in ages. There was an air of excitement about him. Oona wondered if it was a new chick, but these days Anand was steering clear of women, including the ones from his past. Of course, he continued to flirt with them at social gatherings. It was work-related, Oona decided, when she saw that he and Mannuji seemed to be going in and out of endless meetings. She was very curious but didn't want to ask. One day she caught him in an expansive mood. They were having coffee together after ages. She asked Anand, 'Some interesting project? Tell me *na*, what's up?'

'Okay, but first promise you will not tell anyone. Not a whisper out of this room,' Anand said. 'Also not a hint in your column till I give you the go-ahead.'

Oona promised.

Anand told her that he had had several meetings with Sameer Shah and Shah's production house and they were working on a big project together. This was big news and a big break for Anand who, though a respected and successful producer, had never been in the big league with the Shahs and the Khans. He was known as a producer of moderately successful, low-budget films rather than blockbusters.

'Wow!' was all Oona could say.

'Keep your fingers crossed. Lot of money involved and competitors are always ready to pull you down,' Anand said, referring to Badshah Khan.

'Are you also putting in your money?' Oona asked, concerned. She knew the industry's fortunes were fluctuating, and besides, Anand's production house had not been doing too well.

'Yeah. But only a bit. It is mainly Sameer's money. He says he wants to use my expertise because he admires my career graph and knowledge of the industry. And as for me, it's the opportunity of a lifetime to work for such a big banner,' Anand said.

Oona poured herself more coffee and offered some to Anand, who refused. After a while he said, 'But this one's going to be the mother of all projects. It's a love story which blossomed in the Taj Mahal Hotel during the 26/11 attack.'

'Hmm,' Oona said. 'Sounds interesting.'

'Interesting? It is a mind-blowing concept. Shah's flair for a large-canvas romance and my flair for real-life high-tension drama will make a wonderful onscreen confluence. This will be a first in Bollywood. That is why it is top secret,' Anand sounded charged.

'But don't you think the memories of 26/11 are too fresh, too raw? Won't it bring back painful memories for the victims' families?'

'*Arrey* that is the whole point *na*. Can't you see? If we do not cash in on it now, when will we ever? When it is a stale and forgotten subject? Now is the time people will come to see such a film,' Anand said.

'Boy! You guys are so insensitive?' Oona said, disgusted.

'We? *Jaan*, we are not as insensitive as you guys. No one can beat the media for that. You don't allow people to mourn in private, creating a public *tamasha* of death.'

'That I agree with wholeheartedly.' Oona accepted.

'It's also going to be the most expensive and extravagant film in Bollywood so far,' Anand continued. 'After all, Shah has to prove that he is one up on Badshah Khan. Badshah's *Baarish Ki Woh Raat* was such a hit. Now Shah has to prove that if Khan is the Badshah of Bollywood then he is the Shahenshah! Each trying to outsmart the other,' Anand concluded.

'Hmm, it's a strange coincidence that if one makes a film on hockey the other makes a film on cricket; if one makes a film on Chandragupta, the other makes a film on Tughlaq; if one cashes in on the 26 July floods, the other cashes in on 26/11,' Oona observed. Anand nodded.

'So who's the female lead? I assume Sameer will play the male lead?'

'Not yet decided. There is enough time before the film goes on the floor,' Anand replied.

'Have you guys decided on the title yet?' Oona asked.

'Yes. But I've been told not to disclose it to anyone.'

'Oh c'mon, Anand. Tell me *na*. Please?'

'Okay. But promise you will not tell anyone?'

'Promise.'

'*My Name is Khanna.*'

'Honey, don't I know that,' Oona said sarcastically.

'The film is titled *My Name is Khanna*,' Anand repeated.

'Whaaat?' Oona asked. 'You must be joking!'

'No I am not. I like the title a lot but am not sure if everyone else will agree. It is the story of a middle-class Maharashtrian girl working at the Taj who put duty before herself by saving as many guests as she could. Ajay Khanna is the NSG commando who kills two terrorists and saves her in the end,' Anand explained in the typically Bollywood style 'brief story narration'.

A few months later *My Name is Khanna* went on the floors, shot in a huge studio near Panvel where the Taj Bombay was recreated by Bollywood's top set designer, Kiron Dasgupta, in painstaking detail. Sheetal Jha, a new girl from Patna, was chosen to play the lead opposite Sameer Shah after thousands of hopefuls auditioned for the role. Anand spent most of his time in Panvel and Oona and Riz continued to meet regularly.

Midway during the shoot, controversy broke out in the media over the filming of *My Name Is Khanna.* Apparently two journalists from a vernacular daily were barred entry to the sets. The only media person allowed in was Ashwin Sinha, who also doubled as Shah's publicist. Shah retained him monthly and paid him four times what he normally earned from his freelance writing.

Mimiii Saluja slammed Shah for his high-handed attitude to the vernacular media in her column. Obviously Mimiii had fallen out with Sameer Shah since the days of *Chandragupta.* Of late she leaned towards the Badshah Khan camp.

Oona Khanna refrained from commenting on the issue. People began saying that she was losing her integrity and protecting her husband. In reality she was too preoccupied with Riz to bother about Anand's film.

The controversy soon died down. Filming continued.

Four months later, filming was complete for the most expensive film in Bollywood history.

At the editing console, Shah and Khanna realised their blunder. The film did not match their expectations. When the final print was ready a few months later, Shah and Khanna invited ten genuine well-wishers, including Oona, to watch it. Post screening, gauging the reaction of their friends, both realised that the film was not just a blunder, it was blunder of Himalayan proportions.

Back home, Anand asked Oona what she thought of the film.

'Not much,' Oona told him honestly.

'Just keep it to yourself. You have not seen the film. You know nothing. Get it?' Anand told her.

Oona nodded, wondering about Anand's next move. At times like these he could be as slippery as a snake.

Two days later Anand and the great Sameer Shah were deep in conversation in the den. Oona overheard snatches of their discussion while serving them tea and refreshments.

'Oona, being your wife, is no good,' Sameer said. Oona's ears cocked up. 'The press will say she is being partial.'

'They will say the same if Sinha writes. Half the world knows he is on your payroll,' Anand justified.

'I know, I'm not even thinking of him,' Sameer said.

'Our only option is Mimiii Saluja,' Anand said.

'Mimiii Saluja!!' Shah exclaimed. 'But she is in the Khan camp.'

'Camp loyalties can be bought. The media is always on sale,' Anand cut in, 'I have an idea. It is the media which always uses us. This time let us turn the tables.'

'What do you have in mind exactly?' Shah asked.

'Common sense. We use them. Starting with Mimiii Saluja. Later, let us start using one against the other, like Sinha against Saluja. They have no loyalty to their papers. Or their counterparts. Unlike us. They are only loyal to money—a greedy bunch.'

The Daily

> Sameer Shah's latest extravagance *My Name is Khanna,* which will be released in theatres a fortnight from now, is out to cash in on the sentiments of 26/11. That is all very well.
>
> The story revolves around the romance and bravery of a Mumbai chi mulgi and a Punjabi commando, part of the NSG, who rescues the damsel in distress. That is all very well too.
>
> What I fail to see is that while everyone is bleeding the state to death, making the most of the Mumbai pain post 26/11, why isn't the state of Maharashtra benefitting?
>
> The producer is from Punjab. The lead star from Aligarh. All very well. At least he essays the role of a North Indian.
>
> But what about the heroine who is an *amchi mulgi*? Did she have to be imported from Bihar? Like our cabbies? Isn't there a single Maharashtrian girl in this city who could essay the role? What about our Mrunalini Dikshit or Rekha Deshpande?
>
> Jai Ho but not to Maharashtra in this case. Sad but true.
>
> Mimiii Saluja

The next day the Narangi Dal took out *morchas* and went around threatening theatre owners who screened *My Name is Khanna* that they would burn down the place.

Distributors started backing out. No one took the Narangi Dal lightly in Bombay.

Posters of the film were torn down. Effigies of Sameer Shah were burnt.

Sameer doubled his security and Anand got himself round-the-clock cover.

Oona stopped meeting Riz as she was also under police protection.

Daily Mirror

> Mimiii Saluja is being parochial. Why can't Sheetal Jha (though no country cousin of mine) play a Marathi mulgi? Just as Mrunalini Dikshit played a Punjabi kudi in Dil Pe Dil?
>
> Does Ms Saluja nee Apte have a problem with this or with Mr Shah? Personal problems should be ironed out personally and a public forum should not be used to hit someone below the belt.
>
> I have seen the film. And it is brilliant.
>
> Ashwin Sinha

Mimiii retaliated in her next column:

> *I don't care if it is a bloody brilliant film. Marathi sentiments have been hurt.*

Sinha's response in his column:

> *Do we let political sentiments rule over the artistic beauty of a film?*

It was open war now. The Narangi Dal hoodlums were vandalising theatres that promoted the film. Sameer Shah appealed to the public on national television to stay calm. He requested them to watch the film, assuring them of full police protection so that the people would not bow down to regional fundamentalists.

Oona followed the events with much amusement. She wondered why Mimiii Saluja was taking such a stance against the film considering Shah was planning to buy her over. *Did he and Anand fail to buy her out? Or was it just a ploy in a bigger game plan? Anand's favourite Machiavellian line was:* 'You've got to lose the battle to win the war.'

Some days later, Sameer Shah publicly apologised to the people of Mumbai that he had been mistaken in not choosing a Maharashtrian girl to play his heroine. He admitted that it would have lent the role a stamp of authenticity. He publicly sought forgiveness from the Narangi Dal and appealed to audiences to make *My Name is Khanna* a success.

The Narangi Dal supremo accepted Shah's apology via the national channel. He said that mistakes were human and forgivable, so long as people realised their fault and apologised. He requested his Dal workers not to vandalise the theatres and told the public to go ahead and watch the film. He even gave it the thumbs-up, saying Shah had held a private screening for him and that he had enjoyed it.

My Name is Khanna was sold out three days before its release.

For the first time Anand Khanna could not get tickets for himself for the first week's show where he normally sent his domestic staff. He gave them each a 1,000-rupee note instead.

Shah and Khanna were laughing all the way to the bank.

People saw it as a publicity stunt. But Mimiii complained that 'the Narangi Dal was bought over.'

Perhaps it was not a publicity gimmick after all.

A few days later, while rummaging through Anand's bedside drawer for some papers, Oona stumbled upon an interesting piece of information. She noticed his cheque book and, flipping through it out of sheer curiosity, she found that three cheques had been made out to Mimiii Saluja, Dal Seva Comittee and Ashwin Sinha. The amounts were for thirty lakhs, one crore, and one lakh respectively.

Oona was puzzled to find these three strange bedfellows together in Anand Khanna's chequebook. Then she smiled, and picked up the phone to call Shahnaz.

The next day:

The Post
By a staff correspondent

Take this scenario.

2003:

Sameer Shah decided to make the epic *Chandragupta* using his own funds. The film did not live up to people's expectations. With a lot at stake, Shah immediately bought out the entire media along with the star ratings. The film opened as a hit. Then word of mouth got around that the film was terrible. The media was accused of being bought over. And rightly so. *Chandragupta* sank but just before Shah was able to recover part of his money, surviving by the skin of his teeth.

2009:

Six years later Shah's suppressed ambition surfaces. This time he ropes in veteran producer Anand Khanna. Despite Anand's caution, Shah makes another extravaganza, cashing in on 26/11, titled *My Name is Khanna* (nothing to do with the co-producer). Post production they realise the film will not click. But too much money is at stake now. So what does the duo do?

They launch the mother of all publicity gimmicks.

They buy out Mimiii Saluja for thirty lakhs to throw up a regional angle to it. Knowing Saluja and Shah don't get along too well, no one would suspect Khanna and Shah of a marketing gimmick.

Mimiii uses her Marathi card (she was Apte before marriage) and the services of the Narangi Dal to create the hype. This at the cost of a crore.

Finally an unsuspecting Bihari, Ashwin Sinha, is roped in as a sidekick to harp on the Bihari angle and react to Saluja. This for a pittance of a lakh. (Had Sinha been aware of the bigger gameplan, he would surely have upped his price manifold.)

Now the scenario is believable.

Narangi Dal hoodlums create nuisance within reasonable means.

They spread fear.

Distributors want to back out.

The public is curious.

Shah allegedly apologises to the Narangi Dal.

They call off their hoodlums.

Saluja still rants against Shah and Khanna.

The public is now certain the film is genuine. Shah is being unnecessarily framed.

My Name is Khanna is sold out.

Shah and Khanna laugh all the way to the bank.

And so do the Dal Seva Committee, Mimiii Saluja and Ashwin Sinha.

My Name is Khanna bombed.

Anand blasted Oona for the damaging article in *The Post.*

'You cannot blame me. It is by a staff correspondent,' Oona screamed.

'It is you. I know,' Anand screamed.

'How?'

'You think you are very clever, Madam. You slipped up. Mentioning *Chandragupta* was a dead giveaway.'

Oona almost bit her lip.

'I'll see how you survive in Bombay now,' Anand threatened.

Anand Khanna moved bag and baggage downstairs.

Crossroads

It had been six months since Oona and Anand had come to an arrangement that till they officially separated, Oona would occupy the upper floor of the bungalow while Anand lived downstairs. Fawzia Hasan, the women's activist-lawyer had briefly explained Oona's rights to Anand, and he decided not to rub people the wrong way. He was going through a low patch in his career. Mannuji was looking out for promising newcomers to represent, ones who had freshness and '*josh*' or drive. He had only half-hearted interest in the career of a has-been film-maker. The women from his past barely bothered him these days. He had been much more attractive when he could pick them up in a limo. And Oona had finally decided to move out of his life.

Oona had the run of the master bedroom and walk-in closet. They made some changes to the doors and staircases so that she and Anand had their own entrances leading directly into their section of the bungalow. Oona converted part of her bedroom into her study, moving in her old rosewood bureau and laptop and a leather-backed armchair for reading. Anand had taken his fancy home-theatre system downstairs so the empty lounge became Oona's private lounge to entertain the rare guests she called over. Oona turned the mini-gym into a bedroom for guests, mostly with her mother in mind. Sangeeta was getting on in age and Oona now wanted her to live closer. She modified the tiny kichenette to suit her current needs, bringing in the crockery and cutlery from her office. Her old faithful part-timer Renuka bai would come in the mornings to dust and clean the place, run the washing machine and get clean clothes ironed.

Oona had started contributing more than just her weekly column to *The Post*. She often went into the office and worked there if necessary. She was thrilled to be able to breathe free without Anand hounding her every time she stepped out. Of late she noticed Anand spent a lot of time by himself. She still enjoyed the perks of being Mrs Anand Khanna as very few outside their immediate circle of friends knew about their separation. Anand still referred to her as his wife in public and she maintained the same stance.

She put her studio on rent as she now had her own space in the house to work and entertain. The rent was a welcome bonus and took care of her driver's salary and gas bill. She had earlier wanted to let it out to Riz for free, but the latter cautioned her that Anand might become suspicious. Riz frequently came over to Oona's home, and they no longer had to clandestinely meet.

One morning, while leaving for work, Oona went to Anand's apartment to drop Sridevi off. The dog was now the only common factor between them. Anand seemed to have grown quite fond of Sridevi, and no longer abused the poor creature. He had insisted that Sridevi live downstairs so that she could enjoy the lawns and Pandeyji could take her for her walks. Oona took Sridevi up to her apartment whenever she liked. The dog roamed freely around both sections of the bungalow.

Seeing Oona, Anand, who was still at home, called out her name. He was reading the papers. '*Arrey* just read your cover story in *The Post*.' She walked to where he was holding out the day's paper, Sridevi scampering around them both. Looking at the paper, Oona saw it was the exposé she had done of the house-hunting story. It had been an idea that had stayed in her mind since the first time she learnt that Riz was having trouble finding an apartment for rent because of his religious identity. As she read, Anand smiled at her, 'I totally agree with you. Why don't you sit down. *Chai piyogey*? Or coffee?'

'I've just had coffee. Nothing, thanks,' Oona hesitated.

'*Arrey*, another cup won't matter. Once in a while you can have *chai* with me *na jaan*? And don't worry, I won't poison your tea. I'm not taking *panga* with a journalist. Am I crazy? Your *biradari* will hound me to death. Anyway, whatever has happened has happened. Let us at least be friends.'

Anand called to Shanta bai for two masala teas and some biscuits. He knew Oona never drank her tea without a biscuit. Oona noted this but steeled herself. The old Oona would melt with one kind word or gesture from Anand, but the new Oona found that Anand's mere presence angered her. She reasoned it was the years of crassness and meanness she had tolerated, or perhaps Riz's gentle presence in her life. Anand Khanna paled in comparison to Riz Ali when it came to his sophistication and affection for her.

'Like I was saying,' Anand interrupted her thoughts, presuming she was thinking about her story, 'Mumbai is not worth living in anymore. I was telling Rukmandidi to look for a house with land for me. Chandigarh real estate is too expensive, maybe in Mohali or some other place close by.'

This came as news to Oona. 'Why? Are you planning to shift to Chandigarh?' she asked.

'No *yaar*. Are you mad? Was planning to invest in some farmland in Maharashtra. Around Karjat, Panvel or Lonavala. Wanted to set up something like a resort. Now I am having second thoughts. Why invest in this state with the Narangi Dal's anti North-Indian thinking? Today they want to get rid of Biharis and Bhaiyas, next it will be Bengalis and Punjabis. *Kya bharosa*. One is safer in one's own territory. After all, Punjab is where my roots are. You'd also better be careful. Don't put all your eggs in one basket. Look out for options in Calcutta.'

'I don't have too many eggs to invest anywhere,' Oona said. 'Besides, I am so busy earning a living that I have no time to think of investments. And for me, Anand, Bombay is the only place I can think of working and living in now.' Oona said. 'Oh, what was this resort thing you mentioned?'

'Ah that. Bobby wanted to get into the hotel industry. I got him a seat in Dadar Catering College in the one-year intensive course. Had to pull a lot of strings. Hope he lasts the year. Thought of setting up a small resort near Karjat or Khandala. Those places see lots of film shooting but there are no decent cheap lodgings there. Thought Bobby can manage it.' He saw the look of shock on Oona's face and added, 'I know, I know. He is a waster. *Kya karein.* After all my blood *na,* however useless. Besides, I am going to make the bugger slog. I am going to keep an eye on him. I am thinking of doing fewer films now. Planning to retire. I'm practically a senior citizen!' Anand smiled.

You hardly behave like one. She didn't say it out loud, of course. She sat back and focused on finishing her tea quickly. Just then her phone beeped. She had a new message:

Just saw the Post. Wel researchd and wel written. Bold stance. I am touched Oona. Luking 4wd 2 catching up wid u sometime 2day. Take care and have a grt day. Thanks again.

It was Riz.

Anand looked on inquisitively as Oona smiled at the message. 'Some admirer?' he joked.

'No. Just a colleague. Female at that. Just sent a funny joke…' Oona stopped abruptly. *Why the heck am I explaining to him? How does it matter?* 'I'm getting late, I'll have to go,' and she left. As she reached the gate, she heard Anand saying, 'Bye *jaan.*' She yelled back a 'bye', patting Sridevi, who had come to see her mistress off at the gate.

'Hello,' Oona answered a call on her landline.

'Hi. How are you? All well? Was wondering how you are? Why didn't you call? I was worried about you. Deepak will be in Bombay next Tuesday for three days. Do you need anything from here?' Oona smiled as she heard out the rapid fire of questions. When Sonia stopped for breath, she spoke.

'Relax babes, take it easy. I'm fine. No need to send anything from Cal as Ma will be here in a few weeks' time. I want her now to spend more time with me. And to answer your other questions, what were they? Oh, yes, sorry I could not call earlier as I was really busy with work. Got back into investigative news. Tackling soft crimes at the moment. Look up the website. You'll read my latest scoops.'

'I know. I'm up-to-date with your columns too. Didn't quite agree with your take on *Bhishm* though. I thought it was quite a beautifully shot film,' Sonia said.

'No one's disputing that. But there's a big difference between a well-shot film and and a well-made film. The guy was way off the mark on that score.'

'Okay *baba*. I must remember I'm talking to a critic rather than my old pal. But I really miss you babes.'

'Me too,' Oona admitted. 'Tell Deepak to shift base to Mumbai.'

'That is wishful thinking,' Sonia laughed. 'Why don't you come back here? You need not stick around in Mumbai alone now,' Sonia said, genuinely concerned. 'You need friends near you.'

'I know and appreciate your concern, Sonia. But I cannot live anywhere else but Bombay. It has become, oh so…how can I explain? Anyway, I like it here, with or without a man, if that's what you mean. Besides, work keeps me busy and I cannot go elsewhere and start from scratch. Soon Ma will be here and hopefully I will feel a lot better. And Calcutta is only a flight away.'

'I know. I know. Oh, by the way, guess who I met the other day?' Sonia asked.

'Who?'

'Take a guess?'

'Can't. I give up,' Oona said.

'Hector. Hector Bose from Lowes. Remember?'

'Of course I do,' Oona said, feeling that old flicker of excitement. 'How's he? What's he doing? And where's he?'

'He stays in London. Is still flying…I think he mentioned British Airways,' Sonia said.

'Yes. Someone I met mentioned it a while ago. What's with his wife Sonia Singh?'

'He didn't mention her and I didn't ask. We did not get to talk much. In fact he asked about you. I told him what you are doing and even mentioned things were not going well with you and Anand. Okay, *na*?' Sonia asked.

'Ya. Cool. No problem. Then what did he say?'

'Nothing. Just seemed a bit concerned. Took your cell number from me. Said he keeps passing Bombay so he will give you a call someday.'

'Do you have his number?' Oona asked trying not to show her interest.

'No. I forgot to take it. We met at a party so it was rather rushed. But I can get it if you want. No big deal. *Kyon*? Want to touch base with Mr Bose, Miss Roy?' Sonia teased.

'Oh shut up! Just curious. I knew the family so wanted to check on Aunty…'

'Aunty Bose or Hector Bose?' Sonia cut in. 'Just be a little patient my dear and expect a call from the slightly paunchy Mr Bose one of these days.'

The old friends chatted on in this vein for a while. It was always great talking to Sonia. Even if they spoke after months, it seemed like they had just spoken a few days back. They simply took up where they left off.

Oona felt good that Hector still showed an interest in her whereabouts. She of course had not mentioned to Sonia that she had found out a bit about Hector. She thought about connecting with Hector through Victor, whose email address Riz had given her. After all, Hector still remembered her, so she would not sound desperate if she got in touch with him.

Hector Bose. Wonder what he looks like now? Sonia mentioned a little paunchy. What does she mean? Is he still handsome? And charming? Are he and Sonia Singh happy? Are they still together? She was older than him wasn't she? Do they have any kids? Is Sonia also in London? Why did he take my number if he hasn't yet called? He must have heard that I am married to Anand Khanna? Wonder what he thinks of me being a celeb wife? Sonia told him of Anand and my splitting. Is that why he took my number? To console me as a friend? Or take more than a friendly interest? But does Hector Bose really matter after all these years? After all, I'm seeing Riz Ali. Now what will Hector think of that? The plain Jane with the dashing dude!

Oona smiled to herself as she set the coffee to percolate. She had just returned from a day shift and needed to unwind. She was looking forward to some alone time with her favourite brew after a long day. And then of course, Riz would be joining her for dinner. He had just returned from Delhi, and was bringing *kheema* specially made by his mother. She had told Renuka bai to make some parathas and keep it in the casserole. And she would toss a salad. But that was for later. Right now she was excited about Sen Babu's letter, which she had managed to locate in a box of junk papers in the garage. Maybe it would throw some light on her great aunt Ela Sen and her English lover David. Oona couldn't explain why the ill-fated romance fascinated her.

Sen Babu did manage to find a forwarding address left by the gentleman David Oliver. It was 17 Park Lane, Calcutta. Oona wondered where that would have been in 1929. She roughly knew where the present Park Lane was though her road sense of Calcutta was a little outdated. On impulse she decided to call up Moushumi, her friend and former colleague. Moushumi still worked with the *Herald*, now as a senior editor looking after the features section. She had married a colleague,

Soumya, and had two children. They kept in touch with the occasional call or email. Moushumi had always taken credit for Oona's marriage to Anand. Sometime back, hearing rumours of the split, Moushumi had called Oona for confirmation. Oona had sidestepped the question.

Now Oona called Moushumi and made her request, 'I need your help to find out exactly where 17 Park Lane was located in 1929. What happened to the occupants—the Olivers—after they vacated the bungalow?' She remembered Chhordida mentioning that the family had left for England, perhaps to separate David and Ela. 'Did they return to England? Basically you have to find out for me any forwarding address left by the Olivers then. I have a hunch they left for London. I can ask one of my London-based friends to track down their descendants,' Oona said.

'Why the sudden interest in this family? On to a story?' Moushumi couldn't help but ask.

'No. Digging up a family secret. In fact, it would make a wonderful cover story for your Sunday magazine. My great-aunt and her English lover. Also, she was closely associated with Tagore and Bose,' Oona added on the last bit for effect and to arouse Moushumi's curiosity further. 'Just remember, the name was David Oliver.'

'I've made a note of that,' Moushumi said. 'What did you say your great-aunt's name was?'

Oona hesitated. 'Do you need that now?'

'Well it helps, but you do not have to give if you don't want to,' Moushumi said.

'No, no. It doesn't really matter. Just keep it to yourself now—family and all that, right. It's a sensitive *maamla*. Her name was Ela Sen and she was amongst the first batch of women graduates from Cal U if that helps. But I want the Olivers' decendants tracked down. *Bujhli*?'

'Sure, there's this young reporter on my team, Pritish, and this is his kind of thing. He is super. Right now he is a bit busy on another story, but I will ask him to look this up. Just give me a little time. *Aar ki khobor*? What news of Anand? All well?'

'All well,' Oona was curt.

'You know, you can always confide in me as a friend,' Moushumi did not probe further.

'I know. Thanks a ton,' Oona said.

Later that evening, Oona told Riz about Ela and David and Sen Babu's letter. And about her uncanny resemblance to Ela Sen. 'I have her photograph in Cal. I'll tell Ma to bring it. You can see for yourself,' Oona said.

'Would love to. This is interesting,' Riz remarked. 'Let me know what you find,' he said, sipping at his red wine. Oona held a Diet Coke. These days she seldom drank and hardly stored expensive liquor. The days of single malts were over. She either served wine or beer or breezers and whenever Riz felt like a whisky he brought along his locally distilled quarters.

'So your mother's coming?'

'Yes,' Oona replied.

'When?'

'She was supposed to come towards the end of this month, but it's been pushed back to the middle of next month. Why?'

'No. Just wondering. She will obviously be staying with you here, won't she?'

'Yes, obviously. Since the studio apartement is on rent, I'm setting up the guest room for her. The cupboard's arriving tomorrow. Why do you ask?'

'No. Just that our movements will be a little more restricted. What with that crazy husband of yours downstairs and your mother here...I mean...you know,' Riz shrugged.

'I know, but it can't be helped. After all, she's my mother, Riz.'

'I know, honey,' Riz said, coming closer and hugging her tight. 'I didn't mean it that way. It is just that I can't walk in and out as freely as I do now. First Anand and then your mom.'

'But you can come anytime, really. She will know you are my friend.'

'Yeah. But some of our movements will be restricted,' he smiled gesturing towards the bedroom.

'Oh we'll find our ways. Maybe after she's asleep—she goes to bed early you know,' Oona smiled mischievously. 'Yes, but you will have to control your decibel level in bed, my dear,' Riz laughed.

'Oh shut up!' Oona blushed.

Spending the night and waking up to the sunrise in Riz's arms was one of life's glorious moments. It was these moments, apart from her work, which kept her otherwise battered ego and emotions going.

Trouble in Paradise

'Oh, damn!' Oona muttered as she entered the Grand Ballroom. It was the post awards party of the Filmdust Awards. Oona could not attend the awards' ceremony due to some prior engagement. When she had told the magazine editor, Samaira, the latter told her to at least join in for dinner. Oona had told Riz to meet her at half past ten at the reception of the Grand Hyatt.

Hearing her exclamation, Riz looked at her enquiringly.

'Don't turn now, but Anand is at the far end with Mannuji, to your right,' Oona said through clenched teeth, smiling at random people in the crowd. She knew Anand had seen her enter with Riz. Though she was not very comfortable with the situation, she had to pretend nonchalance. 'Let's just be cool honey,' she turned to Riz and smiled brightly. Riz got the drift and nodded.

'Sure, sweetie,' he returned with a wide grin.

Moments later Anand walked up to the couple and extended his hand towards Riz. 'So, the great man himself!' Anand remarked.

'*Ji*?' Riz shook hands rather awkwardly.

'I mean the great supermodel Riz Ali…'

'Please, Anandsaab, don't embarass me. Look who's talking. Your contribution to Indian cinema is astounding. We are just small fish in the pond…'

Oona could not take this. 'Excuse me a moment,' she said as she spotted a journalist friend a couple of feet away. She joined her with an effusive 'hi' and pretended to be catching up on old times, while her one ear remained tuned to Riz and Anand's conversation. She picked up a cola from a passing waiter's tray, just for something to hold.

She overheard snatches of conversation between Anand and Riz.

Anand: So what are you up to these days?

Riz: Trying to do bit roles in Bollywood. Also some modelling.

Anand: Where do you live?

Riz: Yari Road

Anand: Ah, that's where I live too.

Riz: Yes Sir, I know.

Anand: You do? Ah, but of course. I forgot, you are a regular visitor to my house since you are my wife's friend. Yes, my driver and maid do tell me. But somehow I always seem to miss you. Why don't you drop by and have a drink with me some evening? I may not be as attractive company as Oona but I'm sure I'm not all that bad!

Riz: No, no, Sir, I would love to join you.... Just a moment Sir, I'll just be back in a moment. I spotted a friend I must say hi to...

Riz waved randomly and excused himself from Anand's company. Standing with the group of journalists, Oona tried to see which way Riz went, but he melted into the crowd. She turned around and saw Anand coming up to her. She quickly excused herself from the circle and joined Anand.

'Quite a looker,' he smiled wickedly at Oona.

'Who?' Oona asked.

'Stop pretending,' Anand was high. 'He's not good for you though. That bastard has no balls. *Darpok saala*...'

Oona tried desperately to change the subject before it got out of hand. She suddenly spotted Mannuji and before Anand could say anything, she dashed through the crowd towards him. 'Hi Mannuji. When did you come?'

'Ah Oonaji, *namaste*. We came few time back. You met Sirji *na*?' Oona nodded, gesturing towards Anand with a smile. Anand was talking disinterestedly to her journo friend. He scanned the crowd for Oona and when he saw her with Mannuji, he relaxed and continued talking half-heartedly.

'I'll just say hi to Sameer Shah there,' Oona said, walking away.

She hurried out of the ballroom, walking quickly through the lobby out into the porch and asked the bell-desk to call for her car and driver. She kept checking to see if Anand was following her. Once in the car, she dialled Riz. 'Where are you?' she asked.

'I sent you a text. Didn't you read it?'

'Oh, no, I didn't notice. I'm outside in my car, where are you?'

'I'm headed home. You carry on,' Riz told her.

'The situation was getting uncomfortable, good you walked away. Where are you now?'

'I'm in an auto, Oona,' Riz sounded curt.

'Okay. Tell me where I can pick you up, we can go home together and…'

'Oona, please carry on. I'm not up to dinner right now. I'll talk to you tomorrow. Take care.' And he hung up on her.

As she reached home, she got a new message. *Sory was a bit abrupt. Bit rattled. Settling my nerves. Talk 2 u 2mrw. Nite. Riz*

I understand. Tk cr. Sleep well.

The next day she called Riz around noon after waiting to hear from him all morning. He did not take her call. She tried later in the evening but the phone rang out. Finally, she sent him a text to call her as soon as possible. He replied that he would call back the next day.

When he did not call the next day, Oona grew desperate. She called him on the third day. He answered after a long time. 'Where are you, honey?' Oona asked, close to tears.

'I'm with people,' he drawled, 'in Delhi.'

'In Delhi? When did you go there? You never mentioned…' Oona was surprised.

'Yes, I had to come here suddenly as some family matters are being sorted out. I can't talk now. I'll call you as soon as I am free. Take care, Oona,' he said, hanging up before she could say bye.

Oona found his behaviour strange. Why was he being so cagey about meeting her since his encounter with Anand? Oona had always felt Riz grow uncomfortable whenever Anand Khanna was mentioned. Was Anand right afterall? '*Darpok saala*' is how he had described him—'a bloody coward'. Anand had a sixth sense in judging people and 99 per cent of the time he was right.

Damn!

After Riz had been silent for a fortnight, Oona called him up one evening.

'*Hanji. Sab khairiyat*? All well?' It was that familiar nasal voice which brought a glow to her face and still made her go weak in the knees.

'All well. You left suddenly and did not even call,' Oona complained.

'Yeah,' Riz yawned. 'I know. Anyway, I am back tomorrow by the evening flight.'

'Great! I'll come and pick you up from the airport,' Oona said.

'Please don't bother honey. I feel bad if the flight gets delayed and you have to wait. I'd much rather take an auto. Okay? I'll come over in the evening.'

When Riz finally walked in the next evening, he sat down straightaway, reaching for the drink she offered. She had hoped he would kiss or at least hug her after all these days.

'Good to have you back Riz. It's been a while since we have been together. I really missed your company,' Oona said, trying to stay cool.

'Likewise, madame,' Riz said, raising his glass in a toast.

'So, what is this project you are busy with?' Oona asked.

'Well, it's been on my mind for a while now. I want to make a series of thirty-second spots on HIV-AIDS awareness for television,' Riz said. 'I have conceptualised it and need to shoot it. But I need a sponsor. Remember when I first called you to discuss a project?' Oona nodded.

'Yes I remember. We never got around to discussing it.'

'Well, this is what I had in mind. I needed your help regarding the media,' Riz said.

'So you want to feature in the spots?' Oona asked.

'Well, both direct and feature in them. The script is also mine,' Riz added.

'Why suddenly HIV?' she questioned.

'What do you mean by suddenly? It's not a sudden whim. This subject has been close to my heart for a while now. I have been closely associated with NGOs rehabilitating HIV-AIDS victims. I have seen some of my friends suffer the disease at close quarters.'

'I see,' Oona said, still not quite convinced by his reasons.

'Alliance Telecommunications sponsors HIV-AIDS projects in a big way,' Riz said. Alliance was one of the country's leading business houses.

'Wouldn't know,' Oona shrugged. 'I know the Telecom head vaguely though. Rima Banerji.'

'Yeah, I've been meeting Rima for this,' Riz said.

'Oh, so you're on first-name basis?' Oona asked 'I heard she is very snooty and a real bitch.'

'Not at all. But I have been trying to flatter her so that she'll sponsor it,' Riz said.

'How, by giving her blow jobs?' Oona burst out.

Immediately, she was sorry. 'Just joking, sorry Riz,' she mumbled.

'That's okay,' he said, looking away.

The rest of the evening passed in awkwardness. Suddenly Riz got up to go. 'What about dinner?' Oona asked. 'Let me order something. A pizza, maybe?'

'No, I'm not hungry. Besides, my doctor advised me to cut down on alcohol and late nights. I need to look after myself as there is no one to look after me. Even if I have to die, I do not want to suffer,' Riz said.

'Why are you talking like this? Is everything all right, honey?' Oona asked, genuinely concerned.

'Yeah. As good as it can get,' Riz said.

'What is the matter with your health? Would you like to tell me? I am concerned, believe me,' Oona asked.

'I believe you. Maybe we'll talk some other time. I need to go and rest now.'

Oona went up and hugged him. 'I really, really missed you.'

Riz held her, 'Me too.'

'Just hold me tight,' Oona said. Riz tightened his grip around her.

'Shall we call it a day now?' Riz asked.

'Don't leave, Riz.'

'Do you want me to give you a blow job?' he asked.

Oona badly wanted one but her ego made her refuse. 'No. Not today honey. You need to rest.' It took a great effort to let Riz go.

Later that night Oona mulled over Riz's sudden coldness towards her. He had not even bothered to hug her when they had met. Something was wrong. But she cursed herself for being nasty to Riz on the Rima Banerji comment.

She quickly texted him: *Sorry about the nasty jibe. Didn't mean it one bit. Just a slip of the tongue. Been missing you all these days. Concerned about your health. Let's talk about it tomorrow. Anything I can do? Am always there for you. Sleep well! Nite*

Riz messaged back: *That's ok. Quite used to being calld a wimp n a gigolo. I'l look aftr myself. U look aftr urself. Nite -:)*

The Big Book Awards this eve at 7pm. Remember? Follwd by dinner. Pick u at 6.30 near gas stn. Oona

K. C u. Riz.

At 6 pm while Oona was getting ready, Riz texted her: *Sory. Can't make it. 2 much work. Apologies.*

Oona was furious. But she texted back: *Ditcher! Feel like strangling u.*

Already feeling strangled. Lots to do. Riz

Oh her way back, Riz sent her a message: *Stil a while to go at work. Talk 2mrw. Hav a gud nite. Riz.* Oona smiled at his thoughtfulness. She loved him.

Next day Oona messaged Riz: *What about coffee at 5?*

Riz texted back: *In delhi. Sudden plans. Mom's doc's apptmt.*

Oona: *All well I hope.*

Riz: *Yeah. U take care. Wil cal when bak.*

A few days later Oona decided to call Riz and see how he was doing, as he had not called. He answered in his usual, inimitable tone, '*Adaab arz ji. Sab khairiyat*?'

'How are you? Been missing you. When are you back?' Oona asked.

'Well, am back already. Just got back yesterday,' Riz said.

'What? You never told me!' Oona was upset.

'Yeah. I know. One of those things.'

This is so unlike Riz. He usually messages or calls the moment he lands, but this time he's been here a whole day without calling me. What's wrong?

'Let's meet tomorrow?' Oona asked.

'Cannot commit about tomorrow. Maybe the day after?' Riz said.

On the day after Riz called to say he had to meet a friend for dinner.

'I thought you said you were cutting down late nights and alcohol,' Oona asked.

'Yeah,' Riz said.

'Why are you avoiding me, Riz? I feel miserable. Do you realise what I am going through?' Oona almost broke down.

'Listen honey, just take an Alprax. You'll feel better. We'll talk tomorrow. I have to go now.'

Oona almost cried herself to sleep. When she was about to turn in her phone beeped: *Hope u are doing well! Alprax kicked in? Talk tomrw! Sleep well! Riz.* She was glad he had messaged. And fell asleep with a smile on her face.

൭൭

The next day Oona messaged Riz: *Cofee at 5?*

Riz answered: *U hav a gud day. Off 2 pune. Ashram. Wud like to maintain radio silence for next 5 days. Need 2 sort myself out. Explain when I c u! Thx.*

Oona did not know what to make of it. She was really upset at Riz's strange behaviour. Either he was trying to break away from her or something was really bothering him. An illness perhaps. He had mentioned health concerns of late. Oona was worried. She missed his attention too, being used to hearing his voice at least once a day. But she respected his wishes. After five days, she sent him a blank message. He did not reply. The next day, however, he messaged her: *Hi Oona. Hope all goz well wth u. Am still in ashram for another week. Will retrn by thur next. C u thereafter.Regrds. Riz.*

൭൭

To:vicbos@aol.com

Hi Victor,

My name's Oona Khanna. Used to be Roy previously. Was your neighbour from Cal. Stayed in the Mouchak lane. Used to be a friend of Hector's. Knew your parents, Aunty Maive and Uncle Bose and visited them often when you were away in England.

Sorry to hear about Uncle's death. How is Aunty Maive? Where is she? Can you give me her address? I would love to get in touch with her. Is she on e-mail by any chance? And how is Hector? I heard he is in London. Do forward me his e-mail id too.
Oh by the way, just in case you are wondering, I got your address from Riz Ali, a good friend of mine. He happened to mention you and I made the connection with Hector.

Warm regards
Oona

A week later,

To:oonakhanna@vsnl.com

Hi Oona,

Nice hearing from you. It's always nice hearing about Cal. I miss the city. And our house. I have spent some of my best times in Golpark. Do you still visit Kolkata? And Golpark?
Coming back to your queries, Ma is well indeed. She has resettled here in the UK after Baba's death. She stays in Wales to be precise, in a small seaside village called Barmouth with a total population of 2,000. There are twenty-nine shops (restaurants included) and no one ever locks their doors! I can't imagine that, having spent the better part of my life in a city like London! I am sure she would love to hear from you though I must admit she is a bit hard of hearing these days. She is not on e-mail, unfortunately—I am sending you her address. As for Hector, he remembers you. Sends you his love. He will mail you soon. As I write this he is in Kathmandu on office work. He is now working for British Airways, stationed in London, after having logged over ten years as a pilot for Cathay.
How is Riz? Reformed? Or still wild? I pity the poor wife. Is Charmaine back in Bombay or still in Frisco? How's his work front?

Give him a big pat on the back from me. He is a good soul!

Love and light,
Vic

PS: Maive Bose
Aberdale
Barmouth
Wales, UK
Hector's e-mail: whattheheck@hotmail.com

Oona wrote a warm letter to Aunty Maive, Hector's mother, telling her as briefly as she could about the two decades that had gone by since they last met. Maive Bose replied with a three-page letter a fortnight later, delighted to hear from her. She enquired about Sangeeta and asked Oona to send her a recent photograph so that she could see her. She explained her move to Barmouth from London, saying she had wanted to spend the twilight of her life in the peaceful seaside resort. But she missed Golpark, especially during the windy winters of Barmouth. She was worried about her sons: Hector's marriage had not worked out and Victor had chosen to remain a bachelor. But then it was their life and they knew best what to do with it.

Oona replied, sending her a nice photograph, the glamourous one in soft focus taken by well-known photographer Jayesh Sharma which she earlier used for Oona's Take. She deliberately did not send one with Anand. Hector had not yet mailed her. Oona was tempted to shoot out a note to whattheheck@hotmail.com but she resisted the impulse, choosing to wait and watch.

Instead of the 'Thursday next', Riz returned three Thursdays later. From the ashram in Pune he went to Delhi and then back to Pune. He called Oona once from Delhi and texted her a couple of times from Pune.

Oona wondered why he hesitated to call her from Pune. Did he have a girlfriend there?

Just bak. Hope all's well. C u soon. Riz
Ian's art exhib 2mrw. Wine n cheese affair. Wanna come? Oona
Ok. Tel me what time? Riz
6. At gas stn.

Oona picked up Riz from their usual point. 'Hi,' Riz said. 'You are all dressed up!'

'Just wearing a skirt, that's all. A little change from my jeans and trousers look. You seem to have lost more weight, Riz. All well healthwise?' Oona asked.

Riz nodded. 'I ran some tests in Delhi. The reports are fine. But I haven't felt too well lately. I seem to be losing weight despite having a good appetite.' Then he got a work-related call and was busy for the rest of the drive.

At the event, Riz consciously stayed away from Oona. She noticed Jolly Anand, the socialite and casting director of many Bollywood films and walked up to her, motioning to Riz to do the same.

'Hi darling,' Jolly said, in her sophisticated convent accent. 'Good to see you in this part of town. Where is Anand?'

'He is travelling.'

'Great! Then come over to my place tonight for a drink and dinner,' Jolly said.

'Sure,' Oona agreed without thinking.

'Hi Jolly! Good to catch up with you. Hi, Oonaji! What a surprise!' It was Riz.

Oona immediately caught on to Riz's act for Jolly's benefit. She went along with a 'hi' and a hug.

Later, as Jolly was leaving, she asked Oona whether she would like to go with her.

'I have my car, Jolly. And besides, Riz is with me. What do I do?'

'Oh Riz. But I thought you guys just met?'

'Yes. But since he stays in my part of town, he wanted a lift back home,' Oona hurriedly explained.

'That was quick. Trust Riz to be ready with his pick-up lines,' Jolly laughed, 'Bring him along too. No worries.'

As they got into the car, Oona told Riz about Jolly's invitation. 'You go. I'll get off,' Riz said sullenly. 'I'm in no mood to socialise with the likes of Jolly Anand.'

'Hey, I'm not interested in going either. I'll call her and tell her.' Oona dialled Jolly's number and mumbled an excuse.

'It's okay, darling. Some other time,' Jolly said.

Riz took her to a restopub called Ghetto instead. The place was full of youngsters in their teens and quite noisy. Riz led her to a corner table, which was quieter. He ordered a whisky for himself and a spritzer for Oona. Over drinks, Oona decided to speak honestly, 'Riz, I find your behaviour a little strange these days. I can see you are trying to shut me out. It hurts. Please tell me what I've done to offend you.'

'I know. I'm trying to cool off,' Riz said.

'But why?'

'I realised I am too old to just be fooling around. I have had enough of flings and heartbreak and an unsuccessful marriage. You know my reputation. I'm tired of my bohemian ways. I want to settle down. This is not the time to have frivolous flings and link-ups. More so with a married woman. It stresses me out completely.'

There was a silence. Oona's eyes glistened with tears. Riz noticed and looked away. 'Have you ever asked about my feelings in this matter?' Oona finally asked.

'What is there to ask? You are married and settled happily. Right? *Baat toh* simple *hai*.'

'In that case you should have thought about my marital status before getting into a relationship with me,' Oona burst out.

'I did, honey,' Riz patted her hand. 'But I realised you were lonely. You needed a companion.'

'I did. And I still do.' Oona took a sip of her drink. 'I don't know how to say this. I think we are too mature for "I love you" stuff. But you must know that I care for you a lot.' Riz squeezed her hand. Oona continued, 'I may be Mrs Anand Khanna, but for all purposes our marriage is dead. I harbour no feelings for him. I just don't publicise that fact—I'm a very private person.'

'Oh, I'm sorry to hear that, honey. I knew things weren't great, but not that they were this bad,' Riz said, continuing to hold her hand.

'Riz, I'm really madly in love with you.'

'Ouch!'

'I have all the wealth and glamour as Anand's wife. I don't need that from you. But I love the fact that you are sensitive to my emotions and....'

'Yes?' Riz looked at her.

'And that you are essentially a good human being.'

Riz kissed her hand. 'Thanks honey. I appreciate it.'

As Oona reached her bedroom later that night, she received Riz's message: *In life we have a lot 2 lose and very little 2 choose. Whenever u get a chance 2 choose, do it wisely and see that u never lose what u choose.*

Next morning Oona messaged Riz: *Wanna do coffee at 5?*

Riz: *OK. Call u later. At audition.*

At 4.30 p.m. Oona's cell beeped: *Hav left recordg office. B there in 15.*

Oona: *OK. Am home.*

Oona smiled with relief. Looked like the old times were back after months of uncertainty.

She continued to work furiously on her computer, engrossed in her work. Suddenly she realised it was nearly 6 p.m. and Riz had not yet come. Worried, she dialled his number.

'*Hanji.* I was just about to call you,' Riz answered.

'Where are you? You were supposed to be here an hour ago! Am waiting to have coffee,' Oona asked.

'Well, it's like this. On impulse I decided to head to Delhi. Am on the way to the airport. I was about to call you,' Riz said.

'Delhi! But you were just there a few days earlier,' Oona exclaimed.

'Yeah. Just got a few days off from work and was missing my mom.'

His explanation sounded weak, but Oona, though upset, couldn't do much about it. 'Okay, have a safe flight. Call me when you land.'

'Sure honey. You take care.' Riz was his usual polite self.

Oona was fuming. *Acts like a king. Does as he pleases! And what's this mother fixation? He hardly appears to be a mama's boy. Then why is he rushing off to Delhi at the drop of a hat? And where does he get the money to fund his air travel? He says he hardly earns. He complains he is broke. This man is incorrigible.*

ೲ

Jolly Anand called Oona a few days later. 'Want to have dinner? I have coupons for Napoli from CD and am trying to use them.' CD was CD Singh, the owner of hip restobar Napoli next to Oona's place. 'Is Anand around?' Jolly asked.

'No,' Oona replied, 'So it'll be just me.'

'Great! I'll see you at 7.30 at Napoli.'

'Hi darling!' Jolly got up and hugged Oona. 'You look lovely!'

'Thanks Jolly. You look lovely yourself,' Oona said, settling in.

'I often wonder how you manage your life so well,' Jolly continued. 'A young and talented woman left by yourself so often while Anand travels. And you know, don't mind, but there's such an age and intellect gap between the two of you!'

Oona shrugged, 'Such is life, Jolly,' she tried to change the topic, 'Sorry about ditching you the other night. I was keen but Riz had an early morning shoot.'

'Oh that's okay. I was not very keen to have Riz around. Was just being polite,' Jolly assured her.

'Seems the feeling was mutual. He was not too keen to have dinner with you either,' Oona said without thinking.

Jolly stiffened. 'Yeah? Did he say anything else?' Oona shook her head, embarrassed. Jolly continued, 'Oona I think you should keep away from men like Riz.'

'But he's just a friend, Jolly,' Oona said.

'Nevertheless, men like Riz cannot be mere friends hanging around with young women like you.'

'What do you mean?' Oona asked.

Over dinner Jolly enlightened Oona on all there was to know about Riz Ali. That since coming to Bombay over two decades ago, he did more blow jobs than ad campaigns. Oona almost choked on her drink. Jolly didn't fail to notice it. He'd had a string of girlfriends, mostly white, as he seemed to have a thing for '*gori chitti*' babes. Then of course, he regularly disappeared for months, living at the Rajneesh Ashram in Pune while his agency people would despair. There were also rumours that he slept with men, including a fellow model, some Bengali chap.

Everyone had thought he'd settle down when he married the French-American Charmaine, whom he met at the US embassy in Delhi. But Charmaine was transferred to San Francisco and Riz, soon tired of America, returned alone to Bombay, fooling around with women.

'He loves the good life and enjoys dating socialites and bored rich housewives,' Jolly said. Oona wondered if Jolly was one of them. 'You know Romola Marware? Well her marriage broke up because of him. She left her husband Rana for Riz and the poor guy killed himself. What did Riz do? Abandoned her, taking the first flight out to Frisco.'

Oona was a little uncomfortable with this conversation and not entirely sure whether to believe Jolly. 'Wow! Quite a character I must say,' she said lightly.

'A cousin of mine is Riz's neighbour in Nizamuddin, in Delhi. Riz has been pursuing her daughter, Payal, since she was sixteen. Payal was so attractive, and Riz would follow her around on his motorcycle. Naturally, Payal fell for the handsome man. My cousin Julie didn't want Payal to marry a Muslim, and besides, she'd heard that Riz had told his friends, '*Main to uski izzat lootnewala hoon. Thorei ghar basanewala hoon.*' (I intend to have fun with her, not marry her.) So Julie got Payal married to a rich NRI. But whenever Payal would visit Delhi, Riz would show up. Eventually her marriage broke up. She began seeing another guy, but Riz interfered there, too. She's forty now and single. He's caught up with her again and Payal seems to be completely floored by him all over again.'

Oona was completely shattered on hearing this. *That explains his frequent Delhi trips in the last two months. Gosh! He must be with her right now, courting her, maybe even givng her a blow job. Damn!*

In Transit

Oona was in complete depression the week after Jolly's disclosure. She had called Riz some days ago but he had disconnected her call. He texted her later: *Busy. Wud like 2 be left alone. For a bit! Thanks.*

She was dying to hear his voice. It broke Oona's heart that Riz was with another woman while she pined for him.

A few days later she messaged him: *All well? Miss you madly. Still in Delhi?*

He replied: *Yeah. Is this a surveillance?*

Oona was very hurt: *For God's sake! How could you say such a thing?*

Riz replied: *Sory. Been stressd. Wil cal later. Tk cr. Apologies again.*

It was afternoon. Oona put her phone on silent, took an Alprax and cried herself to sleep. When she woke late in the evening, she saw three missed calls from Riz. She immediately returned his call.

'I'm sorry about the comment,' Riz said. 'Been stressed out lately.'

'You want to tell me about it?' Oona offered.

'No, it's okay. Will let you know when the time comes. How's Anandsaab? In town?'

'Yes,' Oona said. 'Off tomorrow to Pune on work.'

'Are you going with him?' Riz asked.

'Nope. How is your health?' Oona asked.

'Okay. My doctor suspects a liver problem and told me to cut down on the alcohol. Anyway, you take care and we'll talk later.'

The 'later' never came. Oona messaged him after a few days: *Hope all's well. Go easy on the alcohol and joints.Love.Oona.* There was no reply.

The next day Oona sent Riz the same message. Still no reply. On the third day Oona texted: *Hope you are going easy on the alcohol and late nights.Truly Concerned.Reply. Take care.*

Riz messaged back: *Ok. But try not to give me unsolicited advice. Have my own people in the field.*

Oona was reduced to tears.

To:oonakhanna@vsnl.com

Hi Oona,

Vic told me you had written to him. He gave me your mail id but I was away for a while and quite caught up with work. Honestly, I had forgotten about writing till I happened to visit Mum and she showed me your photograph. Gosh! You look the same as when I first met you. In fact, more gorgeous now. Marriage does suit you. I read somewhere that you had married Bollywood producer Anand Khanna. Saw a couple of your photos in film magazines some years back when I was in Bombay. Thought I'd look you up but did not make the effort as I wasn't sure you'd remember me. After all, you move in a different social circle now.

As for myself, I flew Cathay for over ten years and left four years back when my marriage to Sonia (Singh) broke down. We'd married soon after I joined Cathay and have a seven-year-old daughter, Shaina. Sonia still flies Cathay as a senior flight attendant. She has remarried and lives with her husband in Hong Kong. Shaina lives with them. I miss her terribly, but I think she is better off with her mum. I don't want to rock the boat at this point.

As for me, I have been with BA since leaving Cathay. Enjoy flying and that has been my saviour. As of now, I am single. I stay with Vic and we kind of manage okay together. Vic and I meet Mum as

often as we can. And yes, we do miss Cal. It's a pity Bose Mansion had to go.
Do you go to Cal often? Check out what's become of our bungalow and let me know, please? How's your mum? Is she still in Cal? Give her my regards. Keep in touch. And if you guys happen to be in London, let's catch up. We'll drink to old times.

Cheers!
Hector

Hector's letter brought some joy to Oona in this low phase. Twenty years earlier, Oona would have touched the sky in joy. Today Hector was part of her past. Her present throbbed with Riz.

To: whattheheck@hotmail.com

Hi,

You finally wrote. I had given up on you. Great to connect after such a long time. Wish you had got in touch when you were in Bombay. There is always a place in my heart for old friends.
All's well in Cal. Ma is okay. Suffering the usual old-age problems like osteoarthiritis. Refuses to come and stay with me in Bombay. You know how parents are—independent and adamant. We visit each other though. Heard about Bose Mansion being sold, will check what's happening there next time I'm in Cal.
I'm very settled in my career as a writer and columnist in Bombay. Can't say the same about my marriage, though I am still married. Sorry to hear about your divorce. Missing your daughter must be painful. Thankfully, we don't have any kids yet.
London's one of my favourite cities. Haven't been there for a while but have lots of friends there so don't be surprised if I just land up someday and take you up on your offer for a drink.

Keep in touch.
Oona

To: vicbos@aol.com

Dear Victor,

Thanks for connecting me to Hector. Great hearing from him after such a long time.
Haven't been to Cal in a while but next time I visit I'll let you guys know the status of Bose Mansion. Golpark is the same and yet not quite the same without us!
Conveyed your regards to Riz. He sends you the same. Charmaine's still in Frisco as far as I know. Haven't met her though. Riz spends more time in Delhi than Bombay so I don't get to meet him that often. Doing the odd film here and there.
Hope to catch up with you guys some day soon.

Regards
Oona

To: oonakhanna@vsnl.com

Dear Oona,

I am glad Hector and you connected because of me. And I agree, Golpark cannot be the same without us! Keep me posted about the place when you visit next and have an extra kheer sandesh *on my behalf from Mouchak.*
As for Riz, the bugger will never learn. He should have taken his career more seriously. As well as his marriage. I don't understand why he hangs around in Delhi doing nothing but faffing with old pals. Always a bit of a waster, this Riz. Anyway, I should not be complaining much since I have not done much with my life either. But that's another story. Riz was always more talented than me. We had some wonderful times together.
I miss him.

Love and light,
Vic

To: oonakhanna@vsnl.com

Hi,

I'm glad you're doing well in your career. And looking forward to seeing you in London sometime soon. How is Sonia? I met her, but it was too brief to really talk about how she's doing.
Do you still listen to Neil Diamond? I am sorry to hear your marriage is not going great guns. But you are still young and lovely (from the photograph I saw) and you have a great future ahead. Look life full in the face. Do not get disheartened. Who knows? Life is full of surprises.
How do you know Riz? Have you met Attiya? What is she doing these days?

Take care,
Hector

To: whattheheck@hotmail.com

Hey,

Good to hear from you. I'm going through a slightly low patch and your letter is like balm. That's what old friends are for I guess.
Sonia and Deepak are happily married with two kids, a daughter and a son. Sonia is busy with house and hearth 24x7. Deepak is looking after the family liquor business.
As for Neil Diamond, I think I've kind of outgrown him. I have some of his songs on my iPod though.
I know Riz through the good old Bombay party circuit. Nice chap. Spends a lot of time in Delhi though. I have not met Attiya but from what I gathered, she is still with Cathay. Brother and sister don't get along much.

Hey, that reminds me, what about sending me your current photo? I want to see how you look now. Not fair, since you know how I look. Mail me one asap.
Ciao

Oona
PS: Regards to Victor

Oona suddenly got a message from Riz one day. *Sorry 4 not being in touch earlier. Had to go 2 mysore suddenly 4 a shoot. Wil cal later. Hope all goes wel. Tk cr. Riz*

Oona was thrilled. *Miss u. Call soon.*

A couple of days later, Riz messaged her: *In Bg'lore. Call me on landline: 080 410 9999 #101*

Oona called back immediately. Riz was polite and distant. Oona tried very hard to control her emotions.

'I'm off to Delhi after two days before I return to Bombay. So *inshallah*, we'll catch up soon.' The last sentence gave her some succour, though Oona was not sure she could trust Riz any longer.

To: oonakhanna@vsnl.com

Hi,

Busy on a flight. Vic will send you some photographs of us.
Am happy for Deepak and Sonia. Give them my regards. Glad to hear Attiya's still with Cathay—she went through a rough marriage. Been a bit wild always. Like brother, like sister.
How's mum? Am glad you have outgrown Neil Diamond. So have I.

Look after yourself. Will call you one of these days. Send me your cell number.

Take care,
H

To: whattheheck@hotmail.com

Victor just sent the photographs. Gosh! You look old, balding and pot-bellied! Middle-age has set in. I just could not believe it was you.
Hey! Caught you by surprise. Just joking. Except for a wee bit of weight, you look handsome as always. I think the weight kind of suits you. But I must say Victor takes the cake. He is gorgeous! What a hunk! Must speed up my London visit.
Meanwhile you fly safely,

Take care,
Oona
PS: my cell: +91 9820000060

To: oonakhanna@vsnl.com

Am in transit in Frankfurt. Just saw your mail.
Thanks, I wasn't aware you found me handsome earlier. Guess we can always make up for lost time.
As for Vic, he's out of bounds for you.
Will call once I return.
My cell: 077862343234

Take care,
H

To: whattheheck@hotmail.com

What do you mean by Vic being out of bounds for me?
Where are you now?

Take care,
Oona

To: oonakhanna@vsnl.com

In New York! Will be here for a week.
As for 'out of bounds', I mean not your type. Ask Riz to explain.
Till then, sleep over it baby!

H

To: whattheheck@hotmail.com

Completely foxed! Please explain. Riz is not around. He's in Delhi.
Besides, I am not in touch with him so often.
Losing sleep over it.

Ciao
Oona

To: oonakhanna@vsnl.com

I don't want your pretty face marred with dark circles. So don't lose sleep over it. If you must know, Victor is gay. As gay as goot. So stop wasting time ogling my bro.
Sleep well tonite.

H

ꕥ

Oona was a mess. Riz's silence weighed heavily on her. Her work suffered. Everything reminded her of Riz. From his favourite armchair to his beer mug. She couldn't listen to music without thinking of him admiring the system. She didn't want to use the mini home theatre he had fixed for her. Coffee time in the evenings became unbearable without him. She would not go to the multiplexes she had visited with him, or the coffee shops and restaurants where they had spent time together.

Though she had officially split with Anand by now, even he noticed Oona's condition when he saw her one day and asked casually if something was wrong. Oona assured him that all was well. She stopped bothering about her appearance. She lost interest in exchanging mails with Hector after the initial banter. She would stare at her cellphone, willing it to display a new message from Riz or hoping to see Riz Ali flash on the screen as he called her. He called very rarely, and her face lit up when he did. But immediately after she hung up, the doubts and insecurities would resurface.

Then one day he messaged: *Bak in B'bay. Hope all's well. C u soon. Riz*

But he avoided meeting her the next few days. Finally Oona called, in tears, 'Riz why are you being so harsh with me? I am going mad. And the problem is you. Don't you realise I'm in love with you?'

'Ouch!'

'You can ouch all you want, but it's true.'

They met up a couple of days later on neutral ground, at a corner table in a sheesha bar.

'I have to tell you that we will have to stop seeing each other. This cannot go on.'

'But that's not fair, Riz. You decided to get into this relationship and you decided to get out of it. You never considered my feelings even once.' Tears streamed down Oona's cheeks.

'Well, I did not exactly lead you up the garden path, did I?' Riz said nastily.

'I know,' Oona mumbled.

'Then? You are old enough to take care of yourself.'

'Is there someone else in your life?'

'No, not at the moment.' Oona knew he was lying.

He looked away and said, 'I think we must go now. I have an early morning tomorrow.'

Sory abt last eve. Am off 2 delhi. Wil talk 2 u later. Riz

Ok, Oona messaged back. She still could not fathom Riz. At least with Anand she knew he behaved despicably all the time. But Riz could be really mean and nasty one moment and then concerned and apologetic the next.

Hector called one day as she sat brooding over her failed relationships. It was fun talking to him after all those years. His voice of course didn't make her knees go weak as Riz's did.

'I normally do the London-New York sector. But am trying to work around a London-Bombay sector so that we can catch up,' Hector told her.

'That would be lovely,' Oona said. She wondered what it would be like to meet up with Hector after all those years. Not half as exciting as Riz. Hector did not have the glamour of being a celebrity that Anand or Riz had. But at least she and Hector had common ground and a lot to say to each other.

To: oonakhanna@vsnl.com

Hi,

All well with you? Long time no news. Just returned from Barmouth. Mum sends you her love. She hasn't heard from you in a while and was complaining. So send her a note. Vic also sends you his regards. Don't bother to write to him, I'll convey your regards! Just joking.

Spoke to Shaina last night. I really miss her. Am trying to wrangle the London-Bombay sector. Then may go over to Hong Kong to meet her. It's been a while.
Will let you know exactly when I am in Bombay.
Hope things are well with you at home. Regards to your mum.
Let me know if you need anything from here. Will happily bring it.

Cheers
H

To: whattheheck@hotmail.com
Just bring yourself, that's all.
Things are as good as they can get. Am surviving.
Will write to Aunty and love and a big kiss to Vic from me.

Ciao
Oona

To: oonakhanna@vsnl.com
Kiss delivered to Vic. He couriers you the same through me. Will deliver the needful when we meet.
You cannot just survive. You gotta rock! I am concerned about you.

Take care.
H

To: whattheheck@hotmail.com
Thanks ever so much for you concern. Need it badly.

Fly safe,
Oona

Moments later Oona messaged Riz: *Sorry but still miss you. Are you in Delhi?*

Riz: *Ouch! Yeah. Wil b here for a bit. Call u when in B'bay.*

To; oonakhanna@vsnl.com

Will be in Bombay on Fri, 21st. Will call the moment I land.

Meanwhile look after yourself.

H

It gave her something to look forward to. But Riz was constantly on her mind.

&

'Hi,' Hector called her on Saturday. 'Just landed midnight last. Been a long flight. Am planning to sleep out the day. Thought we could catch up for dinner. Any plans?'

'No. I've kept myself free knowing you would be here. Dinner is fine by me,' Oona said.

'Great, does 7.30 sound fine?' Hector asked.

'Maybe eight? It's Saturday and Bombay is up all night. Shall I come to your hotel?'

'Sure, I'm staying at Taj. Land's End. Let's meet here and we can decide where to go out for dinner later.'

'Done. See you at eight sharp. Room number?'

'412.'

&

The evening with Hector went off well. He was full of compliments for her, though to Oona these came about twenty years too late. He had retained his good looks but they no longer excited her as before. Now her mind was preoccupied with thoughts of Riz. They chatted in his room over a spritzer and then went down to the coffee shop for dinner. They bumped into other colleagues of his staying at the same hotel and Oona noticed he seemed quite popular with the ladies. After all he was single and eligible all over again. In spite of his flirtatious letters, he behaved like a perfect gentleman all evening, except for a tight hug while dropping her home in the cab. They had planned to meet again the next evening to watch a play.

As she turned in for the night, her phone beeped: *Truly lovely evening. 20 years vanished in a haze! You have not changed and hope you stay that way. Looking forward to the play tomorrow and spending more time with you. Sleep well and talk to you tomorrow. H*

She wished Riz had messaged thus. Nevertheless she texted back: *Enjoyed every bit. Its been a long time since I let my hair down. Thanks for everything. Gudnite. O*

'Gudnite', she noticed the spelling as she typed out the word. It was the way Riz spelt it. Without realising, Oona had got into the habit of spelling it thus.

*

Next morning Riz messaged her: *How r u? In Chandigrh 4 a shoot. Cal me on landline 0172 567771/2/3/4 #202.*

Oona called. Riz said he was busy with a Punjabi film shoot and would be there for a week. He was his charming self. Thank God he is not with that Payal bitch in Delhi. He must be missing me now, Oona consoled herself. She felt good. She had spoken to Riz. He was not in Bombay. She could safely meet Hector without bumping into him. It was a beautiful Sunday!

*

On Sunday evening Hector dropped her home very late after the play and dinner. 'Would you like to come in?' Oona offered politely.

'Some other day. It's too late now,' Hector looked up at her bungalow, impressed. 'Neat place you have here.'

'Only half of it is mine,' Oona clarified.

'Okay, good night,' Hector hugged her and kissed her cheek. 'This one is from Vic,' he remarked naughtily.

Oona laughed. 'And yours?' she asked.

'Some other time,' Hector smiled as he waited till she entered the house.

Have a safe flight tomrw. Bon voyage.Oona

Thx. Was a lovely eve. Got a taste of Bombay glamour. U r popular lady! Feel proud of u girl. Keep up. Wil cal from HK. Take care…H

To: oonakhanna@vsnl.com

Hey girl,

Am back in London. Sorry did not call from HK, it was hectic. Shaina is unhappy as Sonia has a baby boy from her other marriage. He is six months old and both parents are busy with him. So brought her away with me for a bit and then will pack her off to Barmouth to be with mum. We made it to Bombay just in time for my return flight to London, or would have called and met up.

You take care
H

To: whattheheck@hotmail.com

Hi,

Was looking forward to your call, but that's okay. Wish there was time enough to have met with Shaina, though I must admit I am not very good with children. Can just about spoil them rotten with toys and chocolates—that's what I do with my nephews and nieces. Spend some quality time with your daughter and make the most of it.

Was curious to know why is your id what the heck? *Any particular reason or just like that? Anyways, what the heck and how does it matter?*

Lotsa luv,
Oona

To: oonakhanna@vsnl.com

Hi Oona,

Sure missed you too on way back from HK but there will always be many more occasions to meet. I will be doing the Lon-Bom-Lon sector more frequently now.
And don't worry you will meet Shaina soon. She's a delight and gets easily spoilt by chocolates and less. Works on most children—wait till you have your own.
As for the id bit, what the heck, does it really matter? Got it?

Lotsa luv to you too,
WhattheHector Bose!

To: whattheheck@hotmail.com

Hello Mr WhattheHector Bose!

Hope all's well with Shaina. Hope to connect soon. I think I'm too old for babies. And don't forget I'm no longer with Anand.
When are you headed to Barmouth? Give lots of love to Aunty Maive from me.
Remember me to Mr Victor Bose.

Hugs
Oona

To: oonakhanna@vsnl.com

Hey, who said you were old! Weren't we together in high school? So you'd be about my age. And I'm never going to grow old. So that makes you young too. Shaina was born when Sonia was in her late thirties. So you have enough time. Besides, Anand is not the only man around.

Take care and hugs,

H

What does he mean by 'Anand is not the only man around'? Is he proposing to me?

She wished she would hear something like this from Riz.

On an impulse she messaged Riz: *Hi. Where r u? Miss u lots. O*

Keeping a tab on me honey? Back in Delhi. C u soon in Bbay. Riz

It was after a long time that Riz wrote 'honey'. Oona loved it. She chose to ignore the 'keeping a tab' comment.

A few days later, Riz messaged her: *Hi Oona. Arrvd an hour bak. Resting. Talk 2 u soon.*

Oona messaged back: *Grt. C u soon. Missd u.*

In this way, Riz spoke to Oona everyday but avoided meeting her on one pretext or the other.

Oona would message Riz every morning: *Let's meet for coffe at 5 at my pad?*

And he would reply in the affirmative. Then she would spend the whole day focused on her work and happy, waiting for 5 p.m. But invariably, around 4 o' clock, he would message, cancelling the date with something like: *Cant make it 2day. Tired. A nap needed.* Or: *Headin 2 bandra for auditn. Sory!* Or: *Sory! Me busy. Good luk.*

Why the hell is he avoiding me?

One day when she got the usual cancellation message from Riz, Oona called him. 'Since you don't want to meet me, at least we can talk,' she yelled into the phone.

'Sure. Go ahead. Talk.'

'Riz! What is the matter with you?'

'Please, I think we should call it quits,' Riz said. 'Hear me out. I am going through a lot of health problems at the moment and am stressed out. My shrink has doubled my dosage. I do not want added tension.'

'But I'm here to help you, Riz.'

'The only way you can help me now is to leave me alone for a bit. I need to sort out my life. Besides, the tarot card reader told me to stay away from married women as they would cause impediments to my health.'

'I don't believe this! You actually go by bullshit tarot readers?'

'Well, to each his own. You have your beliefs, I have mine. Let us go slow for a bit. You take care and I'll talk to you later, honey,' Riz said.

'Don't fucking honey me!' Oona banged the phone down. She had never been so rude to Riz.

Damn that Payal bitch! Oona had a wild impulse to call Jolly Anand and send a message to Payal that Riz Ali was two-timing her. But that would reveal her own relationship with Riz to Jolly, Oona realised. If Jolly didn't already know, of course.

Oona spent the next few days popping Alpraxes. She just walked around the house in a daze. Hector called from London and she howled on the phone, till he got so worried that he almost decided to fly down to Bombay. That sobered her a little and she dissuaded him from doing so.

'Why don't you come to London?' Hector suggested. 'You can stay with Vic and me or any of your other friends. You can meet Mum and Shaina in Barmouth. I think you need to get away from work and Anand for a bit.' Hector of course thought Anand was the cause of all her troubles.

'I don't know. Let's see.' Oona hesitated.

'Look babes, either you come here and be with us. Or else I'll come down one of these days and bash up your Mr Khanna.' Oona laughed out loud after days at that. She actually felt sorry for making Anand the scapegoat. *Wish Hector would beat Riz instead. Beat the shit out of him.*

'Okay. Maybe,' Oona told Hector.

'Not maybe. It'd better be soon. Or I'll come down I promise. Like Lochinvar. Remember, we had it in the school text?' Both laughed.

When she next bumped into Anand he remarked on her appearance. 'Oona, I'm genuinely concerned about you. What's wrong?'

Oona couldn't bring herself to explain. She had never thought she would need or get sympathy from Anand. She broke down.

'I can't explain Anand. I just feel so lost. I don't want to be in Bombay.'

'Would you like to go to Cal? To your Ma's place?' Anand asked as Shanta bai brought in the *masala chai*.

'No. Not Cal. I don't know.'

'Okay, you haven't been to London for a while, why don't you go now? I'll book your ticket. Meet all your friends. Do some shopping. And the change of scene will do you good. What say?'

First Hector, now Anand. Both had made the same suggestion. Oona decided she may as well head to London.

To: whattheheck@hotmail.com

Sorry for being out of sorts lately. Been under tremendous emotional and mental duress. I need not explain. You know by now. Anand is sending me to London.

I know I can stay with you guys or with friends. But I would like to live on my own for a bit if you don't mind. So you will have

to find me a modest serviced apartment near your place. A studio will do.
Looking forward to spending time with you guys and visiting Aunty Maive in Barmouth. Let me know about the apartment asap.
Also let me know when is the best time to visit in the coming weeks when you will be around as well.

Love to all,
Oona

To: oonakhanna@hotmail.com

Thank God you have decided to come. Best time to be here is the month after next. I will be in London for two weeks then before going to New York for ten days. My handsome bro will entertain you in my absence. He is great fun. You will love him.
I can take a fortnight off after that and take you to be with Mum in Barmouth. She has a lovely cottage. She will be really happy to meet you and you can meet Shaina. We can do Legoland or some such trip after that.
Have booked you a serviced apartment in Collingham Gardens, just across the road from us.
Give me your flight details. We are all looking forward to your visit.

Cheers
H

Oona felt loved just reading the line 'We are all looking forward to your visit.'

To: whattheheck@hotmail.com

Thanks. You are such an angel. You forgot to mention the rate of the apartment though. Have to check whether it fits my budget.Let me know. Love to the family.
Oona

To: oonakhanna@vsnl.com

Don't worry yourself over rates. Will sort that out later. Just look after yourself and bring yourself here soon. Can you manage to bring some sandesh *with you? Vic loves them.*

Take care,
H

To: whattheheck@hotmail.com

Will bring sandesh. *Anything else? For Aunty or Shaina?*

Love
Oona

To: oonakhanna@vsnl.com

Would have asked for alphonsos, but they are not in season! Don't cart anything but yourself. Text me flight details asap.
H

'*Adaab arz. Sab Khairiyat?*' Riz called after quite a while.

'*Ji,*' Oona almost melted at the sound of his voice. But she controlled herself.

'All well at home? How is Anandsaab? You guys aren't going anywhere for New Year's Eve? All the glam brigade is headed to Goa I hear.'

'No,' Oona lied. She did not tell him of her London plans with Hector. In fact she did not mention getting in touch with the Bose brothers at all, though Riz had made it possible. 'Too much work. What about you?'

'Well, nowhere in particular. Just Delhi and back. I just might go to Frisco. But not sure as yet.'

'All well with you healthwise?' Oona asked.

'Yes. As well as it can be. Just wanted to say hi. We will talk at leisure and *inshallah* catch up soon,' Riz said.

'*Inshallah*,' Oona said. She still missed him.

Now that Oona knew she was headed to London, she had something to look forward to. She counted down the days and planned her trip, cheering up knowing she would soon be with old friends. She also remembered her interest in Ela Sen. She decided to follow up with Moushumi on the information she had requested about David's family whereabouts. She had her life to sort out. And some history to dig up. She couldn't wait.

Book Three

LONDON & WALES
2009–2010

London

It was a dull Saturday afternoon when Oona arrived in London. And quite cold. She shivered as she came out of Heathrow and pulled her leather jacket tightly around her. Hector pushed the trolley with her luggage as they headed towards the car park. 'I hope you are prepared for worse days ahead?' Hector asked, noticing her shiver. Oona nodded.

It had been a long flight and rather tiring. She had travelled economy class after ages. Now that she was no longer with Anand, nor was she travelling with him, there had been no need to keep up appearances. Besides, Anand was also cutting corners after losing money on *My Name is Khanna*.

It was the first time she was travelling the familiar freeways to the city without Anand. She glanced at Hector. His hands on the steering, exposing his broad wrists, did make him rather an attractive figure. Oona tried to look away, on an impulse replacing those hands with Riz's in her imagination. The thought made her sad as well as smile.

'A penny for your thoughts,' Hector said.

'Well…just thinking…we've come a long way indeed. From Golpark to London.'

'Yes. I was thinking that too. In fact, I was….'

Suddenly Oona's phone rang. 'Wow! You are popular, lady. Take the call first,' Hector said.

Oona answered, 'Hi Shalini. I'm in London. Will call you later.' Oona hung up. 'One of those most avoidable calls,' she explained to Hector, shrugging. He smiled.

The service apartment was tiny but cosy. Well furnished in soft, warm colours, it had a fairly comfortable living room with a kitchenette, a decent-sized bath and a tiny bedroom—just small enough to squeeze in and get into bed.

'Do you like it?' Hector asked, showing her around.

'Yes. Cute. Except it doesn't have much of a view apart from the neighbouring window,' Oona said. 'But I'll get used to it.' Oona was not very fond of basement apartments, but let it go.

After explaining a few more things about the apartment, Hector said, 'Then I'll take your leave while you settle in. Give me a buzz when you're ready and I'll come over to take you to our place. Vic's looking forward to meeting you.'

'I can't thank you enough. Hector, how do I settle the rent?' Oona asked.

'Oh for God's sake, you've just arrived. You're not running away, nor am I. We'll work it out later. Now just relax. I've left you some provisions in the kitchen and a tuna sandwich in the fridge. Eat it.' He gave her a peck on her forehead and left.

Gosh! I'd never believe this is the same Casanova Hector Bose from Lowes. He has grown so mature.

The evening with the Bose brothers went off well. Oona loved their apartment and immediately felt at home. It was the top-floor apartment of a series of Edwardian mansions in Kensington. Largish, with two-bedrooms and two baths, it also had a tiny balcony that looked out onto the Lexham Gardens. The apartment had a cheery and well-lit feel. The best part was the kitchen—it had a curved atrium in the centre that looked up to the sky.

Victor was great company, witty and charming. He almost reminded her of Riz. No wonder they were friends, Oona thought. Had she not been aware of his sexual preferences, Oona surely would have flirted with him.

'What a waste!' Oona sighed, when Vic left the room for a moment.

'What's a waste?' Hector asked, following her gaze to Vic's retreating figure.

'Your brother. He is sooooo good-looking and such an incredible charmer. What a waste for womankind. As it is there are hardly any charming single men left these days and there goes Victor Bose all gay as goot. Not fair! Are you sure he is gay?' she asked Hector, who was all smiles by now.

'You don't believe me or what? Actually I don't blame you. None of my girlfriends do.'

'Hey!' Oona protested, but he reached out for her hand and, before she knew it, he had pulled her towards him and kissed her lightly on her pert little nose.

Vic re-entered the room at precisely that moment. 'Ouch!' he exclaimed, sounding exactly like Riz. 'Hey don't bother,' Oona called out as he turned to leave the room, 'We won't embarrass you any further, I promise,' she said, wriggling out of Hector's embrace.

Over the next few days Hector showed her around the neighbourhood. There was a nice little park called Collingham Gardens opposite her apartment. Two blocks further and across the road were the Cromwell Hospital and a huge Sainsbury's.

'It's open twenty-four hours, round the week. Even has a Starbucks inside. So you can get your caffeine kick any time of day or night.' His and Vic's apartment was another block away. A good fifteen minutes from his apartment was High Street Kensington. 'For all you smart shoppers,' he joked.

'Wow! That's pretty close by. I'm going to love this.'

On another day Hector took her around the other end of Kensington and pointed out the various museums, the V&A, the Natural History Museum, the Science Museum, and others. He showed her where the nearest tube station was located. Then further down Knightsbridge he pointed out Harrod's, Harvey Nichols and other stores. 'Happy?' he asked as Oona nodded, trying to keep her bearings. 'And if you feel a little adventurous someday, then you can walk some miles ahead and reach King's Road, all the way to Chelsea,' Hector pointed.

'Wow! Chelsea? Hugh Grant lives there, right?'

'Gosh, Oona grow up. You are behaving like those village bumpkins who get thrilled on reaching Juhu because Amitabh Bachchan lives there!'

'Aw! Shut up.'

Hector's time off drew to a close. He had to do the New York—London—LA sector for a week. She had already begun feeling lonely at the thought of his departure.

'I think I'm going to miss you,' Oona told him over the phone.

'Relax, sweetie, I'm only gone for a week. Besides, now you have all the time to flirt with bro,' Hector mocked.

'You bet I will. Thank God for Vic. I guess I will also catch up with my friends. Bond a bit with Sandra and Jo and the kids.' Sandra was her old friend from college and Joseph was her husband. Both husband and wife were lawyers at the Old Bailey. That was another place Oona was keen to see.

'Listen, tonight I want to take you and Vic out for dinner. My treat. And no saying no,' Oona said.

'Okay, okay, though you don't have to. I'll tell Vic. Any particular place you have in mind?'

'Well, I thought of the Boxwood Café, unless you guys have something else in mind?' Oona dropped the name casually.

'Boxwood Café! *The* Boxwood Café? Are you serious?'

'But of course! Why wouldn't I be?' Oona laughed into the phone.

'You know it takes days to get a booking there. How do you think we are going to accomplish that by this evening?'

'I already have a booking for us for 7.30 pm,' Oona said coolly.

'Lady, you've got to be kidding. Just how did you manage to pull that one off?' Hector was astounded.

'Well, I know Gordon Ramsay's chef, Stuart Gilles. He's a good friend. Met him in Bombay. Stuart's cooked a great meal for us and we partied out together. I called him and that's it,' Oona explained.

'I am impressed!'

Oona had known he would be.

Victor and Hector were most impressed by the preferential treatment they enjoyed at the Boxwood Cafe because of Oona. Gilles personally came to their table, chatted for a bit, and recommended his specials.

As Oona cut into the asparagus tart, one of Stuart's specialties, her phone beeped.

Hi Oona. How is everything? Just wanted u to know that I am back in Bombay. It's been a while. Let's meet soon. Let me know when. Riz.

Oona almost dialled his number but refrained as she did not want Hector or Victor to find out about her and Riz. Nor did she want Riz to know she was with the Bose brothers. She messaged back, her face glowing: *At dinner with friends. Call u tomrow. Ciao.*

Her cell beeped back: *Dinner? Rather late @ 2am? Partying without me?*

Oops! She'd slipped up. She let out a soft giggle.

'What's so funny?' Hector asked.

'Well, this friend of mine does not know I'm in London. So I messaged her saying I was having dinner and she was surprised, because it's 2 a.m. in Bombay!'

They laughed and Oona messaged back: *Yep! School pal Reema's b'day. Gals hanging out in her pad. N u? So late? Cheers.*

Riz texted back: *Just got back from the airport awhile ago. Talk in the morng. Ciao.*

Morning for Riz will be way past midnight for me. I'll be fast asleep with the phone on silent mode. Good! He'll think I'm playing hard to get. But at least he's still concerned about me. Or is he just trying out his luck with me again? Maybe Payal's giving him a hard time. Serves him right. I'm not falling so easy again. I'm trying to get over him. And I am happier this way.

It was nearly half past ten when Hector drove Oona up to her apartment. Vic had got off near Knightsbridge to meet a friend for a nightcap. Oona wondered if she should invite Hector over for a nightcap too. The few spritzers she'd had made her a little light-headed. As he pulled up in front of the gate, Oona hesitated before asking, 'Would you like some coffee?'

'I was afraid you wouldn't ask and I'd have to invite myself in. Anyway, you go right ahead and put the coffee to percolate while I just put this baby on the lot,' he said referring to his swanky BMW.

She set about making coffee for Hector, but was brewing tea for herself when he walked in.

'I thought you love coffee. What's with this tea now?' he asked.

'I do love my coffee. But after sunset just a drop of it will have me rocking the whole night. You'll leave and I don't want to lie wide awake in bed.' The words were out, and she was surprised at her own last remark.

'Well, I won't leave if you tell me not to,' Hector remarked naughtily with a wicked grin. Oona blushed. She wondered whether she was giving

Hector all the wrong signals. In fact she was not sure what she wanted from Hector. She lacked the security of being Mrs Anand Khanna and she felt emotionally bereft after Riz. She wondered whether Hector could fill in for both. Hector had been giving her the comfort and protection she desperately needed in the past few months as she coped with her troubles. At times she felt a strong physical urge to be with him. But she was not sure about her current emotional state. *Have I truly got over Riz? Or for that matter Anand? Will it be fair to get into a relationship with Hector now? What if it doesn't work out? I'll be devastated. Or will I not? Can I be that calculating? After all, Hector himself is no angel. But will it be fair on him?*

As she sipped her tea, she felt Hector come closer to her.

'A penny for your thoughts.'

'Just wanted to th…thank you for every…for standing b…by me….' Oona stuttered.

'Just a dry thanks. Won't do.' Hector smiled, towering over her five-foot frame at his six feet two inches.

'Tell me what you want. I can cook you a nice Bengali meal….'

'Who said anything about food?' Hector said, setting his cup on the kitchen table so that he could hold her close. He gently took the cup from her hand and placed it next to his. 'A way to a man's heart need not always be through his stomach.'

'Oh really! Then how?' Oona tried to laugh it off boldly, but she was tense.

'Like this,' Hector said, tilting her face towards him and kissing her gently on the forehead. He then kissed her eyes, nose, and finally rested his lips on hers.

Against her mouth, he murmured softly, 'Do we add a spice component to this sweetness or would you rather keep it at this level?'

'I don-don't know,' Oona said, haltingly.

'I say the sweet content is far more apparent and enjoyable when contrasted with the occasional spice,' Hector whispered.

His lips crushed hers and she responded by hugging him tighter. He let out a soft moan. Before she knew it, Hector swung her up and walked towards the tiny bedroom as she helplessly clung on to him. He laid her down on the bed and kicked off his loafers while Oona tried to pull off her Blahniks. Hector helped her and as soon as the shoes were off, she swung her legs up, rolling to the other end of the bed. Hector caught up with her and pulled her to him. He ran his fingers through her short crop. 'I miss your long hair. You'll have to grow it again for me.'

'I didn't realise that you had a crush on my hair!' Oona said.

'Forget your hair, I had a crush on you since I first set my eyes on you!'

'Liar!' Oona giggled.

'I swear!' Hector murmured, starting to unbutton her shirt and reaching for her bra clasp. 'Especially these,' he whispered as he started to suck on her right nipple. 'These have grown since the Golpark days.'

Hector continued kissing her nipples and Oona moaned in pleasure. Emboldened, Hector tore away her remaining clothes and soon, Oona felt Hector Bose throbbing inside her. He completely enveloped her with his huge frame, and was gasping her name between thrusts.

Minutes later both lay naked, completely spent of 15 years of suppressed passion as their clothes lay strewn across the bed.

The first thought that hit Oona as she stared into the dark ceiling, holding Hector, was that she must remember to take the i-pill which she had carried as a precaution. It was too early in their relationship for her to risk a pregnancy with Hector.

Next, she wondered how her friend Sonia would react if she saw her and Hector in this state. For Oona it was a minor victory of sorts.

Oona tried to stack the papers neatly on the dining table while Victor made himself comfortable on one of the armchairs in the living room. 'Something to drink?' she asked him.

'A cup of tea will be fine. Thank you,' Victor said. 'Busy with some paperwork?'

'Well…kind of. It's something to do with family history,' Oona said, placing the kettle to boil. She explained briefly to Victor about the ill-fated romance of her great aunt Ela Sen and her English lover David Oliver and their letters in her possession. Of how Ela's staunch Brahmo father refused permission for her to marry David. The tragic death of Ela under mysterious circumstances. Ela Sen's death had been officially recorded as an accident, wherein she fell into a gorge, people speculated that it had been 'suicide' or even 'murder'. Oona told Victor about the pendant with David's photograph and how it had helped her trace David's address to 17 Park Lane in Calcutta.

Moushumi's colleague had been able to find out more and had sent Oona a report some weeks back. The report said that the occupants of 17 Park Lane, David's parents and sister, left India in the mid-1920s, much before Independence. David's father, Vincent, had been a Company officer and wanted to return to his homeland due to the unrest and anti-British feeling that had begun building in India by that time. According to the report, David stayed back in Calcutta, living on as a tenant in the same house that his father had sold to an Armenian family, the Ezras. Old correspondence between the Ezras and the Olivers revealed that the Olivers' address in England was 212 Edgeware Road, London.

'I plan to check out what's left of 212 Edgeware Road and what became of the Olivers and their descendants. If I can trace them that is,' Oona summed up.

She noticed Vic frowning. 'I hope you didn't get bored. You look a bit preoccupied,' she said apologetically.

'Oh, not at all. It's quite an interesting story. Good material for a novel. I was wondering how I could help you track down the Olivers.'

'That's precisely what I was thinking! A historical romantic thriller. But, the idea is mine!'

'Of course!' Victor cut her short. 'No one is denying that. It's just sheer curiosity on my part. I would like to know what became of David and his descendants. How did he cope with your great-aunt's death? Did he find love after her? Did he marry? Did he have children?' Victor shrugged. 'I'm now just as curious as you to track them down. 212 Edgeware Road did you say? Well, let us locate it first,' Victor said, noting down the address using his phone's memo function.

Oona was happy that she now had Victor as a partner in this endeavour. She shared a great comfort level with Victor and of late she seemed to have developed a close bond with him, maybe because he was Hector's brother or Riz's friend, or simply because he was Victor Bose. The rest of the afternoon went off well and Victor relished the prawn *malai* curry with rice that Oona cooked for lunch. Hector was away but Victor looked her up often—this was the second time in a week that Victor had dropped in on Oona. He had taken Oona to watch *Art*, starring Albert Finney. Oona enjoyed every moment in his company and especially loved the envious glances she garnered from many women who noticed her handsome date. It felt like the good old early days of her and Riz's romance. This time however with no strings attached. Whatsoever.

Her phone beeped.

Is that all u miss? I have a lot more to give than that ☺

Hector's message. She had texted him that morning saying she was cooking prawn curry for Victor and was missing him, knowing he loved prawn curry. She smiled and to Victor's questioning look answered, 'That's your brother, envious of us having a good time.'

'Oh. Tell him not to fret. We'll have to tolerate his company soon.'

Vic says hi and c u 2morow. Hope all's going well. Oona messaged back.

Longing to get my hands on you is how it is going. ☺

Oona blushed. Victor gave her a knowing smile as he got up to leave.

'I'll call when I get some info on the address. Meanwhile take care and we'll catch up when Hector's back.' Victor hugged her. As he stood up to kiss her, he noticed a love nick near her cleavage, '*Bhalo theko*, and don't let my brother bully you too much,' he said with a knowing smile.

ꕥ

Hector was back and this time he spent more time with Oona in her apartment, making love to her through the afternoons. In the evenings they would go for long walks in Kensington Park and occasionally catch a film or a play. Most evenings, Oona cooked with the brothers at their apartment and supped with them. Both brothers were good cooks and fed Oona many scrumptious meals. When Victor was not home, Oona and Hector made wild love on Hector's queen-sized bed. On other occasions Hector would walk her across to her service apartment and spend the night in her arms. He always kept a change for the night in her closet and would slip out in the wee hours of the mornings, kissing Oona as she slept peacefully. Sometimes he would wake her up, making love to her like a 'raging bull', as Oona described his early morning fervours. After that he would bring her bed tea and cook up a nice Scottish breakfast of bacon, eggs and roast potatoes. At other times he would slow-cook a pot of porridge, topping it up with nuts and sliced bananas and yoghurt.

For the first time in many years, Oona felt pampered like a princess. In the early years of their courtship, Anand used to pamper her thus, but without the finesse of the Bose brothers. He had always been worried about the press and his image. With Riz it was worse, as he was always edgy given his fear of Anand. Here, for the first time, Oona felt completely at ease, with no one to tell her what to do or how to behave. In spite of the dank dark weather, when most moods were sombre, Oona was like a fresh burst of sunshine. There was a glow on her face and a spring in her gait. She was falling in love with Hector. But more than falling in love, this time her happiness came from the idea of being in love itself, with the near fulfilment of the ideal of love. She didn't know if she was jumping into the relationship too fast, nor did she care.

Sometimes she wondered whether Hector was coming on too strong. She loved Hector and revelled in his possessiveness but at times found his ardour stifling. If they were alone, Hector would make love to her even if she was tired and unwilling. Even outdoors, he never missed an opportunity to paw and caress her. PDA, as all Bollywood journos called it: Public Display of Affection. This contrasted sharply to Hector's earlier restrained image. His obsessive appetite for sex amazed her and left her sore. With no breathing space between their love making sessions, she sometimes could not enjoy sex with Hector.

She reasoned that being much younger than Anand and Riz, and having been single for a while, Hector just had a lot of pent-up passion. But she could not explain away his refusal to wear a condom and attempts to stop her taking birth control pills. This despite Oona's insistence that she did not plan on starting a family for the next couple of years. Hector also took offence to Oona's low necklines and once at Sandra and Jo's he told her rather rudely that she looked much better in *salwar-kameez* than the skinny jeans she lived in. She decided not to dwell on such thoughts, choosing instead to look forward to meeting Aunty Maive in Barmouth soon. Hector was leaving for Hong Kong in a couple of days and would bring Shaina back with him. They all planned to visit Barmouth together.

Oona was a little apprehensive about meeting Shaina, having nurtured no fondness for children. She prayed Shaina would be an easy-going child and not try her patience much and fervently hoped for her and Hector's sake that they would bond well. But that was still a week away. Right now she was waiting for Hector to leave for Hong Kong so that she could recover from the soreness of his love making and spend some easy hours with Victor, perhaps even dig up something on the Olivers.

Riz had been texting her on and off. For a change he was curious about her whereabouts. She decided she might as well tell him she was in

London, though she had earlier pretended she was in Calcutta. She called Riz a couple of times but his phone was busy. Deciding to try again later, she headed off for a bath. When she had bathed and dressed, she checked her phone to find nine missed calls from Riz! Between Hector's ardour and Riz's concern, Oona's face glowed in a warm smile as she dialled his number.

'*Adaab*,' Oona said to his '*adaab arz*'.

'You called? All well with you?' Riz asked.

'Yep. And you? What's up?'

'Well not much. Was in Delhi with mom. Just got back. You said you were in Cal. Are you back?'

'Well, yes I did get back,' Oona lied. 'Then I decided to take a break. Am in London. Just chilling.'

'In London! Wow! Good for you. And when are you returning?'

'Well, I've been here for nearly three weeks, but I plan to be here another couple of months. Catching up with old friends, a little personal work, and basically just relaxing. I needed to get away from Bombay,' Oona trailed off.

'Yeah, I know. You deserve it. Does Anand know you are in London?'

'Can we change the topic?' Oona asked coldly.

'Ouch! I'm sorry,' Riz said, sounding sheepish.

'That's okay. Oh by the way I met up with our common friends the Bose brothers, Hector and Victor. Vic says hi to you.'

'Oh did he? Say hi to him from me. Will call him one of these days myself. How is he?' Riz asked.

'As good as he can get. Still the hunk,' Oona said, drawling it out for effect, hoping Riz would feel just a little jealous.

'Hmm. Good for him. All right then, I'll talk to you later. Meanwhile take care and look after yourself. And hope to catch up with you soon.'

'You too. Ciao.' Oona hung up.

Flashback

It had rained and it was dark and cold. Victor and Oona walked down near-empty streets, deserted in this weather. Victor had called Oona to say he had located 212 Edgeware Road and that if she was willing to brave the weather he could take her to see it. She would have much preferred to take a cab, but Victor insisted they walk. Oona had bragged to Victor that she loved walking, and now she had to keep up appearances. Though she did wish she didn't have to wear this heavy overcoat. It weighed her down and made her feel really short.

Well, maybe I'll shed a few kilos now that I rarely do my surya namaskars.

Victor looked as dapper as always in his well-cut long coat, swinging his umbrella casually when he came to fetch Oona. She had a tough time keeping pace with his long strides. In fifteen minutes' time she was a good ten feet behind him, forcing him to slow down. 'Sorry,' Victor apologised. 'I did not realise I was walking too fast.'

'Oh. That is okay. It is just that…'

'My daddy long legs! I know. Can't help it,' Victor patted her encouragingly. 'Okay. Let me slow down while I tell you what I have found out about the Olivers.'

'I'm all ears,' Oona smiled.

'But before I tell you all that I have unearthed in this saga, which, let me tell you young lady, is far more fascinating than you bargained for…'

'Really?' Oona cut in, her curiosity getting the better of her.

'Really, Oona. It makes me wonder why you embarked on this journey. Especially after so many years. Answer me honestly.' Victor asked.

'To tell you the truth, pure coincidence. I was bored, had nothing much to do and Ela Sen's letters came out of the backburner. Actually, the back drawer. The journalist in me was tickled and I decided to dig up Ela's story. Who knows what might come of it. A novel maybe. I am tired of being an honest writer and the brickbats that come with it. There's so little honesty left in journalism these days, just sycophancy. I'm so disillusioned.'

'Ah, I thought as much. That is quite a novel idea!' Both laughed. 'Jokes aside, is that all?'

'Well...yes and no.'

'Tell me.'

'People have often commented on my uncanny resemblance to Ela Sen. That's part of why she fascinates me. Unearthing her story was a way of getting back to my roots, or destiny...well I don't know how to explain.'

'You have, kind of. I know what you are getting at,' Victor assured her. 'Now listen to this.'

'You will be amazed to know what has become of 212. Take a guess.' Victor smiled at Oona.

'I can't. Tell me!'

'It has become a casino! It's called Reel Casino.'

'Oh,' Oona sounded a bit dampened. 'What's become of the Olivers then?'

'Patience, my dear,' Victor said with a smile, enjoying keeping Oona guessing.

'The present owners are two Arab brothers, the Saids. In fact, one of them, Faroukh, was nice enough to direct me to the previous owners, giving me their number and address. The Johns—Tony and Rebecca now live in the lane next to 212. They sold the place to the Saids some seven–eight years ago.

'When I caught up with Rebecca and Tony, they were initially a bit wary of giving me any information about the earlier occupants of 212. In fact, they pretended they did not know and at first turned me away. The next day I called Rebecca, used all my charm, and explained how important it was to my friend, who has come all the way from India, etc., etc. She finally relented and called me the next day saying that she had managed to pull out some information. I'm sure she already had it, but was just acting a bit pricey. I met her when Tony was out visiting a friend in hospital. It is all quite intriguing,' Victor said as he gently steered Oona across the road.

'In the late twenties,' Victor narrated, 'Vincent and Alison Oliver relocated to England. Alison's mother was Indian and her father an Englishman settled in India, whereas Vincent Oliver was from Chester near London. They chose to live in London. All he could afford with the proceeds from the sale of his Chester house and his small savings was 212 Edgeware Road. It was one of the not-so-affluent areas of the city, mainly inhabited by migrants from Arab countries and India, though it was the slightly more educated and affluent Indians who moved here—mainly professionals. Vincent was happy to be among Indians, even though this was not one of the swankiest areas of London and not many Englishmen lived here. '

Victor went on to say that Vincent and his family lived in their ground-floor apartment at Edgeware Road for many years, till at least the early to mid-forties. Rebecca's grandparents and later parents, the Hartlands, actually lived on the floor above and were quite friendly with the Olivers. Rebecca remembered stories about Aunty Judy, the Olivers' daughter. Her father, William and the other neighbourhood boys were all in love with the attractive girl, though she was much older. 'We called her "Judy O-la-la", and we all wanted to wed her,' William Hartland used to tell his daughter out of her mother's earshot. But that was not to be. Rodney O'Brien, an Irishman, came to live in the rear basement of 212. He was a civil engineer, overseeing the construction of the coal-fired Battersea Power Station located on the south bank of the river Thames near Battersea. Judy and he became romantically involved; soon Judy-O-la-la married Rodney and the two left for Cork.

'Now listen to this bit about your great aunt. A few years after Judy and Rodney's marriage, tragedy struck. The Olivers' son David, who lived in India and seldom came to visit them, died tragically there. The Olivers said it was suicide as David was romantically involved with a native girl, whilst the rumours went it was murder.' 'What?' Oona exclaimed, covering her face in shock. Then she recovered, 'How dare they call Ela Sen a native! She was more educated and cultured than the Olivers or any other British family of the time!'

'I know, I know. But then this is how the common white-skinned man thinks. For them it is only colour, not breeding which scores over Asians and Africans.'

'I guess. Okay, continue.'

'Judy and Rodney visited her parents from time to time. Rebecca's father remembers her two little ones, Charlotte and Philip. Philip was an angel and Charlotte was a riot. But after the death of their son the Olivers, especially Alison—otherwise a spunky lady—lost their love for life. They whiled away their days just for the sake of Judy and her children, but the zest had gone out of their lives. They looked forward only to their India visits, but those stopped too after Alison's mother passed away in Calcutta.

'Alison died sometime in the mid 1940s. She was in her sixties, and Vincent, grief-stricken, followed soon. Aunty Judy retained the house for a while though she hardly visited it. She died in her forties, of breast cancer, and her daughter Charlotte sold off the apartment to William Hartland, Rebecca's dad.' Victor concluded, adding, 'Earlier the Hartlands rented out the Olivers' apartment and continued to live on the floor above. Rebecca and her husband inherited the house, but eventually, childless, ageing and unable to keep a check on a large property, they sold off 212 to the present owners, the Saids, who have converted it into a casino.'

'So where is Charlotte now?' Oona asked.

'She died. That's what Rebecca said.'

'And her brother Philip?'

'No idea. In fact, I did not ask. You ask for yourself when you meet her,' Victor grinned. 'This way. We're almost there.'

Rebecca John must have been quite attractive in her youth, Oona thought when she met her. Tall, slim and smartly casual, with a short crop of neat blonde hair framing her pert features, Rebecca was somewhere in her early seventies. Or maybe late, Oona thought to herself. 'Have another one of them, dear,' Rebecca held out the plate of shortbread fingers for Oona. 'They are fresh.'

'Yes, I know,' Oona said as she reached out for another one, balancing the teacup on its saucer, 'I love Walker's.'

'Oh dearie, no they are not Walker's. I bake them at home. Myself.'

'Wow. Delicious,' Oona crunched out the words.

'As I was saying my love, what a small world. To think your great-aunt was the love of the Oliver boy's life. Ooh, this is sooo romantic.' Rebecca went on. Oona wished she would get on with the facts than go on about mushy romances.

'I thought it a bit surprising that Judy's daughter, Charlotte would sell off the property in a hurry so soon after her mother's death. What about her brother Philip? Did he not have a stake in the property?' Oona asked Rebecca.

'What an intelligent observation! That's a smart lass you have here,' Rebecca told Victor. Both smiled. 'Charlotte had no contacts in London, having grown up in Cork. So she talked to my dad about disposing off this property. My old man did get a little suspicious, because Charlotte was unmarried, and her brother Philip, who was a year younger, was already married. When dad asked about Philip, Charlotte said he had married against his parents' wishes to either a Scottish or a Welsh lass and a very upset Judy had disinherited him.'

'Poor fellow,' Victor exclaimed.

'Yes, I know. Before buying the property my dad made sure she was telling the truth. He looked at Aunty Judy's last will and testament, saw that all was in order, and then bought over the property.'

'When was this exactly?' Victor asked.

'I think 1959 or '60. Could even be '61. I can look up the exact date of purchase for you,' Rebecca offered.

'What about Charlotte? Did she keep in touch?' Oona asked.

'Well, off and on. At some point in time she mentioned the passing away of her brother. She used to send us the occasional Christmas card. Seldom came down though. She remained a spinster. I heard of her death from her nephew, he wrote from somewhere in Wales, I think. I think that must be more than ten years ago, sometime in 1995-96, a couple of years before we sold off the property to the Saids,' Rebecca tried hard to recollect. 'Hey wait a minute. Her brother Philip was married to a Scottish lass. Now I remember. Her name was Rosalind. And Philip's son, Guy, her nephew, married a Welsh girl. I forget her name. But it's all there in the card. I must have noted their names in my old address book. Give me some time to hunt it down and I shall give you their contact details.'

'Oh that will be very helpful,' Oona said.

'But I'm afraid love it's been a long time since I heard from them last. More than ten years ago. Who knows where they're living now,' Rebecca shrugged.

'It doesn't matter. At least we can try to locate them through their forwarding address. Just like we managed to dig out a lot of info on the Olivers from you,' Oona said. 'When I first decided to embark on this journey, I had no illusions. In fact I thought I was being foolish. That I would never find 212 Edgeware Road and even if I was able to locate the address, I expected a new building with new residents who had no clue about the Olivers. And I had a nagging feeling I would be termed a lunatic or turned away rudely,' Oona concluded. 'But thanks to Vic here, we are where we are today.'

'Rebecca honey, I just wondered whether you could locate the Olivers' contact in the next couple of days or so?' Victor asked.

'You mean the O'Briens. Remember Judy married Rodney O'Brien and the deed of transfer was between the Hartlands and the O'Briens,' Rebecca reminded him.

'Yes, yes of course. The reason for my urgency is that we leave next week for Barmouth. And if this nephew lives in Wales and we had his contact address, maybe we could try looking him up ourselves,' Victor said.

'Barmouth at this time of year! It'll be freezing out there!' Rebecca exclaimed.

'It is. But my mom stays there and Oona is here on a fairly short trip. One of the main reasons for her coming here, apart from tracking down the Olivers, is to catch up with Mum. They haven't met in about…two decades?' Victor looked at Oona, who nodded.

'I understand, dear. I'll see what I can do. Maybe you could call me tomorrow morning around ten when Tony's out for his daily stroll. He doesn't like nosey parkers,' she winked at Victor.

'I can quite understand,' Victor kissed Rebecca's freckled hand as they prepared to leave.

'Bye dearies,' Rebecca waved. 'And don't forget to keep me updated once you find out. I am as curious as Anna now,' Rebecca said, referring to Oona.

Oona did not bother to correct her. She just wanted to lay her hands on Charlotte's nephew's, that is, David's great-nephew's whereabouts.

The BA flight from Hong Kong was delayed by half an hour. Victor led Oona to the mini Nero's outlet at Heathrow. 'I'll need a double shot of espresso to deal with what's ahead…You know…Shaina,' he smiled at Oona.

'Oh my God! Don't tell me she is a handful! I am not too comfortable with children myself.'

'Well, not exactly a handful. She is quite a sweet and obedient kid, but she's hyper. Full of questions, rattles on and on. And I'm her favourite Uncle Vic, so she just clings to me. Hector of course is quite happy that way. Between you and me, I think it was a good decision that Shaina stays with her mom. My brother isn't quite the epitome of patience, especially with children.'

'Oh,' Oona said as she ordered her latte. Hector had led her to believe that he was cool with kids. 'But isn't Shaina a little neglected because of her mom's new family?'

'Well, it's Sonia's new baby keeping Sonia and her husband busy. That's just a phase. Things will settle down in a couple of months. Shaina's step dad, Rohan, is actually quite good with her. In fact I think he does a better job than Hector could have done. I think she misses having his attention more than her mum's. Rohan mailed me a few days back, saying he felt guilty about neglecting Shaina. And that, I guess, says a lot about Rohan.'

Oona nodded as she sipped her coffee. This was a complete eye-opener. She herself had begun feeling a little disappointed in Hector. Of late he'd sent her some bold and colourful texts, loaded with sexual innuendos. This was a complete contrast to the Hector she had known in Calcutta, or even a few months ago, when she was in Mumbai. That Hector would send her flirty yet crisp, cute mails, full of concern. The previous evening she'd been with Sandra and Jo at a falafel place, when Hector sent her a text:

Armoured plans fall out of joint
When steel reaches its melting point
Alas! My furnace lacks the power
To liquefy that steel shod cover
So add yours—for beyond it lies
A little piece of paradise.

At first Oona was shocked. Then disgusted. And finally embarrassed by his poor poetry. It was cheesy and she began to wonder whether he had a sick mind. When Jo left the table for a while, she showed the text to Sandra, who was quite excited by it, notwithstanding the bad poetry. Sandra's marriage was placid and predictable and this obviously appealed to her.

'I think Hector is just right for you,' she said. 'Both of you have been married once before. Besides, thank your stars that his daughter stays with the mother. It will be perfect now to settle down and start a family of your own. And just imagine my luck. You will be in London, living close to us in Kensington. What fun!' Sandra rattled off, pragmatic to the core. She didn't realise that Oona was not interested and was not sharing her enthusiasm. She loved Hector no doubt. But she did not want to jump into another commitment so soon. It was not thoughts of Anand or Riz holding her back—it was just that Hector did not excite her enough to want to be with him for the rest of her life. She still felt a strong sexual attraction for him, though he frequently overwhelmed her with his passion.

Gosh! Am I turning into a nymphomaniac? To me a physical relationship always meant a deep emotional commitment. And look at me now .... enjoying sex without caring for commitment. Is Hector's sexual overdrive putting me off? Or have I just matured with age?

'Hey,' Victor snapped his fingers. 'Stop dreaming about my brother. Hector will be here soon.'

'Oh no, no, I wasn't thinking of him,' Oona lied.

'Really! Then who's the other lucky man. Let me tell you Hector's not going to like it one bit.' Victor joked.

'Oh please!' Oona slapped his hand playfully.

'Ouch!' Victor feigned hurt. 'Oh, did I tell you I got Guy's address from Rebecca?'

'Guy?' Oona looked blank.

'Guy. Guy O'Brien? David's great-nephew? Charlotte's nephew?'

'Yes. Yes. Of course. Sorry, I was a bit distracted. Oh good.' Oona said, getting back to the present.

'Guess what?' Victor said.

'What?'

'Guy O'Brien used to live in Wales ten years ago. Barmouth to be precise.'

'What!' Oona exclaimed. 'That's where Aunty Maive lives! What a coincidence!'

'Yes. Quite. I don't know whether he still lives there. But we can definitely find out. The address says,' Victor checked it on his phone, 'Ruskin's Cottage, Barmouth, North Wales. I think I have heard of that one before. Barmouth's such a small place. But I can't recollect the exact location. Mum will know for sure.'

'Oh good! I'm so excited. We're so close to it. I just hope something comes out of all this. Although I don't know what I want it to be,' Oona said. Just then her phone beeped.

Hi Oona. Hope all's well with u. I wanted Vic's no if u cud text it to me. Been ages since I spoke to him. Also tell me when is a gud time to talk to u. Ciao. Riz

Oona smiled as she punched the keys on her cell: *Am with Vic right now. We r at the airport waiting to pick up Hector from HK. U can call now.*

She told Victor Riz might call and almost immediately her phone rang, flashing 'Riz Ali'. After exchanging the usual pleasantries with Riz, she passed on the phone to Victor.

'Hi. Riz. This is a surprise. Oona just told me. Hope everything's all right?'

After hearing Riz out at the other end, Victor replied, 'Oh. I see. What do the tests say?' After nodding, Victor said, 'Keep me posted about the reports. How are you feeling?' Oona saw Victor's face fall and heard him mutter a few monosyllables. Then he said, 'Listen, let me just get back to the apartment and I will call you. We will talk at length. Your number is the same, right? Yes, do not panic. All will be well. I'll call you in a bit,' Victor concluded.

'All well with him?' Oona asked, genuinely concerned, as Victor handed her phone back to her.

'Yes, I guess.' Victor nodded, a little distracted. 'It's a long story. I'll tell you some other time.'

His ashen face told Oona everything was not quite well with Riz. She wanted to call him, but controlled herself as she heard the announcement that BA 137 from Hong Kong had just landed. She got up, squeezed Victor's arm and whispered, 'Let me know if I can help.' Victor nodded, patting her hand. They walked towards the arrival gate.

The evening was quite taxing for Oona. Shaina was a prettily behaved child, albeit a bit precocious. Hector tried to force the reticent Shaina onto Aunty Oona. The little girl clung to Vic instead. Not because she resented Oona, but because she took time to open up with strangers. Vic seemed rather preoccupied, though he had to cover it up for his niece. Shaina had jumped onto Victor like a little monkey at the airport and refused to leave him. Hector had to drive all the way back home. Once home, Oona got dinner ready as Hector showered and changed, leaving Vic to listen while Shaina rattled off stories non-stop on his lap. Oona understood why Vic had needed that double espresso!

After dinner, Hector decided to walk Oona back to her apartment though she was confident of walking back alone. She tried to politely dissuade him by mentioning his tiring flight, but Hector would hear none of it. Neither would Vic, who insisted with a naughty wink that Hector walk Oona home. Shaina wanted to join them, but Vic bribed her back with a story.

Oona had barely opened the door to her apartment when Hector grabbed her and started kissing her furiously. Though taken aback for a moment, Oona soon responded with equal fervour. Hector did not even bother to take her to the bedroom as he started to rip open her clothes. Oona could feel how hard he was and she herself shook with longing. She realised she had missed Hector. At least physically. They made wild love on the couch like forbidden lovers and both came with quick intensity. Much later, after lying languidly on Hector's large frame, Oona got up and headed to the bedroom. While she was changing she heard Hector's phone ring and from what she could hear she gathered it was Shaina wanting him back home. Hector explained to the little girl that Aunty Oona needed him, that he would be back first thing in the morning, and that she should cuddle up to Uncle Vic and go to sleep.

'I think you should go home, Hector. Shaina needs you. I am fine and besides we'll catch up again tomorrow,' Oona said, walking into the room as he hung up. Much as she had enjoyed their love making, which was enough to last her for a few days, she now wanted to sleep peacefully without him bothering her.

'Shaina is fine with Vic. I need you,' he ogled the outline of her body through her diaphanous night dress. Oona blushed as she followed his lustful gaze.

'C'mon Hector. We've just made love. I think you should go,' Oona mumbled as Hector came over and tried to kiss her again. 'Please, not now Hector. I am tired, please,' Oona tried to pull away. Hector abruptly let her go, causing her to nearly lose her balance. She grabbed hold of the lamp stand just in time. Just then, her phone rang. She ran to get it, with Hector following her.

'Who the hell's calling at this hour?' he barked.

'Hello,' Oona answered.

'Aunty Oona,' there was the faint sound of a child's voice. 'Can you please tell Dadda to come home? I want him to sleep with me,' Shaina said haltingly.

'Of course my love, your Dadda will be home with you in a bit, won't you Dadda?' Oona looked towards a shocked Hector. 'In fact darling, Dadda was on his way home. Here, speak to him and tell him yourself to get back home soon.'

She shoved the phone at Hector, who mumbled an I-am-coming-soon-love and clicked the phone shut. He then turned to Oona saying, 'Did you have to do that? I missed you and I wanted to spend the night with you.'

'I know. I am not running away, am I? I think Shaina needs you now,' Oona said.

'How thoughtful of you to think of Shaina. I wish you were as thoughtful about me, lady,' Hector started dressing, sounding upset. When Oona tried to hug him at the door, he brushed her aside and slammed the door shut behind him.

It took Oona a few days to get into Shaina's good books. The child resented Oona's presence at the Boses' and after a polite 'Hi' mostly ignored her. Till the day Oona decided to give Shaina the gifts she had brought her from Bombay. A beautiful *ghagra-choli* with mirror work, a pair of beaded sandals and matching purse and traditional Indian jewellery, including glass bangles, hair clips, et al. Shaina just loved her loot. She immediately put on her outfit and jewellery and preened about the house. From time to time she would admire herself in the full-length mirror in Vic's room and come and ask everyone in the room how she looked.

'Very pretty,' Hector said, most amused.

'I think you look prettier than Aishwarya Rai,' Vic added. Shaina was over the moon.

'Thank you Aunty Oona. Next time get me a *ghagra-choli* in green, though red is my favourite colour.' She hugged Oona tight. Oona knew she was in Shaina's good books. How easy it was to please children, she thought. The innocence of childhood and the happiness surrounding it, begotten through simple pleasures.

Having fairy-taled Shaina to sleep one evening, Oona joined Hector on the living-room couch. Victor was not at home. Hector, a Liverpool fan, was glued to the Chelsea-Liverpool match on TV. He switched off the TV the moment Oona joined him.

'She's asleep?'

Oona nodded. 'Why did you switch off the TV? Let's watch the match,' Oona asked

'We have better things to talk about. After all, it's not an important tournament.'

Oona smiled at Hector's explanation. She had realised Liverpool was losing and knew Hector couldn't bear to watch it.

'I think motherhood suits you well,' Hector suddenly said.

'What?'

'You are great with Shaina. What about us having a baby now?' Hector smiled.

'Please! What's wrong with you? Besides, Shaina and I have just started bonding…'

'So?'

'Well I'm just getting to know her.'

'It will be nice if she has a little brother or sister to play with,' Hector cut her short.

'What's wrong with you, Hector? You know Shaina's just had a little brother and she is feeling left out.'

'Yeah, I know,' Hector cut in. 'That's Sonia's child, not mine.'

'What are you up to? Are you in a child-bearing contest with your ex-wife?'

'And what exactly are you up to? Using me to get over your celeb hubby?'

'For your kind information, he is my ex-husband. And Hector, to set the record straight, I am not using you. I really like you,' Oona said.

'Good to hear that. In that case why aren't you keen on getting married or starting a family?' Hector asked bluntly.

'What's the hurry, Hector? I've just got out of a relationship and it would not be fair on you or myself to…'

'I don't give a damn about fairness. You're in a relationship with me now? Aren't you?' Hector asked.

'Yes,' Oona hesitated. 'But it's not the same as being married. Marriage is a serious commitment. We have to bond emotionally as well.'

'Gosh! What bullshit. Emotions and such crap. Even your sensible friend Sandra thinks it's time you settled down.'

'Sandra doesn't know my emotional needs. I need to heal myself first and I need time, Hector. Only if you give me time can I be fair to you. And myself.'

'To hell with time and fairness and such nonsense. Let's just get married. Both our mothers will be happy for us. You know Mum loves you like her own daughter.'

'I know, Hector. But this is not a question of pleasing moms. It is a question of our happiness.'

'Of course we will be happy. Especially since we've both been badly bitten once before. Trust me Oona.'

She was quiet.

It's pointless explaining to Hector. How can he understand when all he's doing is settling scores with his ex-wife?

'Are you serious?' Sandra screamed over the phone.

Oona had just told her that she wanted to break off with Hector.

'Just hang in there, babes, before you do anything silly,' Sandra said. 'I'm just leaving office and will be with you in twenty minutes. We'll talk.'

'Sandra, please. Don't rush. I'm okay.'

'What do you mean you're okay? I know what you must be going through. Men are such bastards. Always want to have fun without any commitment. But I never thought Hector would turn out like this. Anyway, if need be Jo or I'll talk to him!' Sandra swore.

'Sandra,' Oona said calmly over the phone. 'I think you have got it all wrong here. Hector is not ditching me. In fact he wants to get married. It is I who want to break off with him. I want to opt out.'

'What is wrong with you babes? You've got a chap who wants to marry you, whom you love and now you want to break off. I don't get it.'

'Okay just come over. We'll have tea and I'll explain.'

Over tea, Sandra ate eight chocolate chip cookies with a vengeance as she heard Oona out. Oona realised that Sandra was upset with her decision to leave Hector and therefore ate the cookies more out of despair than hunger. Sandra, like Sangeeta, was always traditional in her approach. She and Jo had had an arranged marriage, both belonging to the conservative Kerala Catholic community. Though Sandra had a romantic streak in her, having grown up on the staple Barbara Cartland and Mills & Boon diet, she had never been in love, apart from Jo or Joseph Anthony. But she had come to love him more out of a sense of duty and because he met her physical needs and fathered her children. She just could not comprehend Oona's complex emotional needs. Especially since they did not arise out of a sense of duty.

'You make a cool pair. He is good looking, well-settled and besides you have had a crush on him since childhood. So where's the hitch?' Sandra asked, still puzzled.

'Sandra, Sandra, Sandra. Grow up! I love Hector but not deeply enough to spend the rest of my life with him. Yes, I did have a crush on him, I admit, but as I got to know him better, I am disillusioned by his behaviour. He can be hurtful. Besides, he is not so much in love with me but...'

'But?'

'He just wants to get even with his ex-wife. Just because she is married he wants to marry. And I seem to be convenient enough and besides...'

'What?' Sandra asked.

'I don't think we have much in common mentally or emotionally. He is just not my type. Know what I mean?'

Sandra nodded. 'When do you plan to tell him?' she asked after a long pause.

'After we return from Barmouth. I'm looking forward to meeting Aunty Maive and don't want to spoil that visit. Once I return, I will tell Hector and he can explain it to his mom. I know she will be upset, but what can I do? Better safe than sorry. Please, Sandra, keep it to yourself for the moment.'

'I will,' Sandra agreed.

'Don't even mention it to Jo.'

'I won't.'

'And please, not a word to Hector.'

'Of course not, stupid. You tell him. Why should I tell him? And besides, it is your life. You know what is best for you. I can only support your decisions since you are my friend.' Sandra came up to Oona and hugged her tight.

'Thanks. I needed this,' Oona's eyes were wet.

'Any time, my friend. And I am keeping my fingers crossed that you will change your mind once you return from Barmouth. I can already hear wedding bells!' Sandra smiled, still trying to hold out some hope for the Oona-Hector romance.

'Please Sandra, please. Stop it. I won't change my mind, that's for sure. As for wedding bells, that's a long, long time away, if ever.'

'Oona!' Sandra reprimanded her, 'Don't say inauspicious things. *Shubh shubh bolo.*'

Barmouth

'Shrewsbury,' Oona read aloud as they passed the board. 'So is this the place where the famous biscuit originated?' she asked as they drove past the little town. Hector was driving Oona and Shaina down to his Aunty Maive's in Barmouth. It was a long drive, over five hours, and the road went through a lot of wilderness interspersed with hamlets, towns and cities, like Birmingham and Shrewsbury.

'What biscuits?' Hector asked. He was in a sunny mood in spite of the dank weather. Driving through the fog was hard enough and Hector was doing it solo. Vic had stayed on in London and would join them a week later.

'You know the famous Shrewsbury biscuits you get in Bombay. They actually come from this old Parsi bakery in Pune called Kayanis,' Oona explained. 'They are buttery and taste somewhat like shortbread cookies.'

'You know, this is strange but some years back I was driving a friend to Barmouth and when we passed Shrewsbury, she asked me the same question. Attiya used to stay in Bombay and she mentioned the same biscuits,' Hector paused. 'To answer your question, though, no I don't think you get Shrewsbury biscuits in Shrewsbury; just like you don't get Russian salad in Russia!' he laughed. Oona thought his quip was rather predictable. 'But we can check it out if you like,' he said as they approached a mall. 'Want to?' he asked Oona.

'Yes, Dadda, please. Let's stop there,' Shaina piped up as she pointed towards the big M sign. 'I want a chicken nuggets happy meal,' she insisted.

'Okay, darling,' Hector assured his daughter as he drove in to the mall. 'And let us see if we can get some of those biscuits for Aunty Oona.'

'Attiya, did you say?' Oona was still preoccupied with Hector's earlier statement.

'What?'

'Didn't you mention your friend Attiya from Bombay?' Oona asked.

'Yes. Why? You know her?'

'No. Not really. I know her brother though. She's Riz Ali's sister, right?'

'Yes. The same one,' Hector said as he collected his parking ticket from the slot. 'You know Riz, don't you? Vic happened to mention it the other day. How well do you know that rogue, lady?' Hector laughed.

'Rogue? Why?'

'Oh what else can you call him? He's a bloody gigolo,' Hector said as he parked the car.

'Well, I don't know him too well,' Oona lied. She did not want to break Hector's sunny mood. 'Just the usual party circuit…the hi-bye types,' Oona tried to sound casual.

'Hmm,' Hector said. 'Good. Now let's get both my girls some goodies.'

A little known town on the shores of the Cardigan Bay, swept by the warm current of the sea, perched precariously on narrow ledges of the cliff which juts boldly out from the mountain range, sits pretty along the broad estuary of the river Mawddach. Balancing on these ledges are ancient stone cottages that make up a fishing village, known as Abermaw, or the popular watering-hole: Barmouth.

It was wet and windy as Hector drove up and parked his car at the bottom of a tall cliff, a few yards from a pub called The Last Inn. As Oona got out, Hector explained that the pub was named thus because in older times it used to be one of the last watering holes before people travelled onwards, further north.

'This must be at least four hundred years old. The present owners, Greg and his wife Debbie bought it a few years ago. Maybe eight or ten. They have redone the interiors and set it up as some sort of a cultural hub of Barmouth. Every Wednesday, they have a quiz contest and at the end of the year, there is the grand finale where the winning team gets a free two-night stay at the inn. All meals thrown in. They also have a beautiful inn above the pub,' Hector explained.

'Wow. Just reminds me of Cal,' Oona said as she took in the beauty of Barmouth in spite of the dark wetness. 'Remember all those inter-club quizzes at DI—Dalhousie Institute?'

Hector nodded. 'Yeah. You'll enjoy meeting Debbie. She's a local beauty. They call her the Princess Diana of Barmouth.' Hector winked. 'Okay, I'll bring up the luggage later. First let's go and meet Mum. She must be looking forward to meeting you, and Shaina here can't wait to meet her grannie,' Hector said as he hauled Shaina up on his shoulders. Shaina loved her perch and drummed on her father's head in excitement. 'Okay, honey that's enough,' Hector gently admonished his daughter.

'Let me warn you, Oona, it is a steep uphill climb and very windy. So walk slowly, look around carefully, keep to the sides of the hills and don't go near the edge. A sudden bout of strong wind can blow you away,' Hector warned Oona. 'Just follow me.'

Oona cautiously began wending her way up. Halfway, she could hear herself panting. 'Are you okay honey?' Hector asked. He stopped several times on the way to allow Oona to catch up with him.

Climbing up a thousand feet, through steep steps and narrow twisty passages was an effort, but once in the warmth of the low gabled cottage, named Primrose, an entirely different experience awaited Oona. The cold weather was more than compensated for by the warmth showered by Aunty Maive. It was Oona she embraced first and then her granddaughter.

'Oh look at you!' Maive patted Oona on the face. 'You have grown up so much!'

'For God's sake Mum. Don't embarrass Oona,' Hector told his mother.

'It's okay,' Oona gestured to Hector. She then bent down to do a *pronam* to Aunty Maive.

The latter was touched. '*Thak, thak*. Stay well, my child,' she blessed Oona.

The years had indeed taken a toll on Aunty Maive. She no longer stood ramrod straight. A little bent, her face had quite a few wrinkles. Oona noticed her wrinkled hands. She remembered beautiful, soft-skinned hands. Was it nearly two decades ago? How time had flown!

'How time flies!' Maive seemed to echo her sentiments. 'It just seems like the other day in Golpark! No?'

As Oona sat by the kitchen table, nursing a hot cuppa while half-heartedly biting into a slice of Aunty Maive's famous carrot cake, what amazed her was the view. The windows opened upon a brilliant expanse of sea and sky with the mountains glimmering in the distant horizon. This was indeed paradise.

Hector went down to bring up their bags and Shaina wandered around the familiar rooms while Aunty Maive and Oona caught up over all that had happened in the years since they last met. For Uncle Bose and Aunty Maive, who had spent all their lives in a big city like Calcutta, it was love at first sight with Barmouth when they visited the place about fifteen years ago. Aunty Maive's sister and her husband lived here, having moved in from Ireland. Maive's family was Welsh and while she had married an Indian, her elder sister Sinead had married an Irishman who was part English and part Scottish. The couple, like the Boses, had also fallen in love with the place some years earlier when they came here on vacation.

Some years before Uncle Bose passed away, the Boses had bought a stone cottage located on one of the highest points on the cliff. A couple of miles away, Sinead's cottage was actually the highest cottage in Barmouth. 'You've come here at the wrong time of year, my dear,' Aunty Maive said. 'It is windy and stormy and dark. Tell Hector to bring you here in summer. 'It is so beautiful with long days stretching into the night,' she told Oona.

'In spring, we have daffodils and primroses and in autumn, the bramble leaves turn scarlet and gold and it is simply breathtaking,' Maive continued. 'My sister Sinead was the one with the green fingers and used to have the best roses in her garden.'

'Used to?' Oona asked.

'Yes. Used to. She died two years ago,' Maive sighed. 'We were both widowed around the same time. Your uncle died of pancreatic cancer and my brother-in-law died two months later of a galloping liver cancer. Sinead and I rarely met after our college days. And that was more than forty-five years ago.'

Oona realised that after the hullabaloo of Golpark, Barmouth could be frighteningly lonely. It had probably been a long time since Aunty Maive had a decent conversation with someone willing to hear her out.

The old lady carried on, 'We grew up in the fashionable Swansea in South Wales. Sinead went to London to study dentistry but never got around to completing her course. She fell in love with my brother-in-law, an Irishman, a practising dentist who was visiting London. Sinead got pregnant and followed her boyfriend to Cork and settled down to home and hearth, bringing up two children. A boy named Keelan and a girl, Rita. Keelan stays in London though he comes here often. Thank God he has decided to retain his parents' cottage. Rita lives in New York, working with a big publishing house. Both have not married. I don't know what it is with us Llewellyns. That's my maiden name, dear. Except for Hector, no one seems to be in a hurry to marry. They forget that age is catching up with them.' Oona laughed.

'Like I said, Sinead and I hardly met. I went to Oxford and that is where I met your uncle. We married and then I moved to Calcutta and she stayed in Cork. In the next decades we met maybe once or twice in London. No wonder Hector and Victor hardly connect with Keelan even though all three are in London. Hector of course says Keelan is strange in his ways, espousing socialist causes. Victor meets up with him occasionally. Keelan's a highly intelligent boy. Was a Slade scholar at Oxford. It's sad that the boys do not bond as family.

'When I moved to Barmouth, and later, when Sinead and I were widowed, we thought we'd make up for the lost years. We did of course. Spent some wonderful times together. Drove down to Scotland and Ireland. Several times we took the train to London. Went on a conducted tour to Morocco, Turkey and Spain. I was planning to take Sinead to India. Show her my foster country. Show her Calcutta, Golpark, Bose Mansion. Then she died. Of a massive attack. Just like that. In minutes she was gone!' Maive's eyes welled with tears. Oona got up and hugged her.

'Why is Granma crying?' Shaina suddenly popped in and jumped on Maive's lap. She kissed her grandmother. 'I hope you did not make my Granma cry? Naughty Aunty Oona,' Shaina asked, worried.

'Oh no, darling,' Maive ruffled Shaina's hair with a weak smile. 'Aunty Oona loves me a lot, just like you love me.'

'Now will you show Aunty Oona her room?'

'Which one is Aunty Oona's room, Granma?'

'The one next to Dadda's. The guest bedroom.'

'Oh, I know that one,' she jumped off Maive's lap and pulled Oona by the hand, 'Let me show you the guest room.' Both Maive and Oona laughed.

'Please, for God's sake no, Hector, no . . . ' Oona tried to pull herself away. But Hector pinned her hands down and started kissing her all over her face and neck, smelling strongly of Guinness as he got on top of her. Oona responded briefly before pulling her face away.

'Bitch,' Hector muttered. 'You want it as much as me. Then why the *natak*? All the drama?'

'It's not *natak*,' she gestured towards Shaina who was lying on the bed next to them, sleeping peacefully. Earlier on in the evening, soon after supper, Oona had been reading a story to Shaina in her room, and the little girl eventually fell asleep. Maive suggested they let her spend the night with Oona. 'Just call me if she wakes up in the middle of the night,' Maive advised.

'Oh, don't worry, I'll manage,' Oona had assured her.

Now with Hector wanting to make love to her in the presence of his sleeping daughter, Oona felt extremely uncomfortable. The thought of Shaina waking up in the midst of their act embarrassed her. But Hector didn't seem to mind. 'Hector, please. Let's go to your room,' Oona pleaded.

'I can't hold on till then,' Hector groaned, and forced himself into her. 'I can't hold on forever, you bitch. You'll have to come soon.' As Oona began to respond, Hector came and called out her name and bit her cheek. Oona let out a little scream. In the commotion Shaina woke up crying. Hector roughly disentangled himself and threw on his clothes as he hurried across to comfort his daughter. Oona felt embarrassed and hurt. And deeply humiliated.

She got out of bed and ran into the bathroom, half naked, and closed the door behind her. Suddenly she burst into tears, realising that Hector only desired her physically. He had no finer feelings for her. As long as she could gratify him sexually, all was well with Hector Bose. The moment she held back, he revealed his mean self. And it had happened once too often.

'God! Will any man ever love me for my...for myself?' she sobbed.

'You okay?' Hector knocked after a while.

'Yes,' Oona responded blankly.

'Mum's taken Shaina to her room. Don't worry about her. You can come out now. Sleep well. Goodnight.'

When she came out a few minutes later, she noticed the door to Hector's room was ajar and he was sprawled on his bed, snoring. She made her way to her empty bed. He had no need for her now.

Oona got up in the morning with a nagging headache. She had slept fitfully through the night. Suddenly the previous night's incidents hit her again, and she hid her face in her pillow, embarrassed and saddened. It was already eight. Half an hour later, she dragged herself from bed and went to the toilet. Washing up, she walked towards the kitchen with a strip of Disprin in hand, her head thudding. Maive was already busy with breakfast.

'Good morning, Aunty,' Oona said.

'Good morning love,' Maive replied. 'Did you sleep well? Sorry Shaina kept you up.'

'No. No. It's okay.' She had no idea what explanation Hector had given his mother. 'I need some water,' she said. Maive saw the tablet strip in her hand and gave her a glass, motioning towards the tap. Oona half-filled the glass and popped in two tablets. She waited for it to melt and fizz up and after swirling the mixture, drank it.

'Where is Shaina?' she enquired.

'Sleeping. I'm in a rush to make breakfast. Hector's been called. He has to leave. Filling in for a colleague who has suddenly taken ill. He'll be doing the Lon–NY sector the coming week. He's in the shower—will leave for London in an hour and then fly out to New York tonight. Poor boy has a long day and night ahead.'

This news came as a big relief to Oona. She had lost sleep over how to deal with Hector for the rest of her stay. She had never felt as grateful to God as she did that morning in Barmouth. The next piece of good news was when Aunty Maive told her that Vic had wrapped up work in London and would be in Barmouth by the next day. All Oona wanted was a tight hug from Vic.

When Victor arrived the following evening, Shaina as usual clung to Uncle Vic like a little chimp. Oona also hugged Victor tight and would not let go of him for a few seconds.

'Please, I need a hug,' Oona told him.

'All well, I hope,' Vic kissed her on the forehead. Though Oona nodded, Vic felt something was amiss. The next day, as Oona sauntered onto the little terrace outside the cottage early in the morning, she saw Victor sitting there, reading the paper. Seeing Oona, he got up, hugged her and said, '*Chalo*. Go change and let's go.'

'Where?' Oona asked surprised.

'I'm going to show you early Barmouth. This will be the only quality time I can grab with you as Shaina is sleeping. I'll tell Mum, you get ready.'

As they wended their way down the hill, Victor holding Oona's hand from time to time, he told her about the little town. 'These cottages have been here for more than five hundred years and have withstood the harsh and stormy winds, rarely suffering any damage. Though it is dark and windy in the winters, the summer months are beautiful. Long, sunny days. We love Barmouth and its languid lifestyle, though I must confess it does take a bit of getting used to, especially after London and Calcutta. The people are so warm and trusting that we seldom keep our doors locked here. The total population is about 2,000 people and everyone knows everyone. In summer though, the town is bursting with people—more than 20,000 at times!'

'Oh!' Oona exclaimed.

'Yes, every inn is booked well in advance for summer and most houses double as little guest houses. We keep having friends pouring in, so most summers Mum has company. A beautiful place, clean air to breathe and simple and friendly people, what more can one ask for?'

Down in the town, Victor showed Oona the main street, starting with The Last Inn at one end, followed by the tuck shop, the post office and Tony's Hardware. 'There are exactly twenty-nine shops, with a Woolies at the further end of the road,' Vic said, pointing towards it.

'This is where Barmouth comes to shop. You can call it High Street Barmouth,' he joked.

'Good you told me,' Oona said.

'Yes. You have enough time in the next few days to scour each one of them since there isn't much to do here anyway. Oh by the way, it's Wednesday today, right? Remind me to take you to Debbie and Greg's...it's their weekly quiz night tonight.'

'I know,' Oona said. 'Hector told me. I am so looking forward to it.'

'What about some coffee? I need my double espresso shots,' Vic asked.

'Sure. I would love some coffee. And maybe a croissant,' Oona said.

'I'll take you to Mrs Bunce's bakery. Quaint little place. And she bakes these wonderful buns, somewhat like the hot cross ones but crunchier. The locals call them the Barmouth buns. You'll love them, take my word.'

'Mmm, they are truly delicious. I'm going to have them every day I'm here,' Oona crunched into her bun. They had settled in one corner of Mrs Bunce's tiny bakery. Patricia Bunce, the owner, came up and after being introduced to Oona, hugged her saying, 'Yes, Maive has been telling me about you. She was so glad you were coming. Enjoy yourselves dearies.'

As Patricia went to attend to other customers, Vic gave Oona a I-told-you-so look. 'Everyone knows everyone here and very soon everyone here will know about you Oona. The pretty Indian girl who is dating one of Maive's boys!' Vic laughed. He noticed Oona seemed to tense up at the last statement.

As they drank their coffee, Vic asked Oona what was bothering her. She explained her current emotional state and her confusion over her relationship with his brother.

'I can see Hector isn't being of much help. What you need now is to heal yourself. Completely. Then you can get into a relationship. Why don't you ask Hector to give you some time? Maybe six months, maybe a year. Things will improve, I'm sure,' Victor suggested.

'Yes, I know. But your brother seems in a tearing hurry to settle down. I need my space right now.' Oona was almost in tears.

'I know, I know. It all started with his ex-wife marrying. Now he wants to do the same. Just an ego issue, I guess. But marriage is serious business, my dear. You want me to talk to him?' Vic asked, gently patting her hand.

'Should you? You think it will be okay?' Oona asked.

'I'll try. He does respect my advice, for what it's worth. Anyway, we still have a week to go before Hector returns. Meanwhile you take it easy and enjoy the countryside.'

'And what about checking out on the Olivers' descendants here in Barmouth with the address Rebecca gave us?'

'Oh blimey! I almost forgot about that,' Vic exclaimed.

'Ruskin's Cottage, did you say?' Maive echoed Victor. 'Wait a minute. That's part of the Talbot Cottages where Aunty Sinead lived. In fact Sinead's cottage *is* Ruskin's Cottage.'

'No way, Mum. You forget, it's called Aberdale,' Victor interjected.

'Aberdale is what Aunty Sinead and Uncle Guy called it after they moved in. But the original name of the cottage is Ruskin's Cottage. The locals still refer to it as Ruskin's Cottage. The social thinker, John Ruskin.'

'Really? That's news to me,' Vic shrugged.

'Since you guys hardly come here often, you do not bother with the history of the place,' Maive said, as the three of them sipped their tea around the kitchen table. They had just finished lunch and Shaina was watching television in the family room. Without getting into the whole story, Victor had decided to ask his mum for assistance in locating the address Rebecca had given him.

'Uncle Guy? Ruskin's Cottage? Doesn't that ring a bell?' Oona asked Victor. 'Remember, Rebecca said that Charlotte's nephew, that's her brother Philip's son, Guy, lived in Wales and was married to a Welsh lass?'

'Yes of course, but that was Charlotte's nephew Guy. Charlotte O' Brien died a spinster, so obviously her brother's son would be an O'Brien. Guy O'Brien. Uncle Guy was Llewellyn. Guy Llewellyn.'

Victor had barely finished when Maive cut in, 'Says who?'

'What?' Victor looked at his mother in surprise.

'Who says Uncle Guy was a Llewellyn? We are Llewellyns, Sinead and me. Guy was as Irish as they come. Guy O'Brien.'

'Whh..aa…t?' Both Vic and Oona exclaimed together.

'No way! I don't believe this!' Vic thumped the table hard.

Oona put her hand on her mouth in shock, saying, 'It can't be true. Tell me I'm dreaming, Vic. Pinch me hard.'

'How stupid of me! I should've have connected this long ago. I always kind of presumed Uncle Guy was a Llewellyn. Now I remember, when I once visited Keelan's apartment in Holland Park many years ago, the nameplate read Keelan O'Brien. Damn,' Victor said aloud to no one in particular and yet for the benefit of Oona and Maive.

'That's okay. Better late than never. We would still have come to Barmouth,' Oona said to console him.

All this time Aunty Maive had been trying to figure out what they were talking about. She finally gave up. 'What's all this? What's going on between the two of you?' she looked from Oona to her son. Oona was too excited to talk and went up to Vic, hugging him tight.

'Will someone please tell me what is going on?' Maive demanded.

As Oona clutched Vic's arm in excitement, he slowly narrated the story of Ela and David to Maive, describing how Oona was looking for the Olivers' descendants.

'Imagine going through all that when the truth was right at our doorstep! Isn't it uncanny? I still can't believe it,' Oona laughed.

'Wait till you meet Keelan, my cousin. He lives in London and might just dig up more family history for you. There may be more skeletons in the cupboard. Can you imagine, Mum, cousin Keelan's great-granduncle went all the way to India to romance Oona's great-aunt!'

'And what a coincidence that Mr Oliver's great-grandnephew's cousin is romancing Ela Sen's grand-niece now! History does come full circle,' Maive said with a wink. Vic noticed that Oona did not seem too pleased with the last comment.

'Yeah, fate does indeed take strange turns,' Victor said, trying to divert his mother's enthusiasm from her younger son's relationship with Oona. 'I'll call Keelan right away,' he said, looking up the number on his phone.

'Wait.' Oona stopped him. 'Call and say what?'

'Yeah, good question. Call and say what?' Vic echoed.

'Well, just call and say hello,' Maive suggested. 'Say you're in Barmouth and that if he's here too you'd like to meet up. You could mention that Oona's visiting from India and is keen to see Ruskin's Cottage. Just keep it casual.'

'Thanks Mum but it'll sound a bit awkward since I hardly ever meet up with or call Keelan. He'll wonder why I'm suddenly doing so now.'

'Then you can tell him Ela was doing some research on the East India Company, and that she happened to stumble upon his great-granduncle's name, or something like that,' Maive added helpfully.

'Actually, it was David Anderson Oliver's father, Vincent, who was with the East India Company. So that makes him Keelan's great-great-granduncle,' Oona said, trying to be as historically correct as possible.

'Let me just call Keelan,' Victor said, dialling his number and went to the next room.

'Come to think of it,' Aunty Maive said slowly, 'Sinead did casually once mention that her father-in-law was disinherited from his parents' inheritance because he married a Scottish lass way beneath his station. That the family had a house in London which went to her aunt by marriage, Charlotte, who sold it. Later, when Aunty Charlotte died a spinster, she left everything to her only nephew Guy. Charlotte would often visit their place and Sinead found her cranky, albeit harmless. Gosh. Small world, ain't it?'

Vic walked in. Both Oona and Maive looked at him expectantly. 'Keelan's in Brussels. That's what his voicemail says. I have just left a message asking him to call me ASAP. I also sent him a text. We'll now have to wait for him to call back,' Vic explained. 'I think today has been a very fruitful day, historically speaking,' Vic ribbed Oona and they laughed. 'I think I'll catch up on my forty winks now. Mum, I'm taking Oona to the Last Inn for the quiz tonight.'

'Oh that'll be lovely. You'll enjoy it, Oona.'

Though the Bose brothers didn't visit Barmouth much, everyone seemed to know Victor. His affable nature made him popular with the men and his good looks won over the ladies.

'Good ta seeya young man. Where haveya been hiding after breaking my daughter's heart,' a beer-bellied inebriated old man slapped Vic hard on his back.

'I was busy breaking other men's daughters' hearts, Bill,' Victor joked back.

'And who's da pretty lady withya Sir Vic?' Bill asked looking at Oona.

'Leave the boy alone, Bill,' a gentleman arrived to rescue Vic and Oona, adding, 'That's his brother's fiancée.'

'Hi Peter. This is Oona. Oona this is Peter Bunce, you met his wife Patricia at breakfast,' Vic introduced.

'Yes of course, Peter. I think your wife makes the best buns in the world,' Oona said.

'Well, then you should come home someday. She's a super cook too. We were thinking of calling you over one of these days,' Peter said with his *pucca* English accent.

'Peter and Patricia are from London,' Vic told Oona. 'They have been here for more than two decades now. He's also the chairman of the local town council. Oona here is a keen student of history and architecture,' Vic winked at Oona. 'Maybe Peter can help you with more information on Ruskin's Cottage.'

'Well, you take her there yourself, since Keelan is your cousin. Where's the boy? I haven't seen him in a while,' Peter asked.

'He's in Brussels at the moment,' Vic replied. 'Hey Peter how about you, Oona and I form a team for this evening?'

'That's fine by me, since my quiz buddies are not coming today. So what do we call our team?' Peter asked.

'Beer Bellies,' Oona said suddenly, inspired by Bill's ample belly.

'That's a good one,' Peter said as he and Vic laughed.

The evening went off fine. Their team came third. Greg of course slipped in a partial question in Oona's favour: 'What is the new name for Bombay?' which Oona promptly answered. Afterwards, Oona joined Peter and Vic for a beer. Vic had a Guinness while she stuck to her Budweiser. She noticed the Bose brothers' penchant for Guinness. Later Oona walked home, feeling light and giddy, cracking up at Vic's silly jokes. As she reached the top of the cliff near Primrose, she stood by herself, staring into the darkness, where the sea and sky had merged into one big black canvas.

Dark. Frightening. Mysterious. Awesome.

Oona wanted to throw her palette of colours on it. For Fun. Happiness. Good Cheer.

After a while she looked around for Victor and saw him sitting a few feet away on a stone, engrossed in his own world. She went and sat next to him. 'Something worrying you?' she asked, lightly touching his shoulder. In her worries, she had forgotten that he had seemed worried about Riz. She suddenly had the urge to mother him. 'You seemed upset about Riz's call at the airport that day. All well with him? You want to tell me?'

Victor patted her hand, 'It's a long story. You want to hear it?' Oona nodded. 'I don't know why I'm telling you this, even Hector doesn't know,' Vic said.

It was too late to call up Riz. It would be way past midnight now in Bombay, but Oona still had a strong urge to hear his voice. Lying in bed, trying to sleep, she just wanted to hold him tight. Sit on his lap and ruffle his hair. What Victor had told her about Riz was disturbing. Having led a promiscuous life, Riz was diagnosed as HIV positive some years back. A recent check-up had revealed full-blown AIDS. Victor had sworn Oona to secrecy, so discussing it with Riz was out of question. Besides, she did not want to arouse Riz's suspicions by trying to suddenly be sympathetic towards him. But she really wanted to talk to him. Just hear his voice. Just hear him say '*aadab arz*'.

The little jigsaw pieces were suddenly falling into place. How he had been cagey all the time. Kept one part of his life a big secret though he was privy to all her secrets. She now realised he had refused to have sex with her the first time as he was unprotected. That was why he insisted on wearing a rubber subsequently. Gosh! It made sense at last. She was grateful to him for not exposing her to the perils of the disease. He could have been callous. Like Hector. After all Hector was also promiscuous. But Hector was heterosexual, while Riz was bisexual. A shocking revelation for Oona was that Riz and Victor had shared a strong physical relationship several years back. Who would have thought it of Riz? People were truly strange, one never knew what was going on under the surface. These thoughts lulled Oona to sleep.

The next morning she sent a text to Riz: *Gud morng. Hope all's well. Am in Barmouth, vacationing with the Boses—Vic and his mum. Hector's out on a flight. This place is beautiful. Pure paradise. Wish u were here. U in Bbay or Deli? Tk cr. Ciao.*

Minutes later he replied: *Gud morning to u too. Enjoy your paradise and say hi to all. Am in deli with mom as attiya out on a flite. Tak cr and hope to talk to u soon. Luv. Riz*

Oona decided to leave it at that. Next time round she would talk to him.

As she lay lazing in bed, still a little disturbed at the thought of Riz's illness, Vic entered, bright as the sunshine. He pecked her lightly on her cheek and said, 'My Lady, I bring you good tidings early in the morning.'

'What?' Oona smiled, happy at Vic's happiness.

'Keelan sent me a text. Here see it for yourself,' Vic handed her his phone. Oona read out: *Got both your voice message and text. Am in Brussels. Back to London tomorrow. Planning a trip to Barmouth over the weekend. Let's meet for a drink on Saturday evening at my place. Your friend from India is most welcome to Ruskin's Cottage. I will take her around myself. Love to Aunty Maive and all.*

Best.

K

'I can't wait for Saturday to arrive,' Oona said as she stretched herself in laziness and flopped back into her pillow. 'What did you tell him about me?'

'I told him that you are an old friend from Calcutta, a journalist and travel writer, working on a story on Barmouth. You had heard of Ruskin's Cottage and were keen to see it for yourself and find out more on the place,' Victor explained.

'Did you mention Ela Sen? Or that I was interested in the Olivers' history?' Oona asked.

'Not yet. Let's meet Keelan first, see what he knows about his family history and how receptive he will be to your questions. Then I will reveal your identity. Get me?' Oona nodded. 'Till then, take a chill pill,' Victor smiled as he left the room.

Keelan

'Hey! Good to see you Vic. Been a while!' Keelan O'Brien said, thumping Victor on the back. Vic nodded and lightly hugged his cousin. As Victor moved aside, Oona noticed Keelan for the first time. Slim-built, he had pert and neat features with a charming smile framed within a firm jawline and a receding hairline, which somehow added to his cute looks. Didn't he remind her of someone? Oona could not immediately recollect. What she did notice, however, was that Keelan was not as tall as his cousins or aunt. While Victor towered at six feet four inches and Hector stood six feet two inches tall, Keelan was much shorter. Even shorter than Riz's five foot eleven or Anand's five foot nine frame. Keelan could not have been more than five feet five inches at the most. Just about Aunty Maive's height. It hardly mattered, except that he appeared much shorter than his cousins.

Oona held out her hand and put on her most charming smile as Keelan turned from Vic to greet her. And to her surprise, he stared at her almost in shock. As their eyes connected, Keelan seemed to quickly recover, briefly looking embarrassed. He shook her hand, smiling a soft 'Hello, I'm Keelan. Do come in.'

'Hi. I'm Oona,' she said, feeling a little awkward herself.

Victor did not fail to notice this.

They made their way into the small, cosy parlour where Oona settled herself into an oversized, faded armchair. She looked around and the thing that struck her the most on entering the place was its singular character:

a delightful mix of a doll's house and a farmhouse. The furniture was all in oakwood and in country style—sturdy and functional. It was not from Ikea, evidently handmade, lending it that inherent rustic charm. While Oona was soaking in the ambience, she could hear the cousins exchanging family news. She felt Keelan's gaze wandering towards her from time to time as he conversed with Victor.

Later, as Vic settled down in an armchair, Keelan asked Oona whether she cared for a glass of wine. 'Will a cup o' tea be too difficult? I can make it myself if that's okay,' Oona asked.

'No problem, I'll be back in a moment,' Keelan motioned to Victor to follow him. Minutes later, Keelan entered with a tray and a gleaming silver tea service with a pretty tea-cosy covering the teapot. Victor followed with a bottle of Bordeaux in one hand, clinking two flutes in the other. As Oona poured her tea into the fine blue porcelain cup, she remarked, 'What a pretty tea-cosy. Looks familiar. I think Aunty Maive has something similar.'

'Yes. Quite right. My mum stitched it. One for herself and one for her sister. She always made two sets of anything she stitched. One stayed in Aberdale and the other went to Primrose. Right?' Keelan looked at Victor who nodded in agreement.

'Aberdale, did you say?' Oona asked as if on cue. 'Isn't this Ruskin's Cottage? Named after John Ruskin?'

'Yes, of course it is. But that's a story in itself,' Keelan said as Victor handed him a glass of wine. 'Thanks.'

'Tell me. I am fascinated ever since I embarked on my story of Barmouth,' Oona said.

'Why did you choose Barmouth of all places? That's unusual for a travel writer from India,' Keelan tried to gauge the reason for her interest.

'Well, primarily the reason for Barmouth in the dead of winter was Aunty Maive. For someone who was so ensconced in Calcutta to resettle deep in the heart of Wales did whet my curiosity. And second,

I like the offbeat, non-touristy track.' Keelan seemed satisfied with her honesty and intelligence.

'At this very moment, my lady, you are sitting in Ruskin's Cottage where the great socialist and philosopher John Ruskin lived. And at this exact moment you are sitting in Ruskin's armchair sipping English Breakfast!'

'What!' Oona almost jumped, spilling a few drops of tea. Keelan smiled and Oona realised the resemblance. Of course, he looked like a younger and trimmer version of the Scottish author William Dalrymple, whom she had met some months back in Bombay.

Getting back to the moment with a sip of her tea Oona said, 'Tell me more. I'm all ears now.'

'Ruskin was a Slade Professor in Oxford in the 1870s,' Keelan began in a soft Welsh lilt, though the accent was very Oxbridge.

'You too were a Slade scholar, weren't you?' Oona interrupted.

'Yes. How did you know?' Keelan asked surprised.

'I think Aunty Maive mentioned it,' Oona said.

'Some homework you've been doing there,' Keelan remarked.

'But of course, I'm a journo, don't forget. Love sniffing around,' Oona said.

'Well what a pretty sniffing around it would make with a pretty nose like yours,' Keelan added charmingly.

'Well,' Oona blushed flirtatiously as she tilted her head to one side on purpose, so that the little diamond on her nose glinted. The silver bangles at her wrist jangled as she tried to run her fingers through her hair. Casually contrived. Oona had decided to wear her false nose-pin along with some ethnic silver jewellery, coordinated with her ethnic outfit of *salwar-kameez*. She was tired of wearing jeans and wanted to relax in her *desi* outfit. Victor frowned inwardly as he noticed her flirty mood, but let it go.

'Ruskin tried to save England with his ideal scheme of social life and envisioned the health, wealth and happiness of the British people through a common way of life,' Keelan continued, looking at Oona from time to time. 'Those were his words, not mine. In 1874, Ruskin came to the little idyllic Welsh village of Barmouth because he wanted the movement to spread to the countryside. To use his words, "From cities and luxurious life to laborious days and the education of the heart and mind" was his dream.' As he spoke, Oona saw in Keelan a real scholar, with depth and understanding of his subject.

'When Ruskin came to Barmouth, one Mrs G. Talbot offered Ruskin fifteen-odd cottages and some land. He set up the St. George's Guild in 1875 to preach and practise his socialist theory without disturbing the existing cottages. Instead he decided to "assist them", as he put it. In other words to maintain them as they were. And thus these few have remained unchanged in the last five hundred years or more.' Oona was mesmerised as Keelan spoke, and he, too, gazed at her in fascination. Victor noticed Keelan's interest in Oona. Both seemed engrossed in each other, hardly aware of his presence.

'When my parents first bought the cottage over two decades ago, it was in shambles. It was dank, cold and nothing worked. My sister Rita and I wondered why they had invested in this ruin. Slowly, they made it more habitable, with my father making all the furniture in his little room out there,' Keelan said as he gestured towards a room to the right of the parlour. 'And Mum with her eye for aesthetics and her exquisite collection of crockery, hand-embroidered cushions and throws added the warmth and beauty. She was particular about every little detail. And all along they kept in mind the quaintness,' Keelan paused to sip his wine. 'After all, that is what we all liked best about the place. Therefore we adhered to Ruskin's promise to Mrs Talbot of "assisting" and not "disturbing" the character of the place.

'Come, let me take you around,' Keelan said, as he held out his hand for Oona. She found his manners quaintly charming and rose to take his hand. 'May I?' Keelan looked at Victor.

'Go right ahead,' Vic said, winking at Oona. He noticed Oona was a little extra coyly charming in an attempt to impress his cousin. Keelan took her around, explaining. As he led her into his room, he pointed to the open closet with clothes in hangers against a stark stone background. 'That was mum's idea. It was a fireplace originally, which was converted keeping the stone structure intact. Clever isn't it?'

'Brilliant,' Oona said. 'You miss her don't you?'

'Yes, I do. Terribly,' Keelan's eyes were moist as he looked at Oona intently. She blushed, and her response was not lost on Keelan.

The next morning Oona was busy making breakfast. Aunty Maive had gone to attend Sunday Mass. Oona had decided to surprise everyone by making *luchi-aludum,* the traditional Bengali Sunday breakfast of puffed fried bread and boiled potatoes peppered with cumin seeds. But not finding all the ingredients she wanted, she decided to opt for the easier breakfast of bread *upma.* Just cut slices of bread into small croutons, and sauté in oil peppered with mustard and cumin seeds, and add a dash of turmeric powder and salt. Lo and behold, a spicy *desi* treat. She knew the Boses would be impressed. Shaina was still asleep and Victor was out on the terrace garden sipping tea and reading the paper. As she set the plates on the table, Oona heard the front door open and guessed Aunty Maive was back. What took her by complete surprise was Keelan entering along with Maive attired in his Sunday best. A complete contrast to his well-worn pullover-and-faded-jeans look from the previous evening.

Oona was delighted to see him. She shook his hand and noticed that this time he held her hand a little more firmly. Maive explained that she had insisted on Keelan joining them for breakfast after meeting him in church. 'It's been ages since I attended a Sunday service,' Keelan shrugged by way of explanation.

As Oona made ginger and *masala* tea, which she insisted would go down well with the *upma,* Maive caught up with her nephew. Keelan stopped answering Maive's questions every once in a while to exclaim how delicious the bread upma was. When he sipped the tea, the first thing he said was, 'I just love *masala chai.* Mmm....' Though there was nothing Indian about Keelan, Oona realised he seemed well versed with Indian cuisine. Both spoke animatedly about food, exchanging recipes and laughs. Victor noticed his cousin was quite different from his usual restrained self, and Oona was at her flirty best.

When Keelan left, Victor took Oona aside and remarked on this change. Oona feigned ignorance at first, but she could not deceive Victor and broke into a smile. 'He's pretty charming. And very well-informed. It's not often one meets someone one can talk to so easily.'

'Hmm, no doubt. Only my brother may not like it that...'
'Please Vic, not again,' Oona interrupted.

'Only joking,' Victor backed off. 'But I've never seen him so outgoing in the few times I have met him. And he seems to be quite taken by you. On a serious note, just think it over before leading him on. What is it that you are looking for? A little fun on the side or a complete break from Hector?'

'Please. It's nothing like that. I have just met him twice,' Oona replied.

'But the vibes are very strong, very there, from both sides. Know what I mean? Give it a serious thought,' Victor said as he hugged her.

Oona nodded. 'I don't know about feelings anymore...but he is nice.' Suddenly, she asked, 'Do you think he would be aware of David and Ela?'

'Search me,' Victor shrugged. 'Now that, lady, is for you to find out.'

The following week Keelan was back at the Boses' twice. Maive was a bit surprised but thrilled at her nephew's frequent visits. Keelan always had so much to talk about. Between Oona's bubbly chatter and Keelan's lilting tone, there was a freshness in Primrose which Maive enjoyed. One day over dinner, after Keelan had left, Maive innocently remarked, 'Oona, I am so grateful to you.'

'For what?' Oona asked, surprised.

'You got my nephew to bond with me and his cousin here,' she said, pointing towards Victor. 'I have never seen so much of Keelan in all these years as in the past week.' Maive continued, 'Thanks to the Oliver-Sen romance the Llewellyns are getting to know each other better. Right, Vic?'

Victor smiled and added, 'Yes Mum. And I spent more time in Aberdale this last week than I have in the last decade!' He looked at Oona, who blushed and looked away.

One afternoon Oona was reading Amitav Ghosh's *Sea of Poppies*. Maive and Shaina were napping and Victor had just stepped out, when Keelan dropped by to say hello. Noticing her book, he asked about it and Oona, being a Ghosh fan, went into ecstasies about her favourite author: 'Not only is he a master story-teller, his facts are so solid. Being an anthropologist, he writes each work of fiction like a historical document, minus the boredom.' She went on to elaborate on the background of the *Sea of Poppies*, set in imperial India during the days of the East India Company. Keelan listened with interest adding a bit of information here and there and correcting Oona's facts a couple of times. Oona was impressed. 'I thought you were a Ruskin scholar. I had no idea you're so well-informed about British India.'

'Purely out of personal interest. The history of imperial India, more precisely, Calcutta, and that of my forefathers has been inextricably linked by fate.'

'How?' Oona asked, suddenly on the alert.

'Well, that's a long story. Will take a day to tell. Another time I promise. I would very much like to share it with you for whatever it's worth. I haven't discussed this with anyone yet,' Keelan paused. 'And now, why don't I take you out for a cup of tea? Have you tried the Barmouth buns?'

'I have but I wouldn't mind one now. They are yum.'

'Let's go to Patricia's then?'

Keelan was charming company and more than anything Oona felt she could go on and on talking to him and listening to him without either of them getting bored. Something she shared with Victor and to a small extent with Riz. But never did she have this parity with Anand or Hector. She felt he was not just flirting with her but did genuinely find her attractive as a person. Or was she jumping to conclusions too fast? Either way, there was a strong undercurrent of attraction from both sides, partly intellectual and partly sexual. At least that was what Oona felt when she was with him. After tea, Keelan dropped her off at Primrose with a hug. Oona noticed it was tighter and he lingered on a little more than was needed. She coloured, and he noticed it. She wondered whether she was giving herself away too easily.

Meanwhile, Hector called to say that he would be delayed. Employees of a certain sector were on strike due to recent lay-offs and he had to take up extra sectors to make up for their absence. He apologised over the phone. 'I know, babes, I should not have taken on the extra hours, but things are in a bit of a mess here. Sorry for this, and I'm gonna miss you like hell, already am.' Oona tried her best to sound upset as she earnestly explained to Hector that duty came before self.

Hector asked about her plans. Since Victor was leaving for London the next day, he suggested that she go with him. 'Shaina can stay with Mum. You must have had enough of Barmouth by now,' Hector said.

'Actually, no. I kind of like it here. I'll get bored stiff in London. Vic's taking up this new assignment and will be busy, and Sandra and Jo are busy at work. At least here I have Mum and Shaina and I can catch up on my reading.' There was not a mention of Keelan.

'Good girl. You know what's best. Yeah, London can be boring all by yourself. You enjoy Mum's company and I'll come pick you up myself once I am through with this,' Hector sounded very impressed.

Over dinner, she told Victor about her change in plans. 'I need to find out from Keelan about the Olivers, so I'll stay back. Besides, I'll be bored alone in London. I would rather spend time with Aunty here....'

'I think you had better put a stop to this Oliver nonsense,' Victor cut in rather rudely.

'But what's wrong with probing into her family's past?' Aunty Maive asked. 'Besides, Oona has a point. What will she do alone in London? Hector's not there, you'll be travelling, at least here she will have us. Oona, you are welcome to stay as long as you want. Don't listen to him,' Aunty Maive admonished her son.

As the family sat around the fireplace after dinner, Victor suddenly got up and announced he was off to bed as he had a long drive the next day. He hugged Shaina, who was half asleep, and kissed his mum. As he left the room, Oona ran to catch up with him outside. Turning to her, he hugged her and said, 'Take care. I hope you know what you're doing. Don't do anything you'll regret. I am not saying you should follow your mind, but....'

'Please Victor. I'm trying to follow my heart,' Oona said.

'By all means do follow your heart, but...' Victor hesitated.

'But what?'

'But...don't follow your impulse. It might hurt.'

'I know. I'm hurting already. I don't want to be hurt anymore. I will give it a serious thought,' Oona said, as she hugged Victor. 'Don't misunderstand me.'

'Don't worry. I will always be there for you—with or without Hector,' Vic said, kissing her forehead. Oona smiled, trying to hold back her tears.

Primrose was not the same without Victor. Oona missed his presence in spite of the little uneasiness she had felt with him over Keelan. She was looking forward to spending quality time with Keelan. She had to be careful not to arouse Maive's suspicions about her interest in Keelan. Strangely, he did not come by or even call after Victor left. It had been almost four days since she had heard from him. Oona was restless, as if precious moments were fleeting by.

Hector of course kept calling each time he had a halt, mainly to see how she was doing. She appreciated his concern and actually felt far more comfortable talking to him over the phone than having him around or receiving his kinky texts. Most of them would embarrass her as they were too explicit and she would immediately delete them. Sometimes he would keep texting her to respond, but she ignored those messages. He called one night, a little tipsy, and insisted on having sex with her. 'But how?' Oona was amazed.

'Over the phone, you sexy bitch. Now do as I tell you,' Hector said hoarsely.

'I'll have to hang up. Aunty's just walked in,' she lied, hanging up quickly. The next day Hector called, very upset, 'What's the point of having a girlfriend if you won't fulfil my needs? Shall I go to a whore?'

Oona was shocked. Was that all Hector saw in her? She was hurt. Humiliated. It was as if Anand was back in her life. She again questioned her relationship with Hector. Marrying him meant she would live the humiliating life of Mrs Anand Khanna all over again.

Oona was confused. Depressed. One day her phone beeped.

Hope all's well with u my dear. Been madly busy the last few days. Did u manage to catch up with Keelan. Say a hi to him. And sorry about being abrupt....just go ahead and live your life...don't go by anyone's moral judgement. And that includes me. Cheers. Love.

It was Victor. Oona smiled. On an impulse she called Keelan.

'Yeah!' Keelan answered.

'Good morning!'

'Good morning,' Keelan replied. Oona sensed a certain coolness in his tone.

'Just wondering when we could catch up. I needed to talk to you.'

'Right,' Keelan sounded aloof. 'I've been busy. Tied up a bit. Will let you know once I am free. Meanwhile have a nice day.'

'You too…' Oona barely finished before he'd hung up.

She was shocked at Keelan's coldness. She wondered what she had done to deserve this. She was low and depressed the whole day. She called up Sangeeta and told her how much she missed her. Maive also noticed her low mood and asked whether she was all right. When Hector called she refused to take his call. Later, she heard Maive telling Hector over the phone that Oona wasn't well and was resting. Oona popped an Alprax and forced herself to sleep.

By evening she woke up fresh, but felt a nagging sadness about losing Keelan's company. She missed his soft lilt. She missed the little compliments he showered on her. She even missed the tea he used to make, which she'd grown to love. She refused to eat dinner and slept fitfully. At three in the morning she suddenly woke up to a thudding headache. She sat up in bed and cursed God and the men in her life. First Craig for taking advantage of her innocence when she was resisting Kobir's advances. Then Anand for humiliating her and ruining her life. Riz for letting her down badly when she needed him most. And Hector for not living up to her expectations. And now, finally, Keelan.

But she did not know what to blame Keelan for.

My goodness, I think I'm falling in love with him! Shall I tell him? But what if he doesn't feel the same way? I don't want to lose his friendship. It's rare to have a friend who excites me and with whom I share a chemistry. It's past three in the morning. I wish I could talk to him now. But I should wait for a decent time. Or should I just not say anything to him? Keep quiet and let time run its course?

Feeling restless and uneasy, Oona went down to the kitchen, popped two Disprins dissolved in a glass of water and headed back to her room. Her phone was charging. She unplugged it and typed, against her self-restraining conscience:

Is there anything I have done to hurt or upset you, unknowingly, let me know. U seemed cold towards me today and I am upset and hurting badly. I value you as a friend for whatever its worth. God Bless. Love. Oona

She sent the message. It was 3.24 a.m. Relieved to have spoken her mind, she lay back, dug her head into the soft pillow and snuggled under the quilt. She had just dozed off when her phone beeped, startling her awake again. She reached out for it and looked at the message, her heart pounding like never before:

Every day of our friendship is valuable to me. Sorry if I hurt your feelings, I didn't mean to but am currently in a confused state of mind. I will tell you. We need to talk. Sleep peacefully tonight and don't fret. Tomorrow will be a beautiful day.

K

Oona smiled with relief. She was tempted to call Keelan but instead texted back: *Thanks. Much relieved. U too sleep well. Take care.*

Tomorrow never came for Keelan. He did not call Oona the next day or the day after. She was growing restless and wondered whether it was a good idea to stay on in Barmouth after all. She realised she was a little snappy with Shaina and abrupt with Maive. She decided to return to London. Maive was a little surprised at her sudden change of plans but did not pry. 'But how will you go?' she asked.

'I guess I'll take the train, Aunty.'

'Okay. But who will take you to the station? You don't know your way around here. I will tell Keelan to put you on the train.'

'It's okay Aunty, don't bother. I'll ask Peter to see me off.' But Maive was already on the phone to call her nephew. 'When do you plan to leave?' she asked Oona as she dialled Keelan's number.

'Tomorrow. By afternoon latest,' Oona said, leaving for her room.

Back in her room she pulled out her case to pack for London. She neatly folded her clothes and settled them in her soft-top Samsonite. She looked around the room as she packed.

Wonder whether I will ever be able to come here again. Not after I tell Hector off. I wonder whether I will ever be able to face Aunty Maive after this.

As she was immersed in her thoughts, she heard her cellphone's message tone. She decided to check it in a while and continued with her chore. Two minutes later it beeped again. She ignored it. Two minutes later it beeped a third time. 'Someone's really desperate,' Oona thought out loud. She went over to her phone and looked at the three messages in her inbox. They all read Keelan O'Brien.

The first one read: *This is my third text. Please respond. K*

The earlier two messages read the same: *Can I meet you in 15 minutes for a cuppa. K*

K, Oona typed, without thinking. The next thing she did was brush her hair and put on a dash of lipstick. And she quickly changed her tee to a more trendy shirt. By then Keelan had arrived.

Maive was surprised at her nephew's arrival so suddenly. 'Since Oona's leaving tomorrow, I just want to take her around to a couple of spots she's likely to have missed out.'

Maive nodded, though she did not seem quite convinced. But she let it pass. Keelan gently led Oona outdoors.

'I thought you were going to show me around some historical spots. Why did you bring me here?' Oona asked Keelan, after they had settled into the familiar comfort of Ruskin's Cottage. All the way from Primrose to Aberdale, Keelan brushed aside her questions saying he would explain once they reached home. Oona tucked her feet into John Ruskin's chair and accepted Keelan's offer of a cuppa.

While nourishing the warmth of the tea cup in her hand, Oona asked, 'So? What's up?'

'You tell me,' Keelan coolly retorted.

'Tell you what?'

'Why are you leaving tomorrow?'

'Because I'm bored here. And besides, how does it matter to you? You don't even bother to call!' Oona blurted out.

'Oh. If I'd known that was the reason, I'd have definitely called you several times a day,' Keelan replied with a mischievous glint in his eye.

'Oh stop joking!' Oona was upset, exasperated and angry. 'I want to go home.'

'You are home,' Keelan said with a smile.

'What?'

'You heard right. Relax. Get a grip on yourself. And tell me what's bothering you.'

'Nothing.'

'Then say nothing,' Keelan said. Oona glared. Keelan continued to look amused.

'You want to hear about my miserable life, do you?' A tear rolled down her cheek. 'So that you can laugh at my expense.'

'I can only decide on that if you tell me, Oona.'

Her name had never sounded so gentle as when it rolled off Keelan's tongue.

As if the floodgates of her troubled mind had burst open, Oona narrated her journey. From the gawky Golpark teenager in love with Hector to the adventurous young girl who slept with Craig, partly out of love and mainly out of a sense of sexual desperation. Of the time she met and married Anand and how she regretted her life as Mrs Anand Khanna. Of Anand's sexual abuse and mental torture. His philanderings and chauvinism. How she felt stifled and landed straight in the arms of a man like Riz, who seemed just the ideal man and yet could not protect her. She told him about her reconnecting with Hector and how Hector shattered the image she'd had of him. Her disappointment with Hector and her complete disillusionment with life.

'There must be something terribly wrong with me,' Oona concluded with moist eyes. 'You must be bored stiff listening to my miserable story,' she said, smiling at Keelan while trying her best to hold back the tears.

Keelan got off his chair, came towards Oona and gently pulled her up towards him. He held her close. Tight. Oona felt pleasantly suffocated as she let herself be held thus. She was drawn to Keelan and could tell that he reciprocated her feelings. Both sensed a strong sexual undercurrent. But both held back. Neither of them wanted to spoil this moment. Suddenly Keelan gave her a kiss on her forehead. Oona smiled as she extricated herself from his embrace.

'Sorry,' she barely whispered.

'For what?' Keelan asked softly.

'For making a fool of myself. I really don't know what to say.'

'There is nothing left to say now. Only feelings.' Oona looked away.

After what seemed like a lifetime of silence, Oona turned to Keelan. 'Thanks anyway.'

'For what?' Keelan looked bemused.

'For hearing me out. I don't know what made me tell you all this. I really haven't known you long enough.'

'Maybe you were meant to. Who knows what brings two people together. Maybe destiny.'

'You still want to go back to London tomorrow?' Keelan asked Oona. She nodded as she pulled her jacket tighter in a slight shiver. Keelan held her close as they walked down the cliff from Ruskin's Cottage.

'You sure?' Keelan asked again as he held her close. Oona nodded.

'Why? Why do you ask?'

'Oh, I thought we could return together. I'll be leaving in a couple of days' time myself,' Keelan said, waiting for Oona's answer as the latter mulled over Keelan's offer.

'Well.... it wouldn't look nice now, especially after I told Aunty Maive I was leaving. She'll wonder why I changed my mind, and with you taking me out, you know, she will start wondering...' Oona trailed off.

'I understand,' Keelan nodded. 'That's a wise decision.'

'Also I wanted to sort myself out. I needed a little time to myself.'

'Of course,' Keelan said.

Oona looked around the Talbot cottages nearby merging with the dark sky in the distant horizon. The roofs of the cottages were the only specks of colour. She smiled.

'Much as I want to stay on, I think I should head back. This way it will be easier for all of us. Especially to call off my so-called "engagement" with Hector and to break the news to Aunty Maive, and maybe even for us.'

Keelan nodded. His hold on her arm tightened.

'But you know what?' Oona broke herself free of Keelan, 'I feel like some sort of a homecoming here. And I will be back soon.' Oona ran ahead, turned around to smile at Keelan and, with hands raised heavenwards, she ran backwards in excitement, dangerously close to the edge of the cliff, laughing, 'This is indeed paradise!'

'Wait. Stop! Just hold it there Ela, don't go further!' Keelan screamed like a maniac, as he ran and grabbed Oona.

'Oh my gosh!' Oona turned pale as she realised how close she had come to toppling over the edge. She clung to Keelan. 'Oh my God! I could have died!'

'I wouldn't have let you,' Keelan said as he ran his hand through her hair.

'I cannot thank you enough. You saved my life Keelan.'

'No Ela, no. I just did what I had to do. I just could not lose you this time, Ela. I will not let you leave me Ela,' Keelan cried softly into her soft hair.

'Keelan, are you all right? This is me. Oona.' She held his face in her hands.

'I know.'

'But you said Ela.'

'Did I? Sorry. I meant Oona,' Keelan seemed a bit confused.

'Then who is Ela?' Oona asked.

'Ela? Oh. No one. I'll explain everything another time. Please Oona, not now.'

'Okay Keelan, but you must tell me about Ela.'

'I will, Oona. Soon.' Slowly, they walked hand in hand down the hill to Primrose.

The Revelation

The first thing Oona did on returning to London was to call Victor, who was out of town, and tell him how Keelan had called her Ela. She skipped over the preamble, of course.

'Strange. Why would he do that?' Vic asked.

'I don't know. But a number of my relatives have remarked that I do have an uncanny resemblance to her.'

'And do you?' Vic asked.

'I think so,' Oona pondered. 'This proves that Keelan does know about David and Ela.'

'Hmm. Looks like your search is over. Now, just ask him upfront.'

'I did. He said he'd explain later. I'm just biding my time. Waiting for the right moment.'

'Hmm. Quite right. *Aar ki khobor*? What's new? Did Hector call?'

'As a matter of fact he did,' Oona said, trying to sound as distant as possible. 'He says he'll be back next week. Thursday to be precise. And when do you return?'

'Me? In another three to four days' time. Been busy, but nicely so.'

'Good. I'm glad to hear that. And Vic, honestly, I miss you.'

'Really!' Victor laughed on the other end. 'More than you miss Mr O'Brien?'

'Mr O'Brien? Oh, Keelan. Aww, shut up! I'll clobber you.' Both laughed.

Hi Oona. Hope you have settled in. Just got back from Barmouth. Thought I'd let you know. Will call by soon.

K

Oona received Keelan's text the next afternoon. She hadn't spoken to Keelan since she arrived in London. She had called him but he disconnected her call and later texted her saying he was in a meeting. She had sent him a text informing him that she had safely reached her apartment. Keelan acknowledged her text but did not call back.

Now Oona immediately dialled his number. His earlier, formal greeting had been replaced by a more familiar 'Yeah.'

'You never told me you were returning today! This is a surprise,' Oona said.

'That was the intention,' was Keelan's answer.

'Hmm. That's nice. I was beginning to miss you,' Oona cooed.

'Just beginning to? I'm surprised you did not…'

'Well, actually I did,' Oona cut him short as she blurted out her feelings.

'Did what?' Keelan asked.

'Miss you,' Oona muttered.

'What?' Keelan asked again.

'I missed you, Keelan,' Oona was clear and louder this time.

'What did you say?'

'Keelan,' Oona sounded exasperated. 'I just said that I…' she heard him stifle a laugh, 'but of course you heard me,' Oona said. 'Stop pretending.'

'Well, of course I did. But I want to hear it again Oona.'

'Well Mr O'Brien, I cannot remember what I just said.'

'In that case Miss Roy let us meet for dinner tonight and get my impaired hearing and your failing memory back on track. I'll come pick you up from your apartment at seven. Just text me the address.' That was so typically Keelan. He did things without warning.

'Hmm. Will do.'

'Take care Oona and see you soon.' Keelan hung up.

'Hi sweetie, all well?' Vic asked. He was returning Oona's call. He had a missed call and a text from her, asking him to call ASAP.

'Yeah. Okay,' Oona replied, though she did not sound quite okay.

'What's the matter? Something wrong?' Vic asked

'Vic, Hector called,' Oona sounded teary.

'Yes?'

'He got to know from Aunty Maive that I was back in London,' Oona paused.

'So?'

'So nothing. He just kept going on about this and that.'

'About what this and that? Will you be more specific as to what is upsetting you?' Victor asked.

'Well, he says he wants to settle down. By early spring,' Oona informed. Victor did not reply. 'Vic are you there?'

'Yes, Oona. I'm listening. What did you tell him?'

'I didn't say anything. Please Victor, please help me out,' Oona pleaded.

'What do you want me to do?'

'Talk to Hector, please. Explain to him,' Oona said.

'What do you want me to tell him? That you want some time before you decide to marry him? Or that you don't want to marry him at all, Oona? Should I tell him to wait for you or should I tell him to go ahead and find someone else and settle down? What do I tell him?'

'Vic, I'm sorry. I'm confused. But I cannot see myself with Hector, though I am fond of him. Besides, I am also fond of you and Aunty Maive and of course Shaina. I don't want to lose you guys,' Oona sounded distraught.

'You will not lose me, honey. Mum will be upset but she will get over it. She is quite fond of you. Thinks you are the best thing that happened to Hector. Never mind that. The problem is trying to explain to my brother. He can be moody and difficult at times. Don't say anything to him right now. We'll handle this when he returns.'

'Thanks Vic.'

'That's all right. How is Keelan? Is he back?' Victor asked. 'Yes, just got back. I haven't met him yet though,' Oona said. She did not mention the evening's dinner appointment with Keelan.

'Say hi to him when you meet him. You take it easy and I will call you once I am back. See you. Ciao.'

'Ciao. And love you lots Vic.'

'Likewise.'

Oona looked at herself in the mirror as she tried to twist an unruly lock into place. She was wearing a maroon woollen *phiran* or loose Kashmiri coat with delicate gold embroidery along the v-shaped neckline, teamed with a pair of black trousers. She threw a black Kashmiri shawl over her left shoulder that matched the gold embroidery of the *phiran* along its borders. This delicate handwork was so typical of Kashmir. Oona felt bad that the beautiful valley was no more a safe tourist destination due to insurgency for the past many years. There was a time when the 'Switzerland of India' was the locale for most romantic Bollywood films.

When she gave herself a final look in the mirror, she noticed that her neck looked a little bare. Oona rummaged through her jewellery box on the dresser, wondering whether she should wear the delicate match-head pearls with gold balls, which were her all-time favourite or the bigger, bolder string of South Seas which sat snugly around her neck. Suddenly she noticed Ela Sen's delicate gold chain and pendant. On impulse she put it on, smiling at herself in the mirror as the phone rang. She looked to see Heartbeat calling.... Hector had replaced his name with 'heartbeat' in Oona's phone once at Sandra's place. That was some weeks back. However since, his calls no longer set her heartbeats racing, she thought to herself, 'I must remember to change that,' and ignored the call. The phone stopped ringing, and the next instant it beeped with a new message. She almost ignored it, thinking it was Hector, but realised he couldn't have sent a message that quick. It was Keelan:

I am across at the park. Just come around as there is no parking space.

K

On my way, Oona messaged back, smiling. She checked her watch and realised Keelan was ten minutes later than the appointed 7 p.m. *Not as punctual as Riz.*

As she picked up her purse and put her keys and phone in, the landline rang. She was on her way out and instinctively turned back, but realising it would be Hector, she turned and left as the phone rang on.

'Hmm,' Keelan looked at her appreciatively.

'Hi,' Oona said as she slid into his car.

Keelan kissed her hand lightly. 'I love your perfume, lady.' Oona smiled back.

'And you're looking lovely,' Keelan held on to her smile.

'Excuse me?' Oona asked impishly. Keelan continued to smile.

'I didn't hear you. You'll have to say it again.'

'I thought I was the one with the impaired hearing. Anyway, can't remember what I said.'

'But wasn't I the one with the failing memory?' Oona joked. Both laughed.

'We are contagious, to each other,' Keelan said, squeezing her hand.

Her cellphone beeped. It was from 'Heartbeat'. *Where da hell r u? Tried u @ home. Not pickng ur cel. H*

In the theatre, watching a film. Talk 2 u latr. Oona messaged back.

A couple of minutes later he messaged back: *Alone? Or wid whom? Sandra's home. Just chekd.*

'Damn,' she muttered under her breath as she typed out angrily: *Yes alone.* She also wanted to add 'fuck off' and 'none of your bloody business', but she refrained.

Keelan looked at her enquiringly. 'All okay?' he asked. Oona nodded.

'Yes. All good,' Oona said, noticing that Keelan was an over-cautious driver. Not at all relaxed like his cousins or even Anand.

Damn. Why do I always compare the men in my life with each other... their looks, mannerisms, skills... grow up Oona.

Her phone beeped again: *What film & in wich theatre?*

'Damn,' Oona said aloud as she read the message. She decided not to reply.

'Is it Hector?' Keelan asked in a whisper. Oona nodded.

'Please, Oona, feel free to talk to him,' Keelan said, tensing at the wheel.

'I messaged him to say I'm watching a film,' Oona said. 'Honestly, I don't feel like talking to him.' Keelan nodded, relaxing a bit.

'Where are we going to eat?' Oona asked, changing the topic.

'Home,' Keelan looked at her and smiled, 'Unless you want to go out somewhere?'

'No, not at all,' Oona added quickly. 'In fact, that's what I was looking forward to. I just want to let my hair down.' She gently slid her fingers through his as they waited at the red light at Nottinghill Gate. Keelan responded with a gentle squeeze.

Keelan's apartment was charmingly old-fashioned, overlooking Holland Park. It was on the first floor of a Victorian mansion. Unlike the Bose brothers' apartment, which was furnished with light period furniture in pastel hues, Keelan's was old fashioned with a lot of rugs and cushions thrown in. The furniture was carved, at times ornate. The furnishings heavy. The rugs and carpets an eclectic mix of the Occident and the Orient. There was bric-a-brac from all over the world, spread over the side tables, shelves and showcases kept at various intervals in the living room. The entire length of the corridor was lined with books and between the books were more curios. Built in the early years of Queen Victoria's reign, it was a large and spacious apartment, and despite so many things occupying virtually every corner, the place did not look cramped.

Keelan, Oona learned, had bought the apartment along with most of the furniture from an old English gentleman more than seven years ago. 'He was a scientist, honoured with a baronetcy by the Queen. Lord Hamish, that was his name, was quite a collector,' Keelan said, pointing to the assorted collections. 'Especially those eggs there, he had two expensive Russian Easter egg replicas, one from Kashmir in *papier-mache*, and a painted ostrich egg. He was so old and frail when I bought this apartment. An eccentric bachelor, he wasn't on very good terms with his relatives. Somehow, he took a liking to me and parted with his prized possessions,' Keelan smiled.

'Oh, this is all so charming. I could spend hours, maybe days looking at all this stuff,' said Oona, who was completely taken in.

'I am so glad you like my house. Because I'm very house-proud myself,' Keelan said.

'I can see that,' Oona said. She had noticed that everything in the house had a rightful place and was aesthetically appealing. Just like Ruskin's Cottage had a deliberate rustic charm, Holland Park had a deliberate old-fashioned urban charm.

'So, Oona, would you like a drink?'

'Yes, some wine please. You have a great collection of books here,' she said, pausing before a bookshelf. 'And quite an interesting mix of genres.'

'Yes. Those are mine and not Lord Hamish's,' Keelan winked. 'Red or white? Or rose?'

'White. A spritzer, if it's okay?' Oona asked.

'With soda?' Keelan crinkled his brows. 'Okay, if that's what you want,' he shrugged.

Oona walked around the house as she heard Keelan in the kitchen and the combined sounds of glass and ceramic and wood and steel emanating from in there. 'Need some help?' she called out.

'Oh no. I'm fine,' Keelan answered.

Meanwhile, Oona took in the geography of the house. The well-lit sitting room led into the dining room which further led into the kitchen. A book-lined corridor ran along the entire length. All the rooms opened onto the corridor. Oona noticed two other rooms on the other side of the corridor. One looked like the master bedroom whilst the other was a study. Keelan's Mac was the only modern gadget on a roll-top desk. On one of the book-lined shelves lay a Bose Worldspace. Oona felt it was Keelan's private space and did not want to intrude any further. She returned to the living room and casually walked up to the baby grand Steinway that stood in one corner.

'Do you play the piano?' Oona asked, as she lifted the cover and tinkered with the keys.

'Not really. Just a bit. That's also a legacy from Lord Hamish,' Keelan answered back, barely audible. 'Do you play?'

'Not really. Maybe a couple of pieces from memory,' Oona replied, sliding back the cover.

The assortment of family photographs in sepia, black and white and technicolour in various frames of silver, pewter and brass on the mantel of the fireplace caught Oona's attention next. The inhabitants of those frames were as varied as the frames.

'Keelan?' Oona yelled.

'Yes?'

'All family in these photographs here on the mantelshelf?' she asked, already assuming they were.

'Yes,' he answered.

'Come and explain them.'

'Give me a minute, Oona. I'll soon introduce you to my family members,' Keelan called back.

Oona's eyes ran over the frames lightly.

She knew his parents Sinead and Guy from the photographs she had seen in Ruskin's Cottage and also on Maive's dresser. She also knew his sister Rita from her earlier photographs at Ruskin's Cottage. There was one black and white picture of a little girl and even younger boy in a sterling silver frame. Must be Keelan and Rita as children, Oona thought to herself. Then there was an old sepia print of a young couple in a green stone-studded beautiful Russian pewter frame. She admired the frame till her focus shifted to the occupants. Must be his grandparents, she decided, wondering whether they were from Sinead's or his father's side. Then she saw an antique brass frame in tarnished gold with another young couple and guessed that those must be the other set of grandparents. She began studying their features to find likenesses with Sinead and Guy, to identify all of them correctly. It was like solving a jigsaw puzzle.

As she tried to gauge their identity, her focus shifted to a small tarnished silver frame containing the profile of a handsome young man. The print was really old and frayed at the edges. There was something scribbled at the bottom in faded blue ink, barely legible. She began mumbling to herself to get the family tree straight based on what she remembered of Victor's notes.

What was Uncle Guy's father's name? I think it was Philip. Yes, yes, Philip. And Philip's father was Rodney O'Brien, who was Judy's husband. Could this be Keelan's great-grandfather Rodney? And Rodney was married to Judy who was David's sister. Wait a minute, this gentleman does look familiar. Where have I seen him before?

Oona took the frame off the wall and looked closely at it. On a hunch, she set it down, pulled out the chain hanging around her neck, opened the little clasp of the locket and looked at the photograph.

Damn. They match. It's the same gentleman. This is David Anderson Oliver.

'Oona,' she heard Keelan call her name softly behind her. It shook her out of her reverie and she turned around, dropping the frame and locket guiltily, like a child caught stealing a cookie.

Keelan stood there smiling. Obviously he had been observing her for a while. He noticed the look of shock on her face and his smile was replaced with a look of concern.

'What is it Oona?' Shaking, Oona hugged him. Keelan held her tenderly. 'Get a grip on yourself, Oona,' Keelan said.

'I am scared,' Oona said, almost sobbing.

'Of whom?'

'I don't know.'

'That is ridiculous,' Keelan was calm. 'Just relax and tell me what is bothering you.'

Oona released Keelan, picked up the silver frame and asked, 'Who is this? I mean, who is he?'

'Oh him. That's my great-uncle, David A…'

'…Anderson Oliver,' Oona completed.

'How do you know his name?'

'Was he born in Calcutta during the British Raj? Was he in love with an Indian girl? Was her name Ela Sen? Was she Bengali?' Oona blabbered in quick succession.

'Yes, yes. How do you know all this, Oona?'

'Ela Sen is my great-aunt, Keelan.'

There was a stunned silence.

Keelan kept staring at Oona the way he had when they first met at Ruskin's Cottage. Oona, still shaking, still trying to comprehend this long-awaited moment, said nervously, 'Say something.'

'There is nothing to say, Oona,' Keelan said, calm as ever. 'Except that I knew it the day I first met you at Barmouth.'

'Knew what?'

'I knew that destiny had brought you to me. That you were Ela Sen's kin.'

'What? Then why didn't you tell me?'

'What would I have said? Should I have asked if you had a relative who romanced my great-uncle almost a century ago? You would have taken me for a mad man. I did not want to frighten you off. Besides, I wasn't sure myself,' he trailed off.

'Well, at least you could have shared your thoughts in our subsequent meetings.'

'Yes I know, but I decided to leave it all to destiny. I wanted to see what destiny had in store for us like it had for our grandparents.'

'Oh! You know, Keelan, when I went to meet you, I had already done my little research on the Olivers' descendants. That's what brought me to Ruskin's Cottage. My wanting to meet you had nothing to do with travel writing.'

'I suspected that all along,' Keelan said, hugging her close. 'You naughty Ela!'

'The name is Oona.'

'Yes, yes. I know. Oona,' he said her name softly, planting a soft kiss on her forehead.

'And now my search is over, Oona.'

'But my search, Keelan, has just begun.'

Two Worlds Collide

'I need a drink,' Oona said, still a little shaken by the recent turn of events.

'Here's your spritzer,' Keelan said.

'Can I have a malt whisky instead?' Oona asked.

'Sure, I'll get you one,' Keelan replied, arching his eyebrows. 'Do you take it neat or diluted?'

'Neat. Just two cubes of ice, please.'

When the drink arrived, the first thing she did was to take two large swigs. 'Hey, go easy on the drink, honey,' Keelan said, having never seen Oona take more than a few sips of wine at the very most. 'Here,' he said, lifting his glass of red, 'To the future.'

Oona nodded as she raised her glass.

It was a memorable evening.

An evening when destiny brought them together, erasing geographical and historical boundaries.

An evening when the past and present met.

An evening when two worlds collided.

And merged.

As Oona settled down with her drink, Keelan told her his story.

Many years ago, when he was around fifteen–sixteen years old, he had a strange dream. He was somewhere in the Himalayas, a grown-up man walking with an Indian lady friend who wore a *saree* and carried a parasol. He was wearing a light tweed jacket and muffs and a bowler hat as he walked in the mountains with her. All of a sudden his friend slipped and fell off the edge of a gorge. He tried in vain to save her. He could not remember her name, but her face, full of pathos and helplessness, was etched clearly in his mind. He woke up, disturbed. After a while he had forgotten about the dream. A few months later, the same dream occurred. He thought it strange, but this time he was less disturbed. So he let it go.

But the dream kept coming back every few months. He told his parents, who took him to a psychoanalyst. There was nothing to worry about, the analyst said. Perhaps something he had read as a child had got embedded in his subconscious and was revealing itself now. As long as it did not disturb him, it was all right.

As time went by, Keelan began to anticipate the dream. The same sequence of events, the same duration. Nothing more, nothing less. Almost playing out like a film negative. He tried to see more details, to register the conversation between his lady friend and himself on their walk that led to the gorge, but in vain. After some years, he learnt to live with it.

He went to university, lectured, travelled and worked, but the dream kept haunting him every once in a while. He never let it bother him much, though he was a bit concerned.

His father's aunt Charlotte, who visited from time to time, gifted him an old box one day. It contained letters belonging to an ancestor who had lived and worked in India.

'My grandfather served as an officer with the East India Company in Calcutta,' Charlotte had told him. 'His name was Vincent Anderson Oliver. Though he loved India he was forced to return to England when the natives revolted against us. He came and settled in London with his wife, my grandmother Alison, and his daughter, my mother, Judy. My mother married an Irishman, your grand-dad Rodney. As children we heard about my mother's only brother, David, but we never got to meet him. Uncle David, Mum said, had refused to return to England. The main reason was that he was in love with an Indian girl and wanted to marry her and settle down in Calcutta. Unfortunately, her father refused permission for her to marry Uncle David and it was rumoured that he had both of them killed. After Uncle David's death, his possessions were sent to us and Mum kept them safely. Much later, she read some of the letters written to him by his Indian girlfriend as well as his last note and told us that Uncle David and his girlfriend were not murdered. That it was only a rumour and not true. And that he committed suicide. Since my grandmother Alison was dead against Uncle David marrying an Indian, and could not believe her son would kill himself for an Indian girl, she insisted it was murder.

'Mum used to say Grannie went half-mad with grief when Uncle David died. As a scholar of history, perhaps you would find these letters interesting. I don't want them to get lost,' Charlotte had concluded, bequeathing the letters to her grand-nephew.

Oona nodded. 'Yeah. I also became the keeper and inheritor of David's letters to Ela in a similar fashion. Bequeathed to me by my grand-aunt along with a similar story,' Oona said. 'Ever since, I have been curious to read Ela Sen's letters to David. That is partly the reason I embarked on this journey. Now that you have them, I would love to go through them.'

'Sure,' Keelan said. 'But first let me finish my story. What will follow is quite fascinating,' he took a sip of his wine. I travelled to Barmouth soon after that and read some of the letters at random. There weren't too many, and mostly had trivia about imperial India. Also some love notes and letters of endearments. And then I chanced upon a little velvet pouch. On opening it, out slipped this gold pendant and chain,' and Keelan pulled out a chain from around his neck. It had been hidden under his sweater and was similar to the one Oona had, just slightly larger. He laid it on the table before Oona. 'Similar to the one you have.

But this one belongs to my great-uncle David.' Oona nodded and opened her mouth to speak, but Keelan stopped her, 'Let me finish first.'

'The instant I unclasped the gold pendant, the face of the woman in my dreams stared back at me. The same helplessness and pathos in her expression. It was uncanny. I could not sleep for days, wondering whether it was more than a coincidence. After going through the letters, I realised that through my dreams, my mind was replaying the last moments of David Oliver and Ela Sen.

'Why me? I could not comprehend. But the strangest thing was that after seeing Ela's photographs, and there were a couple more in the box mind you, the dream stopped. It's been quite a few years, perhaps more, and that dream has never recurred.'

'Strange,' was all Oona could whisper.

'You know something, Oona?' Keelan asked.

'What?'

'You look so much like Ela Sen from her photographs. It's uncanny.'

'I know,' Oona said. 'A lot of my relatives have told me, and even I can see it for myself.'

'That evening when you walked into Ruskin's Cottage with Victor, I thought I was seeing Ela Sen's ghost. It was as if you walked right out of my dream, right out of Ela Sen's photograph…'

'I was wondering why you kept staring at me. I had no idea you were aware of David and Ela's romance. I thought I alone was privy to this knowledge and this was my journey of discovery. I was keen to learn what happened to the Olivers' descendants. After all, their forefathers were inextricably linked to mine!'

Keelan smiled. 'I am sure it is your knowledge, your journey as much as it is mine. I too embarked on a similar journey the day I chanced upon those letters. I read all there was to read about British India and the Brahmo Samaj, looked up all possible sources on Somenath Sen and his family. Because I was, in a strange way, as curious as you Oona. Only…'

'Only what?'

'The only difference here is that you beat me to this quest. While you embarked on a journey which led you to my doorstep; I just stood here and let the answer arrive, walking right in through my door.'

'So true, Keelan. And well put,' Oona was overwhelmed. 'But there's one thing I want to know, just so that my ancestors rest in peace. Was it murder? Their deaths? Or suicide or accidents? I want to clear the air once and for all.'

'That, my dear, I will let you know in a moment,' saying this, Keelan went to his study and returned with a small wooden box. He rummaged through it and took out some frayed and yellowed papers, giving it to Oona to read. 'Be careful. They are brittle. David's last letter before he died. I'll get myself another glass of wine. Want a refill, honey?' Oona nodded. Keelan took her glass and headed to the kitchen.

It was a four page letter in cursive long-hand. The ink was almost fading.

Dated: 22 July 1930

Ela,

I know you are no more. And yet I write to you. No, I am not insane. I write in all my sanity. Life has no meaning for me without you, just like it had no meaning for you without me.

You could not go against your family and I do not blame you for it. You were caught in a dilemma between the two men in your life...your father and me.

I do not know whether you took your life because of this. Nor do I wish to know. I would much rather believe it was an accident. But I blame it on myself, my helplessness, my cowardice. I let you die whilst I stood selfishly, fearing death myself.

As I returned home, I realised that while your family would find out about your death and grieve, I have nothing left to mourn or grieve for you. For me time stood still the moment you were gone.

For me life stood still the moment your life ended.
For when you died, life in me died.
Since we could not be together in this life, there will always be another time, another life where we will realise our unfulfilled dreams. Till then my dear,

I will always be yours
David.

The last sheet contained a note to his parents:

Dear Mum, Dad and Judy,

Forgive me for the pain I will cause you with my death.
Nobody is responsible for my death except me.
I love you all dearly and will miss you.
God has given me the best family. Perhaps I did not deserve you and the happiness you gave me.

I love you all deeply.
David.

Oona's eyes were moist as she finished reading David's letters. Keelan set her refilled glass on the table and gently wiped a tear from her cheek. Oona smiled and held his hand.

Destiny Wills

Oona looked at her watch. It was almost twelve. She never woke up this late, however late she went to bed. Then she caught sight of the beautiful sapphire and diamond ring Keelan had given her the previous night.

After Keelan and she had discovered all there was to discover about the ill-fated romance of Ela and David, Keelan had gone back to his study and returned with a small black leather box. He handed the box to Oona. 'Open and see,' he answered Oona's questioning look. She saw Harry Winston inscribed in gold on the box. Inside, she found a gold ring with a deep blue, round sapphire encircled with diamonds. She looked up at Keelan who smiled and said, 'Keep it. It's yours. Or at least, it's your great-aunt's.'

'Then how did you get it?'

'That's a long story. Another time,' Keelan said, as Oona admired it. 'Why don't you wear it?'

Oona slipped the ring on the third finger of her right hand. It was a little loose, but she could wear her silver band above it to make sure it didn't fall off.

'Are you sure you want me to have it?' she asked, holding out her hand to look at the ring.

'Absolutely,' Keelan said. 'It looks beautiful, back where it belongs.'

It had been a little after midnight when Keelan dropped her at her apartment. He had waited for her to let herself in. Oona asked whether he would like to come in for a nightcap, but he just smiled, gave her a light hug and a kiss on her forehead saying, 'Some other time. We have an entire lifetime for nightcaps.'

Sitting up in bed this morning, Oona smiled. She found his ways charmingly old-fashioned. Though they were both physically attracted to each other, she could feel Keelan trying to control himself, even as she grew impatient. While she had given enough signals to Keelan to show that she was willing, he did not seem to be in a hurry. But he seemed to enjoy teasing her.

Apart from platonic kisses on the hand or forehead, he has never kissed me deeply on the mouth. Even if he wasn't rushing into relationship, at least he could kiss me on the lips. Also, when he gave me the ring, it would have been the done thing if he had proposed to me. Otherwise what man parts with such an expensive gift without a long-lasting promise? Besides, he need not have told me it belonged to Ela Sen. I would have been none the wiser. It must cost a bomb, and he just gave it to me, just like that. As if it were a trinket. Why didn't he propose? I hope everything's all right. I hope he isn't gay? Oh damn! I must banish such thoughts!

Stretching lazily, she reached for her phone and turned the sound on. She saw three missed calls. Two were from Hector and one from Keelan. Then she saw three new messages, two from Keelan and one from Hector.

Oona read Hector's message first:

I tried you last night. What time did u return? Hope all well? Call back asap. She messaged him back, knowing it must be some unearthly hour in New York.

Hector I know it sounds rude, but please, please leave me alone. I need some time on my own to sort out my life and I hope you understand. I want to be left ALONE for a few days. So please do not keep tabs on me by calling me or texting me. I will call you once I am sorted out. Thanks and take care.... Oona

She next looked at Keelan's messages. The first one read

Tried calling you. But you must be sleeping. I woke up late myself. I wanted to tell you something. I'll call you later.

K

That was sent nearly an hour ago, at 11.10 a.m. The next message followed soon after, at 11.21 a.m. It was a long text: *I'm afraid Oona, I'm not…*

Oona's heart skipped a beat, wondering what would come next. Did Keelan want to break off with her like Riz? She closed her eyes in a silent prayer before reading on: *I'm afraid Oona, I am not a romantic in the conventional sense. Nor am I well-versed with social manners, having been on my own, literally, for so long. Last night when I gave you the ring, I meant to say something. But I just could not bring myself to say it. I don't know how to put it. Oona I meant to ask if you will marry me. I know this is not the best way to propose, but you will have to forgive me for not going down on my knees and all. But I mean it sincerely all the same.*

Keelan

Oona messaged back the very next instant. She looked at her watch. It was 12.17 p.m.

YES.

O

Two minutes later her phone beeped.

That is such a relief. It was the worst waiting hour of my life.

K

Sorry to set your pressure up, I just woke up. It is the most beautiful day of my life because I LOVE YOU very much Keelan.

Oona

I love you too Oona. Very, very much. Talk to you later.

K

The first thing Oona did was call Victor.

'Yes? All well sweetie?' Victor answered.

'Yes. All well. Vic do you have a moment to spare? I have to tell you something,' Oona said.

'Yes. Go ahead. I'm all ears. I hope it's something good?'

'Vic, Keelan asked me to marry him.'

'What! When?'

'This morning. And I said yes,' Oona said.

'Are you sure? You hardly know him. Oona, this is crazy....'

'No, Vic, no. I'm not crazy. And I'm not doing it to spite Hector or on the rebound or something. I really like him. I liked him the day I first met him. And Vic, he does know about David and Ela. He showed me some of her letters. I don't know, I know it sounds strange but it seems we have some cosmic bond from our previous lives. You know what I mean?'

'I'm trying to understand this. I knew something was up the moment you two met, but darling, are you sure? You still haven't quite broken off with Hector yet...' Victor trailed off.

'I know. But I am very sure of Keelan. I enjoy his company and Vic, believe me, I do love him. We haven't even kissed each other. You might find it weird, but Keelan's very shy. Yet I want to spend the rest of my life with him. I know it. I will be happy with him.'

'I wish you all the happiness. You have to be sure of what you want. Oh, by the way, congratulations!'

'Thanks,' Oona blushed on the other side. 'One more thing, Vic. You'll have to help out, with Hector,' Oona said.

'I knew that was coming. Tell me,' Victor asked.

'I've sent him a text saying I want to be left alone and am not going to take his calls. You'll have to tell him about Keelan and me and that we're...oh, I don't know,' Oona broke off.

'That's going to be difficult, but I will try my best. Let's see...there are still some days before he returns. All right, you take care and congratulations once again. Bye.'

You not only show zero social manners by proposing to me through a text, you also did not give me an engagement ring Mr O'Brien. Howzzat? But I still love you lots. O

Then what is the sapphire and diamond doing on your ring finger, my lady?

K

But that you said belonged to my great aunt Ela Sen, Mr Scrooge!

Well not really. It was bought for her by my great-uncle David as she liked the colour of sapphires. But he could never get around to giving it to her because of the tragedy… he mentions it in one of his letters to her. Which also he never got around to delivering to her….That is what I also wanted to tell you last night Oona.

K

Ouch! I am sorry. I take back my words. So what David Oliver could not deliver eight decades ago, his nephew managed to achieve. That should go down in the Guinness Book as the longest courtship… what say you Mr O'Brien?

I'll file the story to the Guinness guys. Take care.

K

Oona's next call was to Sandra, who was shocked at first, but eventually very happy for Oona.

'Doesn't matter who you marry,' Sandra laughed, 'As long as you are happy. Besides, I am glad you will still be in London. But you must tell me how it all happened, you wicked girl!'

After that, Oona called Sangeeta. Taken completely by surprise and upset at the prospect of Oona settling far away, she nevertheless gave her blessings. 'As long as you're happy and know what you're doing is right,' Sangeeta said in her typical maternal fashion.

'Call up Aunty Maive,' Keelan called her later in the day. 'I spoke to her and explained everything. She was a little surprised at first but she's happy for us. I think she'll do anything for her sister. Bless her soul.'

'Oh that is a relief. I was most worried about her,' Oona said. 'And by the way, where are you? We've barely got engaged and you disappear!'

'Busy all day today. Will catch you tomorrow,' Keelan said.

'That's not fair,' Oona grumbled.

'Sorry darling, but you will have to get used to my strange ways…unless you want to change your mind….'

'No, no, no,' Oona yelled. 'I love you with all your eccentricities. Wait till we get married. I'll fix you.'

'Is that a threat?' Keelan asked.

'Absolutely. Big time.'

Oona was exhausted with happiness by evening. It was barely nine o'clock and she wanted to turn in. She picked up a celery and prawn fried rice from the Chinese takeaway near her apartment after a walk around the park. She ate it while absent-mindedly watching TV. Suddenly, her phone beeped. Distractedly she looked at the message: *Vic just calld. You bloody bitch. You're worse than a slut.* It was from Hector.

The most beautiful day in her life was ruined with this message. A tear trickled down her cheek as she forwarded it to Victor, adding below: *Your bro sent it to me.*

He messaged back: *Shocking. U relax n take it easy. Nite nite.*

One World

Three weeks later, on a rainy Thursday afternoon, Keelan O'Brien, great-nephew of David Anderson Oliver, married Oona Roy, great-niece of Ela Sen, in a London court. It was Oona's second marriage and Keelan's first. Keelan's cousin Victor and Oona's friend Sandra were there to witness the event. Later the foursome had a hearty lunch at Veeraswamy's.

Later that evening, Oona moved out of her Collingham Gardens apartment and moved into Keelan's Holland Park residence.

A beautiful church wedding followed on Sunday, this time at Barmouth. Victor was Keelan's best man and Sandra's daughter and Shaina were the bridesmaids. Peter Bunce gave the bride away and Maive shed tears on seeing Oona and Keelan pronounced man and wife for the second time that week. Sitting beside her were Patricia, Greg, Debbie, Sandra and Jo. Hector was not present. Surprisingly that morning, there was a hint of sunshine in the otherwise dank town.

Oona wore a simple white gown which she had got fitted at a Chelsea boutique where Sandra took her. When the pastor pronounced them 'man and wife' and said 'you may now kiss the bride', Oona realised her three-day-old husband looked shy. His lips trembled on Oona's, who firmly yet discreetly ran her tongue into his mouth. 'That was wicked,' Keelan mumbled, with an impish look.

The guests walked up to Primrose where Maive served her famous berry pulao with chicken butter masala. In the evening, Debbie and

Greg hosted a dinner for the newly-weds at the Last Inn where nearly all of Barmouth was present. The menu, of course, did not deviate from Debbie's famous fish 'n chips with mashed potatoes and peas. Oona wore a peach chiffon saree as she cut the wedding cake for dessert.

As the newly-weds drove off in the groom's battered Honda SUV towards Ruskin's Cottage, Oona turned round to see half the town waving them goodbye. Tears rolled down her cheeks as she headed towards Ruskin's as Mrs Keelan O'Brien. Or was it Oona O'Brien? She liked the ring of her new name as she played it in her head.

'A penny for your thoughts Mrs O'Brien!' said Keelan.

'You just said it,' Oona replied.

After a quiet honeymoon in Swansea, Oona and Keelan returned to Barmouth a week later, on their way to London. The following evening they were to catch a flight to Calcutta, where Sangeeta was arranging a small Bengali wedding for the couple. This was at Keelan's insistence. He was very keen to dress up and play the Indian bridegroom. It would be their third wedding in less than a month. But thankfully to each other.

An hour out of Barmouth and a little before Birmingham, as Keelan tried to steer through a deep bend in the hills, he suddenly lost control. Before either of them knew what was happening, the car skidded, hitting a tree. 'Oona' was all Oona heard before she blacked out.

The first thing she saw as she regained her senses was a heavy bandage on her right wrist. A dull pain throbbed in her head as she realised she was lying in a clinic. A doctor stood by, smiling encouragingly. Keelan was sitting by her side, and bent forward to kiss her on the head.

'You'll be fine, honey,' he smiled.

'Where is…what happened?' she asked, as she remembered the run-up to the crash. 'Are you all right?' she asked him, noticing a small piece of sticking plaster on his forehead.

'I'm fine,' Keelan said. 'It's just a nick. Nothing to worry about. Want something to drink?'

Oona nodded, 'Water.'

I'll get some,' the doctor said. 'You dearies take it easy till your transport arrives.'

Keelan explained to Oona briefly about the accident and how they had managed to come out nearly unscathed. The car, of course, was badly damaged. 'You'll never believe anyone could survive that wreckage,' Keelan told her. 'I was worried about you. It took a while to get you out. For a moment I thought I had lost you,' he said, pausing to take a deep breath, 'but you did well, just a few stitches,' he said gesturing towards her wrist.

Oona looked at the plaster on her right wrist. She looked at her left hand which was all right, the gold wedding band gleaming on her third finger. Suddenly she looked at the third finger of her right hand. The sapphire and diamond ring was missing. She gasped.

'Keelan,' Oona said.

'Yes?'

'Where's the ring?'

'What ring?' Keelan asked.

'The sapphire and diamond engagement ring you gave me. Uncle David's ring! Shit, it must have come off. Let's go and check in the wreckage.'

'It's okay, Oona,' Keelan calmed her down. 'Just relax. I'm just glad we're alive. Forget the ring.'

'But it's....'

'Oona,' Keelan interrupted. 'What happens, happens for the best. Maybe the ring was not meant for you. Maybe it was supposed to go. Maybe the sapphire brought ill-luck to David and Ela. Who knows?' Keelan kissed her. 'Look at it this way. Its loss will perhaps bring peace to David and Ela's souls. And who knows,' he shrugged, 'maybe lots of happiness to us.'

'Why maybe?' Oona smiled, 'Certainly.'

'Yes, certainly,' Keelan echoed.

Bibliography

Burnell, AC and Henry Yule. *Hobson-Jobson: A Glossary of Anglo-Indian Words.* Rupa.

Chandra, Bipan. *India's Struggle for Independence.* Penguin Books.

Chandra, Bipan, Mridula Mukherjee and Aditya Mukherjee. *India After Independence: 1947–2000.* South Asia Books.

Chatterjee, Jayabrato. *Kolkata the Dream City.* UBSPD.

Hubner, John and Lindsey Gruson. *Monkey on a Stick.* Onyx.

Moorhouse, Geoffrey. *Calcutta: The City Revealed.* Phoenix.

